Out of
Her Hands

Out of Her Hands

Megan DiMaria

TYNDALE HOUSE PUBLISHERS, INC.

CAROL STREAM, ILLINOIS

Visit Tyndale's exciting Web site at www.tyndale.com

Visit Megan DiMaria's Web site at www.megandimaria.com

TYNDALE and Tyndale's quill logo are registered trademarks of Tyndale House Publishers, Inc.

Out of Her Hands

Designed by Beth Sparkman

Edited by Lorie Popp

Published in association with the literary agency of Alive Communications, Inc., 7680 Goddard Street, Suite 200, Colorado Springs, CO 80920.

Scripture taken from the HOLY BIBLE, NEW INTERNATIONAL VERSION®. NIV®. Copyright © 1973, 1978, 1984 by International Bible Society. Used by permission of Zondervan. All rights reserved.

Library of Congress Cataloging-in-Publication Data

Out of her hands / Megan DiMaria.
   p. cm.
ISBN-13: 978-1-4143-1888-2 (sc)
ISBN-10: 1-4143-1888-X (sc)
1. Mothers and sons—Fiction. 2. Mate selection—Fiction. I. Title.
PS3604.I4645087 2008
813'.6—dc22   2008020380

Printed in the United States of America

14 13 12 11 10 09 08
7 6 5 4 3 2 1

For Carl,
Dan, Kathleen,
and Liz.
Without you,
there would be
no words

ACKNOWLEDGMENTS

My writing journey is even more exciting than I ever dared to dream it could be. But the best part of this journey is being able to share it with my family. Carl, Dan, Kathleen, and Liz—it wouldn't be nearly as much fun if I couldn't share this joy with you.

To my wonderfully supportive DiMaria clan: Thank you for being my East Coast marketing team. You're a huge blessing in my life.

Thank you is not enough when it comes to acknowledging the work and support I get from the amazing team at Tyndale House Publishers. Jan Stob, Lorie Popp, Mavis Sanders, and Babette Rea—you're the best!

Thanks to my literary agent extraordinaire, Beth Jusino, for being so wise, so helpful, and so much fun.

Thanks to my critique partners—Marion, Angie, and Frances— you keep me on my toes. The encouragement and support of all my American Christian Fiction Writers and Words for the Journey writing friends is precious. You know who you are. God bless you.

Jan P., what a blessing you are! You're always available to give me a pep talk and plan a good promotion (providing I don't call before 11:00 a.m.).

Thank you, Pastor Jack Serr of Castlewood Canyon Church, for taking the time to discuss the issues parents face with their young adult children. Your wisdom is greatly appreciated.

One of the wonderful experiences of this journey is the new friends I've made along the way. Thank you, Auna Jornayvaz, for your enthusiastic support. I look forward to watching your career bloom.

Thanks to Belle for being so Belle-ish.

Thank You, Jesus. Thank You for blessing me with life, love, and words. It's all because of You that this journey continues.

And now these three remain: faith, hope and
love. But the greatest of these is love.

1 CORINTHIANS 13:13

• • •

Some days I imagine that the hundreds of details dancing in my brain will make my head inflate like the Mr. Magoo balloon in Macy's Thanksgiving Day Parade. *Didn't he explode one year?*

Can I round up enough fairies by Thursday to repair those halos and wings? And are the ice pixie dresses ready to go? *What a job.* It's always something.

I focus on inputting the correct security code into the control panel and scoot out the door of Dream Photography, my home away from home. I pull my jacket closed and double-time it toward my car in the lamp-lit parking lot. Loaded down with my purse, lunch box, and a folder full of portraits, I shift my burdens to dig my ringing phone out of the depths of my bag, fumbling to keep a strong grip on the folder, when the cell slips from my hand and skitters under my car.

Oh, goodness, I've done it again. Like Grandpa always said, "No sense being dumb if you don't show it."

So here I stand, amazed that the silly phone still works and annoyed that it's singing from beneath a three-thousand-pound vehicle. A glance around assures me that no one witnessed my lack of finesse. Irritation prickles my scalp. Anyone who saw this embarrassing display wouldn't believe I produced a daughter who is on an award-winning competitive cheerleading team.

A late October breeze dives beneath my hem while I squat beside the soiled sedan, yards of fabric from my favorite green broomstick skirt billowing out like a ship's sail on the high seas. The muffled tones of the "Hallelujah" chorus taunt me as I grasp toward the cell phone that sits inches beyond my reach. I lean over as far as propriety allows, stretching toward my goal. *If only . . .*

I know. I'll swat at the phone with my ice scraper. I retrieve what my son, Nick, calls the mother of all ice scrapers from my car. At nearly four feet long, this thing will surely do the trick.

I squat again and get a visual on the now-silent phone. Leaves scud past me as I hear footsteps approaching.

A tall shadow falls across the asphalt. "Excuse me?"

I pause in my efforts and look up to see a thirtysomething businessman peering down. Is that pity in his eyes? "Yes?"

He leans toward me. "Can I help you, ma'am?"

I smile and push my hair behind my ear, pasting on a competent expression to displace any suggestion that I'm a total dimwit. I raise my monster ice scraper. "I've got it under control. Thanks."

Mr. Helpful cocks his head.

I chuckle and explain. "I dropped my cell phone."

"Oh, sorry." He stays planted to the pavement.

Keep moving, fella. There's nothing to watch here. "Uh, thanks again."

"Night, then."

"Good night." I smile and nod, waiting for him to walk away before I resume my awkward pose and retrieve my phone.

But he addresses me once more. "Too bad you couldn't have just moved that car."

"Uh, yeah." I'm grateful the cool breeze has already colored my face so he can't see the telltale blush travel to my hairline. He heads toward his car, and I gently push my phone out from under the Taurus. I pick it up, brushing debris from the silent device, pretending to test out the phone, waiting for him to drive away.

After all, I can't have him see me get into the offending vehicle.

Move the car. Too bad that simple suggestion never crossed my mind. *Sheesh.*

I pull onto the freeway and head east to Pine Grove, putting the car on cruise control. Ever since that last speeding ticket, I don't take any chances. Jerry's just about the most patient husband in the state of Colorado, but one more blip to our insurance premium may put him over the edge.

I plug in my hands-free device and access my voice mail. It was a call from my friend Deb Hinesley. "Hi, Linda. I'm sorry I missed you. Listen, I was wondering if you and Jerry are free for dinner Saturday night. Keith and I were hoping you'd join us to try out the new sushi restaurant in Denver. It's very hip. Reservations required. Call me."

Sushi? My scientist husband turned college professor is pretty cautious and is more of a meat-and-potatoes guy, but maybe I can convince him to try something new.

Deb has been my best friend since college. But it takes every ounce of self-control and Christian love to face her husband, Keith, and pretend I don't know his dirty little secret. And to think I used to be jealous of their so-called romantic marriage.

Not too long ago I thought Jerry could use a boost in the romance department, but I've since discovered—or shall I say *rediscovered*—just what a gem I have. Now, I'm not saying he hits the mark all the time, but at least he tries.

I'm feeling warm and tingly toward my husband as I arrive home. I know both my children are out tonight—Emma at cheerleading practice and Nick with his college buddies. Today's one of Jer's short days at the community college where he teaches science.

I'd love for my honey to greet me at the door, but the only one who seems to care is our Jack Russell terrier. I scratch the top of her head. "Hi, Belle. How's my girl?"

The kitchen is in darkness, and there are no delicious aromas assuring me that dinner is being prepared.

Ooh, maybe Jerry's cooking up a special surprise—upstairs.

Belle dances around me while I hang my jacket in the closet. I go to the pantry and toss her a treat. "Jer?"

I hear his muffled response come from our bedroom.

My heart beats a little bit faster as I hurry up the stairs. What could this surprise be? Strawberries dipped in chocolate? A candlelit massage? The door's ajar, so I gingerly push it open.

I can't believe my eyes. Every surface of the room is covered with plastic drop cloths. Jerry's standing on a ladder, white speckles staining his face and hair, painting our bedroom ceiling. He couldn't look more pleased with himself. "What do you think?"

My heart rate remains accelerated. I know how this man's mind works, and this is his way of being romantic. Okay, maybe I would have preferred champagne and roses, but . . .

He descends the ladder, walks over, and gives me a quick kiss.

I'd love to throw my arms around him, but I'm not willing to ruin the wool blazer I'm wearing. "What made you do this?"

He angles his head and gives me that smile I've loved forever. "Don't you think I listen to you?"

"Huh?"

"I heard you and Emma talking about painting your bedrooms." I follow him to the bathroom, where he washes. "My class dismissed early today, and I went to The Home Depot to buy some paint. I saw that article you clipped from the paper."

I love this man. "You mean the room-makeover article based on the colors in this season's Hollywood movies?"

He dries his hands and strips off his paint-splattered sweatshirt. "That very one. Except I didn't know if you wanted blue or apricot for the walls."

I can't remember the last time I felt this attracted to him. I hustle to the walk-in closet and change into my sweatpants. When I step into the room, half the drop cloths have been cleared away.

The sound of his cheerful whistle echoes from the first floor. A mouthwatering smell greets me at the top of the stairs and escorts me down to the kitchen.

Jerry's sitting at the table. He gestures toward a large cheese pizza from our favorite joint. "Dinner's served."

Could there be a more perfect ending to a stressful day? I try not to think about the folder of portraits that needs to be arranged before eight thirty tomorrow morning and concentrate on the simple meal and the man sitting before me. I adore my kids, but there's something wonderful about a quiet dinner for two. Even if it's delivery pizza.

Jerry says a blessing and passes me a napkin.

I savor the first delectable bite and hop up to retrieve the newspaper clipping hanging under the Dream Photography magnet on the refrigerator. I take my seat and push the article toward Jerry. "See that color blue? I think it will look beautiful with brown and green accents."

He nods while he chews, pulls the clipping closer, and points to the picture. "Yep. That's the color I thought you liked."

I run my fingers through his thinning hair and give him my come-hither smile. "How about I help you wash the paint from your hair?"

Jerry looks intrigued. "I should do more painting around here."

I'm about to lean in for the kiss I'm dying to steal when I hear a key in the front door.

Emma breezes in. "Pizza? Great."

This girl's timing is unbelievable. And I thought her having a driver's license would give us fewer interruptions and more privacy. For the past eighteen months, living with her has been like living with a jack-in-the-box. You never know when she's going to pop up.

She washes her hands at the kitchen sink, all the time editorializing about life at Pine Grove High. She sits next to me and helps herself to a slice. "Oh, you're not going to believe what I heard today." She pauses for effect, looking us each in the eye.

Spit it out, girl.

"Hillary had to leave school for an orthodontist appointment, and before her mom brought her back, they went to Starbucks. And guess who she saw?" Emma takes a bite of pizza.

Jerry looks confused. "Who's Hillary?"

Oy. For an intelligent man, he can never seem to remember our kids' friends' names. "Hillary Seer, a girl from cheerleading." I take a nibble of pizza. "Who did she see?"

Emma obviously enjoys her moment of power, taking a sip of cola to wash down her pizza. "Nick."

"And . . . ?"

"He was with a girl. A very pretty girl."

Jerry waves off her announcement. "Is that a crime? He has lots of friends he meets for coffee. For all we know, it's just a classmate."

Emma straightens, pushing her shoulders back. "Yeah, just a classmate . . . that he kisses?"

"Are you sure it was Nick she saw?" I can't imagine my son kissing someone in front of other people. He's so contained. So careful about the way he appears in public. And wouldn't he mention someone he was interested in?

She rolls her eyes. "Hillary knows what Nick looks like. She's been over here lots of times when Nick's around."

Jerry gives me his let-it-drop look. "Emma, unless you want Nick to tease you about your boyfriend, I suggest you go easy on him."

She pouts for a moment but lets the subject slide.

I sit at the kitchen table organizing the photographs into piles.

Emma meanders in, pulls out a chair, and sits, dropping a textbook on the table. "Whatcha doing?"

I answer without looking up. "Organizing photos."

"Why?"

"We need to have a file on each set we do for our Special Edition promotions."

She points to a pile. "Which one's this?"

I fan out the portraits. "Victorian Christmas."

Emma studies the images of a replica Victorian living room complete with an exquisite Christmas tree, an ornate fireplace decorated with satin stockings suspended from a bough-laden mantel, and three young children dressed in elegant, custom-made outfits. "Cool." She hands back the photos. "Can you help me with my English homework?"

"In a few minutes, honey. I need to finish this."

She sighs. "I need to do math homework too. Can't you help me now?"

"Why don't you do your math homework until I'm finished?"

"Well, I wanted to do this first because—"

She's interrupted by the sound of the front door opening. Nick's heavy footsteps come down the hall. "What did you have for dinner?"

Before I can respond, Emma says, "Hillary saw you this afternoon. At Starbucks. Kissing a girl."

I steel myself for the fireworks I fear will explode.

Nick shrugs. "I don't know what you're talking about. I wasn't at a Starbucks today."

Emma frowns. "Really? Hillary said she saw you."

He rummages through the refrigerator. "I don't know who she saw, but it wasn't me."

"Are you sure? She knows what you look like."

Nick gives her a blank stare. "Hillary's an idiot."

"She is not—"

I put my hand on Emma's arm to stifle her objections, and Nick leaves the room.

She turns to me, eyes wide with indignation. "Why would he lie?"

"He's not lying. Your friend must have been mistaken."

Emma shakes her head. "Sometimes you can be so naive."

We sit in silence. I hear the shower running in my room. Jerry must be washing his hair. So much for a little romance tonight.

I thought I'd be the first one in to work this morning, but my boss, Luke Vidal, beat me. He's pinning a notice on our staff bulletin board when I enter the office. It's no doubt something more for me follow up on. As office manager, I barely have time to catch my breath around here.

"Morning, Linda." Luke arranges the extra pushpins on the corner of the corkboard.

I drape my jacket over the back of my chair. "I didn't expect to see you this early."

"I had to cancel Carol Ball's appointment last week, and the only time she could reschedule was for first thing this morning." He reaches for the bin that holds his mail.

I drop the thick folder of photographs on my desk.

Luke lifts the cover on the folder and leafs through the images, which are separated according to theme in several labeled file folders. "Good job."

The door chime rings, and Luke glances at the clock. "That's probably the Balls. Give me a few minutes and then send them back to my studio."

As he rounds the corner, I hear the commotion that always accompanies the Ball family. I smile as I greet one of our most high-maintenance clients. "Hi, guys."

Carol Ball walks in carrying a garment bag in one arm and

holding the hand of one of her eight-year-old twins. She lays the bag across the back of a chair and greets me with a hug. "I'm going to need help choosing our wardrobe. I meant to call you last week, but I got too busy and didn't get around to it."

"No problem. Let's see what we have here."

Carol and I move over to the marble delivery counter and unzip her bag. She pulls out an assortment of clothes in various sizes and styles. This woman has exquisite taste. We settle on black pants and russet shirts.

I escort Carol, her husband, and their three children to our dressing room and go back to the office. Carol demands 150 percent from the merchants she frequents, but I discovered that she can be just as giving as well. A while back when my world had tilted on its axis, Carol intervened, persuading an acquaintance to drop the criminal mischief charges she had filed against my daughter. And for that, I'll be forever grateful.

I nearly bump into Traci, one of our associate photographers, as I walk into the office. She holds the day's schedule in one hand and a clipboard in the other. Her face brightens. "Can you do me a favor?"

That should be my title here—favor doer. "Sure."

"I need help tearing down the set in the window-light studio and assembling cowboy Christmas. Could you please call in some fairies?"

I scribble my notes. "When do you need them?"

She gives me dates and times, and I open my e-mail program to do a mass mailing to our list of nighttime fairies. They're clients who are addicted to having their children's portraits taken and trade their time for portrait credits. They love the various Special Edition sets that rotate throughout the year—intricate representations of unique childhood fantasy concepts that have mothers flocking to us to capture their little angels as, well, among other things, little angels.

I hit Send on the e-mail and ponder how I became the studio's fairy herder. It's not an easy task, believe me. These clients can be quite a challenge to organize.

There's never a dull moment here. But that's what makes this job such a kick.

"Linda?" Jill stands in the doorway, shifting from one foot to the other. "Can you help Barb in the lobby?"

"I'll be there in just—"

"Uh, this can't wait." Jill's face is the color of cheap farm-raised salmon.

I rush to her side. "What's the issue?"

"Pauline Lincoln is in the lobby complaining to everyone about how bad the cropping, the color, and the artwork are on her son's senior images. Code red. This woman's nuts."

At times it seems I have a love/hate relationship with our clients, but truth be told, most of them are sweethearts. Unfortunately, Pauline is not one of the sweet ones.

I take a fortifying breath and head out to the battle. I'm always ready for the challenge of my position, but I could do without some of the drama that goes along with it. "Ms. Lincoln?"

An impeccably groomed, designer-clad woman in her late forties turns her attention to me as though I were a bug on the windshield of her Jaguar. She sizes me up in an instant but remains silent.

I approach her, smiling. "My name is Linda. I'm sure I can address your concerns."

The other clients in the lobby are all conspicuously quiet, no doubt hoping to witness an altercation.

She straightens to a height about four inches taller than me. "First, I have to say that for all the money I spend here, I hate your huge logo splashed across my five-by-sevens." She peers at me to see if I'll pick up the gauntlet she threw.

Huge logo? Give me a break. I doubt it's three-quarters of an inch long. I act as though she's invited me to tea. "You know, it will be much easier to discuss your issues where we can spread out a little bit more." As I speak, I collect her portraits that are fanned across the top of the coffee table. "Let's go into the conference room. May I get you a bottle of water? some coffee?"

Fortunately, Pauline follows me in silence. We enter our elegant conference room that could be mistaken for a suite on the twenty-fifth floor of a Manhattan skyscraper overlooking Central Park. The carpeting is so plush, it's as though you're walking in a sound-insulated booth. Heavy wooden chairs surround the enormous cherry conference table, polished to a mirrorlike sheen. On one side of the room is a stocked wet bar with an assortment of beverages and a fresh plate of chocolate macadamia nut cookies.

I put her portraits on the table. "Mineral water, tea, soda?"

"Mineral water, with lemon." She gives me a smug look.

Come on. Give me a challenge. "Sure thing." I open the refrigerator beneath the wet bar and take out a bottle of mineral water and a plastic container of fresh lemon slices. I hope that creature comforts will soothe this savage beast. I put ice cubes in a crystal tumbler, pour her beverage, and set it in front of her on a custom-made Dream Photography coaster.

One finely shaped eyebrow twitches.

I decide to go on the offensive. I pull out her client file. "Now, you signed the front of your file where it says that our company logo will appear on all portraits."

Her eyes narrow as she snatches the file from my hand and reads the fine print. "I didn't see this."

I force myself to remain calm in the face of her building fury. "Every portrait studio displays their logo on their products. Before we move on to your other issues, I need to tell you that if you object to our logo, I'll be happy to give you a full refund in exchange for all the portraits."

Pauline looks at the images spread before her with longing.

Aha. I know I've disarmed her. Once clients get to see the beautiful work our upscale studio is known for, they're hooked. I smile and regard her as though I'm awaiting her reply.

Her manicured fingers tap on the table. A fine line of perspiration beads her upper lip. "Several of the five-by-sevens will be framed together, and that huge logo will be distracting."

I riffle through her file. "Oh, dear. Were those images supposed to be matted and framed? Then the mat would be signed, and the portraits wouldn't have the logo. If that's the case, I apologize for the error."

Pauline sighs and glances at the images of her smiling seventeen-year-old son. His personality leaps off the paper. And that's something only a great portrait artist can accomplish. No cookie-cutter images for Dream Photography, thank you very much. "No, I didn't order them to be framed."

Hmm. Yeah, not here, but I bet you were planning to run across town to the cheap framer and have our lovely images slapped into a cut-rate frame to hang on the walls of your million-dollar home. "Oh."

I let her stew over the situation for a moment. "Well, what would you like to do, Ms. Lincoln? Shall I issue you a credit in exchange for the portraits?"

She fingers her necklace as she seems to organize her thoughts. "Perhaps I will have four of those pictures matted together after all."

Gotcha. We're nothing if not gracious here. "You know, I'm sorry for the misunderstanding. If your image consultant knew you were planning to have them displayed together, she should have shown you some framing options." *Although I'm sure she tried.* "And I would like to offer you a 10 percent discount on the frame for your troubles."

Pauline sits back. I can practically see the gears clanging inside her head. "How long will it take?"

A little appreciation would be nice, but I just want her to walk out the door smiling. "If you choose an in-stock mat and frame, how does fifteen minutes sound?"

13

She glances at her diamond-studded Rolex. "Fine. I have to run a quick errand. I'll be back within a half hour."

I'm sitting at my desk ordering my priorities when Thomas interrupts me. He lugs his camera bag in, drops it, and plugs the studio cell phone into the charger. He talks over his shoulder. "Saw your son this morning."

"Really?"

"Yeah, I was shooting downtown by the Performing Arts Center. Doesn't he go to CU?"

I open my mouth to answer, but he continues his monologue. "Well, we were walking over to the 16th Street Mall to take some shots by the D&F Tower, and Nick comes strolling down the sidewalk with his arm around a gorgeous girl."

I'm dumbfounded. "Are you sure it was Nick?"

He raises his eyebrows and nods emphatically.

I feel a flush creep up my neck. "Are you positive?"

"I don't forget a face." Thomas smiles and leaves the office as he always does, with a flourish. My heart feels waterlogged. Could two people in as many days be mistaken about seeing my son fawning over a young woman? Why would he keep this relationship from his family?

I push personal thoughts aside and grind on through the day. By the time I leave work, it's late. Again. Fortunately I have an understanding family that doesn't mind eating takeout at least once a week.

I'm so over Chinese food. But I've found a new joint that satisfies my nostalgia as much as my appetite. When Jerry and I went to college in Pennsylvania, we developed a taste for Philadelphia cheesesteak. My mouth waters just thinking about the shaved beef with caramelized onions on an Amoroso bun, smothered with Cheez Whiz. I'll be the first to admit it's not health food, but sometimes you just have to feed your soul. I can't tell you how thrilled I was to discover this little sandwich joint—inside a gas station, of all places.

The only negative to Yeah Philly! is the owner, not that JR isn't a lovely gentleman. You could say he's just a little too enthusiastic about his hoagies. The first time I went there, he forced me to read an essay about the proper way to build a sandwich. I've since discovered he makes every new customer read his sandwich manifesto. I can appreciate a quirky person, but JR raises quirkiness to an art form.

A few weeks ago, I phoned in my order as I was leaving work, expecting to run in, pay for my food, and leave. Unfortunately, that's not the way JR does business. I arrived to find that he hadn't started cooking my french fries. "I will cook no fries before their time," he told me.

So tonight my order didn't include fries. Two cheesesteaks, a meatball hoagie, and an Italian hoagie. Nice and straightforward. There are no customers ahead of me when I stroll into the shop. "Hi. Order for Linda, please."

JR nods as he works over his grill. "Linda, Linda, bo-binda, banana-fana fo-finda, fee-fi-mo-minda. Linda!"

Oh, please. Don't tell me he's going to sing. I smile, hoping he'll get on the ball and deliver my sandwiches.

"Now, you ordered a meatball hoagie?"

"Yes."

"Okay." He turns from the grill, grabs a bun, and slices it down the middle.

What? "Is my order ready?"

JR shifts his Phillies baseball cap on his head. "Just about. The meatball hoagie is a very delicate sandwich. You can't make it in advance."

"You know, that's okay with me. I'd rather have my sandwich a little soggy and be on my way."

JR looks at me as if I asked him for a veggie hoagie with creamy coconut saffron sauce—a request which I'm sure would give him a heart attack. "What? Are you kidding me? I learned my craft from the best, and they're all up there watching me now." He points toward the ceiling, and I half expect to see the clouds part and the ghosts of hoagie chefs past scowling down at me. He narrows his eyes. "There's a right way and a wrong way to make a hoagie, and I always do it the right way."

Oh no. Now I've done it.

He gestures with his spatula. "Ah, like brown mustard on an Italian hoagie—that's just not right. A hoagie is supposed to be a symphony of flavor, not a symphony of flavors. There's no gestalt in a hoagie with brown mustard."

Did he really say that?

He assembles my meatball hoagie while he rants, and I hold out my credit card to pay for my order. But does he take it? No. He continues on and on about the shops he's worked in on the Jersey shore and how people on the boardwalk would never consider telling a hoagie chef how to build a sandwich. "This ain't Subway, you know."

I wave my card in front of him.

"And earlier, a chick came in and asked me to hold the tomato on her hoagie. Can you believe that?"

I move the card closer to him. "Uh, no."

JR finally takes my card and runs it. While I'm signing the slip, he grabs a marker and draws a line down the top of each sandwich wrapper and puts them in a bag. "Remember, line up. We don't want the juices to run the wrong way." He hands me the bag. "Hold it like a baby."

• • •

My family's eager for dinner when I arrive home. I try to tell them about JR, who must have been the inspiration for the soup Nazi on *Seinfeld*, but they won't hear it.

Emma slaps the table. "Don't put the ban on Yeah Philly!"

I shake my head. "I'm not going to ban it."

Jerry speaks around a mouthful of cheesesteak. "Don't go crazy on us. We all love these sandwiches."

I roll my eyes. My family makes too much out of my boycotts of certain businesses that I don't think deserve our patronage. I work too hard to throw away money on stores that don't appreciate me.

We discuss inconsequential things, but I really want to know about the girl who seems to have captivated my son's attention. And why hasn't he told us about her? "Nick, Thomas says he saw you on the 16th Street Mall today."

He looks at me. "Um, I didn't leave the campus until I came home."

Why is he lying? "Really? Thomas was sure it was you. Said you were walking with your arm around a very attractive girl."

Nick shrugs and takes a bite of his sandwich.

Emma points an accusing finger. "Hillary was right. You were with a girl at Starbucks yesterday."

"Shut up."

Jerry glares at Nick. "Don't speak like that."

Silence descends on us, and my appetite flies out the window. We've always had a good relationship with our kids, and I plan to keep it that way. I put down my sandwich and lay my hand on Nick's arm. "What's going on?"

He drops his hoagie and pushes away from the table. "Do I have to tell you every detail of my life?"

Whoa. A little defensive, Son? "No. But if you're seeing a girl, I don't know why you'd want to keep it a secret."

"I'm twenty-two years old. Could you try to respect my privacy?"

"Don't be like that."

My words fall short of his retreating back.

3

I'm left alone in the kitchen to clean away the greasy wrappings from our sandwiches. What's happened to my relationship with Nick? We used to be able to discuss anything. And it's not like this is the first girl he's dated. So why the mystery?

After finishing my final wipe of the table, I tie up the garbage and take the bag to the garage. On my way back inside, I nearly trip over two gallons of paint sitting along the wall. *Oh, gracious.* A smudge of awful teal paint on the lid proves that my husband does not have a single design gene in his body.

I sigh. Jerry's design challenges will have to wait for another day. Right now I'm going to get to the bottom of Nick's issue with his new girl.

I knock at his door. "Nick?" Then I turn my ear toward the door to better hear his reply. There is none. So I knock again, harder this time.

"Yeah?"

"Can I ask you a question?"

"What?"

For someone who wants his adulthood respected, he sure is acting childish. "Can you open the door?"

Nick doesn't respond, but I hear his bedsprings squeak and the sound of feet shuffling across the room. He opens the door, but instead of allowing me to come inside, he stands at the threshold, barring me from entering.

I put my hands on my hips. "Why are you being so rude?"

"Sorry." He turns sideways and allows me to walk in, then flops on the bed.

I sit in his desk chair and fold my hands, trying to come up with the least confrontational way to ask him why he's been so secretive. Out of the corner of my eye I see Emma standing in the doorway.

Nick leaps to his feet, crosses the room, and slams the door in her face.

Emma's muffled response is punctuated by her kick to the door.

I open the door, then glare at Nick. "Apologize to your sister right now."

He looks as though he's coiled to spring to the attack. He spits out an apology.

Emma makes a disgusted face and retreats.

I reclaim my seat at his desk, and Nick perches on the foot of the bed, his arms folded across his chest. *What's happened? How did my pleasant son turn into this morose stranger?* "What's going on?"

He looks past me at the inky darkness beyond the window. "I've met an amazing girl. I think I'm falling in love."

I had imagined this news would make me leap to my feet in joy because I've always wanted my children to find love. I'm certain the words I utter in the next moment must be carefully crafted. Instead of the warmth of emotion the circumstance should have, I feel a sort of cool dread. I force a smile. "Tell me about her."

His countenance softens, and a sparkle comes to his eyes. "She's wonderful. She's smart and thoughtful and fun to be with."

"Why, then, have you kept this under wraps?"

Nick's expression turns wary. "She's my ideal woman, but I'm not sure she's yours. But keep in mind I'm the one spending time with her."

The hairs on the back of my neck stand at attention. Nick's

always had such high standards. How could he choose someone he has to make apologies for? "What's wrong with her?" As soon as the words leave my mouth, I know they're a mistake.

"There's nothing wrong with her. Really. This is what I was afraid would happen."

"I'm sorry. I didn't mean for it to come out that way. I'm sure there's nothing wrong with your new friend—"

"Girlfriend," he growls.

"Okay, your new girlfriend. But you're the one who said she was less than ideal."

"No, I said you might find her less than ideal."

This conversation isn't going well. My brain feels sluggish, not up to the mental acrobatics that Nick is playing. *Give me wisdom, Lord.*

We sit in strained silence.

Finally I clear my throat. "We've always trusted you. I'm sure she's a wonderful girl."

"She is."

Is this conversation going in circles, or what? "Well, tell me—what's the issue? Why are you being so guarded?"

Nick looks down at the pile of books on his floor. *This can't be good.* He raises his eyes to mine. "She's not a Christian—yet."

My heart drops. "I've given you the same advice my mother gave me—don't date anyone you wouldn't marry."

He shakes his head. "Ease up. I'm not marrying her. We're just dating."

I reach out and pat his knee. "Okay. But if you marry the wrong person, you'll be sorry for a long time."

"Mom!"

"Okay. Good night." I drag my weary self out of his room, closing the door behind me.

Jerry's folding laundry on our bed. I pick up a pile of towels and stow them in our linen closet.

When I return, he glances at me and raises his eyebrows.

"He's seeing a girl and thinks he may be falling in love."

I can see the wheels turning in Jer's head as he processes that information. I tell him the rest of the story. "And she's not a Christian."

"Oh, boy."

Well, that's an understatement if I ever heard one. "Yeah. I can't believe this."

Jerry puts the laundry basket on the floor by the door. "Don't jump to conclusions. This relationship may not go anywhere, and we don't need to make a mountain out of a molehill."

His advice is sound, but I have a passel of prairie dogs running circles in my stomach. I nod.

"So, what's this mystery woman's name?"

"I don't know. Nick never told me. I think he was too interested in finishing our conversation and getting me out of his room."

I pick up the basket and walk down the hall to the laundry room. As I pass Nick's door, I hear him speaking. He pauses, and his musical laughter fills the air. He must be on the phone with Miss No-name.

I need some help here, Lord. I don't want to handle this situation the wrong way. I don't want anyone leading Nick away from his heritage of faith. So please guard my mouth and Nick's heart.

4

Jerry's forehead furrows in concentration while we drive north on
I-25. Our reservations at Sushi Sasa are at six thirty, not late enough
to miss the end of Denver's rush-hour traffic. I know he's not
thrilled to be trying something new, but he's going along with plans
to meet Deb and Keith at the newest sushi restaurant in town.

He glances at me. "What exit do we want?"

I rustle through the papers stuck between the seats to find driving
directions. "We're going to exit 211—west 23rd Ave."

Traffic slows as we approach the curve by Colorado Boulevard.
"Turn on the radio and see if you can get a traffic report, Linda."

We listen to the dismal traffic news. A disabled semi has the
south lane stopped dead, and the northbound traffic is slowed
because of all the rubbernecking.

Jer's lost in thought, so I silently replay the conversation I had
this morning with Nick. His mood improved considerably from
last Tuesday. He even told me the name of his new heartthrob—
Amber Webber. His face lit up as he rattled off her good qualities
and listed some of the challenges she's had in her life. I forced a
smile, but my heart was heavy in my ribs. My son has been dating
Amber for months, and we're just finding out about it now. Could
he have a guilty conscience? Deep down, does he know that Amber
may not be the right girl for him?

Our car continues to creep forward. I reach for my cell and call

Deb. It goes straight to voice mail. "Hi, Deb. We may be a little late. There's an accident tying up traffic. Hope to see you soon."

My gaze follows a light-rail train as it passes the snarled traffic. *Lucky them.* As the train leaves the station adjacent to the highway, I see a young couple walking arm in arm. Of course my thoughts go to Nick and Amber. I can't help myself, and a deep sigh surfaces from my lungs.

"What's wrong?"

"Just thinking."

"About . . . ?"

"Nick and Amber."

Jerry nods. "Don't put too much energy into their relationship. I have a feeling it's not that serious."

"You're probably right." I don't believe my words, but it's easier to say that and avoid a lecture from Jerry.

Traffic loosens, and Jer punches the accelerator to make up time. Before too long we're at our exit.

Good news: we're off the highway. Bad news: we're back in snarled traffic. *Sheesh.*

We creep for another half mile and find a small parking lot a block from the restaurant. I spy Keith's car parked across the street.

Jerry and I enter the eatery and queue up to wait our turn. Jerry inquires about our table. The sharply dressed host nods and gestures to a waiter, who leads us through a door and down a narrow stairway. We round a corner, and I spot Deb and Keith sitting at the far end of the dining room.

Keith stands as we approach the table. He shakes Jer's hand and leans over to give me a hug. I maneuver my purse between us and manage to escape with an air kiss.

After we take our seats, I look around to get my bearings. The small room is filled with tables that run along the walls. The sound of laughter from a nearby group disrupts the rest of the diners, but no one seems to mind. I think we're in the upper age bracket for the diners; most of the others look to be in their thirties or early forties. *Whatever. Fifty is nifty, right?*

A hip, young waiter strolls over and takes our beverage order.

When he walks away, I realize that he didn't leave menus. "When he comes back with our drinks, we need to ask for menus."

Keith holds up his right hand, palm out. "No need."

"Excuse me?"

Keith smiles. "The chef is preparing a five-course meal for us. Chef's choice."

Jerry looks a little worried. Personally, I love California rolls and new experiences, but Jer has successfully avoided Japanese food for fifty years. He's always had a fear of sushi. It's never been an issue with us because this is a battle I've chosen not to wage. There are so many other culinary delights that we agree on.

With the mood I'm in right now, this evening could go downhill—and fast. *Give me patience, Lord.* I take a cleansing breath. *Hmmm. Smells good.*

Deb loops her arm around Keith's. "I forgot to tell you. Dinner will be our treat."

Jerry leans in. "Thanks. But let me split the bill."

Keith puffs up. "No, I insist on paying for this one."

This dinner date may have been a mistake. I'm not feeling the love for my best friend's husband. But I'll try. If he wants to pay, let him. "Uh, thanks."

Keith yammers on about some great business deal or something. Jerry and Deb are mesmerized. The flame from a candle at a nearby table catches my eye.

A middle-aged couple smiles broadly as a waiter places a dessert in front of the young woman sitting at their table. She takes in a deep breath and blows the candle out, then turns to kiss the young man sitting at her left. They look so—

Ouch. Jerry just threw an elbow in my ribs. *Of all the . . .*

I focus my attention on my husband, but he's such a good actor, he seems unfazed. I tune in to the conversation.

". . . three days later!"

Everyone at the table erupts into laughter. Despite being clueless, I join in.

Keith turns to me. "What about you?"

Oh, rats. What were they talking about?

Jerry puts his arm around my shoulders. "Linda's not that kind of girl."

They laugh again.

Jer squeezes my shoulder. I don't understand what actually transpired, but I know he just pulled my fat from the fire.

A young waiter stops at our table with a tray of fragrant soup. He carefully places a small bowl in front of each of us. "Miso soup." He beams as if he actually made the soup himself and leaves.

I speak to his retreating back. "Excuse me?"

The waiter stops and turns around.

I give him that yeah-I'm-waiting-for-you-to-come-back smile.

He returns to our table in three strides. "May I help you, ma'am?"

"We don't have any spoons."

He tucks his tray under his arm and leans toward me, clasping his hands. Sotto voce he says, "The soup is in sipping bowls, but if you're not comfortable with that, I can bring spoons."

Well, that's something new to me, and I don't want Jerry to feel awkward. "May we have two spoons, please?"

The waiter nods and walks away.

Keith grins as he picks up his bowl and slurps a sip of soup.

What's that supposed to mean? Does he think he's better than we are? I glance at Jerry, and he gives me his irresistible smile.

The soup is as delicious as it smells. I almost don't mind being one of only two people in the room using a spoon. Next time I'll know better.

We navigate through a maze of unfamiliar dishes, each more scrumptious than the last—albacore tataki, masago unagi, ebi fry, ikura this and hotategai that. The more full and happy my tummy gets, the easier it is to stomach Keith.

I know I should be more compassionate toward my friend's husband and I've promised Deb that I would try, but my skin still crawls when I recall the evening Deb called me to fess up to Keith's stinking shenanigans. I could imagine her looking regal in the beautiful jewelry that he showered upon her, sitting in her luxurious home, surrounded by the expensive furnishings and decorations he often bestowed. His countless gifts. At that moment, I wanted to gift his jaw with my fist. What a sham it all was.

She made excuses for him. "It's not as if he's cheating on me."

Oh, but it was. Words failed me. The best thing I could do for my friend was to let her know that I'd stand by her no matter what. Never in a million years would I have thought that Keith would be the kind of man to confess his attraction to other women and then shower his wife with empty words and stupid trinkets. The idea of him lusting after the attractive bank teller and later giving Deb a new Michael Kors bag makes me seethe. She makes excuses, goes to counseling, and pretends it will be all right. Maybe she's a better woman than I am.

It's such a challenge to summon up polite feelings for Keith, but I need to keep trying.

I hope that each day I continue my journey with the Lord, I become a better person. But in reality, it's more like each day I see how shallow I really am.

5

Dappled sunlight plays through the autumn leaves during the drive to church. The foliage is just past its glory, blazing colors before surrendering to a season of dormancy. Emma chatters about the party she's going to this Friday.

As usual, Nick drives his own car. Our harsh words ring in my head. I didn't mean to pick a fight this morning. All I did was ask if Amber would be joining us.

My eyes adjust to the change from brilliant sunshine to artificial light as we enter the building. Jer leads me by my elbow, and Emma escapes to the company of the youth group.

"There's Nick." Jerry gestures to the right, where our son is engaged in a lively conversation with old friends.

I catch Nick's eye. He holds up his finger to stop our progress toward the sanctuary. While we pause, I regard my son, so handsome, so self-assured, so poised. He and the young man talking to him do that macho shoulder-touch thing.

Nick turns toward us and crosses the room. "Sorry, Mom."

My response is a smile, and we walk together into the sanctuary.

I give myself over to the moment. The sermon is thought provoking, the music inspired. Unfortunately, my mind keeps wandering. Despite the fact that Nick is sitting next to me during the service, I feel like he couldn't be farther away. He's so secretive lately. And his lies push him farther from the family.

As soon as the service is over, Nick's out the door, a quick kiss on the cheek my farewell. Off to spend the day with friends and with Amber.

Jerry escorts me to the car, where we'll wait for Emma.

"I don't know why Nick didn't invite Amber to church with us."

He points his keyless remote at our car. "Yes, you do."

"Why do you say that?"

The car beeps and flashes its headlights. We climb inside, and he puts his hand on my shoulder. "My guess is that he doesn't want to put his new girl in an awkward position."

I'm stunned. "Awkward? As in going to church?"

He shakes his head. "No, awkward as in he thinks his mother dislikes his girlfriend."

It's my turn to shake my head. "That's not the issue at all." There's no reasoning with this man.

We gaze out the window waiting for Emma. It's not even noon, and I wish I could go back to bed. This is not my usual mood on most Lord's Days. Sundays are when I enjoy my family and read a good novel.

• • •

Jerry, Emma, and I pile into the house and change into our casual clothes. I pull cold cuts and salad fixings from the fridge. "Emma, come help me make lunch."

She pounds down the stairs from her bedroom. "What?"

"Can you spin some lettuce for salad?"

Emma makes a face. "Nick never has to cook."

"He helps when he's around."

She snatches the salad spinner out of the cabinet and throws it into the sink. Thank goodness it's made of plastic. "Will he be coming for lunch?"

"Um, not that I know of." I suspect my daughter is trying to make trouble. She knows I'm not thrilled that Nick wouldn't invite Amber to church or to spend some time with the family.

We work in silence. I wonder if Amber will be here for Thanksgiving later this month. Maybe she'll have dinner with us. Nick says she's not close with her family. How odd is that?

My thoughts turn to oven-roasted turkey, Grandma's dressing recipe, garlic mashed potatoes, green bean casserole, cranberry sauce, pumpkin pie, and my loving family all gathered around the table. This year will be Jerry's father's first Thanksgiving without the love of his life. I fight back tears thinking of Theresa, the best mother-in-law anyone could have. She was so sweet and patient and a second mother to me. She and Ross modeled a wonderful marriage and family life.

At least Ross will be joining us. This is such an important holiday for my family—getting on with life after losing Theresa.

Emma begins to hum. Maybe she's thinking about her new crush, Cole. I met him last week. He seemed nice and polite and not in that smarmy Eddie Haskell way, either. I hope my impression is correct, but I trust my mama-bear intuition won't let me down if that's not the case.

I clear aside the Sunday papers and set the table. "Jer! Lunch is ready."

Jerry emerges from the study. His hair is messed up, as if he just ran his hand through it. I know his hair is thinning, but when I look at him, I still see that twenty-two-year-old I fell in love with, and my heart stirs.

He sits at the head of the table and holds out a hand to me and to Emma. We bow, and Jerry says a blessing.

I squeeze his hand when he's finished and continue with a prayer of my own. "Lord, guard Nick's heart and give him wisdom with this new relationship."

As soon as our *amen*s are spoken, Emma starts in. "Good luck with that."

Is she trying to get on my last nerve? "What do you mean?"

She rolls her eyes, something she's been doing much too often lately. "I think Nick's too far gone for any wisdom."

I sit up straight in my chair. "Really? Well—"

Jerry interrupts. "Girls."

My mouth snaps shut and I turn to him.

He helps himself to tossed salad. "I think you're both getting a little carried away."

"Why are you in denial?" Before he can get a word in, I continue. "Nick told me he thinks he's falling in love. Don't you think this is an important issue?"

As usual, Jerry remains calm while I go into a tizzy. "Lin, don't get ahead of yourself. Just let this play out a bit before you go off the deep end."

"Whatever." *Let him stick his head in the sand.*

"Ease up. It's not the end of the world." Emma takes a bite of her sandwich and gazes at the magazine section of the Sunday paper.

Hmm. Thanks for your support. "Em, do you have any plans for the day?"

"Don't you remember?"

She doesn't need to sound that annoyed. "Remember what?"

Emma closes the paper and stares at me. "You told me I could borrow the car to go to the movies with my friends."

"Oh, sorry." The car she inherited from Jerry's mother is in the shop again. "Yeah, you can take the car. Is your homework finished?"

She shrugs.

"What does that mean?" Jerry asks. "Is your homework finished or not?"

She crosses her arms. "Don't worry about it. It's just a one-page paper. I can do it later."

I can practically see the shroud of irritation fall over Jerry. Emma should know better than to try to pull that haughty number on her father.

"That's not an attitude we tolerate around here," Jerry says, "and you know it. If your homework isn't done, you won't be going to the movies."

"I can get the assignment done in no time at all, later tonight."

My gaze bounces between my daughter and my husband. This is one argument I don't want to take part in.

Jerry maintains his posture, his expression stony.

Emma throws her hands up and glances at me. "This is not fair."

Uh, thanks, girl. I really don't need to referee this one.

Jerry slices the air with his hand. "You can leave your mother out of this. If the assignment's so easy, do it before you go to the movies."

They both turn to me. *Have I mentioned I want to go back to bed?* "What time were you leaving? Maybe you can get your homework done before you go out."

She jumps to her feet. "I can't believe this. I'm supposed to leave to pick up the girls in less than two hours."

Oh, brother. "Well, then I suggest you get yourself up to your room and do your homework."

Emma stomps from the room.

"So much for a peaceful lunch." Jerry stands, pushes his chair under the table, and walks toward the study.

Great. They argue, and I get stuck cleaning up the kitchen. Thank goodness for paper plates. I clear the table and put away the salad dressing. Before I can wipe off the table, the phone rings.

Caller ID says it's Nick. "Hello?"

Laughter floats across the line. "Hold on." It sounds like he's talking to someone else.

"Nick?"

His voice is still laced with laughter. "Sorry."

"What can I do for you?"

More laughter, and it sounds like he's muffled the phone. "Oh, sorry again."

My stomach turns sour. "Hello? I've got things to do. What do you want?"

My attitude must have traveled through the phone because he suddenly sounds a bit more serious. "I was calling to let you know I probably won't be able to make it for dinner."

Disappointment falls over me. "When we made our menu for the week, you specifically requested baked ziti. Why can't you make it? Would you like to invite Amber?"

"Uh, thanks. But that won't work. Maybe another time. Gotta go." He disconnects the phone, and I'm left alone in the kitchen.

What's going on with Nick?

6

I snap my book shut. I've read the same page three times and still can't tell you what it said. The house is too quiet. Jerry's in his study grading homework, Nick's gone, and Emma's off to her movie.

The moment I enter the kitchen, Belle is at my heels. *Shameless beggar.* After putting a pot of water on the stove, I assemble my ingredients for dinner. I don't think I've ever prepared ziti in the past twenty years without Nick eagerly awaiting the hot, delicious pasta.

I always thought I'd look forward to the empty nest, but seeing my son stretch his wings makes my heart feel heavy. It's not that I don't want my children to mature and venture out; it's just that I never imagined either one would choose someone with such an apparently different view of spirituality.

Why can't I shake this mopey feeling? Fortunately I've made ziti enough times that I can do it by rote. I set the tray of pasta on the counter and clean up my mess.

Even Belle's deserted me. She's sprawled at the top of the stairs, surveying the neighborhood from the window above the foyer. I step over her and go to my closet. This is the perfect time to clear out old clothes, especially with the mood I'm in.

In no time at all, I've filled a trash bag with fashions of seasons past. A light blue swatch of fabric at the end of the rod catches my eye. It's Nick's little seersucker suit, size eighteen months. How sweet he was.

Memories shake free in my mind like the dust that sifts from my closet shelf. Nick dancing in his little suit with short pants and saddle shoes. Nick playing soccer on a warm autumn morning. His first day of junior high, when he tried so desperately to look cool and assured.

Once the bag of clothes is tied up, I lug it to the basement and stow it at the foot of the stairs. Then I head to the kitchen to put the ziti in the oven. Belle comes downstairs and scratches at the back door. I let her out for a few minutes to the cool afternoon. The sky is growing dark, and fat snowflakes are drifting down to cover the ground.

Jerry joins me in the kitchen. "When's dinner?"

"When Emma gets home."

He fills a glass with water. "I've got some more work to do."

"Go ahead. I'll call you."

Jerry goes back to his study, and I set the table. Only three plates. The table looks empty. I toss Belle's kibble into her bowl and turn on lights to ward off the coming dark.

The hum of the garage door lets me know Emma's home safe and sound. She bursts through the door. "I can't believe how hard it's snowing."

I push aside the curtain and look at the snowy conditions. My barbecue grill is shrouded in a mantle of white. "How are the roads?"

Emma hangs her coat in the closet. "I was a little nervous. It was getting slippery on Pine Grove Road, and the streets in our neighborhood are pretty bad." She walks to the family room and pushes Belle aside from the fireplace.

I follow her. "Did you have the radio on? What's the forecast now?"

She holds out her hands to the warmth. "I hope school's canceled tomorrow."

"Is a big storm forecast?" I know it's November and I live in Colorado, but the big storms usually come in December or after.

She shrugs.

I'm searching the couch cushions for the television remote when the oven timer chimes. The weather forecast will have to wait.

Like one of Pavlov's dogs, Jerry appears in the kitchen.

"Did you see the snow?" I ask him.

He carries a pitcher of iced tea to the table and calmly takes a seat. "Snow?"

You gotta love a man who can get so involved in his work that everything else passes away. "Yes, it's snowing out."

He pours himself a drink.

Doesn't he see the implications? "We have to call Nick. He needs to get home before the roads are too dangerous."

"Is it that bad?"

"Emma said it's already pretty bad."

"Why don't we eat dinner first?"

"I think we should call him right now so he can get home safely." I reach for the phone.

Jerry's upheld hand stops me. "Finish dinner. He's not a million miles away, and besides, how do you think he'll feel about mommy calling him home?"

I suck in my breath and take my seat. "I'm surprised that you don't care if our son could be in a dangerous situation."

He covers my hand with his. "Sweetheart, he's a big boy, and he's a cautious driver. If you're still nervous, call him after dinner."

Emma joins us and Jerry prays for our meal.

As I serve him some pasta, he gazes at his plate. "Ziti?"

"Yeah?" He knew what the menu was.

"Don't you think you should have waited for a night Nick would be home?"

I shrug and dig into my delicious meal.

"Are you trying to get back at him?"

"Why do you say that?"

"It's his favorite. You made it knowing he wouldn't be here. Just wondering if you're trying to serve up a portion of guilt."

His question sucks the air out of my lungs. I settle down and try to enjoy dinner. I turn to Emma. "How was the movie?"

She stuffs a forkful of pasta into her mouth and shakes her head. "What?"

She dabs her mouth with a napkin. "It wasn't great. We left early and went to Starbucks."

Emma and Jerry talk about the movie, but I can't stop thinking about Nick. When I asked Jer if he didn't care that our son might be in a dangerous situation, I wasn't just thinking about the weather. I was thinking about him becoming too involved with a girl who doesn't share our faith.

The brass wind chimes that hang outside the back door begin to clang like mad, cutting into my thoughts. "Wow, the wind's really picked up." I put down my fork and push away from the table. I slide open the door and step out onto the patio to retrieve the chimes from their hanger. A strong wind whips my hair, and snow stings my eyes.

As soon as I step back inside, Jerry closes the door behind me, takes the chimes from me, and places them on the counter. "It looks pretty bad out there. Maybe you should call Nick."

I raise my eyebrows but don't tell him *I told you so*. I'm above that. Instead I pick the receiver off the wall mount and dial our son.

The phone rings and finally goes to voice mail. *Great.* "Nick, it's Mom. The weather's taken a pretty bad turn. Emma was out this afternoon and said the highways are getting slick. Call me when you're on your way." I hang up.

Jerry starts to clear the table, and Emma and I load the dishwasher.

I spend the next hour packing a lunch for tomorrow and preparing my wardrobe for the week. Wind batters the windows and howls down the chimney. The phone rings at eight thirty. I answer on the first ring.

"Hi, this is Lyndsay. May I speak to Emma?"

"Sure." I pass the handset off to my daughter so she can speak with her best friend. I grab my novel and make myself comfortable on the living room love seat. Within minutes, I'm carried away in the fictional world of Miss Mimi and her troubles.

The chiming clock pulls me out of my book. *Ten o'clock?* I can't believe it's that late. And Nick's not home. Where did he say he was going to be? At a coffee shop? Or did he mention someone's apartment?

Jerry ambles into the room.

"Did I miss hearing the phone? Has Nick checked in?"

"Nope."

I don't waste any time getting to the phone. I hit Redial and wait while his phone rings. Finally he answers.

"Didn't you get my voice mail?"

"Mom?"

Duh. "I called hours ago. Have you looked out a window? It's storming pretty badly. You should come home."

"Oh, okay. I'll get going in a few minutes."

"I think you should leave right now."

"Sure." To my surprise, he hangs up without a proper good-bye. Maybe he didn't want to look like a mama's boy in front of his friends.

I let Jerry know Nick will be on his way and go up to bed.

The sound of an aspen branch slapping against the side of the house stirs me from my sleep. I slide out of bed and throw my fleece robe around my shoulders. The hallway is dim, only lit from the light we leave on in the foyer. Nick's door is wide-open. *That's odd.* I pad down the hall and look inside. His bed is neatly made.

He's not home? Or did he fall asleep in front of the television? Not that I hear any noise coming from downstairs.

I hurry down the stairs. The family room is dark and the

television is off. I peer out the front window toward the driveway. His car's not there.

I rush upstairs and turn on the light in my bedroom. "Jerry!"

My husband is blinking back sleep. "What?"

"Nick never came home. I hope there hasn't been an accident." My hands are shaking, but somehow I manage to dial his number.

When he answers, I can tell I woke him.

"Where are you? We're both worried."

"Sorry. By the time I started to leave, the roads looked dangerous, so I decided the safest thing to do was sit tight. No worries."

Are you kidding? "Why didn't you call?"

He yawns over the line. "I didn't want to wake you."

"Nick—"

"I'll see you tomorrow. Good night."

Thick silence comes through the receiver.

Stunned, I hold the phone and look at Jerry. "He hung up on me. He didn't leave when we asked him, and then the weather was too bad to travel."

"So where is he?"

"I wish I knew."

7

After a fitful night's sleep, I awake, feeling dazed. The digital clock reads six thirty, and sunlight squeezes through the edges of my shades. At least the snow has stopped. I turn off the alarm and lie in bed. My heart dips when I realize only one of my children is under my roof. *Where is Nick?* I'm glad he's not off on the side of a road, encapsulated in a wrecked car, but is he in a safe place?

I drag myself from the warm bed and put on my robe. Jerry's snore is peaceful, like a purring lion.

I make a cup of tea, raise the shade. The sun reflects on the snow, turning the front yard into a mystical, bejeweled landscape. I settle in the living room rocking chair. Snowdrifts swirl around the evergreens, and the road holds evidence of at least one pass through with a plow. Still, the wind is whipping snow back in the street at a furious rate. I try to calm my heart and get into a good place to pray, but my mind is too frantic. *What's going on with my son?* I pray for the right attitude and the right words that I'll need at dinnertime when I see Nick.

Emma comes down the stairs. "This stinks. School's not canceled, only delayed." She plops into my Victorian chair, her face a study in adolescent disappointment.

"Sorry, kiddo. Want to join me for breakfast?"

In the kitchen Belle prances between us. Emma feeds the dog

while I cook oatmeal. I take maple syrup out of the fridge, and we sit at the table.

She looks at her cereal as if she's formulating her thoughts. "Did you know that Nick's not home?"

"Yes." I gaze at the white landscape. "He said the roads were bad, so he stayed where he was last night."

She presses her lips together and digests the information. I'm quite surprised that she's not making a big deal about it.

I don't know if it's sleep deprivation or something hormonal, but I can't hold back my tears. I swipe my eyes with a paper napkin. "Sorry."

"Nick's a good guy. I'm sure this will be all right."

I study Emma's face. She's talking about her big brother, her hero. Nick has always stood beside her like a sheltering tree. I can't express my doubt about his choices to her. "Yeah, you're probably right."

• • •

I slip and slide down our street and head north to E-470. My car creeps at a cautious pace. Idiots in SUVs speed along, oblivious to the fact that no matter what kind of vehicle you drive, ice is ice.

Thirty minutes later, I turn into the parking lot of Dream Photography. Not too bad, my commute only took me an additional fifteen minutes. The parking lot is sparsely populated. I guess I'm one of the hardy souls.

The door chimes as I make my entrance. Luke is sitting at the reception desk, retrieving telephone messages. He waves as I walk past. I settle at my desk and pull out my cell phone to call Nick. The call goes directly to voice mail. I disconnect and drop my phone into my purse.

The pile of folders on my desk captures my attention. I open the first folder and get down to business.

Thank goodness our receptionist, Barb, made it into work, even though she was late. The phone's been ringing off the hook with clients canceling their appointments. It's one thing to schlep across town for a doctor's appointment on a snowy day and another thing to venture out in the snow to a portrait sitting.

The phone rings again. I look and see two lines already engaged. "Dream Photography, this is Linda. May I help you?"

"Yes, I picked up our pictures on Friday, and I really didn't look too closely at them before I left."

"Is there a problem?"

"Well, I've always loved the pictures we've bought there, but we're not happy with this one."

Just spit it out. "What is it that you don't like, ma'am? And to whom am I speaking?"

Nervous laughter filters through the phone.

Oh, come on. It's not as if we torture our clients.

"This is Tricia Riso."

"What exactly is the issue, Tricia?"

"I was looking at the twenty-by-twenty-four picture again, and . . ."

It sets my teeth on edge when clients refer to our beautiful portraits as pictures. They're art, not pictures. I try to put a smile in my voice. "What's wrong with your portrait?"

"It's my husband's head. It's too big."

I'm probably the last person who should deal with troubled clients today. Is it our fault that she married a man with a big melon? "Too big? Are you saying this is a lighting problem or a camera angle problem?"

"I don't know what the cause is, but I can't possibly hang this in my living room."

"Well, you know we have a 100 percent satisfaction guarantee. Why don't you bring it in, and we'll see what we can do?" *As if there's a cure for a big-headed man.*

"Thank you. Will you be in later this afternoon?"

"Yes, but really, anyone here can assist you."

"You sound so nice. I would rather work with you."

I hate it when clients bond with me. "I'll be happy to assist you. My name is Linda."

We end our conversation and I try to focus on work again, but all my thoughts are about Nick. Why didn't he call my cell this morning? We often talk while we're both on our morning commute. Where did he spend the night? And with whom?

"Linda?"

I look up to see Traci standing over me. "What?"

She shakes her head and laughs. "I asked you if you were ready for your lunch break. Twice."

"Sorry." I stuff my paperwork into a folder and stand. "Lunch sounds good right now."

I join my friends in the break room, and we sit around the table. Traci and Jill talk about preparing for the holiday rush. It gets so busy around here that we don't even plan our company Christmas party until January.

Traci sits up straight. "I know how we can keep clients from biting off our heads when things get rough."

Well, she has our attention now.

"We can all wear a uniform to work, and—"

Jill cuts her off. "Are you out of your mind? Why would we want to do that?"

Traci sighs. "Before I was so rudely interrupted—"

"Who would pay for uniforms?" Jill adds. "I can barely—"

"Will you give me a second?" Traci laughs at our friend who too often lets herself get carried away. "The uniform would be red tights, a green jumper with a zigzagged hem, pointed shoes, and a little Santa hat with a bell on the end."

We sit in silence trying to visualize Traci's design.

Traci cracks me up. "You've just described elf costumes!"

Jill puts a hand to her chest. "Good one, Traci. You had me going."

"As if that's difficult."

We all burst into laughter again.

8

I usually have better manners, but I speed-dial Nick twice during lunch. Both times the call goes to voice mail. I appreciate him turning off his cell when he's in class, but I'm pretty sure he's out by now. My concern is morphing into anger. I turn off my phone. I've got to stop obsessing.

This month's frame order forms are spread across my desk. I'm grateful for all the canceled appointments today. The studio is quieter than usual, and I'll be able to get some work done without interruption. I grab my calculator and mentally shut out the world.

The signal tone from our intercom disturbs my concentration, and a static-filled voice barks out my name.

I lay my ruler on the paperwork to keep my place on the form. "Yes, I'm here."

"Ms. Riso is here to see you."

Who? Oh, the woman married to the man with the size-large noggin. She would have to show up right now. Why can't someone else take care of this client?

I walk to the lobby, where a stylish sixtysomething woman is standing by our delivery counter with an enormous Dooney & Bourke bag hanging from her arm and a large portrait leaning against her leg.

She smiles when I approach her. "Linda?"

I extend my hand to meet her outstretched one. "Yes, hello. Tricia, right?"

She nods, seemingly pleased I recalled her first name. "Here's the picture."

I place the wall portrait on the easel that sits on our marble delivery counter. "What a beautiful family."

"Thank you. Our daughter and her family were visiting from Maine." Tricia gestures to a family of four sitting to her right in the image. "The others are my two sons and their families."

They're quite a group, thirteen people in all. What a handsome family, all shiny and well-groomed. And their choice of wardrobe is impeccable. Tricia and her husband sit in the middle of their progeny looking as proud as can be. *Wait a second.* "Your husband . . ."

"Yes, do you see the problem?"

My mind tries to wrap around the image before me. She's right. Her husband's head is too big. Unnaturally so. "Did you have any special artwork done?"

"Excuse me?"

"Any head swaps?"

She nods.

Bingo! I feel laughter bubbling from my gut and practically hold my breath to keep from cracking up. "It looks like an imaging error. I'm very sorry."

"Oh, dear."

I stifle my chuckle. "Don't worry. I'll put a rush on this and have it reprinted. It should be ready in two weeks. Is that okay?"

"I appreciate what you're doing, but . . ." Tricia examines the portrait.

"But?" *Out with it, woman.*

"Well, you see, we're having an anniversary party in twelve days. It's our fortieth. I wanted to have it hung over the fireplace."

"I'll personally make sure your new portrait is back in the studio within a week. If you don't have time to pick it up, we'll deliver it to your house."

She beams as if I handed her a million dollars. "Thank you, Linda."

Tricia is barely out the door when my resolve crumbles, and I nearly collapse in a heap of laughter. Fortunately there are no other clients in the room.

Barb rushes to the delivery counter to see what's tickled me. She sucks in her breath. "Oh my."

I reach for a tissue to swipe the tears from my eyes. "Yeah, you could say that." I can't wait to show this to the girls in the back.

When I enter our workroom, I'm still laughing. Heads turn, and I know my progress is being followed. I sidle up to Jill, who's framing a portrait while singing her own off-key version of "Don't Worry, Be Happy" as though she's the only one in the room. She glances my way and turns around to concentrate as she fires the last few staples into the ornate frame, securing the large image. She pushes the portrait aside and lays down her staple gun. "What's up?"

I prop Tricia's portrait on the framing counter, leaning it against the wall. "Do you notice anything unusual about this?"

Jill cocks her head. "Is it not level in the frame?"

"No, it's level."

She steps back and squints. "Should the tan line on that lady's neck have been smoothed out?"

I focus on Tricia's smiling daughter. "I didn't see that. You're right. But do you notice anything else?"

By now we have a small group standing around us. From behind my right shoulder, Traci laughs. Jill shoots her a look. "What? What do you see?"

Pam positions herself in front of the portrait. She tilts her head and places a finger on her chin. Pam's one of our top salespeople, so if there's a flaw, she usually spots it. Her shoulders begin to shake, and she tosses her head back before letting out a very unladylike guffaw.

Jill spins to Pam. "What am I missing?"

Pam shakes her head. "If you're our only quality control, we're in big trouble."

Mottled clouds of scarlet color Jill's throat. Her mouth opens to respond.

"Sorry," Pam says. "Don't take it so seriously."

Our sweet framer's expression softens.

Pam points to the portrait. "It's Big Daddy. Look at his head."

Jill moves closer to the portrait. "Why, it's—"

Pam completes her sentence. "It's huge. That's what it is. This poor man has a head like Shrek!"

"Oh no!"

We all turn and see Audrey, the imaging artist who started working with us during the summer. Her expression of horror is mixed with embarrassment. "I am so fired."

"No, you're okay," Traci says. "You have to mess up really badly to get canned around here."

Audrey lifts the portrait. "How could I have not resized that head after I swapped it from the other image?"

"Don't sweat it. I'll retrieve the file for you. It can be fixed this afternoon and sent to the lab. We can make it right." I pull open our *R* file drawer and sift through the envelopes of client files.

Jill grunts while she pulls the portrait out of the frame and breaks the image in half, then stuffs it into the garbage can.

"Whoa. Hold up there, Sparky." Traci snatches a jagged half of the Riso family portrait from the trash, lays it on the framing counter, and reaches for a straight-edge. She holds the scrap of portrait securely with one hand while she scores the image with the razor.

Jill puts her hands on her hips. "What are you doing?"

"For our wall of shame," Traci responds.

We follow Traci through the workroom down the short hallway leading to the break room—out of sight of any client who may come into our work area. Jill carries her hammer and a small nail. We stop in front of a large corkboard, and Traci holds up the part of the portrait with Mr. Riso's image while Jill pounds home the nail, securing the fragment. And there it hangs, next to the discarded portrait of the handsome little boy with a big piece of snot dripping from his nose.

"Hold on." Jill sprints back to the workroom. A moment later she returns with the label maker. "It's missing a caption." Her fingers fly over the keyboard. She prints the label and sticks it on the bottom of the image.

Mr. Bobble Head.

9

The days get shorter and shorter. The distant mountain peaks obscured by the silhouette of dark clouds sitting on the horizon mirror the heaviness in my heart. I hope I can find the right words to speak to Nick tonight. I can't believe how inconsiderate he's being. Where was he last night? Will he even tell me the truth?

Behind the spine of the Rocky Mountains, the sun fades in a splash of pink and gold. I start my car, turn on my cell phone, buckle my seat belt, and ease out of the parking lot. Most of the snow has melted from the roads, and brake lights reflect streaks of red on the wet pavement. The tune that indicates I have voice mail plays from the seat next to me. I pick up my earbud and access my message.

"Mom, sorry I missed you." Nick's voice sounds relaxed and pleasant. Doesn't he know the rift he's causing in our relationship? "I stayed with a friend last night, and I probably won't see you later today. I'm running home to shower and change clothes, and then I'm meeting the guys in my group project for dinner. I might be home late. Don't wait up."

Why does it seem Nick treats our home like a boardinghouse? Is it his girlfriend? Is he lying to us about where he's spending time?

When I get home, a delicious aroma drifts from the back of the house.

Emma's in the kitchen, standing over the stove, stirring a pot of tomato sauce. "Hi, Mom. I was in the mood for spaghetti. I hope you don't mind."

I drop my lunch box on the counter and give her a hug. "Are you kidding? This is the best thing that's happened to me today."

She smiles that grin I remember from her Brownie days, the one she'd flash whenever she received another badge.

"Guess what."

I raise my eyebrows.

"Grandpa's coming to dinner."

No wonder she's in a good mood. Ross is one of her favorite people. I'm crazy about him too. "Great."

"He called a half hour ago and asked if he could join us."

And no one loves a good spaghetti dinner more than Ross Revere. Hence, her choice of menu.

"Can you make a salad?"

Yeah, now that Emma's cooking, she wants someone to help her. I could mention how nice it is to have a sous-chef with a good attitude, but I won't. "Sure. Let me get changed first." Halfway up the stairs, I pause on the landing overlooking the family room and yell down, "Have you heard from Dad?"

Belle glances up at me from her spot on the corner of the sectional.

The sound of cabinet doors punctuates Emma's reply. "He'll be home in a few minutes. I asked him to stop at the store for fresh bread."

Interesting. This girl certainly can rise to the occasion—if she feels like it. But this might give her pause. "What about dessert?"

"Dad's picking up coffee ice cream."

Ross's favorite. I'm not surprised she remembered.

The doorbell rings twice—Ross's signature announcement. I'd answer the door, but I know I'd be run over by my daughter.

I pick up a towel to dry my hands and follow Emma to the foyer.

My father-in-law catches his granddaughter in a bear hug. He looks over her shoulder at me. "How are you, sweetheart?"

Emma holds his hand, but with his free arm, he draws me into an embrace. Having him over for dinner is bittersweet. It still breaks my heart to see him alone, without his beloved Theresa. They did everything together. I don't think I'll ever get over missing my mother-in-love.

He slips out of his overcoat, and I hang it in the closet.

As we're walking back to the kitchen, Jerry comes in from the garage. "Pop." They give each other a brief hug.

We gather in the kitchen, where Emma takes her place by the stove. She tastes the sauce and closes her eyes while she savors her creation. "Hmmm, more basil." She opens the cabinet door and searches through the spice turntable.

"You made dinner? It smells delicious." Ross looks impressed, and Emma blushes under his praise.

"Hey, I made the salad." As soon as the words fly out of my mouth, I realize how juvenile I sound.

Ross winks at me.

Jerry looks at the table. "Four place settings?"

"Yeah, Nick won't be home for a while." I busy myself cutting the loaf of bread and putting it in a basket.

When we finish saying a blessing over our meal, Ross turns to me. "And where is my grandson?"

"He's working on a midterm project with some classmates."

I sit back and enjoy the banter around my table. Ross and Jerry are so alike, and Emma loves to dive into conversation with her grandpa.

"Guess what, Grandpa?"

He glances at Emma while chewing his salad. "Hmm?"

"Nick's got a new girlfriend." She grins, surely thinking Jerry or I will fill in the blanks.

Thanks for nothing. "Pass the bread, please."

Ross helps himself to iced tea. "Ah, young love. Who is the lucky young lady?"

I smile sweetly at Jerry. If he knows what's good for him, he'll pick up the thread of conversation.

Jerry lays down his fork. "Her name's Amber. We haven't met her yet, but Nick has nothing but good things to say about her."

"He must really be in love, Grandpa. They've been seen kissing in public."

If I were sure I'd get the right leg, I'd kick Emma under the table.

"Really?" Ross asks.

"So, Pop, what's new with you?"

Thank goodness for Jer. If we continue to talk about Nick and Amber, my head will explode. At least Emma didn't mention that Nick never came home last night.

"Well, I do have some news." Ross rests his hands on the table and hesitates.

If it weren't for the smile hinting at the corners of his mouth, I'd think he's about to give us bad news.

"What is it?"

"Nick's not the only one in the family with a new girlfriend."

"What?" Emma appears confused.

"Are you dating?"

Before he can respond, Emma interrupts. "What about Grandma?" She swallows, apparently making an effort to maintain her composure.

Ross stares at his plate and sighs. "Your grandmother was the love of my life, but I'm a lonely old man. I want to dance again."

Jerry looks pensive. "Then I guess you have to dance."

The rest of the meal is eaten under the strain of forced levity. I understand that my father-in-law is young at heart, but it's hard to think of him dating someone else.

Why is nothing easy anymore?

10

Okay, breathe in through the nose, out through the mouth. Unwind.

I let each part of my body relax bit by bit. My neck, my face, my ears, my forehead, my scalp. *Sigh.* I'm still wide-awake. Jerry, on the other hand, started snoring about eight seconds after his head hit the pillow. *Sheesh, it's a little chilly in here.* I pull up the afghan lying at the foot of my bed. The digital readout on my clock says 10:57. Soft shadows play across my bedroom ceiling, and a car occasionally cruises down the street. Is there a dimmer on this stupid clock?

I flip my pillow over. The cool cotton of my pillowcase soothes my poor, stressed head. My clock taunts me—11:15. I think the emerald glow of the digits is burning into my retinas.

I can't imagine seeing Ross with another woman. I love him, and I want him to be blessed and happy. When he said he wants to dance again, my heart squeezed. I remember the first time I saw Ross and Theresa dance. It was at a family wedding a few months before Jerry and I married. I was sitting at a table when someone said, "Wow. Look at that couple dancing."

Jerry was sitting next to me. "I bet it's my parents."

We looked, and sure enough, he was right. Ross and Theresa waltzed in perfect harmony and with such grace and style that other dancers moved off the floor to give them more room.

Dancing was their thing. Despite being out in public on a dance floor surrounded by other people, when Ross and Theresa danced, it was as though they were the only ones in the room. Like they entered a special world of music and rhythm and a very private love. And now Ross wants to dance with another woman.

Outside my bedroom door I hear Belle whimpering in her sleep. No doubt dreaming of that elusive squirrel that razzes her from the aspen trees.

What time is it now? 11:39. *How long does it take to work on a group project? Doesn't Nick have to get up early tomorrow?*

• • •

"Mom?"

I jerk awake. Fingers of sunlight reach into my room, and Emma's bending over me. "What?"

"I need twelve dollars for a field trip."

"Did Nick come home?"

"Yeah. Can I take the money out of your wallet?"

I wave her on. "Whatever."

By the time I enter the kitchen, the coffee's almost finished brewing. I'm glad Emma's acquired a taste for java. She's sitting at the table eating a toaster tart. *Bleh.* "I'm making poached eggs on toast. Want one?"

"This is fine." Emma turns the page of a magazine she's reading. "Thanks."

How can she be related to me? "Good food in the morning will keep you running all day long."

She looks at me as though I'm crazy. "I'm not a baby."

Hmm. Yeah. I grab my favorite latte mug and put it in the microwave. There's nothing worse than pouring hot coffee into a cold mug. At least to me. Unless it's eating a breakfast with zero nutritional value and even less flavor than the cardboard it's packaged in.

Emma nibbles on her pastry and turns a page. Her hair drapes the side of her face, and she pushes it behind her ear. The morning sunlight falls across her features, accenting purple smudges beneath her eyes.

"Are you okay?"

She gazes up at me.

"Aren't you sleeping well? You look tired."

She shrugs and returns her attention to her magazine. After a few minutes, she closes the magazine, drains her coffee, and loads her dishes in the washer. "Oh, don't forget. I'm getting a ride with Sara. We're going to go to the mall right after school." She runs upstairs to get ready.

I hear footsteps on the stairs, and my heart beats a little faster. Who would have ever thought I'd be nervous to have a conversation with my son?

"Morning."

Oh, it's Jerry. "Hi."

He pours a cup of my favorite Jamaican Blue Mountain blend. "Is it my imagination, or are you less than thrilled to greet me this morning?"

"Sorry. I thought you were Nick." I begin to heat water for our eggs. "Throw some bread in the toaster." I turn my back to Jerry and continue cooking. Out of the corner of my eye, I see him leaning against the counter, watching me. "Hello? Bread in the toaster—aren't you going to help me?"

He cocks his head. I know the look.

Guilt settles into my weary bones. "I'm sorry. I don't mean to be bossy, but why aren't you doing anything?"

He pushes off from the counter and draws me into his arms. His stubbly chin scratches my forehead. "I know this is a tough situation. It bothers me too. We have to trust that we raised Nick well and he'll do the right thing."

Do the right thing. That's exactly something Ross would say. Like father, like son. I hope that pattern continues to the next generation.

As if on cue, Nick walks into the kitchen. He grins and pours himself some coffee. "Hi."

Jerry loosens his embrace, and I face Nick. "Hi? That's all you have to say?"

Nick freezes, his coffee mug halfway to his mouth. "What's wrong?"

My jaw drops. "Are you kidding me? How about an explanation about where you were last night? And with whom?"

He sets his mug down hard, spilling some of the coffee on the counter. "Is this any way to treat an adult?"

Don't try that on me, Sonny. "If you want to be treated like an adult, you should act like one."

We stare each other down.

"Nick, it's not very adult to allow people who love you to worry about where you are all night."

"I called."

"Yeah, you called—after I left you a voice mail."

"I can move out if you want me to."

Jerry takes over. "You don't need to move out. You'll be doing that soon enough. You've only got another semester of college left."

Nick squares off. "I can't be calling you every ten minutes to let you know where I am. I'm not in junior high anymore."

"Age has nothing to do with letting us know where you are. It's about being thoughtful." I take a seat and wrap my hands around my mug. "When I leave the house and you ask where I'm going, I don't just say 'out.' I let you know where I'm going because I'm not rude. If I'm late, I don't want to worry you."

He seems to consider my words for a moment. "Okay. I guess you're right. Sorry."

I pause to let him fill me in on where he's been keeping himself, but he just slides the newspaper over and starts to read.

"What's going on, Nick? You usually don't stay out so late or all night long."

He sighs deeply and looks like he's reining in his temper. "I was with friends. And, yes, Amber was one of them."

I'd push for more information, but Jerry's hand on my back tells me to ease up. I stand and return to the stove. "Eggs, Nick?"

"Yes, please."

I attend to our breakfast while my two guys sit and read the newspaper. On the surface, it seems like another average morning, but I know different. The truce we have is uneasy.

I hear Emma riffling through her schoolbag in the living room. She sighs loudly. I leave the kitchen and find my daughter stationed by the front window, watching for her ride to school. Her stance looks weary. She's disguised the purple smudges beneath her eyes with foundation, but I know something's up. "Emma, are you sure you're all right?"

She turns and smiles, fingering the antique necklace that used to belong to Theresa. "Yeah, I'm fine. Just sad. And confused."

I open my arms, and we hug. "I know exactly how you feel, sweetie. But we have to support Grandpa. His days are long and lonely without Grandma."

A car honks from the curb.

I smile at her. "We'll talk later. Have a good day."

Emma rushes out to her friends. I stay by the window and watch the car drive down the street and out of sight. The welcoming comfort of Grandma's Victorian chair calls out to me, and I sink into it. Everything around me seems to be changing and so quickly.

Some days I miss Theresa so much that I can't help but weep. Nick is moving on in ways that hurt, creating an emotional distance that I don't know how to bridge. And this August, Emma will be off to college—one away from home. It used to feel like my little family would be together forever, but now loved ones are passing on and growing up.

Jerry calls to me, "I'm turning off the coffee. Want the last cup?"

I brush away the tear from my eye and return to the kitchen. Jerry and Nick are in the midst of a conversation.

"Yeah. Probably on Saturday." Nick loads his mug in the dishwasher.

"What did I miss? What's happening on Saturday?"

"Nick's bringing Amber over to dinner," Jerry says.

"Wonderful. I look forward to meeting her."

Nick seems pleased as he walks from the room.

I pour the last cup of coffee from the pot and join Jerry at the table. "How did you pull that off?"

"I didn't. It was Nick's idea." He shakes his head. "You better adjust your attitude, girl. You aren't in competition with Amber."

"I know that!"

"Then start acting that way."

What nerve. He can't be right. Can he?

Jerry's given me plenty to think about on my drive to work. But dwelling on Nick and Amber will give me heartburn. So instead, I dial Debbie.

She answers after two rings. "Hi, Linny."

"Sorry I haven't talked to you in a while."

"Well, if it wasn't for e-mail, I'd think you'd fallen off the planet."

I guess I've been neglecting our friendship. "Yeah. Thanks again for dinner last week. Who knew Jerry would like sushi?"

"There's a first time for everything. Hey, I was going to call you today. I have news."

I'm weary of news. "Well? What is it?"

"Something totally unexpected."

"Really? Are you going to be a grandmother?"

"No, that's not it. But Keith went in to work early this morning for a meeting, and . . ."

Her dramatic pauses have always killed me. "And that's your big news?"

Debbie clears her throat. "No. There was a secret executive meeting last night—"

"Has he been laid off?"

"Oh, good grief. No."

"What then?"

"Will you let me tell you?" She laughs. "They've decided to do a reorg, and Keith's going to head a three-year project in North Carolina."

"Is that good news or bad?"

"It's good news."

What will it mean for their marriage? "Will you be going with him?"

Her voice grows soft. "Of course."

I want my dear friend to be happy, and I hope that oaf she's married to will see to the job. "This may be a good thing for the two of you."

"Yes, that's what I'm hoping."

"How are Randy and Andrea taking the news?"

"They'll be fine. They've got each other. We'll probably miss them more than they'll miss us."

It wouldn't be fair for me to complain about how much I'll miss Deb, so I don't bring it up. "Congratulations. When do you leave?"

"Thanks. There's so much to do. Keith will leave in a few weeks. I'll stay behind to get the house in order and put it on the market."

"What? You're not coming back here?"

"We may, but we don't want to live in a rental property, and the only way we can afford to buy a house in the east is to sell this one."

"I guess that—"

"Oh, Keith's on my call waiting. Can I talk to you later?"

"Sure. Bye."

We hang up, and I continue on to work. I feel like I'm losing control of my life. Nick's falling in love with a girl I haven't even met yet, Ross is dating, Emma's looking at out-of-state colleges, and now Debbie's deserting me. Thank goodness for Jerry.

When I walk into the lobby, Barb is busy sorting through our clients and their appointments. She gives a weary-looking mother with three young children a friendly smile. "I'm sorry. Your appointment is at nine thirty, not nine."

I scurry by as fast as I can so I don't get involved in soothing hot tempers. We have three studios booked solid all day. Our hectic Christmas season has officially begun.

Sticky notes decorate the perimeter of my computer monitor. One with neon green highlighter scribbled over the words catches my eye.

Linda, where's Santa's purple cape?

As if I know. That's something the photographers are supposed to take care of. And it's Thomas's job this year. I'm not surprised he can't find it. He is a lovely man, but he's the most disorganized person I've ever met. He's always running around, certain that someone didn't put a prop back in its designated place, when in reality he's searching in the wrong spot.

"Oh, there you are." Thomas comes in looking entirely too sweaty for so early in the day.

I offer him a cynical smile. "Yes?"

"Luke wants me to go through all of the Santa clothes and props to make sure they'll be good to go next month. But I can't find the purple cape with the fur hood."

"And you're asking me because . . . ?"

Thomas walks to my desk and grins. "Because you're nice and you'll help me out. Please. I've got a full schedule the rest of the week, and I'm taking Friday off to go to the mountains. Puh-lease help me out."

"I'll see what I can do."

He blows a kiss on his way out the door and disappears down the hall.

I pick up my sales schedule and client files and slip into my favorite image presentation room.

The morning fades quickly. My first sale of the day is a delight, a young family with portraits of their newborn daughter. They have so much ahead of them—moments of joy and laughter, challenges and rewards. How quickly this life passes. I remember my sweet babies. They always seemed to be on my lap or at my feet, but now they're always on my heart.

My next sale is an older couple who came in for portraits to celebrate their sixtieth anniversary. I glance at my watch. *Yikes.* I didn't notice how much time I spent on that young family's sale. I load the Sullivans' images into my computer and dash to the lobby to escort them to the salesroom.

My adrenaline starts pumping in overdrive when I realize I don't have the time we'll need to write up their order. I just know I'm going to lose some of my lunch hour. And I want to conclude this sale quickly so I can call Debbie back.

When I enter the lobby, I see them sitting together on the couch. They're dressed casually, Mr. Sullivan in blue jeans and a sweater, and his wife in a sweat suit. A hearing aid is visible in her ear, and he looks like an old pirate with a patch covering his right eye. They're talking quietly.

I stop in front of them and interrupt. "Good morning. I'm Linda. I'll be helping you today."

They give me the sweetest smiles ever.

"Hello, young lady. I'm Slim Sullivan, and this is my wife, Bert." He pushes himself out of the seat, then reaches over and pulls Bert's walker closer. She inches forward and grasps Slim's outstretched hand. When she stands, he puts a hand on her elbow and guides her into the walker.

Tick, tick, tick. We should be in the salesroom by now. I stifle a sigh and lead them through the lobby, kicking aside toys that have migrated from the play area. As I'm about to turn the corner and go down the hall, I look back. They haven't even made it out of the lobby. I've never seen anyone walk as slowly as Bert Sullivan.

Slim follows Bert, baseball cap in hand. He raises his hand and waves the hat. "Hold on. We're coming." They both laugh.

I force a smile on my face and bite the inside of my cheek. Looks like I'm going to have to practice my patience with this couple. Okay, so I'm running about ten minutes behind schedule, and we won't get to the salesroom for at least another three or four minutes. My stomach begins to churn. I take a few more steps and wait for my clients to catch up. The Sullivans act as though we've all the time in the world. Do they really need to pause and comment on every portrait hanging on the walls?

Traci comes up behind them and glances around Slim. She catches my eye, cocks her head, and turns around.

Yeah, there's no passing these folks. Before I disappear into the salesroom, I turn to make sure Slim and Bert see me go in.

I scan the room to confirm that I'm prepared. Two chilled bottles of our designer-label water sit beside a plate of freshly made oatmeal cookies on the coffee table. Alongside the plate are fanned-out Dream Photography cocktail napkins.

Where are my clients? By the time they get in here, their cookies will be stale. I go to the door and peer out.

"Howdy." Traci pauses in front of me. "I went back out the front door and around the building and still made it down the hall before your clients."

I'm not surprised. "This isn't a race, you know."

She shakes her head and disappears into the studio.

I watch the Sullivans shuffle toward me. Slim waves again. He hovers over his wife as if he's protecting her from an unseen force. As they get closer, I can see that Bert continually glances Slim's way to check on his progress. How long have they been like that? Forever? I can't imagine what it will be like when Jerry and I are married that long.

I make the mistake of glancing at my watch. *Ugh.* I guess I can kiss my lunch hour good-bye.

12

I'm such a jerk. As if that's new information.

My eyes are misty after watching the Sullivans' slide show. The music I chose was "What a Wonderful World." We're supposed to put our clients into an emotional state. I didn't think it was going to affect me too.

The love this couple shares is apparent in their portraits. It stretches over them like a gossamer shell, sweet and soft and sparkly. The last image is of their gnarled hands, resting together on their family Bible. I think the imaging artist gave their gold wedding bands an added glow.

And to think I've spent the past fifteen minutes fussing and stressing over trying to make them conform to my pitiful schedule.

Slim and Bert sit in upholstered chairs, facing the big screen. When the music fades, Slim swipes his good eye with a plaid hand-kerchief. "Oh, Bert, you're beautiful."

She turns to him. "What? I didn't hear you."

He leans over the arm of his chair, pats her knee, and shouts, "You're beautiful, baby."

Bert waves off his compliment and shakes her head, probably the way she's done for over sixty years when he sweet-talks her.

We begin to weed through their forty-five images. The first set is of Bert sitting in front of Slim. Dear man, his one good eye seems a bit googly. It looks off in a different direction in every image.

"I like that one," Bert says.

Slim holds up his hand. "Nope, not good."

We struggle through four similar images and then switch to a new pose. They're gazing at each other with natural light falling softly on their forms. I almost feel like a Peeping Tom seeing them together in such an intimate setting.

"That's perfect," Slim says, pointing to the screen. "That one; that's good."

"No, it isn't. You look sad."

So we struggle through the images, neither of them agreeing on which is best. My nimble fingers fly over my keyboard to compare poses as these stubborn octogenarians squabble.

It finally dawns on me. "Bert, why do you like number twenty-two so much?"

Bert turns to me. Her face is wreathed with a smile. "My husband looks so handsome in that picture."

My eyes fill up again. Just as I thought. Slim's choosing the images in which he thinks Bert is most beautiful, and Bert's selecting the ones that show Slim at his best. Could there be a sweeter example of love?

By the time we settle on four of their favorite poses, my lunch hour is nearly over. I can eat my tuna sandwich at my desk, and I'll call Debbie on the drive home.

I'm sitting at my desk while I finish my paperwork for the Sullivans' order. They are clients I won't forget for a long time.

Barb's voice squeaks over the intercom. "Your next appointment is running late."

Some days are like this. "Thanks for letting me know."

I toss my empty sandwich bag and munch on a few grapes. At least now I've got time to look for Santa's purple cape. I walk down the hall to our wardrobe room that is stocked with bins of accessories and small props. Clothing racks stretch in three rows from one side to the other. We've got clothing for just about any type of portrait and for any size client.

I push some garments to one side of a rack and sort through them. This room is a mess. Fairy costumes are mixed in with little fireman coats; Harley jackets hang with princess costumes. At the end of one of the racks is a pile of clothes that fell from their place because the stopper at the end of the pole came off. And no one thought to put it back together?

I squat and begin to go through the mountain of costumes. My mind wanders back to Slim and Bert. Walking them to the lobby took nearly five minutes. But it was a joy. They chatted about their portraits and how excited they are to give them to their children and grandchildren.

Thinking of the Sullivans makes me want to go home and hug Jerry. I hope my children find a love as wonderful and enduring. I'm anxious to finally meet Amber. What kind of girl is she? How could Nick possibly think he could have a promising future with a girl who doesn't share our faith?

Sound in the room is muffled, probably because of the yards and yards of fabric taking up space. Muted conversation hums as people walk by the door. I work in the marshmallow silence until the sound of voices catches my ear, as if someone's standing by the door. Words drift my way. "Sneaking . . . ashamed . . . hit the fan."

I poke my head up and see Thomas gesturing wildly while he speaks. I can't see whom he's talking to, but he seems awfully excited, the way he does when he's passing on particularly juicy gossip. *Oh, dear.* I wonder who the victim is this time.

I've organized a portion of the clothes by category and set them in bins while I finish going through the heap of various shirts, dresses, and costumes. A glimpse of fur catches my eye, and I grab the garment from the pile. Santa's purple cape. I shake it out and search for a hanger to hold the ornate velvet cloak. A portion of the fur has come loose from the hood. Thomas better get the seamstress to fix this. I drape the garment over my arm and head to the door.

Yowsa. The hook of the hanger catches on another costume, and I'm nearly pulled off my feet. I fall back and kneel to disentangle this mess.

"Excuse me. Coming through," Luke booms in the hall.

I can hear the casters on the bottom of his rolling tripod clip over the hardwood floors. From the corner of my eye, I see Thomas and our assistant, Katrina, jump into the wardrobe closet to escape being run over by our boss.

"Anyway," Thomas says, "Linda's a prim and proper lady, and . . ."

Me? He's talking about me?

"She's just going to die when she sees the hot little number that has her claws into her perfect son."

What? I lean into the softness of spring dresses and settle between two of the racks. *Why is he gossiping? What have I ever done to him?*

My feet are growing numb, but I don't want to stand and give away my position. It will be more embarrassing for me to catch Thomas in his evil act of gossip.

Uh-oh. It's dusty in here. I feel a sneeze coming on. What was it the doctor told my cousin to do when he broke his nose and didn't want to sneeze? I remember—rub the roof of your mouth with your tongue. I slide my tongue around like crazy. *Rats.* I don't think it's going to work.

Once my sneeze erupts, I know it's going to have at least two more encores. My sneezes are loud enough to wake the dead. I stand up from my hiding place and look toward the door.

I've never seen a face develop a blush as fast as Katrina's. She scurries away.

Thomas looks surprised, but he quickly recovers and bounds over to me. "What have we here?" He holds out his arms for the cloak, and I drop it into his waiting hands. "Linda, you're a sweetheart. Thanks."

I'm numb with shock. He's just going to pretend that I didn't overhear his snippy conversation? I don't think so. I cross my arms and look him in the eye. "Thomas, you must realize—"

"Oh, Linda, there you are." Barb sticks her head into the wardrobe room. "Your next appointment is here."

I look from Barb to Thomas, and in that split second, Thomas takes his leave.

Well, that's the last time I'm going to do him a favor.

13

I'm thankful Barb called me away to help my next set of clients.
I might have said something to Thomas that would have really
blown my testimony. He makes me so angry. I'd prefer to form my
own opinion about Amber rather than take his word for it.

It's drizzling when I leave work, making me long for a cozy fire,
a cup of hot tea, and a good book. I point the car toward home
and call Debbie.

She answers right away. "Sorry I blew you off earlier."

"That's okay. Any more news?"

"No, it's just a million details to deal with. Should we store stuff
or have a garage sale? What Realtor should we use? You know, moving stuff. What's new with you?"

Boy, that's a loaded question. "Can you get away for lunch tomorrow?"

"What's wrong?"

I laugh weakly. "Oh, nothing really."

"Now you've got me worried."

My best friend knows me well. I turn onto the highway and set
my cruise control. "I just need to vent. And who better to do that
to than you, my dear?"

"All right. How about twelve thirty at the tea shop?"

"Tomorrow, then."

I turn on the radio and punch the button for the oldies station.
Music blares, and I turn the volume down a bit. Thirty years ago

I hated that song and hate it just as much now. I punch another button. Commercial. *Moving on.* Within nine seconds, I've gone through all the buttons on my radio. I turn it off.

When I feel a familiar heart tug, I know I need quiet time with my Lord. I've been running ahead of myself, worrying and not trusting the One to whom I can carry my burdens. It's a lesson I should have learned once and for all by now. I'm such a weak vessel. My thoughts filter into prayers, and I try to let go of some bitterness toward Thomas and fear that the changes happening to my family might make for rough times.

I let myself into the dark house and feed Belle. *Where's Jerry?* I thought he'd be home early today.

What's that smell? Wet paint? Oh no. Were those awful cans of paint sitting along the wall of the garage when I got home? I fly upstairs.

Plastic drop cloths lie over my furniture like shrouds. The walls of my bedroom glisten with a fresh coat of that ghastly teal paint. I'm queasy. I don't think this color has been seen in public since 1975. It's suffocatingly awful. I can barely draw breath. How can I wake up to this dated-looking nightmare every morning? And how can I get rid of this awful shade without offending my husband?

Where is that man?

I slip into my sweats and head downstairs to make dinner. The drizzle has let up. I think I'll barbecue burgers. I toss frozen fries into the oven, form the patties, and step outside to turn on the grill.

When I get back into the kitchen, Emma and Nick are walking through the front door together.

"Grandpa? Dating?" Nick looks to me for confirmation of Emma's news.

"Yeah, it seems that way."

The phone rings. Both of my kids casually leave the room. Their friends usually call on their cell phones. I grab the receiver. *Good, caller ID says it's Jerry.* "Where are you?"

Megan DiMaria

"Hello to you too. Is Emma home yet? Can I park in the drive-way, or will I be blocking her?"

"She just pulled in."

"Thanks. I'm on our street. I'll see you in a second."

He sounds so happy. He's probably proud of his paint job. I decide to meet him and step out the front door. Usually the sight of his approaching SUV makes my heart lift. But right now I want to get to the bottom of this paint disaster.

Jerry parks and exits his SUV. He's wearing an old flannel shirt, paint-spattered pants, and ancient tennis shoes. "Did you see what I did?"

Boy, did I. "Uh-huh."

"Well? What do you think?"

We walk toward the house, and I turn the question on him. "What do *you* think?"

"I think we'll need to buy a new bedspread and curtains if they're going to match the walls."

I'm speechless. I don't want to encourage him on this crazy scheme. Besides, I don't think there's any chance he can find linens to match that color.

"Maybe when we redo the bathroom, we can get a new vanity top to match." Jerry looks so excited.

"That might be a little too much. . . ." I don't even know what to call that color. How could anyone sell that ugly paint?

Emma opens the front door. "What are you guys doing out here?"

I walk in past her. "We were talking about the paint job Dad did in our room."

"Really?" She takes the stairs two at a time.

I'm eager for her opinion. Did I hear her gasp?

"Dad! You've got to be kidding!"

Jerry and I join her in the bedroom. She looks as though she's going to puke. I can only imagine the insult this color is to her tender design sensibilities.

Jerry appears sheepish. He turns to me for my opinion.

I cross my arms for emphasis. "It's not exactly what I had in mind. I'm sorry for all the work you've done, but . . ."

Emma steps forward, hands on hips. "Come on. He's a big boy. Tell him the truth, Mom."

Jerry seems to have regained his footing. He cocks his head and studies me. "Yeah, what's the truth?"

I take a deep breath. I should make the most of his generosity. But I never asked him to paint my room. And now I've got to deal with this dreadful color and . . .

Wait a minute. He's got that look. He's up to something. I screw up my face. This is one of my expressions that he'll understand.

Jerry throws his head back and laughs.

I can't maintain my stern composure either, and I join him in a good chuckle.

"You people are so weird." Emma shakes her head, turns on her heel, and leaves.

Jerry puts an arm around my shoulders. "You think it's awful, don't you?"

"It's beyond awful. It's absolutely atrocious. Whatever made you choose this disgusting color?"

He tries to rein in his grin, and he stares down at his paint-stained shoes. "When I went to buy the paint, they had a section with discounted cans, and—"

"Oh, you didn't. Tell me you didn't try to save a few bucks by buying someone else's mistake."

His eyes meet mine. "Guilty."

"You realize that you're going to have to repaint this room, don't you?"

"I just went to the store to buy more paint but decided maybe you should pick it."

Now he's thinking. "Thanks. I'll be happy to oblige."

"Yeah, I—"

He's interrupted by the shriek of our smoke alarm. *Oh, rats. The fries.*

I hurry out to the landing and see a wave of smoke rise to meet me. I lean over the railing and yell downstairs, "Open the kitchen windows." I grab a magazine on my nightstand and hurry out to the landing beneath the screaming smoke detector.

I'm about to start fanning when Jerry grabs my arm. "I'll do it." He fans the detector until its wail begins to falter and finally silences.

I shrug. "No problem. We can toss a salad to have with the burgers."

Jerry and I walk downstairs together.

Emma stands at the open kitchen door, exaggerating her efforts to breathe fresh air. "Aren't we having burgers?"

I get the salad spinner from the cabinet. "Yeah. I'll toss a salad to go with it."

"Did you start the grill?"

I grab the plate of burgers and head toward the door. "Yes. And we should get these cooking while I make a salad."

Emma gestures toward the grill, Vanna White style. "And when was the last time we bought gas?"

I push past her. The warm glow of the flame should be apparent, but the appliance is dark. And cold.

I come back inside. "Grilled cheese, anyone?"

Jerry and Emma groan. They're so spoiled.

I love the time of night when everyone is tucked in bed and the house is still. Jerry bounces as he rolls over, taking the comforter with him. I jerk my portion back.

The heat turns on with a roar. Outside, the autumn wind beats the house. I'm glad both my children are under my roof tonight.

I recall our dinner conversation. Nick was beyond excited to talk about Amber. His face lit up the way it used to when he watched fireworks on the Fourth of July, knowing each explosion would be better than the previous display.

I settled back and observed my family. Jerry and Emma seemed enthralled at his proclamations. I forced a pleasant look.

My mother's intuition is acting up. Could there be storm clouds on our horizon?

14

Deb pulls into the parking lot of TeaTime right behind me. I exit my car and wait on the sidewalk. As usual, she looks like a million bucks.

We hug and enter the restaurant. The lunch rush is in full swing.

Debbie turns to me. "I have to leave by one fifteen. I'm meeting a Realtor at home."

My heart dips. I'm really going to miss her. "You're really leaving, aren't you?"

She cocks her head. "Oh, you can't—"

"Good afternoon. Two?" The hostess picks up menus as she greets us.

We follow her through the maze of tables and sit by a rear window. "All right then, ladies. Today's soup is stuffed green pepper." She nods while she hands out the menus as if she expects us to give her no-nonsense English culinary choices our utmost attention.

When she walks away, Debbie leans toward me and lays her hand on mine. "It's not as if I won't be a part of your life anymore."

She looks hopeful, but I know how it is when people move away. I try to match her enthusiasm. "We'll always be friends. I know that."

"Of course we will. And we'll be coming back to Colorado to visit our kids."

"Yes, that's true." Maybe she's right.

A waitress appears. "Can I start brewing tea for you ladies?"

Deb orders black Lapsang souchong, and I choose a green passion fruit blend.

I glance at the shelves of showpiece teapots, cups, and mugs. This has been one of our favorite meeting spots. I wonder how many more times we'll have lunch together here.

"Okay, spill the beans. What's going on?"

I place my napkin on my lap and take my time straightening it. "Nick."

Deb gazes at me as if I just announced I was getting my tongue pierced. "What's wrong?"

I launch into my explanation. "He's falling in love. And she's—"

Deb's face lights up. "How exciting."

Argh. How do I find the words to explain? Exciting is when something amazingly good is going to happen. Or when a new experience will yield a positive result. Not when a mystery girl may be poised to lead your son away from his spiritual heritage.

Deb must realize my countenance doesn't match hers because her enthusiasm wanes. "What's the problem?"

I shake my head, take a breath, and continue. "She doesn't share our faith, and I don't think Nick sees the long-term implications."

"Meaning what, exactly?"

"Well, the main thing is that she doesn't seem to be a Christian. Nick told Emma that she's never really gone to church. Ever. Her whole life."

Her expression stills. "Oh."

"See?" At last, someone who doesn't think I'm overreacting to this situation. I knew Deb would help me sort out my feelings and worries.

Our waitress beelines to our table. We pause in our conversation while she places our teapots and cups before us and sets a small timer on the table. The sweet fragrance of tea drifts over me. I wait for her to be on her way before explaining further.

"After twenty-two years of praying for my children's spouses, I can't believe she's the answer to my prayers. What if they marry? And have children?"

The timer bleats out its alarm. Deb and I remove the infusers from the pots and pour our beverages.

She absentmindedly stirs sugar into her tea. "What's Jerry got to say about this?"

"That's the frustrating part. He refuses to worry. Says this may come to nothing."

Deb nods and blows at the steam gathered on top of her teacup. "He may be right." She holds up a finger to stifle my objections. "But he may be wrong. How about Nick? What does he say?"

"He thinks he's falling in love. But they've known each other for such a short time."

"What's she like?"

"I'll find out on Saturday. Amber's coming for dinner."

A shadow falls across our table, and the waitress stands poised, pen by her pad. "Have you decided?"

I don't have much of an appetite. Deb orders soup and a sandwich, and I ask for a cup of soup. I'm not sure I can even stomach that right now.

"If you haven't even met her yet, why are you so concerned?"

Et tu? "What if our relationship gets off on a bad note?"

She shakes her head. "Why would you say that?"

"What if we don't have anything in common?"

"For one thing, you've got Nick in common."

I must be giving her one of my dumb looks because she continues. "You both care for Nick. That's a start. And who knows? She may be as nervous as you are."

"I never thought of that. You could be right."

"I'm sure of it. Remember how awkward it was for me when I first met my daughter-in-law?" Deb puts down her tea and points at me. "Besides, you raised Nick right. Maybe it's time for you to let go and trust that he'll make the right choices."

The dark clouds are lifting from the horizon, and I can see beams of sunlight reentering my life. I'm so thankful for Deb. She knows how to put things into perspective.

She smiles knowingly. "Oh, girl, what am I going to do without you?"

The reminder that I won't be able to meet with Deb and enjoy our girl talk for much longer tempers my happiness. I'm really going to miss her.

A young woman in a TeaTime polo shirt and denim skirt plunks our lunch down before us.

Why did I order only a cup of soup? I'm starving. "May I have an order of scones, please? With clotted cream and raspberry jam?"

• • •

The afternoon sun stabs my eyes on the drive back to work. What's wrong with me? Why did I put myself through so much angst the past week? I bet I'll feel better after meeting Amber. Jerry and I have always trusted Nick's judgment before. I have to believe he knows what he's doing.

As usual, chaos reigns at the studio. I clock in, stow my purse, and lunge for the ringing phone. "Dream Photography, this is Linda. May I help you?"

"Just the woman I wanted to speak with." I recognize the voice, but before I can respond, she rushes on. "This is Carol. How are you, dear?"

I feel a smile warm my face. I like Carol—now. A couple of years ago, it was a different story. And she always gives her first name, as though she's our only client named Carol. But then, Carol Ball is in a league of her own. "Hi, Carol. I'm well. What can I do for you today?"

"First, I want to thank you for taking such good care of Katrina. She's so happy to be interning at Dream Photography. I guess you could say it's a dream come true for her." She pauses to laugh at her own joke.

Katrina is the daughter of Carol's old college roommate. Two years ago Carol requested I assist Katrina in securing the internship. Katrina did so well that she was invited to stay as a photographer's assistant after graduation. And no one or nothing stops Carol from getting what she wants. She's a ball of fire. I'll never complain again. Carol has surely done enough for me too.

"I'm glad you steered Katrina our way. I know she's been a tremendous help as a photographer's assistant. We all love her."

"That's nice to hear. The reason for my call is that her birthday is coming up, and I was hoping you'd give me a hand at making it a special occasion for her."

It boggles my mind that Carol would ask for assistance planning any kind of event. She's made a career out of raising millions of dollars for her pet charities over the years. "I don't know what I could do for you, but—"

"Thanks. It seems that Luke has some silly promotion coming up, and he's making everyone on staff work next Saturday. Be a friend and see what you can do so Katrina gets the day off."

A cement brick lodges in my gut. Luke's evolved into a good boss, and he doesn't make a lot of demands, but once a year he insists that the entire staff works during a promotion that helps raise funds for homeless families. "Oh, I don't know if—"

"Tsk, tsk. Let's not have a defeatist attitude. I know you can help us. Besides, her mother wants to surprise Katrina by dropping in."

"I'll do what I can, but no one has ever gotten out of helping during holiday portrait day."

Her gentle laugh comes through the line. "I knew I could count on you."

"I'll do my best, but please don't make any plans yet. Even *I've* never gotten out of working on that day."

Carol chuckles and murmurs words of encouragement and ends the call, promising to check back with me on Monday.

I would love to help out Carol, but this may be too much. Luke has a soft spot in his heart for homeless families, having suffered that fate briefly as a child, and he pulls out all the stops to raise money and assistance for others in that situation.

The sound of shuffling feet yanks me from my thoughts, and I look up.

Luke drops an invoice on my desk. "Will you find this portrait for me? She called earlier to request that it be waiting in the lobby for her, and she's already here." He doesn't bother to wait for my reply and strides from the room.

I search through the files. Of course it's not in the slot where it belongs. I start at *A* and sort through each portrait.

Barb sticks her head in. "The client wants to know how much longer it will take to find her portrait."

If I knew where it was, she'd already be on her way. "Tell her I'm doing my best."

I hear Barb's high heels clip-clop down the hall to the lobby. The peace I regained after my lunch with Deb evaporates as I inch my way through a mountain of portraits. I ignore the ringing phone and move on to the *G* file.

Bingo! There it is. I brush my bangs aside and walk to the lobby to face the music.

Only one client is in the lobby. She's perched on the end of an upholstered chair, checking her watch. I really don't need to have my head chewed off this afternoon.

When I approach, she rises and clutches her hands. "Oh, thank you."

I start to recite my standard apology. "I'm sorry for the inconvenience. The problem—"

She waves her hand. "No, I'm relieved you've found it. Thank you so much." She steps forward and relieves me of her portrait as if it were diamonds. "Thanks again."

Go figure. Some days are blessed.

15

Wednesday is one of Jerry's days to come home early. When I arrive, he's already got pork chops baking in the oven, potatoes peeled and boiling, and the table set. He's standing at the stove with his back toward me while he coaxes canned green beans into a saucepan.

"Hello, handsome."

He turns around, still holding the empty can, and smiles. "Well, aren't you in a good mood?"

He's got that right. I unload myself of my purse and lunch box and saunter up to him. "Why shouldn't I be in a good mood?" After all, our meeting with Amber might not be the fiasco I feared. I'm thankful for good friends. Deb's saved my sanity again.

Jerry puts the can down and allows me to snuggle into his embrace. He smells delicious, like garlic and spices.

Except for the murmur of the boiling potatoes, the house is quiet. "Where are the kids?"

"Emma's doing homework, and Nick's in the basement on the treadmill." He leans back and locks his warm brown eyes onto mine. "Why?"

It's amazing that his gaze still has the ability to turn me to jelly after more than twenty-five years of marriage. "Just curious."

He gives me a little squeeze. "What do you have on your mind?"

I shove him away and toss him a playful smile. "Well, aren't we the flirt?"

As I start to go, he grabs hold of my arm and spins me to face him. He's got one of those looks in his eye. "I can be if you want me to."

Oh, good night. "Jerry!" I pull away from him and march out of the room. His laughter follows me up the stairs.

I change out of my work clothes and knock on Emma's door. "Dinner in a few minutes."

She yells a yeah from behind her door.

Nick passes me in the hall, his face red from exertion and his hair plastered to his head. "Give me five minutes for a quick shower."

I can't recall a dinner as pleasant as the one we share tonight. Emma's excited about the college applications she's preparing, and Nick's all chatty about Amber.

He takes another portion of mashed potatoes. "Mom, what are you cooking on Saturday when Amber's over for dinner?"

Panic grips my mind like the killer brain freeze I got from the Ben & Jerry's Vermonty Python ice cream I had on vacation last year. This dinner could have important ramifications for all of us. A lot can be told by what a hostess serves her guests. I glance at Nick, who's looking at me with the broadest smile I've seen him sport in weeks. "I don't know. Do you have any requests?"

"Uh-uh."

"Well, what does Amber like to eat?"

Nick stares at me as if I asked him a geometry question only a PhD could figure out.

"Does she have any food allergies? Is she a vegetarian?"

Jerry bursts out laughing. "Lin, this is a simple meal, not an inquisition. Simmer down."

Am I putting too much emotion into this? I don't think so. Jerry doesn't realize that this meal could be the beginning of a complicated relationship. I focus on Nick. "A little help here."

He gazes into the distance. "Hmm. How about spaghetti and meatballs?"

"Maybe." Grandma's spaghetti recipe is to die for. But would Amber hold it against me if I served something messy?

Emma chimes in. "Why don't you grill some salmon?"

"Yeah, I've got a great salmon recipe or I can—"

Jerry waves his fork. "You should make that shrimp dish we had when the neighbors came for dinner."

"All right, enough. I'll go through my recipes tonight and figure something out."

Emma passes me the last dish to load into the washer. "I've written my college application essay." She sounds tentative.

That's been hanging over her head for weeks. "That's good, isn't it?" She sighs.

"What's wrong?"

Emma strolls to the table and takes a seat.

This must be important. We may as well get comfortable. I close the dishwasher, turn on the teakettle, and spoon some Earl Grey into my infuser. I pull out a chair and sit across from her. "Tell me about it."

She picks at a paper napkin until it's a tiny pile of nubbins on the table in front of her. "I thought it was a good idea at first, but now I don't know." She pushes the paper pieces into the shape of a triangle.

This girl will be the death of me. She can never just come out and say something. "Well, what's the topic?"

Her eyes flutter, and sparkling tears slip down her cheeks.

"Oh, Em, what is it?"

She plucks another napkin from the holder in the middle of the table and swipes at her eyes. "It's about Grandma."

How could anything about Theresa be bad? "I don't understand."

"Before Grandma died, we had some conversations. About life. About love. About choices."

My emotions mirror my daughter's, and I grab a napkin to dab at my tears. "And?"

"I don't want Grandpa to get mad."

"Why would Grandpa get mad?"

Emma twists her napkin. "I don't want him to think I'm broadcasting personal stuff."

"May I read it?"

She gives me a look that makes me think that was the point of this whole conversation. She jumps up and rushes to her room.

The teakettle screams for relief. I pour the boiling water into my pot and place the plastic cover over the infuser to allow the tea to brew. While I'm waiting for Emma, I take two mugs out of the cabinet and retrieve the milk from the fridge.

By the time Emma returns, I'm pouring our beverages. She hands me the printed essay—"Everything I Learned about Dancing, I Learned from Grandma."

"Interesting title."

She pours milk into her mug. "I'm going to do homework. Tell me what you think of it later."

"Sure." I begin to read.

> *My grandma was the greatest dancer in the world. She never took a lesson, never entered a contest, never won an award. For Grandma, dancing was more than taking one rhythmic step after another—it was the way she moved through life.*
>
> *"Baby girl," she would say to me, "don't slog on through your life—dance!"*
>
> *Some of my earliest memories are of being held in Grandma's arms, swirling around her garden while she*

sang nursery rhymes. But dancing wasn't just something for happy times. It was a balm for difficult moments. When my nana died, Grandma held me in her strong arms, rocking me back and forth, swaying to a softly hummed gospel tune. "It's okay. It's God's time. Your nana wants you to keep dancing, keep moving on to your glorious future."

And so we danced together through good times and bad. While I would like to think I was Grandma's only dance partner, she twirled and rocked with everyone she loved. . . .

. . . and the last day I took her out in her wheelchair, she had me spin her around to view all of God's beautiful nature. The autumn leaves fell from the trees like teardrops from heaven, knowing that Grandma would never dance in an earthly garden again.

"Dance with all your heart, baby girl. No matter what happens, dip and sashay, spin and jump. Don't ever stop putting one happy foot in front of the other."

Even today, when difficulties surround me, I remember Grandma, and a song stirs in my heart and my feet start to tap—and I know that this next dance, whatever it may be, will be just one in the long musical that is my life.

I sniffle and reach for another napkin. How I wish Theresa were still with us. What would she have thought about Ross taking a new dance partner?

16

Whatever shall I serve Amber tomorrow? *Pasta primavera? Too presumptuous. Chicken enchiladas? Too spicy. Linguine with shrimp? Maybe.* But then again, I do tend to end up wearing my pasta sauce. That wouldn't do. *Meat loaf? Too bourgeois. Roast beef? Too over the top. Panini? Too casual.*

Shall it be a formal meal? with good china and crystal? What about appetizers?

Hello? I could just slap myself upside the head. Is the stress of this dinner morphing me into June Cleaver or what? We'll eat on our everyday stoneware like a normal family. I know I've prayed about this, but my heart feels no peace.

I thumb through my index file of tried-and-true recipes and page through my favorite cookbooks. The book that sits open before me lists meals for every conceivable occasion . . . except meeting the girlfriend. I select a stained, yellowed index card stuffed into the front of the file box. *Oh, this looks good—stuffed flounder.* And I can serve it with mashed potatoes. It doesn't hurt that it's simple to prepare, and the fact that it's one of Nick's favorite recipes is a bonus.

I'm cleaning up the table and putting my references back in the pantry when Jerry comes into the room.

"You're up late."

"Yeah, I had to figure out what I'm serving for dinner tomorrow."

He pours himself a glass of water. "Oh, that's right. The big dinner."

I nod. "I want to start the day early so I can get the house spruced up and not feel rushed."

He yawns as he shuffles out of the room. "It's no big deal. We've had Nick's friends over for dinner before. I'm sure whatever you decide to make will be fine."

I watch him head down the hall toward the stairs. Sometimes life's not as simple as it seems. Good thing I've got women's intuition, or this family might be in big trouble.

• • •

It's a perfect autumn morning. My prayer is to get through Wal-Mart with a minimum of frustration.

I accept a cart from the smiling greeter and dive into the chaos. Of course, I would have to get the buggy with the gimpy wheel. For about three seconds, I consider going back to exchange this clunker, but I'm hitting my stride, and I need to shop from one end of this airplane hangar–size building to the other in less than an hour.

I coast up to the deli counter. It's impossible to see the selection of goods through the mob of people restlessly waiting their turn. I turn and maneuver my way through the produce department.

"Excuse me." I smile at a weary-looking woman monopolizing the display of fresh strawberries.

She scowls at me and turns to pick through the cellophane containers.

I try to sidle up to her to take a look at the strawberries myself. Just as I'm getting close to the display, she shifts from one foot to the other, effectively blocking my way.

Are you kidding? Is she Mrs. Wal-Mart, and do the rest of us peasants have to wait until she's finished taking her sweet time making her selection?

Her whining children distract her for a moment. She glares at them. Their whines turn to whimpers, and she focuses again on the fruit, selects a package, and drops it into her cart.

I take advantage of the opportunity when she turns away and begin to peruse my choices. These berries will make a beautiful dessert; they're so fresh and red.

"Excuse me." The scary lady glares at me. "Am I in your way?"

"Huh?"

"Well, I'm not finished."

Being the vertically challenged, lightweight woman I am, I grab a cello pack and back away from the strawberries. I'd like to give this bully a piece of my mind, but she frightens me.

The rest of my shopping experience doesn't get much better. By the time I leave, my head is pounding and I'm exhausted. I'm glad I've got the rest of the day to clean the house and prepare dinner. Maybe I can even squeeze in a nap so I'll be refreshed when Amber arrives.

I turn onto my street and reach for the garage door opener that hangs from my visor. What's that? A car parked in my driveway right where I want to pull in? Who on earth could this be?

I park in front of the house and pop the trunk. I hitch my purse on my shoulder and drape as many bags over my arm as I can hold. As I'm marching up to the front door, I pause to examine the white Hyundai Elantra taking my space. The bumper looks like it's been in more than one scuffle. The car probably belongs to a young man in one of Nick's classes. He must be an aggressive driver. My eye is drawn to the top of the rear window, where a bright red decal declares: Raft Naked. *Oy*. I've got to meet this guy.

By the time I reach the front door, my hands are numb from lack of blood flow to my extremities. My arm is so weighted down that I can barely lift it high enough to insert the key into the lock. I drop a few bags on the porch and ring the bell.

Jerry opens the door and grabs the dog by the collar in one smooth move. "Linda?"

"Who else did you expect?"

"I guess I lost track of time."

I nudge the grocery sack on the porch with my foot. "A little help?"

"Sorry." He releases Belle and takes the bags I'm holding.

I return to my car and collect the canned goods that have escaped their confinement, tossing them back inside a bag. Jerry joins me, and we burden ourselves with the last of the groceries. He slams the trunk closed, and we walk toward the house.

Jer makes an effort to come alongside me without letting the liter bottles of soda fall out of his bag. "Amber seems like a nice girl."

"Amber? She's here?" I freeze on the front sidewalk as panic grips my heart. "I can't meet her for the first time looking like this!"

"Like what? You look fine."

I step into the middle of the sidewalk to prevent him from deserting me. "My lipstick is worn off, my shirt has a stain from brushing against a dirty box in the store, and . . . I'm just not ready."

The front door opens and Nick appears. In the shadows behind him is the silhouette of a young woman. "I'll help you with that." He glides out of the house and relieves me of my bags.

Amber steps aside and holds the door, studying me with icy blue eyes.

My feet have sunk into quicksand, and my head is filled with cotton candy. Jerry nudges me forward.

As Nick strolls into the house, he says, "Mom, meet Amber."

I muster up a smile and put one foot in front of the other until I'm face-to-face with the young woman.

I hold out my hand. "Hi, Amber. It's nice to finally meet you."

Amber pauses before extending hers, then glances down at our clasped hands. "You too."

She makes me feel like I should have washed my hand before offering it to her. Is it my imagination or does she really think she's better than me?

17

I regard the beauty standing before me. If I'd seen a portrait of Amber, I'd have thought that her skin was retouched, her eyes were highlighted, and her lips were enhanced. Her long brown hair shimmers and falls in perfect lines, like she just stepped out of the beauty shop. And her body? Well, you can say it's every man's dream. No wonder Nick thinks he's falling in love. What's not to like?

She releases her limp grasp on my damp hand, and we stand like two idiots, smiling at each other as if we were vacuous socialites about to go for the jugular over the last pair of twelve-hundred-dollar Versace leather boots.

I nod. "Shall we go inside?"

In response, she turns and leads the way through the door. *Really?* Proper etiquette would have had her deferring to me and following me into the house. Into *my* house.

We walk to the kitchen. Jerry and Nick are unloading the groceries and putting them away in the cabinets and pantry. Nick pauses when we enter the room and blesses us with one of his most disarming smiles. Uh, rather he blesses Amber with that smile.

I join them and start to file away my purchases.

Jerry kneels to remove water bottles from the case I purchased and arrange them in a lower cabinet. "Did you buy a jar of pickles?"

"Were they on the list?" My voice is pinched and nasty. Why am

I taking my foul mood out on him? "Sorry. I think they're still in the last bag on the table."

He glances at me, and I can read a whole novel in that look. He's not pleased.

What am I turning into? I dust off my hands and say a silent prayer. The knot of tension in my chest begins to loosen, and a calming breath flows from my lungs. I look at Amber. She's standing in the corner of the kitchen, worrying a ring on her right hand.

I'm such a jerk. If it's possible, that poor girl has shrunk four inches since I came into the kitchen burdened with my eighty pounds of angst. "What would everyone like for lunch? Sandwiches? Soup?"

Nick moves to Amber's side. "Thanks. But we're meeting friends for lunch."

I feel as if I just got a reprieve. "Oh, okay. We'll see you later then. For dinner."

Jerry crosses the room. "It was so nice to finally meet you, Amber."

She gives him a dazzling smile. "You too, Mr. Revere." She turns to me, and her smile dims. "Bye, Mrs. Revere."

I put on my company smile and try to speak gently. "Have a nice afternoon."

As they walk out of the house, Nick drapes his arm across her shoulders.

I drop into the nearest chair. I know my husband's going to have something to say to me.

Jerry finishes loading vegetables into the fridge and takes a seat at the table. After a dramatic pause, he drums his fingers on the table. "That could have gone a little better—don't you think?"

What pearls of wisdom. "I know. It was awkward enough. Do you think she felt unwelcome?"

We both turn at the sound of slippers padding across the tile floor. Emma saunters into the kitchen, looking more asleep than awake. "Who? Who felt unwelcome?"

"Good afternoon, sweetie."

She screws up her face. "It's only eleven forty-five. Who just left the house?"

This girl is like a dog with a bone. "Nick."

Jerry shoots me a glance. "And Amber."

Emma slides into a chair. "Really? What's going on?"

I affect a casual pose. "Amber stopped by to pick up Nick. They'll be back later for dinner."

She looks from me to Jerry. "What did I miss?"

"I think I'd like some soup. Anyone else?" I stand.

"Mo-om." Emma folds her arms across her chest.

My little act isn't fooling her. "I may have gotten off on the wrong foot with Amber. Not that I said or did anything intentional. I was just surprised to find her here." I'm relieved by my confession, but Emma cocks her head and furrows her eyebrows. I'm as confused by my behavior as she is.

I elaborate to fill in the blanks. "I didn't expect to see her so early, and I had hoped I could clean the house and refresh myself before I met her. But when I got home from the store, she was already here." I glance at Jerry. "Did you see the decal on her car?"

"No, I didn't notice it."

"What did it say?"

I face them to give them the full impact of my words. "Raft naked."

Emma giggles. "Oh, Mom, don't be such a prude."

Jerry just looks pained.

Yeah, put that in your pipe and smoke it. "Nice girl. Real nice."

I go about my business and heat a can of soup, but by the time it's ready, I'm the only one interested in eating. I rush my meal and spend the next ninety minutes sprucing up the house.

I override my previous decision and opt to serve dinner in the dining room on my mother's china. Hopefully it's not too much, but

I do want to make up for the lukewarm greeting I gave Amber earlier. The table looks beautiful. I even polished my silver teapot-shaped salt and pepper shakers. For a moment I wish I had fresh flowers for the centerpiece, but I don't want to go overboard.

I glance at my watch. They better get home soon. I take advantage of the few minutes I have before they arrive to whip up heavy cream for my homemade strawberry shortcake.

"Wow." Jer walks into the kitchen and grins.

I bask in his approval. "I wanted to make her feel welcome."

I just have time to fill the water glasses before Nick and Amber come through the door, both looking flushed. I'm not sure if it's the cool autumn air or something else is going on. Amber's hand is held tightly within Nick's grasp. As if he has to protect her from us.

"Hi, kids. Nick, why don't you hang Amber's jacket up, and you can both wash up for dinner." I turn toward the stairs. "Emma! Dinner's ready."

Jerry helps me bring the food to the table. It looks like a holiday meal: seafood stuffed flounder, garlic mashed potatoes, green beans, and fresh applesauce.

We all take our seats. Amber places her napkin on her lap and looks around. Without a word, we bow our heads, and Jerry says a blessing.

I know I shouldn't, but I sneak a peek at Amber. Her head is bowed, but she appears to be staring at her lap. *Interesting*.

I place my napkin on my lap. "Amber, do you like stuffed flounder?"

She glances at the feast before meeting my eyes. "Uh, it all looks wonderful, but I don't eat flounder."

Oh, what have I done? "I'm sorry. Nick didn't tell me you didn't eat fish." I could kill him.

She takes a heaping helping of applesauce. "It's all right. I eat most fish. Nick didn't know. Everything else looks delicious."

We smile as if it's an everyday occurrence that a guest refuses an entrée that's offered.

I can't help but wonder what else my son doesn't know about his girlfriend.

18

"Would you help me clear the table for dessert?"

Emma looks at me like I've condemned her to summer school, but whatever.

Amber doesn't miss a beat and continues her conversation with the guys about the horrors of eating flounder. *What nerve.* Has she no idea of etiquette?

Em and I load our arms with dishes and file into the kitchen. She turns to me. "Uh, I'd rather hear the end of that story."

I raise my eyebrows, and Em huffs. I hope she knows better than to follow that line of thought with me. *"Flounder is a bottom feeder, yada yada yada." Really.* As if I would deliberately consider putting dangerous food into my family's diet. *Humph.*

I run warm, soapy water to soak the china while Emma clears the rest of the food from the table. I shake suds from my hands and stick my head into the dining room. "Coffee?" Everyone nods, and I turn on my prepared coffeemaker.

Emma assembles the dessert plates. I made Nick's favorite treat— strawberry shortcake. From scratch. The glistening strawberries sitting on the homemade biscuits topped with fresh whipped cream look like something out of *Martha Stewart Living* magazine. *Perfect.*

Emma and I proudly present our pièce de résistance to the diners. Nick grins when he sees what I'm serving. Chalk up a few points for me.

I take my seat across from Jerry and prepare to taste culinary heaven. My tribe begins to inhale one of the Revere family favorites, Grandma Theresa's shortcake recipe. The clang of forks on my elegant china is evidence that at least this part of the meal is a hit.

Or is it? Amber forks through the perfectly plated confection, separating the berries from the biscuits and cream.

"Amber?"

She looks at me with her big, beautiful eyes—perfectly still and trembling at the same time.

"Is there something wrong with the dessert? Don't you eat sweets?"

"Uh, this looks great."

I lay my fork down. "What seems to be the problem?"

Amber bobs her head and gives me a bashful grin. "Are these organic strawberries?"

This girl is too much. "No, they're not. Do you only eat organic ones?"

At least she has the good grace to allow a blush to travel up her neck and paint her cheeks. "Conventional strawberries give me a stomachache. You really shouldn't eat them. No one should. Out of all the conventional produce on the market, strawberries retain the most pesticides."

My head is going to explode. "I'm sorry, Amber. The next time you come for dinner, I'll clear the menu with you beforehand." *Did I really say that out loud?* A glance at the rest of my family assures me that I truly had a malfunction between the editing mechanism in my brain and my big mouth. I laugh to clear the air. "Sorry. Just kidding."

The poor girl seems to relax a bit, but Nick throws daggers at me with his eyes. He must have recognized my laugh as phony. Even I think I sounded crazy.

I hope Amber doesn't ask if the coffee is organic fair trade Nicaraguan blend or if the half-and-half has been tested for antibiotics and comes from cows not treated with bovine growth hormones. If so, I may truly lose it. I'm hanging on to my sense of propriety with barely a shred of dignity.

Is this meal over yet? And how long will she linger here? I'm looking forward to the silence of the kitchen while I clean up from this disaster.

Jerry makes small talk with Amber about her major courses and graduation requirements. We finally finish the last of our coffee and push back from the table.

"Thank you very much, Mrs. Revere. I appreciate your hospitality."

I begin to stack dessert plates. "You're welcome, Amber. Please call me Linda." I hope our relationship can overcome our differences. After all, she may be around for a while.

She smiles. "Okay. Linda."

We stand and nod.

Nick puts his hand on the small of her back. "What say we get going?"

Amber looks at Nick with obvious affection. "Shall we drive my car?"

Nick opens the closet door and pulls out their jackets. "I'll follow you home and then drive us to the party."

We travel en masse to the front door and bid them good night. Jerry closes the door after the young couple, folds his arms, and stares me down.

Yeah, like I need that in my life right now. I feign innocence. "What?"

"Sell it to someone who's buying, sister."

Busted. "I don't know what's gotten into me."

He follows me into the kitchen. "I don't know what's gotten into you either. You're not like this maniacal, overbearing mother you're portraying. What's going on?"

I wish I had a good answer. Or at least one he'd understand. "It's a gut feeling. This isn't a good relationship for Nick. Can't you see that?"

While I speak, I sift through papers on the kitchen counter. *Hmm. University of Colorado at Denver. Has Nick registered already for next semester?* I pick up the computer printout and scan the page. "Oh, good grief!"

"What?"

"Nick's midterm grades. They're terrible. Look." I pass off the condemning document to Jerry.

His face goes slack with disappointment. Good performance in school is important to him. Nick's always been a dean's list student, but now most of his grades are Ds and Cs.

Silence echoes through the kitchen while Jerry rereads our son's grade statement.

I lean on the counter. "Well, I can tell you one thing. His grades didn't take a dive until Amber came into his life. All this running around and staying out all night long has taken its toll. And what are we going to do about it?"

19

Last night was a challenge, but I was able to calm Jerry down enough to enjoy another helping of strawberry shortcake. We planned on discussing Nick's grades and study habits when he arrived home. Unfortunately, we had to turn in before he returned.

Belle's whimpering wakes me when the sun's rays have barely crept across my comforter. I slide out of bed and close the door behind me as I leave the room. My poor husband tossed and turned last night, no doubt thinking about our son and the downward spiral his grades have taken. Not that I got more rest than he did. I kept waking, listening for Nick to come home. He never did. At least I didn't hear him come clomping in like he usually does.

Belle rushes to the back door and nearly accordions her body while waiting for me to let her out. The cool morning air stirs my senses. My little dog picks her way across grass covered in a glistening frost. While she's out, I shrug on my jacket and run for the paper at the foot of the driveway. Right where Nick's car should be. I don't have to wonder too long to guess where he is.

When Jerry comes into the kitchen, I'm on my second cup of coffee and have nearly finished reading the Sunday paper. He pours a mug of coffee and sits across from me. His expression makes me sad. Not that I'm happy about it, but I think he finally sees my point. Amber is no good for Nick. "Do you think we should give him a call?"

Jer takes a sip of coffee and shakes his head. "Why bother?"

Argh. "Because he could be dead on the side of the road."

He puts down his mug. "Not likely. If there was an accident we'd have been told by now."

That's shallow consolation.

"Is there enough coffee for me?" Emma enters the kitchen, her hair slightly matted from a good night's sleep. She pulls a mug from the cabinet and drains the last of the pot. "Are we going to church or what?"

Her words spur us to action. We can mope about Nick's poor choices later.

• • •

Nick's car is sitting in the driveway when we return from church. As we pull into the garage, Jerry puts a hand on my arm. "Play it cool."

"Don't worry. I will." I smile at him. He's right. As usual. Still, Nick is becoming more like a stranger. He's definitely not perfect, but he's usually pretty responsible.

"Humph." Emma editorializes from the backseat.

"What?" If she's got something to say, she should just come out with it. I glance over my shoulder at her.

She looks defiant. "The world won't come to an end if Nick dates a hot girl."

"That's not the issue, missy. Your brother's grades have fallen dramatically. Along with his values."

Jerry finishes my thought. "We need to help Nick make choices that won't adversely affect his future. He's got one more semester to go. He doesn't need to hit the skids now."

Emma makes a face but doesn't continue the discussion. We parade into the house through the side door.

"Nick?"

My call goes unanswered.

I check the buffet table in the foyer, where he usually tosses his keys. They're not there.

Jerry walks to the foot of the stairs. "Nick!"

We stand mute, staring at each other. The only response is Belle prancing at our feet.

That's some how-do-you-do. A friend must have picked him up. "Great. It looks like our little talk's been postponed indefinitely."

The flashing light on our answering machine beckons Emma. She pushes Play. Static fills the void, and then Ross's voice comes through the line. "It's Dad. I'm at the Pine Grove Hospital."

My heart flutters, and I clutch my chest as I move closer to the machine.

"I'm here with Doris. She volunteers on Sunday afternoons and asked me to tag along."

Relief floods my limbs. For a moment I feared for Ross's health. I don't know why I would worry. He's as healthy as can be expected for someone pushing seventy-five. "Anyway, we're going to Village Inn for pie and coffee at three o'clock, and I was hoping you and the kids would join us. I want you to meet Doris."

Jerry looks at me. "It's up to you. Do you want to go?"

Ross asks so little of us. How can we deny him something like this? "Sure, but it looks like it might just be the three of us."

Emma thrusts her hands on her hips. "I won't be able to make it."

"Oh, come on. It will only be for a half hour."

She shakes her head. "I've got to go to the library this afternoon to meet some friends from my history class. We're working on a project together."

Is her rebellious body language saying something different? I remember her outburst about Ross dating when he was over for dinner. "You have to go to the library, or you want to go so you won't have to meet Doris?"

She folds her arms and adjusts her stance. "You're trying to pick a fight with me because Nick's not here."

"No, I'm not. I just think—"

Jerry steps between us, obviously trying to head off another mother-daughter confrontation. "That's okay, Emma. Go and do your work. I'm sure you'll get another chance to meet Grandpa's friend."

The three of us pick at a lunch of leftovers. Afterward Emma escapes to the library. We still haven't heard from Nick. He used to be more thoughtful and always left a note when he'd go out. His inconsideration is raising my blood pressure.

Jerry and I drive to the restaurant listening to the radio. At least this way we don't have to talk about Nick and Amber. We've done enough of that in the past twenty-four hours. As we walk in, we see Ross and his lady friend following a teenage waitress to a table.

His hand is barely touching the small of her back. I glance at Jer to see if he notices. I think I see a touch of sadness in his eyes, but he grins and tells the hostess we're meeting another couple.

Doris has taken her seat when we reach the table, but Ross is still on his feet. His face lights up when he sees us, and for a moment he peers around to locate his grandchildren.

"Sorry, Pop. It's just us."

He smiles at Jerry and gives me a kiss on the cheek. Doris is sitting watching us, all smiles.

Ross does introductions and we sit.

Doris shakes Jerry's hand. "I've been looking forward to meeting you and your lovely wife. Ross can't say enough nice things about you and your family."

"Well, hopefully you'll be able to meet our children before too long. They're both students and had prior commitments today."

Jerry nudges my knee under the table. I glance at him, and his eyes hold mine, silently calming my taut nerves.

Doris is smiling at Ross the way the junior high girls flirt with the high school lifeguards at the town pool each summer. She's totally infatuated with my father-in-law.

Ross and Jerry discuss Emma's college application process. Doris looks like she wants to be included in the conversation. She puts a hand on Ross's arm.

I'm not so sure I like this turn of events. Touching? Isn't that a little forward?

Jerry appears as surprised as I feel. He sits back to allow the exchange of conversation. Ross, ever courteous, merely smiles his encouragement to Doris.

I smile politely while Doris dives into the conversation. But that doesn't mean I like it.

What's going on? What's happened to my predictable, boring life?

20

So far this is one of the worst Monday mornings I've had to endure in a long while. Despite consuming an extra serving of strong cappuccino, I still feel thickheaded and slow-witted.

By the time I went to bed last night, I was fit to be tied. Nick never answered his cell phone the many times I rang him. I got voice mail every time. And then he came home long after we were all asleep. I'd talk to him this morning before I leave for work, but I don't trust myself to keep my anger in check. I hate struggling with these emotions.

Today was Jerry's early day out of the house. I'm out the door a bit early, which is nice for a change.

When I enter the lobby of Dream Photography, the place is overrun with fairies putting up our Christmas decorations. We have to get a jump on the season to influence our clients to think about ordering Christmas cards and extra portraits and art products for gifts.

A pleasant thirtysomething woman greets me by name and clearly expects that I'll reciprocate.

I raise my eyebrows to give the illusion that I'm actually wide-awake and refreshed from my weekend. "Good morning." I search the recesses of my cotton-stuffed brain for her name but come up empty. She is still looking at me with an expectant expression, so I know I can't simply walk away. Despite the fact they're surrounded by plastic tubs labeled *holiday decorations*, I ask, "Do you ladies have everything you need?"

She glances at the storage bins that clutter the room, then picks up a photo of our decorated lobby and shows it to me. "Uh, yeah. It looks like we're set."

"Good. If you have any questions, I'm in the office." I don't expect to hear from them because all they have to do is duplicate the image in last year's lobby photo.

As I round the corner, I'm chased by laughter. I could be wrong, but I think the women are laughing at me. Hey, everyone's entitled to one bad day. And this one's mine. Besides, we'll see who gets the last laugh. After all, a lowly fairy should not tick off the fairy herder. We'll see who gets called for the next project. Schemes of revenge run through my sleep-deprived brain as I settle down to work. Who am I kidding? I'm not angry at my client volunteers. It's my son and his girlfriend who are giving me heartburn and brain fog today.

I go through the morning by rote. By midafternoon I'm ready for a nap, but I'm on the schedule to do the two thirty sale. *Fabulous.*

I carry my water bottle and notebook into the salesroom and load my client's images into the viewing program. I glance at the file: Roark, Ben. *Well, Bennie boy, aren't you a handsome fellow?* He looks about fifteen years old—leaving his awkward phase and entering the high school heartthrob phase. I dim the lights and head to the lobby to meet the Roarks.

As I approach, I hear the fairies chattering among themselves. A little too loudly for my preference, but after all, they are unpaid workers. When I arrive in the lobby, I see who I assume is the Roark family standing in the corner, watching the chaos unfolding before them. Christmas tree lights are laid along the length of the couch, and small boxes of ornaments are sitting on the upholstered chairs.

This is definitely not good. We pride ourselves on our superb customer service, and forcing clients to stand scrunched together while waiting to see their images is simply unacceptable. I'm torn between scolding the volunteers and apologizing to the Roarks.

I glance at the women and hope they can read the disappointment in my fleeting look. Then I focus on my clients. "Mr. and Mrs. Roark? Ben?"

Three prickly looking people turn toward me.

"I'm so very sorry for the inconvenience. We're busy decorating."

The fiftysomething man rolls his eyes and urges his family to follow me with a hand to their backs. Ben acts as if he would rather be at the dentist than the portrait studio.

I muster up a smile and lead the way down the hall. The Roarks settle into our comfortable chairs. "May I offer you some water?"

Mrs. Roark speaks up. "Yes, please. And you can call us Joyce and Harry. This is Ben."

"It's so nice to meet you. Please call me Linda." I pass out their water bottles and launch into an explanation of the process we're about to undertake. "Okay, folks. Let's enjoy the show." I turn to my computer station to begin the program when I hear Ben whisper to his mother.

Joyce smiles at me. She really seems like a lovely woman. "Excuse me. Did we smell freshly baked cookies when we arrived?"

"I'm very sorry. They weren't out of the oven a minute ago, but let me get some for you now." I hustle out of the room.

The volunteers have resumed their babbling. I park myself in the midst of their disarray. "Ladies?"

All mouths slam shut and eyes turn toward me.

"I know you're used to working at night when our clients aren't here, but we needed to get the decorations up ASAP. Please remember this is a place of business, and our clients are our number one priority."

Some of the pampered ladies who are used to getting their own way assume the countenance of a spoiled preteen who's been told she can't talk on the phone all night long.

I continue. "Please try to keep your voices down and move the decorations off the seating arrangements."

They clear the decorations off the furniture while I move to the reception desk.

"Here." Barb passes me a pink sheet. "You have a message. From Carol Ball."

I can't believe I forgot to speak with Luke about Katrina getting out of working our charity promotion on Saturday. One more thing on my to-do list. If only my brain weren't like a sieve lately. I release a breath and rein in my disappointment that somehow life keeps getting away from me.

I grab the cookies and rejoin the Roarks. By the time the last image has faded from the screen, half the cookies are gone and Joyce is dabbing her eyes with a tissue. *So far, so good.*

We go through the usual drill and narrow down our choices to eight gorgeous images. I display two of them side by side. Harry and Joyce debate the merits of each image.

Ben's ruddy complexion reminds me of Nick's when he was in his teens.

Nick. My heart feels like a sausage about to burst from its casing.

"Linda?"

I turn toward my clients, and they're all gawking at me as if I'm wearing my pajamas. "I'm sorry. I was distracted. What did you say?"

Joyce grabs the box of tissues from the coffee table and hands it to me. Harry looks uncomfortable, and Ben stares at me with his mouth agape.

I accept the tissues. *What's going on?*

Joyce reaches over and puts a hand on my arm. "Shall we come back another time?"

What planet am I on?

"Linda," she says softly, "you're weeping."

Have I ever felt so foolish? I swipe my eyes with the discount tissues that we go through like water in this joint. "I'm very sorry. I—"

"No worries." Joyce pats my arm like we're old friends.

"Please let me restart the slideshow, and I'll be right back." I escape the small salesroom and zip through the building to the employee lounge. I keep my head down to avoid suspicion. The last thing I want my coworkers to see is me having a meltdown. I did that here once before, and I don't want everyone to think I've gone over the edge—again.

I look pathetic. I blow my nose and push my hair behind my ears. *I need a little help here, Lord, please.* I take a deep breath, repair my mascara smudges, and hurry back to my clients.

I hear a man's voice coming from the salesroom. And it's not Harry's. It's Luke's. I rush toward the door but have to stop in the hallway because my boss is blocking my way.

Joyce is standing, admiring a frame hanging on the wall. "No, there's no problem. I think Linda got something in her eye. She said she'll be right—"

I clear my throat, and Luke turns toward me. "You okay?"

I wave his concern away. "Yeah, I'm fine." I resume my place behind the keyboard. "Sorry, guys. Shall we continue where we left off?"

Luke backs out of the room and closes the door behind him. I have no idea why Joyce is being so kind, but if it weren't for my sense of propriety, I'd give her a big hug.

I square my shoulders and smile at Joyce. "Thank you. I don't know what got into me. I saw that gorgeous image of young Ben, and I took a little trip down memory lane."

She shakes her head. "We all have those days, no problem."

Harry shrugs as though this is a common occurrence.

Have I mentioned that some of our clients are great people? In addition to being some of the nicest people ever, the Roarks spend twelve hundred dollars on portraits of their son. For their understanding nature, I give them a handsome discount on the frame Joyce had been admiring. Despite that, Dream Photography made a considerable profit on their sale.

I escort the Roarks to the door. "Thank you very much for your business—and for your understanding. I—"

Joyce leans toward me and whispers, "I told you not to worry about that. We've all had those days."

A lump forms in my throat. What grace this woman has extended to me. I'm honored. I pull myself together. "We'll give you a call when your portraits are ready, which will be in about four weeks."

Harry's nodding and fishing for his keys in his pocket. "Oh, Joyce. Remember your mom asked if we could collect her pictures too."

"Right. My parents were in here last week. Can we pick up all our portraits at one time?"

I open their file. "No problem. Let me make a note of that. Now, what are your parents' names?"

"Sullivan. Slim and Bert."

My heart warms at the mention of their name. "I helped your parents with their order."

"Yes, I know. They told us to ask that you be our sales associate for Ben's pictures. You were so very helpful and kind to Mom and Dad."

So, now the mystery of why Joyce has such a generous spirit is cleared up. She has such loving parents. "It was my pleasure to help them. I'll call you when I get notice that both orders are ready."

What a legacy of love and kindness the Sullivan family has. Someday I would love to be able to return the consideration this family has shown me.

21

Nick's car is parked in front of the house when I arrive home. Is he really here or are we just a parking service these days? Fortunately I've got my emotions under control enough to say a quick prayer for poise and wisdom. And, boy, do I need it.

I pull into the garage and schlep my stuff into the house. *Peace, Lord. Give me peace.*

Laughter comes from the kitchen. I recognize Emma's musical giggle and another unfamiliar laugh. A door slams upstairs. That must be Nick. Despite my prayers, I feel my blood pressure rise. I'll drop my lunch box in the kitchen and go upstairs to have our overdue chat.

Emma shrieks with merriment. "No, he did not!"

The rest of the sentence is garbled in shared laughter. Emma and her girlfriends can get so silly together, but maybe that distraction is just what I need right now. The weight of anger on my shoulders lightens, and I turn the corner to share a chuckle with my daughter and her friend.

As soon as I enter the room, the mood deflates silently and in slow motion like an old helium balloon left over from last week's party.

Emma and Amber look at me in unison.

I bat my eyes about three times trying to wrap my brain around the fact that the girlfriend Emma's sharing a good time with is the

. . . the person who is leading her brother away from his heritage toward a future of who knows what. I suck in a deep breath and recall the etiquette that has gotten me through many awkward moments. "Hello, Amber. How are you?"

"Hi, Mrs. Rev—I mean, Linda."

I plunk my lunch box on the counter. "This is a surprise." *I wish it were a pleasant one.* "I hope I didn't interrupt anything." *Meaning, what were you girls talking about?*

Amber suddenly finds the floor infinitely fascinating. Silence is challenged by the ticking of the grandfather clock drifting in from the living room.

"Will you be staying for dinner, Amber?" *As if I've got organic produce and natural meat on hand. My pantry isn't stocked to suit her highfalutin tastes.*

She gazes at me through her bangs before raising her head. "Uh, no. I don't think so."

"That's too bad. I'd like a chance to get to know you better." The words are no sooner out of my mouth than I realize they're true. Who is this woman who has bewitched my son?

Amber smiles at me as if she read my mind. It's a little unsettling. She seems to relax and leans against the counter. "Maybe another time. I'm waiting for Nick to finish an assignment so we can meet friends."

Excuse me?

My expression must show surprise because Emma chuckles. "Yeah, Amber's making Nick do his homework."

"Well, I like the sound of that." I wink at Amber. Maybe there might be something to this girl.

I put the meat loaf I mixed last night into the oven to cook and go upstairs to change into comfortable clothes. Then I walk down the hall to Nick's room and knock softly.

"Come in!" he yells from behind the closed door.

I let myself in. He's hunched over his desk, tapping out an

assignment on his computer. I wait for him to pause before speaking. "Long time no see."

"If you're interested in picking a fight, I don't have time right now, Mother."

I beg your pardon? He's never referred to me as *Mother.* "How about a simple hello, or is that too much to ask?"

Nick looks annoyed. "I need to get this essay finished to e-mail to my professor. Can this conversation wait?"

"Sure. Shall I make an appointment with you?"

His hands freeze above the keyboard. "I know you'd like to have an argument, but I have more important things to do." He scowls at me for a moment and then goes back to his work.

I don't care for the dismissive tone of his voice. My heart is heavy as I remember not too long ago when our conversations were as smooth as hot fudge on vanilla ice cream.

I sit down on his bed. "I'm sorry. I don't want to argue with you."

Nick must note the sincerity in my voice because he stops and turns toward me. "I don't want to fight either. But I've got to finish this by six thirty and e-mail it to my professor. Can we talk tomorrow?"

Tomorrow? It's always tomorrow lately. I know the answer already, but I can't help but ask. "Aren't you having dinner with us? Amber's invited."

He continues to type away. "Can't. We have a meeting to get to."

"We?"

Nick pushes back his chair and faces me. "You've got to let me finish this assignment. My grade depends on it."

"Okay." I get up and walk to the door. "We'll talk tomorrow."

On the way downstairs, I pause to listen. I hear a cabinet closing and the sound of scraping. Emma must be peeling the potatoes that are on the menu for tonight. Her conversation with Amber seems easy. As if she likes her. Maybe I should learn how to peacefully coexist with that girl. It doesn't look like she's going away anytime soon.

I pretend all is well and enter the kitchen. *Oh my.* Amber's peeling our potatoes. She and Emma are chatting while my daughter mixes biscuits. I feel like an intruder in my own home.

"We've got dinner going here," Emma says.

"So I see. Thanks." *Is she saying that to get rid of me so she can continue with her pleasant conversation?* I feel at a loss for what to do.

Little Belle runs to the garage door.

A moment later, Jerry walks in. When he sees us all in the kitchen, his smile gets wider. "Hello, girls."

I greet him and accept the hug that I look forward to each day. He glances over my shoulder. "Hi there, Amber. It's a treat to see you. Will you be staying for dinner?"

She seems to bloom for Jerry. "Hi." She gestures with my potato peeler. "I'm helping out. Nick and I have somewhere to go."

I follow Jerry into the dining room, where he deposits his briefcase.

Before I can say a word, Nick comes downstairs. "Hi, Dad." He walks through the room to the kitchen. "You ready, honey?"

Wow. Honey? That doesn't sound like something Nick would say. I glance at Jerry in time to see his head twitch. It looks like that term of endearment caught him off guard too.

We walk into the kitchen together. Amber's rinsing off her hands while Nick stands impatiently jingling his car keys.

Jerry finds his voice. "See you kids later."

They bid us good-bye and are out the door.

I take dishes out of the cabinet and start setting the table.

Emma hums as she kneads her biscuit dough. "Mom, I think you're wrong about Amber."

Her voice is light, as though what she's talking about holds no importance, but I know my girl, and I can see what she's up to. Always the peacemaker, she wants to gloss over the discomfort. Perhaps she's right. Have I misread Amber? "Do you think so?"

Emma pauses to make sure she has my complete attention. "I think she loves Nick."

Jerry whistles through his teeth, and I continue to place forks on napkins and lay the knives down with the blades facing the plates.

I feel their eyes on me and glance up. "What can I say?"

What indeed?

22

I choke down dinner, not enjoying this meal I always look forward to. Okay, I know meat loaf isn't exciting international cuisine, but I've always liked it. Our conversation is bland, usual stuff. I push some corn around for a moment and then scoop up a few kernels.

As soon as I put them in my mouth, Emma glances my way and says, "So. Have you thought about your relationship with Amber?"

Hmm. Did she wait until my mouth was full so I would have time to think before I reply? I roll my eyes and swallow. "My relationship? It's Nick with whom she has a relationship."

Emma tilts her head. "If things continue the way they're going, we'll all have a relationship with her."

Who is this girl? Dr. Phil? That's something I haven't wanted to consider. I draw in a breath and nod. "I guess you're right."

Jerry stares at me as if I just invented a self-cleaning toilet. "Well, it's nice to see the lightbulb go on."

"I'm not quite that naive. It's just too soon to invest in a relationship with her. I want to see if she will have any staying power."
Yeah, that's my story, and I'm sticking to it.

He puts a forkful of mashed potatoes in his mouth and gives me a look that says he knows I'm talking off the cuff. Sometimes it's a royal pain to be married to a man who knows me so well.

Emma shifts in her seat. "I really like Amber. She seems sweet.

And sad." She glances down at her mashed potatoes. "Almost as if she doesn't have the right to be happy."

Emma's so sensitive. I wonder how well acquainted they're becoming.

She points at me. "You've got to give Amber a break."

I'm not crazy about her attitude. "I'm not a bad guy here. I'm a mother who only wants the best for her children."

Emma raises her chin. "But we're not children. You've got to let us go."

Tonight my emotions have swung from irritation to surprise, and now I'm back at irritation. "You don't know what you're asking. I'm only too happy to launch you and your brother successfully from this nest. And if I have to have uncomfortable conversations in the meantime, so be it."

She squints at me.

"If someone I love is standing on the railroad tracks, and I see a train heading that way, I'm going to do everything within my power to get him off that track before the train hits."

Emma cuts her meat loaf with the side of her fork. "I don't think you need to worry. You're such a maximizer. Amber's sweet. She's not going to hurt Nick."

"I don't think Amber's plotting to hurt Nick. My concern is for his future. I want him to make wise choices that are going to help him be happy and successful in life."

She concentrates on her meal. I'm not sure if she's taking what I've said to heart or if she's tired of arguing her point.

After dinner Emma and I clean the kitchen, both lost in our own thoughts. I think back to when I became acquainted with Jerry's family. Was there any conflict between Theresa and me? I don't recall any. We fell into a warm friendship almost from the start. Could it be my fault that Amber and I haven't developed a comfort level in our relationship yet?

By the time I'm finished stocking my lunch box, everyone has drifted to different parts of the house. I remember when we would all gather together in the evenings, even if it was around the television.

I walk down the hall and rap lightly on the study door. I hear Jerry's chair squeak, and the door glides open. "Come in. Sorry the door was closed. I was getting something out of the bookcase, and I needed more room."

"That's okay." I flop onto his old reading chair pushed into the corner. There are school papers strewn about on his desk. "Did I interrupt you?"

He grins. "When has that ever stopped you?"

I laugh. He's got that right. "We still need to speak with Nick about his grades."

Jer shakes his head. "Not anymore. Nick and I had a good conversation the other night. It seems Amber's got him on track when it comes to school."

I guess that's a good thing. Not something I would have counted on, but I'm glad his head is back in the game. Especially since he has only a few months to go. "I was also thinking about Thanksgiving. Do you think we should invite Amber?"

He eases out of his chair, pushes aside my feet, and sits on the overstuffed footstool. "Yeah, you should invite her—especially if you want Nick to be there."

My heart thuds. That's exactly the way I thought it would go down. "Guess so." My eyes fill with tears. I try to blink them back, but I'm not successful.

Jerry lays his hand on my leg. "What now?"

I sigh, trying to get ahold of my emotions. "I'm sorry."

He squeezes my leg.

I swipe at my eyes and unburden myself. "I was thinking of your mom. I never imagined how much I would miss her. It seems unreal that she won't be side by side with me, cooking Thanksgiving dinner. And who's going to make the pies? Mine aren't nearly as good as hers. What will we—?"

Jerry draws me into an embrace. "Shh. It will be all right. We'll be fine. I know it's difficult. But we've still got Pop, and Amber will round out the table."

My head and my heart are in a jumble. I'm glad Ross will be with us, but my feelings toward Amber aren't nearly so thankful.

23

Heavy clouds press down on me like silent reproach from the heavens. I step from my car and walk toward the studio, trying to number the chores ahead of me today, but my mind keeps straying back to Amber. A seed of guilt that sprouted in my heart feels as though it's reproducing like a virus. I'll just have to deal with that later.

I put my purse in my desk drawer and tackle some unfinished business. I refer to one of the pink message sheets in my ever-growing stack and dial Carol Ball's number.

She answers on the third ring. I put a smile on my face, remind myself that we're on good terms these days, and plunge ahead with the bad news. "Hi, Carol. It's Linda from Dream Photography."

"Hello, dear. Thanks for getting back with me to confirm that Katrina can have the weekend off. I can't tell you—"

"I'm sorry. I spoke with Luke, and he's not happy that Katrina won't be working with the rest of the staff on Saturday. It's quite a big deal, you know. Scores of folks have holiday portraits taken. They raise thousands of dollars for charity." I play with the phone cord as I wait for her thoughts.

She finally responds. "This is a bit of a setback. But I have faith that you'll get Luke's approval."

"There's really nothing I can do. Luke's the boss. Do you want to speak with him?"

"No. He's a busy man, and I don't want to bother him with details."

I'm being sucked into a miry pit. As usual, she's not taking no for an answer. "I'm powerless. I can't help. I—"

"Now, now. Don't even say that. Where there's a will there's a way. Talk to you later."

Carol ends the call and leaves me with a coyote gnawing at my gut. Why am I in the middle of this mess?

I try to push the angst from my mind as I exit the office and go to the workroom to put a reorder file into the production queue. As I search for a plastic sleeve to put the file into, I listen to conversation floating over the cubicles.

"Guess what I did yesterday?"

Was that Traci?

Before I can figure out whose voice is about to drop some juicy information, someone responds, "Can you say it out loud?"

I locate what I'm searching for and drop the order into the plastic sleeve. The phone on the workstation rings and rings and rings. Avoiding answering the phone in the back room is an art form here at Dream Photography. I snatch up the receiver before the call goes to voice mail. "Dream Photography, Linda speaking. May I help you?"

A deep voice comes through the line. "Donna, please."

"I'm sorry. There is no Donna here."

"Is this the Beezley Paper Company?"

"No, I'm afraid you've got the wrong num—"

I hear a loud click as the call is disconnected.

The sound of muted laughter drifts over from a nearby cubicle. I guess I'll never know what mysterious deed my coworker did.

When I get back into my office, my cell phone chirps its song that says I have a voice mail. I dig in my purse and push the button to see who was looking for me.

"Hi, Lin. It's Deb. I was hoping to catch you and chat for a while."

Oh, how I'll miss Deb. We've been through so much since we met at college those many years ago. I smile, remembering the joyful call I got from her telling me that Keith's company was moving them from Pennsylvania to Denver. It was a dream come true. But now they're moving on. My smile disappears, and the weight in my heart increases.

I'm struck again with the helpless feeling that too much in my life is changing much too quickly.

24

Darkness has descended by the time I arrive home. My day has left my heart aching, and the inky sky reflects my somber mood. All I seemed to do was go through the motions, without making any significant accomplishments for my efforts.

I'm surprised to find I'm the first one home. I feed the dog to keep her out of my way and check the handwritten menu posted on the refrigerator door. *Ravioli. Perfect. What could be easier?* Boil water, heat pasta sauce, slice French bread.

I lose myself in the busyness of preparing dinner and setting the table. My heart feels as if it's wearing a cement vest. I hate knowing there will be so much distance between Deb and myself. We've always been each other's sounding boards. What will happen when she moves to North Carolina?

Soon my family comes home, everyone chattering and laughing as they pile through various doors.

I manage to get through dinner without trading any harsh words with Nick. Jerry and Emma walk upstairs together. I hear the television in my bedroom squawk on and Emma's cell phone ringing from her room.

While Nick helps me clear the table, I nonchalantly say, "So, is there anything special you want served on Thanksgiving?"

"Well, I won't be spending the holiday here."

"You've always eaten with the family. Why would you say that?"

Nick carefully puts the dinner plates in the washer. "I'm spending the day with Amber—"

I cut him off. "Of course, you know that Amber's invited to spend the day with us."

"Really?"

"Yes."

He eyes me suspiciously. "You didn't mention it earlier, so we made other plans."

"What?"

Nick crosses his arms. "Since you didn't offer for Amber to join the family, I chose to spend the day with her. She's cooking a turkey with one of her roommates."

I feel my face tingle in a blush. "I'm sorry. Please tell Amber she's welcome to come to dinner." When will I learn? If only I extended myself toward this girl more, I wouldn't be dealing with this mess of my own creation.

He studies me for a moment. "Well, I'll mention it to her. Maybe it's not too late to change our plans."

I grasp on to that hope. "No, it's not too late. Besides, I want to get to know Amber better."

Nick takes the garbage out, and when he returns, he puts a new plastic bag in the trash can. "Have you thought about how weird Thanksgiving will be without Grandma?"

Only a million times. "Yes, but we still have Grandpa with us and lots to be thankful for." I feel a little silly giving him such a sappy reply, but I know he won't hold it against me.

His response is a sigh. Nick was close to Theresa, as all of us were.

I cross the room and give him a hug. He pats my back and steps away, looking as though he's taming what he might consider less-than-manly emotions.

"Would you like me to invite Amber to spend the day with us?"

Nick shakes his head. "No, I'll talk to her." He gives me a brave smile and leaves the room.

Jerry's upstairs, stretched out on the bed watching a news program on television. He raises his eyebrows as I walk through the room.

"What?" *Is nothing easy today?* First Deb, then Nick, and now Jerry's questioning me.

He clasps his fingers together and puts them behind his head. "A little defensive, are we?"

I draw a deep breath, close my eyes, and sigh. My chin falls to my chest, and I feel as though I'm being sucked into a void. I don't even pretend to be a strong woman. I know I'm a weak vessel. *Why is so much coming at me so quickly?*

"Lin?"

I lift my head and open my eyes to see Jerry walking toward me, arms open. I fall into his embrace, dissolving into his strength. *What a wondrous feeling.*

He holds me tightly. "I'm sorry. I didn't mean anything. I was just teasing you. What's wrong?"

I wiggle out of his arms and grab a tissue to dry my tears.

Jerry closes the door. "What's going on?"

If only I could tell him how upset I am about Deb moving. Or even tell him about Keith's shenanigans. But I promised Deb, so that tale will remain locked in my heart.

He looks at me, his eyes warm with concern.

"I'm going to miss Deb terribly." It's a relief to pour out my heart about my concerns for Nick and my guilt over not being more welcoming to Amber while we sit next to each other on the bed. "Sometimes I don't recognize myself."

Jerry keeps silent, allowing me to continue.

"I'm not going to pretend that I'm happy with Nick's choice of a girlfriend. After all, she's so very different from the other girls he's dated. But I can't seem to welcome her with open arms. There's something about her, about the situation that just makes me uncomfortable. And you know I'm a bad actor. I can't even pretend to like her."

He clears his throat, but I go on before he can speak. "I'll try to make a better effort." I know it's the diplomatic thing to do, and it's also the right thing to do.

"I'm proud of you, Linda."

"Why?"

He gives me a hug. "I know how difficult this situation with Nick is for you. I'm proud that you're inviting Amber for Thanksgiving dinner. That's a step in the right direction."

I'm not so sure about that, but I don't have the energy to refute him. *What if I'm right? What if this girl's all wrong for Nick?* I try to push the thought from my mind. "I hope they change their plans and join us for Thanksgiving."

"I bet they will. You know how much Nick loves your cooking."

I feel the sting of tears again and bat my eyes to keep them at bay. Jerry turns down the volume on the television. "What else?"

I shrug and try to swallow my fears. "It's too much."

"What?"

"I feel like the changes coming at me are too much and too fast. I feel as if I'm losing my family. Theresa's gone, and now it seems like we're losing Ross to another woman and Nick's ready to stroll out of our lives. And before we know it, Emma will be moving out to college. Life as we know it is about to end. My family is scattering."

He shakes his head. "You're not losing your family. Life changes."

Jerry's hands move to my weary shoulders and gently squeeze. *Ah. Heavenly.* My tense muscles begin to unwind. I tilt my head toward my shoulder.

His breath warms my neck. "It will be all right, honey. Even if it's not okay, we'll get through this together." He punctuates his pronouncement with a kiss on my shoulder.

My last thought before I give way to passion is a prayer that my children will someday have someone to love them, heart and soul, the way Jerry loves me.

25

Panic claws at me like a score of spiders running up my back when I realize that Thanksgiving is exactly one week away. I know I have to pull off a festive, happy holiday, but my heart's not in it. If I could have my way, we'd eat take-out pizza and not think about Theresa being gone or the new faces that will surround our table.

It's bad enough not knowing for sure if Nick and Amber will be joining us, but then I got the surprise of my life when Ross called and asked if he could bring a guest. It's been only eleven months since we lost Theresa, and he wants to fill her seat at the family table with Doris. It seems entirely inappropriate for Ross to be dating seriously so soon after Theresa's death. Of course I've only expressed my concerns to Jerry. I immediately felt sorry for voicing that opinion. I never want to be the cause of a moment of discomfort for him. And did he ever look uncomfortable, but being the man he is, he merely sighed and said the right thing—that Ross is an active adult who wants to enjoy life. He's right, but still . . .

So I've planned a Thanksgiving dinner that's traditional yet simple. I went so far as to advise everyone that we will dress casually. This year, for the first time, I'll wear jeans. My big concession to the day is that my jeans will be brand-spanking-new. Emma's been at me to toss out all my old denim. And then she told me that new designer jeans would make me look slimmer. What can I say? What woman alive doesn't want to look her best?

I leave work at five forty-five and head straight to our retail resort aka local mall. Jerry promised he would pick up dinner for himself and the kids on his way home. Hopefully, there'll be leftovers for me.

Traffic drains out of the parking lot when I arrive at the mall. I find a good spot to park and walk into the glass and brick behemoth.

The window displays assault my senses with Christmas overload. I know I'm dating myself when I say that I remember when Christmas decorations weren't brought out of storage until after Thanksgiving.

Since I parked on the south side of the mall, Macy's is my first stop. I steer clear of the stacks full of my usual Levi's that hug the wall and head toward the designer denim beckoning me from the hanging display.

As I approach, an emaciated woman greets me. "May I help you?" She leans toward me as she makes her request in a clipped manner.

I gesture toward the yards of blue, black, brown, and gray denim. "I need a new pair of jeans."

She looks me up and down, making me feel like I've stumbled into the wrong department. Do you need to have a certain cachet to shop in this department?

She fingers the expensive-looking necklace that falls nearly to her waistline. "These are hand stitched, very fine." Then she pulls out a pair of deep blue jeans that are accented with tiny specks of rhinestones sparkling in an intricate design along the back pocket. *How sweet is that?*

"Oh, that's pretty." I begin to paw through the rack for my size. *Yowsa!* A tag taunts me with a price of two hundred and fifty dollars. That can't be right.

The attendant, still hovering at my elbow, raises her eyebrows. "Is there a problem?"

I'll say. "Well, I wasn't expecting to spend quite as much."

"Shall we take a look at these over here?" She leads me to an adjacent display. The jeans look almost the same as the pricey ones around the corner.

"Thank you." I dive in to find my size.

I squeeze the hangers onto the dressing room hook and kick off my shoes. Emma's advice runs through my head: *"Remember what Oprah said about mom jeans."* She even taped that program for me. Who knew I was wearing the wrong jeans?

I slip my skirt down my hips and reach for the first pair. *Be still my heart.* I didn't think I would ever consider purchasing jeans worth a hundred bucks. Jerry will die—if he ever finds out. But then I can always console him with the knowledge that I didn't spend twice that amount.

The sound of laughter floats over the padded stalls. Young women enjoying a shopping day with friends.

I lean against the side of the tiny room and step into designer denim. The waistband falls perfectly above my hips. *Interesting.* I zip up and turn to see the rear view. *Not bad.* I pick up my purse off the corner bench and take a seat. They're so comfortable. These are definitely keepers.

Voices drift over the handicapped stall that houses the friends shopping together. "You've got to buy that jacket."

A clear voice rings out. "You don't have to sell me on it. I'm already planning what I can wear with it."

I step out of the stall to view myself in the three-way mirror. I'm pressed into the wall when a girl carrying an armload of clothes squeezes past me and into the party dressing room.

I wonder if these pants are too long. *Will my black Aigner shoes make me tall enough?*

"Oh, man. That's unbelievable, Amber."

My ears tingle at the name. That can't be Nick's Amber.

Other voices pick up where the first left off. "That sweater is amazing!"

"It's so sexy."

"Nick is going to love it."

Nick? My Nick? It can't be.

My heart stops when I hear a familiar soft voice. "You better believe Nick's going to love it. He'll especially love it when it lands on the floor."

Laughter explodes in the dressing room, and my mouth goes dry. It is Nick's Amber.

"Move aside. I can't see the mirror."

A flurry of movement sounds from the dressing room. "Why don't you look in the mirror outside?"

Sweet mother of pearl! I have nowhere to go. I can't run onto the floor of the department store, shoeless. And my purse is in here.

Amber announces, "I think I'll stop at Victoria's Secret and buy a bra to go with it."

I can't believe what I'm hearing.

Before I can race back to the safety of my stall, a sales associate walks toward me. "How are you doing in here, ma'am?"

I simply nod. I may be able to escape to my stall if—

The door at the end of the dressing room swings in, and Amber strides out. She's beautiful, as usual. Her hair flows down her shoulders and rests upon the clinging black sweater. Her face is flushed in excitement, no doubt thinking of how she'll seduce my son. As she makes her way toward me, her gaze travels up from the carpeted hallway to my face, and her lips part in surprise.

26

"Hello, Amber." I wish I could tell this tart of a girl to leave Nick alone.

She regains her composure. "Hi, Linda."

I wonder if Amber can hear the frantic beating of my heart. I'm an original mama bear, always ready to defend my cubs and my den with whatever force is necessary. Except until now I've only dealt with shortsighted teachers, neighborhood bullies, and rude people out in public. I have no idea how to defend my son against someone who doesn't share our values.

I wish I could push her out of his life, but now that the true extent of their relationship has been revealed, I know she's not going anywhere—at least for a while. I can't say I'm surprised by this new revelation. We knew Nick was up to something when he'd stay out half the night.

So here we are, two women who both love the same young man, having a standoff in a department store dressing room. Amber's face is colored a shade of red I never imagined on a human being. I wonder if mine is too.

I find my voice. "What a surprise to see you."

Amber licks her lips as if she's parched. "Yes, a surprise."

I smooth out the front pocket of the designer jeans I'm wearing. "I'm buying new jeans."

"Oh? I'm thinking of buying this sweater." She pulls on the bottom of the knit.

Good grief—that just makes the neckline dip lower. Let's hope she doesn't do that too often.

We stand like a set of mismatched china teacups accidentally put together on the same table. A definite design flaw and clashing in pattern.

We both start to talk at the same time, then fall silent, neither of us completing our sentences. Another unpleasant moment.

We must share the same thought, because we awkwardly shuffle around one another, me rushing back to my dressing room and Amber moving to admire herself in the three-way mirror. If this were happening on the silver screen, it would be laughable. But it's not happening to some pathetic make-believe person; it's happening to me.

I strip off the lovely jeans and determine to buy them. At least something can be salvaged from this fiasco. As I pull on my skirt, I decide to wait for Amber to return to her stall, so I sit on the corner seat in the dressing room. My gaze roams the small area of my confinement. Someone, probably a teen girl, wrote *Tiffany loves Peter* on the back of the stall door. I count the number of straight pins on the floor. The sounds of whispers and chuckles intrude on my discomfort. Those girls who are with Amber must have put two and two together and are laughing at our bumbling equation.

I can just imagine Amber out there, standing in front of the full-length mirrors turning this way and that, admiring the fit of the sweater and the curves of her well-proportioned young shape. And I can imagine that she's playing the movie in her mind of when Nick sees her new sweater fall to the floor. *Ugh.*

I shake my head to dislodge that troublesome thought, but it clings to my brain. I look down and see Amber's stocking feet and form-fitting jeans walk past my stall and toward the one holding her giggling gang of girlfriends. Hopefully I never have to meet any of them.

The stall door clicks shut and all-out laughter erupts.

Grabbing my purse and new jeans, I rush out of the dressing room. The attendant who previously helped me steps forward. I give her a goofy grin and keep walking, hoping she doesn't trail me. The last thing I want is to see Amber and her friends. I hop on the escalator and walk down the moving stairway to hasten my escape. I'm sure I can pay for my jeans in another department.

Once I'm on the first floor of the store, my breathing slows and my heartbeat begins to return to normal. *Oh, my goodness. What just happened?* I hope this doesn't cause any trouble between Nick and me. Will I ever be able to have a normal relationship with Amber?

I stroll down the aisle between pint-size mannequins wearing adorable holiday dresses with matching shoes and purses. How I used to enjoy dressing up my children. Especially Emma. She loved to get all fancied up to visit friends and family.

I get in line behind two young women, each pushing a stroller and keeping track of an older sibling. One of the ladies is talking with her young daughter, a sweet little girl who looks five years old. They are admiring the black velvet dress with a fur-trimmed collar that they are about to purchase. The tot's eyes are shining with excitement, and she holds a tiny purse as if it were made of gold.

A thought intrudes on my pleasant memories: *Did Amber's mother dress her up for the holidays? Who were the people who admired her velvet dresses and patent leather shoes? Did she have those sweet memories of knowing she was the prettiest little princess in the room?*

From what little information Nick's told me, Amber's young life was not filled with satin and bows, and she was never her daddy's little princess. Despite my gut feeling of not liking that young woman, my heart aches for what she never had. Would those experiences have made her a different person?

My cell phone chirps from within my purse. I dig through the jumble of stuff to retrieve it. A call from home. "Hello?"

"Mom, did you wash my cheerleader uniform?"

"Yes, I—"

"Well, I can't find it!" Emma's voice is high-pitched, like it gets when she's stressed or upset.

"What's wrong?"

"I can't find my uniform, and we have to wear our breakaway pants and pullover vests tomorrow. What did you do with them?"

"Calm yourself. They're probably in the dryer. I did a load of laundry before going to work. Take a look—"

"Oh, there they are. Thanks." She hangs up without even saying good-bye.

Something's up with that girl. I'll investigate further when I get home.

I check the customer-service counter. Only one woman is in front of me. I work on my patience while I wait my turn. The cashier seems to be flustered as she tries to input information into her cash register. *How much longer can this take?* I just want to go home.

● ● ●

By the time I'm on my street I've practically convinced myself that the bizarre event of the evening was an elaborate figment of my overactive imagination. Or at least I wish it were.

Nick's car is missing from the driveway. Well, at least I know who he is not with this evening. I park in the garage, grab my things, and walk into the house.

Jerry's nodding off on the family room couch.

I glance toward the kitchen and cringe. Styrofoam cartons and dirty plates litter the table. "Emma?"

From the corner of my eye, I see Jerry startle from his rest. Belle runs down the stairs, followed by my daughter—the girl who should have cleared the table and loaded the dishwasher.

"Sorry, Mom."

I drop my purse on the buffet in the foyer and toss my bag by the bottom of the stairs. "You know it's so much easier to clean the dishes before the food gets crusty."

She stops in her tracks. "What's wrong? Are you mad at me?"

"No, I'm sorry. I've had a rough night."

She raises her eyebrows. "A rough night shopping?"

I wave my hand in dismissal. If I don't admit to the catastrophe that the shopping trip turned into, did it really happen? I know I'll never speak of it to anyone.

I change the topic. "What's up with you, sweetie? You sounded a little upset when you called looking for your uniform."

Emma piles the plates and carries them to the sink. "Cole and I had a fight."

Jerry sits up straighter. I know he's listening to our conversation.

I toss the paper napkins in the trash can. "Can you tell me about your argument?"

She nods. "It was a stupid fight. Over Keira Knightley."

"Really?" This is going to be interesting.

"Who?" Jer isn't even pretending he's not listening.

We both turn toward Jerry and at the same time say, "The girl who was in the Pirates of the Caribbean movies."

"Go on, Em."

"Well, we watched that movie last weekend at Lyndsay's house, and we were talking about it on the phone tonight. And I said, 'Ew, why doesn't Keira Knightley ever get braces for her crooked teeth?' And Cole said, 'She has crooked teeth?' Like he never even noticed."

Jerry stands up. "Keira Knightley has crooked teeth?"

"It's always bothered me too," I say.

He screws up his face as if he's trying to evoke an image of the young actress. "Crooked teeth?"

Men. "Yes, have you never noticed?"

Emma turns to me and puts her hands on her hips. "See what I mean?"

27

I drive to work thinking about what I'll face during the next two days. Tomorrow's our big Santa Charity event, and if all the details aren't perfect, the blame will fall on my head. As if I need one more thing to stress about.

The rental truck's coming this morning at ten to take our sets, lights, and reflectors to the church hall that hosts the event. I hope the fairies who volunteered are present and ready to work. This is no small undertaking, and each year it gets bigger and better. Luke partners with two other portrait studios in town, and the church hall is transformed into six shooting bays, each with a slightly different holiday theme. Each of the studios mans two of the bays. We hire three naturally bearded Santas, and they move like clockwork from one set to another, posing with excited children.

It takes all the manpower we have to pull this off. We set up tables for a reception area to check in the families who have made appointments and to schedule the drops-ins that always show up. Once families complete their portrait session, they're led to a snack area, where they enjoy cookies and punch while they wait for the imaging artists to select the best poses to view. Salespeople print out the final images and go over the selections with the clients.

The families who have portraits taken pay a fee for their session and buy reasonably priced packages. If they choose to bring in a donation for the charity, they get bonus images. Luke had a great idea when he decided the more generous the clients were, the more portraits they would receive. That Luke, he's great at coming up with amazing ideas. But then he passes them off to me, and I get stuck—er, I mean, I get the responsibility of executing those brilliant plans.

I'd like to say this promotion is like a delicate ballet with all the pieces meshing seamlessly, but it's more like a crazy square dance with me calling out the moves to teams of professional photographers, anxious parents, and excited children. The day is always a blur of activity and anxiety. And there's always a long waiting line.

The parking lot in front of the studio is nearly full. I specifically asked our fairies to park in the periphery of the lot so clients would have the choice spots. I park in the farthest line of spaces and head into what I know will be a stress-filled day of work.

Christmas music blares from the sound system in the studio. Two school-age children are dancing to the tune of "A Holly Jolly Christmas" while their mother holds a toddler on her lap.

I smile and nod at them all. "Morning."

The hallway is lined with plastic bins full of holiday decorations, and fairies are clustered in small groups awaiting their task assignments for the day. I dart past the melee and into my office. I had hoped this room at least would be an island of tranquility in a sea of madness, but it doesn't look like it will. My desk is piled with clipboards and manila envelopes. I stow my purse in the drawer, slip my coat on the hook, and drop into my chair to begin sorting through the confusion.

"Excuse me?"

Argh! I didn't even see Katrina come into the room. "Yes?"

She toys with her expensive watch. "I was wondering if you've gotten permission for me to take tomorrow off."

The poor girl looks stressed and hopeful at the same time. I hate to burst her bubble. "I'm sorry. As far as I know, everyone on staff has to work tomorrow."

Katrina's countenance falls. "Carol said that I should expect to hear that my request is being honored."

"Luke was adamant that everyone works. It doesn't look like he'll give you a day off."

I expect her to leave the office, but she stays planted. "Will you speak to him? Please?"

Katrina must be getting lessons in perseverance from Carol. "I don't think—"

"I hesitated to ask for the day off, but Carol has been such a friend to me, and she made plans for the weekend. She insisted that getting time off wouldn't be a problem. And please know I'm humbled by the opportunity I have here. I'm sure that's because of your friendship with Carol."

That's not 100 percent correct, but Carol certainly persuaded me to help the application process. "I doubt there's anything I can do to influence Luke. I'm sorry."

Katrina shuffles out of the office.

I feel sorry for her. Really, I do. If my daughter was away from home and I had the opportunity to surprise her for her birthday, I'd be all over it. But I'm sure Katrina can have a nice dinner with Carol and her mom tomorrow night after work.

I sift through the stack of papers. One of them is stained with frantic marks made by a highlighter. There are lots of exclamation points and underlines. *Oh, dear.* It's a fax from the Rent-A-Santa company. They need information for their files faxed to them ASAP. *Great. One more thing.* I start to fill in the blanks and am distracted by a knock on my open door.

I glance up, putting my finger where I left off on my paper, and see a young man dressed in a gray courier's uniform. I finish filling in our telephone number. "Come in."

"Mrs. Revere?"

My head jerks up at the familiar voice. "Cole. Oh, I'm sorry. I didn't even recognize you in that uniform." I vaguely remember

Emma telling me about Cole's work-study program with the delivery service. The young man looks like he'd rather be a million other places than standing by his girlfriend's mother's desk.

He lays a small manila envelope in front of me and holds out a clipboard for me to sign.

I smile at him. "How have you been? I haven't seen you in a while. It seems every time you come to pick up Emma, I'm out somewhere."

Cole pulls at the collar of his shirt. "I'm good. And pretty busy."

"How's the job going?"

He shrugs. "It's good experience. But this uniform makes me feel like a Boy Scout."

"Well, you look like a professional." I dash off my signature.

"Thanks." Cole snatches back his clipboard. "See you around." His black shoes squeak as he leaves.

I stare at the envelope Cole delivered. It's addressed to me. The handwriting seems familiar, but there's no return address. I open it. The heavyweight stationery stirs my memory. It's a letter from Carol Ball. *How odd.* Why didn't she just give me a call?

> *Dear Luke,*

That's strange. If she addressed it to me, why did she write it to Luke?

> *Katrina told me about the charity function you are running this weekend. What a wonderful idea. It warms my heart every time I hear about another way you are involved with the community, giving of yourself and your talents. I regret that I cannot participate in this worthy cause. I have an old friend coming into town, and I look forward to spending some time with her.*
>
> *In honor of your efforts and to help the less fortunate*

in our community, I am enclosing a donation for your cause. Please accept this small gift on behalf of my family.
    If there is ever anything more I can do for you, just ask. That's what friends are for.

    Very truly yours,
    Carol Ball

I pick up the folded check that fluttered from the notepaper. *Good grief.* The check is written in the amount of five thousand dollars.

I put the letter and check back inside the envelope and focus on my Rent-A-Santa fax. First things first.

A few minutes later, the static of the intercom disturbs my concentration. "Linda, you have a call on line two. Carol Ball."

I toss down my pen, stab the line-two button, and pick up the receiver. "Hi, Carol."

"Linda! How delightful that you are available to take my call."

Hmm. She's an amazing politician. "What can I do for you today?"

She's silent long enough to make me regret my abrupt attitude. "Did you receive my letter?"

"Yes, how generous of you. I'm sure Luke will be thrilled."

Her smiling voice comes through the line. "Good. I'm glad he'll be pleased."

Carol usually doesn't waste her time on casual pleasantries. "If you don't mind my asking . . ."

"Ask away, dear."

"Why did you address the letter to me?"

Carol laughs. "I'm so transparent to you. I bet you can figure out why."

Yes, I bet I can. Don't get me wrong; I really care for Carol. "I guess this has to do with Katrina getting the day off tomorrow."

"Of course." She sounds proud of her declaration. "Before you say another word, let me tell you that I support philanthropy and would be pleased to be kept abreast of Luke's other charitable ventures."

Man, this woman is good. "That's wonderful. Thank you."

"When you speak with Luke, please let him know my intentions."

I'm going to speak with Luke? Is that where this is going? "Yes, I surely will."

"Thank you. I knew I could count on you. After all, that's what friends are for."

I'm beginning to feel like an unsuspecting bug that's been captured in a shimmering, beautiful spiderweb. "Uh . . . yes."

Carol continues, "I'm so glad that we've become friends. Aren't you?"

"Uh, yes, your friendship is valuable to me."

"Then I'm sure you can appreciate how warmly I feel toward Katrina's mother. We've been friends forever. You know I'll do just about anything for a friend."

"I'll be happy to personally deliver your letter to Luke. I'm sure your generous gift will influence his decision to allow Katrina to have the day off."

"And if that doesn't work?"

"Then I will convince him it won't make much of a difference if Katrina's there or not."

"Thank you. Don't forget: if there's ever anything I can do for you, I'll be happy to help."

Ain't that the truth.

28

I experience the thrill of victory as I fax the document to our Rent-A-Santa company. It's not been easy to finish this task, what with all the interruptions I've had.

I walk down the hall in search of Luke and find him by the basement stairs, supervising the moving of equipment.

"Luke?"

He holds up a finger before he grabs one end of a long folding table to help two fairies with their burden. When the volunteers are on their way toward the truck, he dusts his hands off on his jeans and faces me. Despite the busyness of the day, he seems stress free. "What do you need?"

"Can I speak to you about something?"

He nods. "What's up?"

I glance around at the activity that surrounds us. "May I speak with you in private?" The last thing we need is for other employees to hear that the assistant (of all people) gets the day off tomorrow.

Luke looks concerned as he ushers me through the hall to his office. When we enter, he gestures to a chair and sits opposite me. "What's wrong?"

I wave my hand to minimize my issue. "Actually, I have great news. Carol Ball had a courier deliver this." I hand him the envelope.

Luke takes out the check, unfolds it, and whistles. "Wow."

"Yeah, I know. But there are strings attached."

His countenance goes from pleasure to confusion. "What?"

Oh, this isn't the way I wanted to present the information. "Well, not exactly strings. That was my characterization. But it has something to do with Katrina. Read the letter."

I settle in while he withdraws the letter from the envelope and reads it.

A small frown creases Luke's forehead. "Of course I'd rather not have to give Katrina the day off. This is a dangerous precedent."

That's fairly obvious.

"I don't want to offend any other staff members. But . . ." He sighs and scrubs his face with his hands. "The only thing that makes me uncomfortable is that I'm nearly being blackmailed."

I feel for Luke. More than anyone else, I know the power Carol can exert over another human being. "That's true, but look at the other side. She's been surprisingly benevolent. That's a lot of money."

"You're right. Carol's been incredibly generous with the check— $5K. I never would have expected that from her." Luke gives me a small salute, stands, and starts to exit the office. "I've got work to do." After a pause, he turns back to me. "Tell Katrina she can have the day off on the q.t. Have her call in sick in the morning."

"Sure." I follow Luke through the hallway and turn into one of our large studios. Katrina is kneeling in front of a pile of lenses, light meters, and gray cards, trying to make sense of the list she's working from. Beside her are a few more experienced photographers. I stand over them a moment until Katrina looks up. I motion for her to follow me.

I weave through the madness in the hallway and slip into my office. By the time I'm at my desk, Katrina's through the door.

Her face is bright with hope, and her smile is contagious. "Can I have tomorrow off?"

I peer over her shoulder. "Close the door."

The subterfuge seems to amuse her. She pushes the door closed and leans against it. "Well? Carol said she would work something out with you. Did she?"

Oh yes, she did. "What I say must stay in this room. Do you understand?"

Katrina nods solemnly.

"The last thing we want is for the rest of the staff to have any hard feelings because you're allowed the day off. I also don't want Carol's name involved in any gossip."

She continues to nod.

"Don't tell anyone else you won't be coming to work in the morning. And call in sick."

Katrina propels herself across the room and throws her arms around my shoulders. "Thanks. Carol said we could count on you."

My only hope is that this little drama doesn't come back to bite me in the backside.

I'm bone weary by the time I leave work. A soft duskiness has descended on the landscape. My last view of the outdoors was during a short dinner break. The sun was beginning to set, and the clouds hovering over the mountains shimmered with a gold edging so bright that if you saw it in a photograph you would swear it was retouched. Now the mountains are obscured, cloaked with clouds offering only a passing glimpse of a full moon.

I try to locate my car. *Where did I park?* Memories of nearly ten hours ago flood back. My burned-out brain reviews my day from end to beginning like a movie trailer running backward. I grit my teeth and march to the edge of the parking lot.

I toss my stuff on the seat beside me, buckle up, plug in my hands-free, stuff the earbud in, and dial Jerry.

"Hey, Lin," he says just before the call would have gone to voice mail.

Good thing. My patience is stretched pretty thin. "What's for dinner tonight? Who's cooking?"

He doesn't speak.

Sheesh. I didn't even greet him. I know I'm in a crabby mood, so I can't blame him for giving me the silent treatment. "Sorry. It's been a rough day."

He sighs his I'm-such-a-martyr-and-a-wonderful-husband-to-boot sigh. "I'm nearly home, but I don't feel like cooking."

As if I do? "Okay. What kind of takeout should I get?"

We begin the negotiation process. After a couple of minutes of shooting down each other's suggestions, Jerry says, "Oh, I know."

"Do tell." *Finally.*

"What about the new Japanese café? Do you want to try their sushi?"

I can't believe what I'm hearing. "Sushi?"

"It was surprisingly good a few weeks ago at that restaurant with Deb and Keith. Want to get us a platter?"

"I thought you didn't want Asian food?"

"I don't want *fried* Asian food. That's the difference."

"Okay. Is that the restaurant over by Wal-Mart?"

"Yeah, that's where it is. I'll set the table."

"See you at home." We disconnect the call, and I cruise off the highway onto Pine Grove Road. Because it's getting late, the usual traffic snarl has loosened up. *Sweet.* I chug along to the sushi café.

A front-door parking space calls my name. Maybe this day is looking up after all. I push through the wide, glass door. For a café, the decor is quite sophisticated—linen-covered tables, tasteful art on the walls, and a wide granite sushi bar.

I walk to the counter. As I wait for someone to greet me, I help myself to a take-out menu displayed in an acrylic holder on the counter. The brochure is well done. I appreciate a good marketing piece. I scan the menu choices. *Oh, good gravy.* I have no idea what these dishes are. There are certainly enough appetizers. Do the Japanese have an equivalent to crab rangoon? I glance around the busy restaurant. The patrons seem happy and satisfied, and the sushi chefs are working hard, hands flying with knives and equipment.

I look back to the menu. Whatever shall I order? What's tonkatsu? Or beef negimaki? The only appetizer that I can understand is spring roll. And the salads—kani salad? Seaweed salad? What on earth are they?

"May I help you?"

I jerk my head in the direction of the musical voice. "Uh, it's my first time here, and——"

The young Asian woman looks as if she's forcing a smile. "We've only been open a week." She doesn't say it with pride of ownership but with that inflection in her voice that I've heard from my kids when they think I've said something stupid. This I don't need in my day.

"Ah yes. I need to take food home for dinner, but I'm not sure how to order."

She pulls out an order pad. "Sushi or entrees?"

"Sushi, please." *At least I know that much.*

She shifts to lean against the counter. "And what would you like?"

Did I not just tell her that I don't know how to order? "I don't know. What do you suggest?"

She rolls her eyes and moves to the other end of the counter to confer with another employee.

A tall Asian gentleman with an authentic smile approaches. He looks elegant, dressed in a black shirt and sharply creased black trousers. His long, dark hair is tied at the nape of his neck in a ponytail that falls halfway down his back. He inclines his head. "May I help you?"

Finally, someone who knows a thing or two about customer service. "Yes, please. I need some sushi to take home to my family."

Mr. Tall-Dark-and-Handsome nods. "How many will be eating dinner?"

"Four."

"Any with large appetites?"

"Yeah. One of my guys could eat a bear."

The man's eyes light up. "Shall I design a sushi platter for you, ma'am?"

At this point that suggestion sounds heavenly. "Oh yes, please. And may I have a glass of iced tea while I wait?"

I take my tea and scoot onto the last barstool at the sushi bar to watch my meal being prepared. As usual, my attention strays to the other patrons, and I lose myself in the pleasure of people watching. Surreptitiously, of course.

"Madam?"

I turn to find Mr. Tall-Dark-and-Handsome standing by my elbow. "Yes?"

"Your dinner is ready."

I stride to the other end of the counter and see a large plastic bag holding my platters. I peek inside. "This looks beautiful!" I've never seen food presented more artistically in my life.

I slide my credit card out of my wallet and hand it to the beautiful, disgruntled young woman. She seems a bit happier now. She pushes the receipt toward me, then takes a pen with a silk flower taped to the end of it out of a bean-filled vase and extends it to me.

Eighty-nine dollars! The sushi sticker shock has my heart beating like one of those huge Japanese drums. I never imagined a sushi dinner would be so expensive, and it didn't even dawn on me that there were no prices listed in the take-out menu. Too bad I didn't get a peek at the bill for the dinner Keith treated us to at that downtown Japanese restaurant. My hand shakes, but I smile and sign the receipt. I grab my sack and walk out of the café with my head held high. From now on, sushi will be a once-a-year treat.

This better be the most delicious takeout ever.

29

Nick's car isn't parked in front of the house. Now I've overbought on some very expensive food. I park my car in the garage next to Emma's and carry my purse, lunch box, and briefcase into the house.

As promised, Jerry's set the table. Four place settings are on a clean table. It's nice to have someone to count on, especially after the day I've had.

Jerry walks down the hall, a frown creasing his forehead. "Where's dinner?"

I refrain from sighing. "In the car. I couldn't carry everything."

We give each other a quick kiss, and I head into the kitchen. The door to the garage slams behind Jerry, and I unload my things.

Emma jogs down the stairs. "I can't believe Dad wanted sushi for dinner."

I smile. "Yeah, who knew he would like it?"

She shuffles across the kitchen in her fuzzy slippers and takes a glass from the cabinet. "I had sushi at a party. It was yummy."

"Yummy but it's also expensive."

Emma draws back her lips in her yikes expression. "Does Dad know?"

"Not yet, and I'm not going to ruin his appetite."

Jerry struts in and places the sack on the table. He carefully extracts the platters. "I feel as if we should take a picture of it before we eat it."

"Yeah," Emma pipes up, "we want to enjoy this meal as much as possible, considering what it costs."

Oh, I could kill her.

Jerry shoots me a look. "What?"

"It was a bit expensive."

He makes a face. "Define expensive."

For a moment I consider softening the blow. But he's the one who asked for sushi. "How does eighty-nine dollars strike you?"

Jerry clutches his heart. "This had better be good."

Wow, he's taking the news better than I expected. "Let's eat slowly and enjoy the meal." I move to the sink to wash my hands. "Have we heard from Nick? I bought extra because of him."

"I don't think so. He may be along soon." Jerry pries the plastic lids off the platters. "At least he doesn't have to heat it up when he gets home."

We all sit, and Jer says a blessing. Without fanfare, we dive into the delicious meal. I can't believe we've deprived ourselves of this scrumptious cuisine for so long. I pop what could be a California roll into my mouth and savor the delicate flavor.

When I hear the sound of a key in the front door, I wipe the corners of my mouth with a napkin. "Well, it looks like this food will be history soon."

Smiling, I turn toward the foyer anticipating Nick's reaction when he realizes what we're serving tonight. But instead of Nick, Amber walks in. I feel my smile freeze to a grotesque mask. I hope no one notices my blush.

Jerry pushes back from the table. "Hello, Amber. I hope you'll join us for dinner."

She smiles at Jerry and glances at me.

Before she can answer, Nick appears. "What's this?"

Emma gets another place setting. "Dad wanted sushi. Can you believe it?" She moves Nick's plate to the side and puts the extra setting next to it. She smiles at Amber. "You eat sushi, don't you?"

Amber glances at me again.

I try to speak in a normal voice. "Yes, you do eat sushi?" But with this girl, who knows? Will she quiz me about where I bought it and if it's all natural and organic?

Nick guides her to a seat. "We love sushi."

I'm not grooving on his proclivity for plural pronouns lately. "Oh, good."

Amber puts her napkin on her lap and looks as if she's about to dig into dinner when Nick grabs one of her hands. "Let's pray." They put their heads together while Nick whispers a blessing. We all pause in our dining until he says *amen.*

I feel like a boa constrictor is wound around my rib cage. *Will Amber say anything about seeing me at the mall last night? Should I mention seeing her? Is that her new sweater she's wearing? No, it was black, I think.*

"Mom?"

I pull myself from my private state of panic and focus on Emma. "Yes?"

"Don't you think that Nick and Amber should go to the charity event tomorrow and have their portrait taken?"

That's not a plan I'd come up with, but . . . "Uh, sure. There are always a few walk-in appointments available."

I study the rapidly emptying tray of sushi rolls and select another. I notice that Amber's taken a set of chopsticks out of their paper wrapper and is expertly wielding the utensils.

Emma notices too. "Amber, can you teach me how to use them?"

They laugh together while Amber tries to position the chopsticks in Emma's hands. My daughter's so cute when she concentrates like that. It makes me smile.

"So," Emma says, "what's the stuff that looks like green ice cream?"

Amber giggles. "It's wasabi, and it's really hot. If you try some, take only a little."

Emma dips a roll into the wasabi and cautiously takes a bite.

She blinks, and her eyes fill with tears. She puts down the uneaten portion of her sushi and grabs her water, gulping a mouthful. She snatches a napkin and as dainty as a queen wipes her mouth. "Well, that was good."

Everyone laughs along with her. The dinner continues on a light-hearted note. Occasionally I catch Amber's eye. *What is she thinking? Is she embarrassed by what happened last night or does she think she's got the upper hand?* If only I could read her.

When dinner ends, Nick and Jerry go out to the driveway to listen to a noise Nick says his car is making. Emma starts to collect the dishes, and I take the empty platters to the trash can. I push Belle away with one foot while I maneuver the large plastic disks into the receptacle. Sticky rice rains from the soiled platters.

"Oh, let me help you." Amber rushes to my side and lifts the plastic bag from the trash bin.

I slide the containers inside and start to take the bag from her to tie it up. "Thank you."

She doesn't release the bag. "That's okay. I can take this out to the garage. I saw the garbage can out there."

I let her have the bag and watch her scoot out the door.

"Don't you think Amber's a lot of fun?" Emma asks me.

Well, I'm sure that's what Nick thinks too. "She seems nice."

My daughter shakes her head. "Will you give her a chance?"

Amber comes back inside. I turn to the sink and finish loading the dishes. As I'm about to reach for the sponge, Amber takes it and wipes off the table.

Emma puts her hand on Amber's back. "I'll see you later. I've got a ton of homework to do." She spins on her heel and heads upstairs.

Oh no. She's not leaving us alone? Where are the boys? Panic begins to inch up my spine like a creeping autumn frost.

Amber smiles at me and pulls out a chair. She sits at my kitchen table as if she expects me to join her. "Linda—" she moistens her lips—"I think we need to talk."

30

"Tea?" I grab my kettle from the stove. "I'd love a cup of tea. How about you? What kind of tea do you like?"

Before Amber can answer, I put down the kettle and retrieve half a dozen foil bags of loose tea out of my cabinet. "Let's see, Darjeeling? English breakfast?" I place my infuser and teapot on the counter, then fill the kettle and turn on the stove. "Do you like flavored tea? I've got a delicious ginger peach. How about orange and spice? Or do you drink decaf in the evenings? I've got a decaf chocolate peppermint that's nice for dessert and a decaf Irish breakfast."

I realize I've developed a raging case of verbal diarrhea, and—*heaven help me*—I can't stop blabbering on. "Or do you like iced tea? I can make any of these into a pitcher of iced tea. You know, Nick loves strawberry green iced tea. I don't know if I have any of that left, though."

Amber looks as though she's watching a bizarre circus sideshow performance. I think I'm frightening her.

Still, I go on and on. "Would you prefer coffee instead? I have regular and decaf. Oh, wait a minute." I go back to my cabinet and rummage around until I find some small sample packets that came in a gift basket. "Look. I've even got gourmet coffees. Let's see. I've got hazelnut, French vanilla, and pumpkin spice sounds nice. Seasonal."

The shrill call of the teakettle stops my inane discourse. I return to the stove, turn it off, and move the kettle to another burner. Man, I'm sweating. I walk to the cabinet by the sink and take down a paper coffee filter. "Well, what will it be?"

"What will what be?" Jerry surveys the scene with a hint of skepticism.

Amber and I turn to see Nick and Jerry standing there.

"I was just making us something to drink." I smile, hoping they'll believe my motives are on the up-and-up rather than a delay tactic to avoid talking about the fiasco at the mall.

Nick looks pleased. If he only knew what transpired twenty-four hours ago. He holds Amber's jacket out. "We've really got to go."

Ah, what a relief. "Too bad. Amber and I were going to visit for a while."

Amber stands as though she's waking from a nightmare and allows Nick to slip her jacket over her arms. "Thank you very much for dinner."

The door closes behind them, and I grab a paper napkin to mop my forehead.

"Linda, what's going on?"

I turn around to face the music, or rather, face my husband. I try to look as innocent as possible. "Going on?"

Jerry crosses his arms and cocks his head. "I know something's up when you start repeating my questions. Spill it."

"Spill it?"

"Linda!"

"Sorry." I collapse into a chair. "I guess I was a little nervous. I've never been alone with Amber. I still need the buffer that extra people provide."

He plops himself in a chair the same way he does when he's about to scold one of the children. "You've got to get over this . . . aversion to Amber."

When he says it like that, it sounds pathetic. "I don't have an aversion to her."

Silence fills the room for a moment.

"Hey, where did they go? Did Nick tell you?"

Jer shakes his head. "They don't have to clear their schedule with us. They're adults."

Now he's getting my dander up. "I know that."

My dear husband can read me like a book. He leans over and places his hand on top on mine. "Who are you? This is not the woman I married. Nick's an adult. We've got to accept his choices."

"He's making a terrible mistake—"

He squeezes my hand. "Let it go. Get to know Amber. She may be around for a while."

That's exactly what I'm afraid of. I'm so frustrated that I feel as if my head's going to explode. Am I the only one who sees that Amber is just not the kind of girl Nick should get serious about? If it weren't for my utter exhaustion, I would explain this to Jerry. Again. "Well, we'll get to know her. She might be spending Thanksgiving with us."

Jerry gives me the look and leaves the room.

I end up making a pot of tea. Maybe Emma will share it with me. Actually, I haven't been able to stop thinking about the chocolate peppermint tea since I mentioned it to Amber. I putter in the kitchen, packing a lunch for tomorrow while the water boils again and then the tea steeps. I pull my wooden tray out from its place between the refrigerator and wall and place my tea service on it to carry up to Emma's room.

The phone rings. I pick up the handset and check caller ID. The number is not familiar to me. I briefly consider not answering it, but my curiosity is too much to overcome. "Hello?"

"Linda? Is that you?" A strange female voice reaches out to me.

"Yes, this is Linda."

"Oh, hello. This is Doris."

"Hi. What can I do for you?"

She laughs as though she's nervous. "Actually I was calling to ask what I could do for you."

"Excuse me?"

"I'm talking about next week. What can I bring to Thanksgiving dinner?"

"You're a guest, Doris. Just bring your appetite."

"Please, I insist. May I bake a pie?"

"No." I immediately realize I've been blunt. "Sorry. I mean, Emma and I are baking the pies." The last thing I can imagine is this stranger taking over Theresa's pie-baking duty. "Would you like to bring something for us to snack on before dinner?"

"That's fine. What does your family like to eat?"

"I'm sure whatever you bring will be fine. Thank you for offering."

"Okay, and what time shall I have Ross bring us over?"

"You know, I haven't thought of that yet. And I'm just about dead on my feet right now. May I call you in a few days or have Ross let you know?"

She graciously agrees, and we end the discussion. Doris really seems likes she's trying to extend her friendship. Now on top of my exhaustion, I'm feeling guilty for being so short-tempered.

I heft the tray and go upstairs. I can hear Emma on the phone as I walk down the hallway. I balance the tray and knock on her door.

She opens the door, and a smile splits her face when she sees my treat. I'm about to walk into the room when she points to the phone and closes the door in my face.

I feel like kicking her door. I stand in the hall and fume.

Within moments, the door opens and Emma takes the tray from me. "Thanks."

I follow her into the room and take a seat on her bed. "What's new with you, kiddo?"

She blows the steam off the top of her mug. "You're never going to believe what Cole said tonight!"

The way my night's been going, do I even want to know?

31

Happy Saturday to me. Not! Did I sleep in? No. Enjoy a leisurely breakfast with my husband? No. And to add insult to injury, when I went out to call Belle in before she roused the entire neighborhood by barking at the squirrel in the maple tree, I came inside with a surprise all over the bottom of my shoe.

It's Santa Charity day, and I'm on my way to work. This is the craziest day of the year for Dream Photography. My jaw already aches from the all-day clench I know I'll suffer through. Jerry was still nestled all snug in our bed when I left the house, and I haven't had the opportunity to speak with him further about Emma's little news. Or not so little news. When I told Jer, he chuckled, gave me a hug, and left the room. Guess he thought I needed to process this new bombshell on my own. The way I've been reacting lately, I don't blame him.

I'm happy for my daughter. She's falling in love. And the object of her affections told her he thinks he's falling in love too. I knew the first big crush was bound to come, and at least it's Cole, a boy who shares our values. She made a point of telling me that they didn't say "I love you." That's a bridge they've yet to cross. I just hope they're taking their time crossing it.

The streets are sleepy, and it's pleasant to drive through the autumn morning. The view of the snowcapped Rocky Mountains, tinted pink from the rising sun, sings the majesty of the Creator.

I thank the Lord nearly every day for the amazing views I enjoy when I drive westward.

The church hall is already filling up when I arrive. I locate the Dream Photography corner of the universe and head that way.

Luke is tweaking the decorations adorning one of the beautiful sets that our volunteers created yesterday. "There you are." He strides toward me, grabbing a clipboard along the way.

"Good morning."

He nods but doesn't bother with pleasantries. "It looks like we have just enough people to pull this off today." He grins. "We've never had so many appointments for holiday portraits before. Today will set a record."

Swell. "Well, it will be a fast day. Busy ones always are." A check in my spirit makes me reconsider my attitude. A successful day will mean more resources to help the homeless in our community. Most days I take for granted my home, my soft bed, and the food in my cabinets.

Luke passes off the marching orders for the day and walks away.

I look down at the Excel spreadsheet I created two weeks ago. I pray the day goes smoothly. My first order of business is to make sure everyone is accounted for and knows their responsibilities.

Thomas is setting up the table in the front of the hall. He's wearing a bright knit sweater with a goofy-looking reindeer on it. Luke insists we all dress in the holiday spirit. I have on the black cashmere holiday cardigan I bought on sale last year at Macy's. I can't wait to wear it for the neighbors' New Year's Eve party. It's almost too dressy for this event, but it's too pretty not to wear as often as I can.

Thomas barely glances at me. "Can you help me straighten this tablecloth?" Without waiting for my answer, he shakes out the red cloth. I stow my purse behind our table and get to work. We pile the table with two computers, our credit card machine, and extra order forms.

As the rest of the employees trickle in, I distribute their assignments to them. Barb brings up the rear, toting an industrial-size coffeemaker, bless her heart.

Three elderly gentlemen with flowing white beards come through the door. *Whew.* Our Santas. We always request Santa Lou, Big Santa T, and Santa Joe early in the year to ensure we get the cream of the crop. These gentlemen have the best beards, the softest paunches, and the perfect dispositions for the day's work.

They greet me with hugs. Sure, they're Santa but they're men too. Jolly, women-hugging men. And a little frisky, I suspect. If they can, they convince the moms to get in on the action. One year Santa Joe proposed that a cute mom kiss him on the cheek on the count of three. She was more than game for that, but as soon as Luke said three, Santa Joe turned to the poor woman and puckered up. Yep, that lady got the surprise of her life. In the photo she looks shocked as she busses the jolly old elf. Thank goodness her husband had a sense of humor.

I direct them to their dressing room and hope they're feeling up to the task of greeting scores of children.

The sound of a guitar being strummed catches my attention. The Broadway Carolers come in looking entirely too eager for the day. Those are professionals for you. They break into a rendition of "We Wish You a Merry Christmas" as they meander toward me. I'm sure they'll enchant our guests with their Dickensian costumes.

At exactly eight fifteen the first clients stroll through the door. *Let the fun begin.*

By nine a line begins to form. The carolers continue singing. I'm optimistic that this event may come off without any hitches.

"Linda?" Traci looks uneasy. "Where are the candy canes? And the cookies?"

I glance over her shoulder and see a family gathered around the end of one of our ordering tables. The children look antsy. As if they're looking for the treat they think they deserve.

OUT OF HER HANDS

I pick up the clipboard and page through my spreadsheet. *Aha. There is it—refreshments.* "The person responsible for picking up our food is Katrina."

"I know," Traci says. "But did you know she called in sick?"

"Uh . . ." *What can I say?* I should have foreseen this problem yesterday. "I'll run to the store."

I can't believe how stupid I can be. After all, I'm the one who made the schedule and the one who told Katrina to call in sick. That girl better appreciate her day off.

I'm just about out the door when Luke bellows my name.

I hurry to the bay where he's working. "Yes?"

"Where are you going?"

I explain about the Katrina day-off thing. "So I'm going to the store."

He frowns. "While you're there, buy more batteries."

I salute and run out before someone else thinks of an errand for me to do. I hope there are no fires that need to be put out while I'm away.

32

I hate grocery stores on Saturday mornings. My plan is to run in, grab what I need, and run out. But first I have to find a place to park. *Are they giving away free groceries, or what?* The lot is jam-packed.

I decide to follow an older gentleman while he pushes his cart to his car. Man, he walks slowly. I don't even need to step on the gas. I ride the brake through the lot. A car behind me honks. *Thanks. As if this is fun for me too.* I wave him on. He creeps around my Taurus, honks at the dear soul trudging through the lot, and speeds away.

I put on my blinker and wait while the little man loads his groceries into his trunk. My cell phone rings. It's a call from home. "Hello?"

"Morning," Jer says. "What time do you think you'll be home tonight?"

"I hope we'll be wrapping up by six. Why?" Maybe he wants to treat me to a romantic dinner for two.

"Dad called. He asked us to meet him and Doris at the Gray Pony for dinner."

Any night I don't have to cook is a treat, but . . . "I'm a little tired. Did you already tell him we'd join them?" I'd rather take it slowly getting to know Doris, just as I hope Ross is doing.

Oh, sweet peas and carrots. As soon as the little man backs out of his parking space, a little glamour girl in a red Mini Cooper swings right in and takes my place.

I honk the horn madly and roll down my window. "Hey, I was waiting for that space!"

The twentysomething girl tosses her hair over her shoulder. "I guess that's what happens when you get old, grandma. Your reflexes slow down." She sashays by my car.

"Lin?"

"Gotta go." I don't wait for Jerry to respond before I end the call, yank out my earbud, and cruise the lot looking for another space. After driving down two more rows, I finally park.

I hope I have Tylenol in my purse. I need it. When I get into the store, there are no available carts. *What's going on?* I walk to the cash registers and decide to wait until someone checks out. I feel like a stalker. Oddly, I see another lady doing the same thing. As soon as a cashier pushes an empty cart to the end of her lane, we both run for it. The other lady beats me.

"Excuse me, madam." The cashier looks down her nose at the cart-race winner. "But we're not finished with this."

The poor lady looks like she wishes she could crawl into a hole. I'm glad that's not me.

The metallic sound of crashing carts alerts me to an attendant who is trying to steer a line of carts into the store. I wait for him to park the buggies. As soon as he's finished, I snag one and head straight to the bakery department. I load up on ten trays of holiday cookies and cut over to the candy aisle. *Is that the little so-and-so who took my parking spot at the end of the aisle? It is her!*

She spots me glaring, and her face turns crimson.

Not so brave now, are you, girlie? Squaring my shoulders, I inch up to the Christmas candy and grab a dozen boxes of candy canes.

When I get to the end of the aisle, I notice that there's hardly a line for the self-checkout. Before anyone can beat me, I queue up.

Not that I like to see others suffer, but I revel in a great sense of satisfaction when I see the line grow rapidly behind me. At least one thing went well on this nightmare shopping trip.

The brilliant blue sky welcomes me back outdoors. I glance at my watch. I've been gone from the church hall nearly thirty minutes. Crinkly leaves race me to my car. I make quick work of loading my trunk. My good luck continues when someone offers to take my cart off my hands.

When I reach the end of the strip-mall lane, the light is green, so I turn right and head back to church. This morning is definitely looking up.

Oh, rats. The batteries. I forgot them. I drive around the block and return to the grocery store. *Just kill me now.* As I'm entering the lot, I see an SUV pull out of a parking space. Right next to the red Mini Cooper. I pull in and run into the store.

If it's at all possible, it's even busier than the first time I arrived. I pick up a basket, locate a directory hanging over an aisle, and search for my destination. I walk through the store as quickly as I can and grab a handful of double-A batteries. Unfortunately, the lines are out of control. I squeeze through one of the cashier's aisles and get in line behind a man at the courtesy counter. Smart thinking on my part. The wait is only about forty-five seconds. I pay for the batteries and am free of this nightmare once again.

When I drop off my plastic basket by the door, I accidentally bump into the lady in front of me. "Sorry."

She turns around. *Wait, that's no lady. That's the little brat who took my parking space.* I am in no mood to put up with this one's nonsense.

She seems surprised. "Oh."

Yeah, it's me—grandma. "Hello." I smirk. This girl is not going to get the best of me again.

She rushes out to the lot.

I heft my bag and follow her, walking toward my car.

Halfway to the car, she turns around. "If you don't stop harassing me, I'll call 911."

"What?"

"My father's an attorney." She walks backward while she speaks. "Don't think you can get away with intimidating me."

"Intimidating you?"

She stops and puts up her hand, palm to me. "Listen. I'm not afraid of you."

What is going on? "Young lady, I'm not stalking you. I'm walking to my car." I point to our vehicles, sitting side by side.

She glares at me, and I glare at her. At the same time, we continue on our way. I go straight to the driver's seat, and she opens her trunk. I start my car and shift into reverse.

"Be careful you don't scratch my car on your way out!" This girl is a piece of work.

I consider rolling down the window, but this chick knows how to wield the power of her daddy, and that's one fight I want to avoid. I shake my head at her and leave.

Who would have ever thought I'd look forward to going back to the chaos of our Santa Charity event?

33

I pop my trunk and dangle the bag of batteries off my arm, take as many cookie platters as I can safely hold, and plunge back into the madness. The Broadway Carolers are walking along the sidewalk keeping the waiting crowd amused. Never before has the line been so long that it stretched outside the building.

The first employee I see is Barb. I hold out my keys. "Can you get the rest of the food out of my trunk? Please?"

The church hall is crowded with families, each trying to keep their children clean, happy, and well behaved. One toddler leaving our Colorado Christmas set is crying hysterically. Either he didn't want to leave Santa or he was afraid of him. The pitch of that kid's howl could shatter glass.

"Linda!" Luke's frantically waving me over to him. When I arrive within earshot, he holds out his hand. "Batteries?"

Could he have waited until I took off my coat? I carefully place the cookie platters at my feet and rummage through the plastic bag to get one of the packages of batteries, then hand it over.

"Thanks. You're a lifesaver." *Aha.* There's his smile. And just in time. I needed a little affirmation. Just when I'm ready to write Luke off as the ultimate curmudgeon, he comes through for me.

I cross the hall, maneuvering around the clients crowding the payment area, and put my purse and jacket on a chair behind the table.

"There you are." Traci approaches me. "Your son was looking for you."

I crane my neck to look around. "Nick's here?"

She points in the direction of Colorado Christmas and shoos me on.

As I'm approaching the set, I hear Santa Joe say, "Come to Santa, honey."

Oh no. I hurry as quickly as I can through the throng of people. I'm almost there when I see several of my coworkers watching the photo shoot. This is unusual. Most families want their portrait session private. The only time we ever view a session is when it's a friend or coworker. I bet they're watching Nick and Amber.

Thomas walks toward me holding a piece of paper.

"Not now." I'll deal with him in a minute. Meanwhile, I continue on my way. I hear a collective gasp. *What just happened?* Now there's an outburst of laughter coming from that portrait bay.

I maneuver around the lights and reflectors to see, of all things, Santa Joe looking chagrined. His eyes are wide, and he's laughing.

"What happened?" I ask Pam.

She's laughing so hard she's crying. "That girl just got the best of Santa Joe. When he puckered up, she went in for the smooch."

I hesitate just long enough to be obvious. The crowd parts for me, and somehow I'm moved forward in the small group.

"Hi, Mom." Nick is laughing with his arm draped around Amber's shoulders.

"Nick, Amber." *Did she have to come here and embarrass me where I work?* Dream Photography is a hotbed of gossip. I don't need Amber adding fuel to that fire. "What's going on?" I feel myself blush. I bet my face is the same color as Santa's suit.

Nick ushers Amber and me to the side of the group. "I told Amber about Santa Joe's little trick, and she thought it would be fun to turn the tables on him."

"That's funny," I say, struggling to smile. *Where's Luke? Did he see this? Did other clients see it?*

"I guess we have to go over there to wait for our images. Do you want to see them when they're ready?" Nick's expression tells me he's looking for me to agree.

What can I do? "Sure. Go have coffee. Help yourself to some cookies. I'll see you in a few minutes."

I slink back across the room to busy myself in the details of the day. I'm grateful for cranky children, ill-tempered clients, and grouchy coworkers. At least it gives me something to do. Thomas is still in a tizzy because the credit card machine ran out of paper. I reach under the table for the emergency box that we take on location sessions and find the tape. I open the plastic door on top of the machine, drop in the new roll, and thread the paper through. If only all my problems were as easy to solve.

I look up to see the first wave of employees who took their lunch break come back into the building.

Rose, one of our salespeople, sees me and walks with purpose in my direction.

What now?

"You're never going to believe what we saw."

Do I want to know? "Do tell."

She crosses her arms before spilling the beans. "We saw Katrina! And guess what? She's not sick. At least she didn't look sick when we saw her strolling down the sidewalk with Carol Ball and another lady."

"Really?"

"Yeah. We all crawl out of bed at the crack of dawn to work on a Saturday, and she enjoys a leisurely morning shopping."

"Shopping?"

"They were loaded down with shopping bags. We were eating at Panera Bread, and we saw them go into Ted's Montana Grill for lunch. Nice, huh?"

"Well?" Rose whispers in a conspiratorial way. "What do you think Luke's going to do?"

"Do?" I catch myself mindlessly repeating her questions. *Why do I do that?*

"You know, disciplinary action?"

I shake my head, at a loss for what to say. I can't very well tell her that Katrina has the day off with Luke's permission.

Rose checks her watch. "Back to the salt mines." She strides away looking less than satisfied.

I'm sure I haven't heard the last of this gossip. It will probably make its way throughout the studio and come back to me ten times worse than it really is.

Traci waves me over to a grouping of chairs where Nick and Amber are studying the paper proofs of their images.

As if I really want to be involved in this. I crisscross the hall to join them. Now, I'm not one to notice a miracle everywhere I look, but in the time it takes me to arrive at their side, my heart has definitely lost some of its chill toward the beautiful girl watching my son admire their images. What I see is a look of unadulterated love on Amber's face. And can that be a bad thing?

34

I still ache from my busy day yesterday. And my pillow-top mattress feels so good. I hear the sounds of morning and roll over to relish the last few moments of sack time.

Thank goodness Santa Charity day comes only once a year. I usually don't spend so many hours on my feet, and I must have crossed that giant church hall a hundred times. Every year there are problems no one could have anticipated. But as usual, I helped clients select the perfect images, organized the staff, and generally did anything and everything to make the event run smoothly.

One of the biggest issues occurred while I sat with Nick and Amber to help them pick out their photos. I smiled my warmest grin at Amber, hoping she's kept secret our little meeting on Thursday night and tried to be as professionally helpful as I could. But can you say *a-w-k-w-a-r-d*? We both more or less talked our way around the conversation by directing our comments to Nick. Not that I think he really noticed. He was pleased that his girlfriend and his mother seemed to be having a polite conversation. To be honest, my heart has warmed up a bit toward her, but what mother's wouldn't? Being in the business I'm in, I know what a loving look is. I see it on the faces of clients as they gaze at the achingly beautiful portraits of loved ones. And Amber looked at Nick that way.

I keep my eyes closed while Jerry climbs out of bed. I know I'm a stinker. But it's so much more pleasant to get up to the smell of freshly brewed coffee.

If ever there was a morning I wish I could sleep in, this is it. But it's also Sunday, and our family always goes to church. Honestly, after all my Savior's done for me, that's the least I can do.

I crawl out of bed, toss on my robe, and float downstairs on the heady aroma of frying bacon and strong coffee.

"Good afternoon." Jerry smirks from his position in front of the stove. He loves to rub it in when he's the first one up.

"Morning. Did you get the paper?" I ease into a chair at the table.

He makes an elaborate show of putting down the spatula and exiting the room. *Why is he so spunky this morning?*

A moment later, he lays the plastic-shrouded paper before me. "There you go, madam. Is there anything else I can get for you?"

You don't even want to know. I smile. "Thanks, hon. How about a mug of coffee?" I know I'm pushing it, and I'm pleasantly surprised when he places a cup before me. Still, I would have preferred for him to heat my latte mug in the microwave, but I'll never say that.

Jerry joins me at the table. "Well rested?"

What's he getting at? "Yeah."

"That's good."

I know he's got a point other than appreciating the state of my health. "What's up?"

He reaches over and taps my foot with his. "I let you off the hook last night because you were so wiped out. But I called Dad and promised that we would meet him and Doris for lunch at the Gray Pony today after church."

Oh, I knew he was up to something with his happy, helpful attitude. "You did, did you? Sweet." I blow the steam off my coffee. I'm trapped like a fish in a net. I doubt there's any way I can get out of this lunch.

Jerry sees through my nonchalance. "You can't stick your head in the sand and ignore their relationship."

Ugh. "I know."

He gives me an encouraging smile. "Let's play nice, shall we?"

"I love your dad, and—"

"Then be the good daughter and get to know his friend."

My eyes sting with threatened tears, but I nod. "How do you feel about this budding relationship?"

Jerry dumps a spoonful of sugar into his coffee. "I love my father. I want him to be happy. And if that means supporting him in his choice to date, then that's what I'll do."

Heavy footsteps on the stairs announce Nick's arrival. I can't tell you how glad I am that he's coming downstairs to share breakfast with the family. Who knows how much longer we'll be able to enjoy this simple pleasure? He looks pretty sleepy, but that's sure to be a consequence of his coming in at 3 a.m. Not that I'm keeping track of his comings and goings.

I stand and put on my perky-morning face. "Coffee?"

He grunts and pours a cup.

"Eggs?" I gesture toward the bowl of scrambled eggs that Jerry made.

Nick walks across the room and lowers himself into a chair. He sips his beverage, then takes about half the eggs in the bowl, four slices of bacon, and an English muffin.

Emma comes into the room humming, helps herself to coffee, and plops down at the table. "Good morning, sunshine." She makes a face at her brother, but I know she's as delighted as I am to have his company. "You going to church with us?"

Nick takes a sip of coffee. "No. I'm picking up Amber, and we're going to a church in Denver."

Jerry nods. He's pleased, and that's his way of showing it.

"That's great." I bob my head like a ninny because I don't want to say anything else that may spoil this moment. I may be an old dog, but I can surely learn new tricks.

After a few moments, I address Nick. "What caused this change of heart for Amber?"

"We've been discussing faith a lot lately, and she agreed to go to church to check it out personally." He pronounces his statement like that's all he has to say about the matter.

I had the impression that Amber wasn't interested in spiritual matters. I wonder if this visit to church will be another step in opening her heart to Jesus. I hope so. I lean forward. "Will you and Amber come to lunch with us?"

"Uh, I don't think so." Nick looks down as if he's trying to avoid a confrontation.

"We're meeting Grandpa and his friend after church at the Gray Pony Inn."

"Really? I haven't met her."

Maybe he'll come after all. I look at him to gauge his reaction.

He shrugs and takes a section of the newspaper. "We have plans to go back to Amber's apartment and have lunch with friends."

Talk about mixed emotions. I'm thrilled they're going to church, but it would be nice if she would join the family for lunch. As much as the thought frightens me, I'm still trying to figure out how to have a relationship with this girl.

Jerry gives me the look.

I dip my head slightly. In his way, he's told me not to say anything, and I've responded with, "I know." Thank goodness for that language long-married couples have.

• • •

I love corporate worship, and my church can rock on with the best of them. I reach into my purse for a tissue to dab at my eyes. I can only imagine the day when my whole family worships together again in the same sanctuary. *Please, Lord, let it happen.*

I'm not spiritually dull, and I can tell when my Father is trying to get a point across. The vision of Amber's face, enraptured with my son, keeps coming to my mind. I know that's how God looks at me, so how can I not try to extend the same grace to Amber?

But to be honest, my stomach still flip-flops when I recall the incident in the dressing room. Should I bring it up to her? Can we pretend it never happened? I should try to concentrate on what the pastor is saying. But I'm doing personal business with God today, so I let myself wander through the Bible in search of guidance. I page through from the New Testament to the Old, but nothing's jumping out at me. I close my Bible and shut my eyes. *What, Father? What are You trying to tell me?*

I hear His voice. And He's telling me to do exactly what I've been trying to avoid. *"Love her, Linda. Like I love you."*

Oh, man.

35

I glance at my watch for the third time. Many of the cars have already left the church parking lot. "Do you think Emma remembers we're meeting your dad?"

Jerry's sitting with his head leaning against the headrest, his eyes closed. "Yeah, she'll be along in a minute. Don't fret."

Hmm. He looks all relaxed and carefree, but if I know him, he's praying for peace. Who knows, Doris may very well become a part of the family. She and Ross seem to be spending a lot of time together. If it's difficult for me to accept, I can only imagine what Jerry feels.

I sit back and enjoy that after-church high. If anyone wants to experience the family of God, they should come to my church.

Unbidden, the image of Amber's face enamored of Nick comes to mind. A tug at my heart tells me I can't ignore what I've been shown.

Emma comes out of the church, pulling on her jacket. Cole is walking alongside her, saying something that makes her laugh. She throws back her head and loses herself in the moment.

I push the button to lower the window. *Crumbs!* The motor's turned off, so the window won't work. I hop out of the car. "Hi, Cole. Nice to see you." I leave the door open and stand in the gap.

He stops and shades his eyes with his hand. "Hi, Mrs. Revere."

"Do you have plans this afternoon? Would you like to join us for lunch?"

He seems slightly uncomfortable to be around his girlfriend's parents. *Why do I have that effect on him?*

"I already invited him," Emma says. "We were coming over to tell you that I'm riding in Cole's car."

"Oh, good." I look at Cole. "Just be sure you're careful at the turn at the new traffic light where Hillside Avenue was extended."

"Mom!" Emma looks embarrassed.

I ignore her discomfort and continue. "I don't mean to imply you're a bad driver, Cole. But with the two turning lanes facing you at the light, you can't see if cars are coming at you in the through lane when you're turning left. Mr. Revere is convinced that intersection is an accident waiting to happen."

"Don't worry, Mrs. R.," Cole says. "I'll be careful."

I have no choice but to trust him. "Okay, see you there." I climb back inside the car and nudge Jerry. "Let's go."

He watches Cole open the car door for our daughter. "That's nice."

Jerry starts the car, and we head down the road. The trees that line the streets sway in the breeze and reach naked arms to the brilliant blue sky as though they are raising hands, praising God. We park the car in the lot by the town gazebo. Most of the leaves from the aged trees that grace the park have been blown, gathered, and mulched, but a few stragglers are clinging to the south side of the structure that epitomizes small-town America. We skirt the pavilion and walk toward the restaurant. "Do you think Ross is already here?"

Jerry glances at the parking lot across the street and gestures. "There's his car." He opens the restaurant door and moves aside for me to enter.

"Don't you think we should wait for Emma and Cole?"

He smiles that grin I love. "I'm sure they'll find us. Now let's get on with this."

Oh, my poor honey. This is bothering him, but being the good son and reasonable man he is, he's dealing with it.

I step through the door and up to the hostess podium. The after-church crowd usually fills up the Gray Pony on most Sunday afternoons, and today is no exception. A perky young woman greets me, and I tell her we're meeting another couple. She refers to her notes and points us in the right direction.

We spot them before they see us. The first time I met Doris I thought she was confident, but her expression today is telling me something different. Ross pats her hand and leans close to speak to her. She nods and stares into his eyes. The scene stops me in my tracks. She has the same look Amber had yesterday when she was gazing at Nick. *What's going on?*

When we approach, Ross rises to greet us. "There they are." He slaps Jerry on the back and gives me a hug. "Where are the kids?"

"Nick's with his girlfriend, and Emma and Cole are coming." I turn toward the older woman and smile. "Hi, Doris."

She greets me and extends a hand to Jerry. He moves closer to her and gives her a casual hug, putting an arm around her shoulders and patting her on the back. I wonder what emotional obstacle he had to overcome to extend himself in that way. My husband never ceases to impress me.

By the time we're seated, Emma and Cole show up. Cole nods his hellos. Emma gives Ross a tight squeeze and turns to Doris. If I didn't know her so well, I wouldn't notice the diminished light in her eyes when she says hello to Doris. At least she's being polite.

A waitress comes by, recites the daily specials, and takes our drink orders. We sit and smile at each other.

Ross toys with his napkin. "Emma, how's school going?"

She perks up. "Fine."

Jerry leans forward. "She's still busy applying to colleges." He turns to Cole. "And what about you? Have you applied to any schools yet?"

"Uh, yes, sir. I've sent applications to three state schools and a few out of state."

We all nod.

Where is that waitress? Shouldn't she be coming back so we can place our orders?

"I'm so glad you invited me to spend Thanksgiving with your family." Doris looks me in the eyes when she speaks. "Since I lost my husband, I've had to travel to be with my daughter's family in California."

"You're welcome. I hope your daughter doesn't hold it against us that you'll be with us here in Colorado."

She takes a sip of her water. "Oh no. Adrianne's fine with that. Especially since we'll be spending Christmas with her."

Excuse me? Did she use a plural pronoun?

Emma scoots her chair closer to the table. "We? Who's we?"

Ross appears uncomfortable, and Doris's gaze darts from one of us to the other like a bunny trapped in a cage.

"Pop?" Jerry looks pained, and I see that tiny pulse dancing on the side of his head.

"Oh, I was going to mention that to you. Doris's daughter invited me to spend the holidays with her family."

"In California?" Emma asks.

Ross smiles weakly. "That's where they live."

Emma's eyes are wide with disbelief. "Why would you do that? Your family is here in Colorado. You don't need to go anywhere."

Cole takes Emma's hand.

"I'm so sorry. Me and my big mouth." Doris sounds like she's going to cry.

Ross drapes his arm across her shoulders. "That's okay. We were going to tell them soon enough."

Jerry folds his arms. "Tell us what?"

He waves his hand as though to soften the blow. "Only that I'm going to California to meet Doris's family. You know, everyone will be gathered over the holiday, and it will be a good time to get to know them."

Emma glares at Doris and then Ross. "What's wrong with you? Why are you doing this? Grandma's not even dead a year."

"Emma!" Jerry shakes his head as if he's trying to keep his emotions restrained.

My daughter hops up and marches in the direction of the ladies' room.

Doris grabs her purse and, still holding her napkin, rushes out the door.

36

Is this really happening?

Ross and Jerry are obviously upset. Cole looks shocked. Several of the diners glance at our table, no doubt watching the drama.

I push myself to my feet and head in the direction of the ladies' room.

Before I can walk past our table, Jerry grabs my arm. "No." His expression is resolute.

I twitch my head. "What?"

"Doris. Go to Doris."

Is he nuts? Our daughter is still grieving over her grandmother, and now she has to face the fact that another woman is stepping into her place. And Jerry wants me to go to Doris? "But Emma . . ."

Cole gets up from the table. "I'll go to Emma."

Wow. I never expected that from him. "Cole, Emma's in the ladies' room." *Did he not notice that?*

"I know." His long legs carry him across the room.

Jerry stands and gives me a little shove toward the door. I glance over my shoulder as I leave the room and see him sit beside his dad.

When I step outside, I try to locate the little lady wearing a dark purple cardigan and black pants. Doris is nowhere in sight. And I'm sure Ross's car is locked. I broaden my search to the park across the street.

There she is, in the gazebo. She's leaning against a railing with her back to me. I glance up and down the road and jaywalk across Main Street. A car honks at me as I skip onto the sidewalk on the other side. *Nice.* As if I need a little more adrenaline surging through my system right now.

The curving sidewalk meanders through the grand old park, giving it a cultured feeling. Guilt nips at my heels as I step off the concrete and stride through the grass toward Doris. I try not to stumble over the roots that have escaped the grip of earth and snake across the leaf-scattered grass.

I see her bring the restaurant's burgundy napkin to her face. *Is she weeping?*

The snap of a twig underfoot alerts Doris to my arrival. She sees me and begins to walk away.

"Doris! Please don't go."

She pauses, then turns around. When I catch up to her, she's sitting on one of the benches near the gazebo and staring off into the distance, her eyes red rimmed.

I take a seat beside her. I don't know what else to do. *What am I going to say to this woman?* I am so not being a comfort to her.

"Well, I guess there's no fool like an old fool." Doris swipes at her eyes again with the napkin and sighs.

"Don't say that." *Should I put my hand on hers? or my arm around her shoulder?* I have no idea since I've only spoken to this woman twice before, once at the Village Inn and the other night on the phone.

Doris reaches into her pocket and pulls out a little package of tissues. Her hands shake while she withdraws one and blows her nose.

The early afternoon wind dances around our shoulders, gently tossing our hair. A leaf scrapes across the patio and plasters itself to Doris's leg. She leans down to brush it aside. "Thank you, Linda."

Huh? "Oh, I haven't done anything." *Really, I haven't.*

Her sigh seems to release the last of her pent-up anxiety. "I appreciate that you didn't blather on with tidy little platitudes. I'm grateful you've given me a moment to gather my thoughts."

Go figure. I did the right thing. Even if it was unintentional. *Still, what should I say?*

Doris pulls on the cuffs of her sweater, then runs her hand through her short hair. "To your family, I'm sure it must seem like I'm swooping in to bamboozle Ross."

We both watch the families gathering at the colorful playground a short distance away. How simple life used to be but not anymore. Things change.

I glance at the woman seated next to me and recall her expression when I walked into the restaurant. She's falling in love with Ross. And who can blame her? The Revere men are solid, level, and trustworthy.

I scoot a bit closer to her and pat her arm. "I'm sorry if we didn't make you feel more welcome." All I could see was that we'd lost Theresa, and I never noticed how lost Ross was. He's a man who's been well loved for decades. How can I blame him for wanting to be loved still?

Doris nudges my arm and points toward the corner of the park. Emma and Cole are standing beneath a large cottonwood, deep in conversation. They're holding hands, and Cole is gesturing widely with his free hand. "Do you need to go talk with your daughter?"

"Nope. It looks like they're doing well on their own."

Emma bows her head and covers her face with her free hand. I know she's still heartbroken over Theresa's death. Cole pulls her into an embrace and smooths her long hair with his hand.

"That young man has some quality character." Doris crosses her arms against the breeze.

"So it seems." I watch Cole rock Emma ever so slightly. "They're falling in love."

From the corner of my eye, I see Doris smile. I guess she can relate to that.

Cole and Emma release their embrace and walk through the park toward us. I can see that Em's been crying, but her eyes are dry and her expression is composed.

They stop in front of us, and Emma squats in front of Doris. She puts a tentative hand on Doris's knee. "I'm so very sorry. Can you forgive me?"

I'm stunned. I'm sure Cole's had something to do with her turnabout.

Doris takes Emma's hand in her own. "Of course. I'm sorry that my relationship with your grandfather has caused you any pain."

Emma stands. "No, it's not your—"

"I understand that your grandmother was a wonderful woman. I'm sure you loved her very much. It must seem insensitive for me to be a part of Ross's life so soon after she passed."

I turn in my seat. "That's not for us to judge. Please, let's go back to the restaurant. I'm sure the boys are wondering what's going on."

We all stand.

Doris smiles at Cole. "Young man, you have your own car here, don't you?"

"Yes, ma'am."

"Would you please be so kind as to drive me home? I don't live very far, and I'll pay you for gas."

What? "No, Doris. Please come back to the Gray Pony with us and have lunch."

She shakes her head, a sorrowful expression crossing her face. "No. Thank you. I can see that I've been too hasty. I was only thinking about how lonely I was and not considering that perhaps Ross hasn't had the proper time to mourn his wife."

"Please come back to the restaurant. Ross has always been deliberate. I'm sure he's given your relationship great thought. I've never seen him rush into anything."

Doris continues to shake her head. "Have you ever seen someone move on from losing the love of their life? It's the most difficult situation anyone can face. I'll just bow out. Yes, that's what I must do." She turns her sad eyes toward Cole. "Young man?"

He holds out his elbow and she slips her hand through his arm, and the two of them walk toward his car.

Emma and I stand gaping after them. She turns to me. "Wow."

"Wow indeed."

"Mom?"

"Yeah?"

"Who's going to tell Grandpa?"

I feel ill. *What shall I say to Ross and Jerry?*

As Cole's car pulls out of the parking lot and turns down Main Street, I wish I could run after them, stop the car, and drag Doris back to the restaurant. I feel such distress at the demise of this relationship.

Emma yanks my arm. "Let's go."

We march across the park. I feel as if I'm heading to an inquisition. *Oh, what have I done? Could I have done anything differently?*

When we enter the restaurant, I'm surprised by the feeling of warmth. I didn't realize it had gotten so cold outside. We walk through the establishment to the side room where our table is located, and Jerry and Ross spot us right away.

When it becomes apparent that it's just Emma and me, I see disappointment fall over them like the smoke from mountain fires that hovers over my neighborhood.

I try to smile, but I'm sure my face is a grotesque mask of false emotion. Emma and I sit down.

"What's going on?" Jerry asks.

Emma looks to me.

I guess I've got to give the bad news. "Cole drove Doris home."

Ross appears devastated. "Why? Is she embarrassed?"

What can I say? "I'm sorry."

Jerry pushes aside a plate of appetizers that he must have ordered after I went after Doris. "Sorry? Why?"

I glance from one man to the other. "Doris has decided to bow out."

"Bow out of dinner? Is she ill?" Jerry seems to struggle to keep his voice low.

I wish that was it. "She thinks your relationship is premature, Ross. That you need more time to grieve Theresa."

Ross slumps as if he received a physical blow. He stares at the table, shaking his head. "Why would she think that?"

Jerry turns to me. "What did you do?"

Oh, great. Blame me. "Nothing. I—"

"Well, you had to have said something."

"Dad!" Emma says, then faces Ross. "I'm sorry. I think it's all my fault." Her face crumples, and tears flow down her cheeks. "It's me. I shouldn't have said that—about Grandma."

My heart breaks for Emma and Ross and Doris.

Ross is on his feet, red faced and wallet in hand. He tosses a bill on the table.

"Ross, wait. Let's talk." I reach out to him.

He points at Emma, pain clouding his features. "You're right. It is your fault. I finally find a reason to get out of bed in the morning, and you chase her away with your selfish behavior."

Emma holds her hand over her mouth in shock. I've never seen Ross this angry.

Jerry stands. "Pop, don't go."

Ross turns on his heel and waves us off with his hand. His retreating form seems smaller and more slumped than ever before.

What a miserable group of people we are. Jerry tosses a twenty-dollar bill on the table, and we follow him out of the restaurant. As we step onto the sidewalk, Ross drives by without even looking in our direction.

What a mess.

• • •

As soon as we enter the house, everyone scatters. Emma runs
upstairs to her room, no doubt to call Cole. Jerry retreats to his
study and slams the door, and it looks like I have the pleasure of
making lunch. I take cold cuts out of the refrigerator to make sandwiches. Belle dances around my legs, begging for scraps. I put the
sandwiches on a platter and place it on the table.

I walk to the foyer and yell up the stairs, "Emma? Lunch!"

I'm sure Jerry heard me call Em, but I knock on his door anyway.
"Come in."

I open the door and find him sitting at his desk, thumbing
through his well-worn Bible. At least he seems to be going in the
right direction for guidance. "Lunch, Jer."

He glances up. "Can you bring it to me?"

How rude. "Don't you want to eat in the kitchen with Emma
and me?"

He pauses. "Not right now."

"Oh, come on. We're all upset. Don't give us the silent treatment."

"I'm not sure I'll be good company."

I sit on the upholstered chair across from his desk. "Jer?"

He rests his hands on the arms of his chair. "Pop said he never
thought he'd be able to exist without Mom, and then he met Doris.
Did you know that Mom urged him to find someone to love?"

"No, he never told me." I can imagine Theresa saying something
like that, though.

"She gave Pop her blessing to love again. And now he's found
someone, and somehow my family has managed to chase her off."

"Oh."

"Guys?" Emma's standing in the hall.

I stand. "We'll be right along." I grip Jerry's shoulder. "Coming?"

He follows me to the kitchen, where Emma is perusing the pantry. "Don't we have another bag of chips?"

Jerry takes a seat, and I bring a pitcher of iced green tea to the table. Emma joins us with an unopened bag of Lay's. We sit and out of habit bow our heads.

After a moment, I glance at Jerry. He looks deep in thought. "Jer?"

"Oh, sorry." He clears his throat. "Lord, bless this food. Thank You for all You've given us. Please be in the situation with Pop and Doris and show us how we are to minister to Pop."

We each grab a sandwich and begin to eat.

The doorbell rings, and Emma leaps to her feet. "Put another plate on the table." She rushes to the foyer, yelling over her shoulder that Cole's joining us.

Jerry gives me his what-else look, and I put another place setting beside Emma's.

Cole follows Emma down the hall, and Jerry and I greet him.

"Folks." He hangs his jacket on the back of the chair and eases himself down.

Emma pours him a glass of tea, and he helps himself to a turkey sandwich.

We concentrate on eating for a while. After consuming his third half sandwich, Cole takes a big swallow of tea. "I've been thinking."

Oh, goodness. Seventeen-year-old wisdom. "Yes?"

"I think I may know how we can get Doris and Mr. Revere back together."

Jerry shakes his head. "That's awfully good of you to care. But I think it's best to stay out of my father's business. He's a proud man. And right now I think he needs his space."

As usual, Jerry is so thinking like a man. Put up the walls and batten down the hatches. Sometimes romance needs a helping hand. "Well, I'm interested in hearing what you have to say, Cole."

38

Another weekend gone. I spend my time driving into work thinking of Ross and Doris and of Cole's crazy scheme. There's no way on earth any of us would be party to that plan. I should have known better than to get my hopes up that a teenager would know how to navigate the road to romance. Oh, how I wish I could make everything right again.

The matching topiaries planted outside the front door of Dream Photography are decorated with Christmas ornaments shimmering in the sunshine. I enter the building and sidestep the clients in the lobby.

A cream-colored, heavyweight envelope sits on my desk. My name is written on the front in Carol Ball's handwriting. I slit the flap at the fold with my letter opener. Carol has custom thank-you cards. *How classy.* Inside is a note thanking me for allowing Katrina to have the day off on Saturday. I still have not evaluated all the fallout from Luke's decision.

Laughter drifting from the workroom catches my attention. I put Carol's note in my desk drawer and head down the hall.

When I enter, everyone's gathered around Jill's framing table. "What's going on?"

A few of the seasonal employees blush and dash from the room. *Do they think I'm an ogre?*

Jill stares at me as though I'm the last person she expected to see.

Now I know something's going on. "What are you looking at?"

Jill looks as if she's about to choke. She seems reluctant to share the object of everyone's amusement with me.

"Well?"

Jill steps aside, and I walk up to the table. It's a picture of Amber in what appears to be a passionate encounter with Santa Joe.

Thomas peers over my shoulder. "Oh, Linda, that's got to be embarrassing."

Thanks. I decide to fib my way though this awkward situation. "Not really. It was all in good fun."

He raises his eyebrows as though he knows what I'm up to, shrugs, and walks away.

I put my hands on my hips. "So why are we all wasting time looking at Santa Charity images?"

Everyone glares at me as though I'm the Grinch who stole Christmas, but they get on with their duties and leave me with the opportunity to put this print away. I only hope that there aren't multiple copies that will come back to haunt me.

Static breaks the silence of the workroom when Barb's voice comes through the intercom. "Is Linda back there?"

I move to the desk and pick up the handset. "Yes. Can I help you?"

"You have a call on line three."

We disconnect, and I stab the button to activate the call. "Hello, this is Linda."

It's our prop supplier with a tracking number on a late order. I grab a pen out of a small bucket on the counter and scribble the number on a scrap of paper. Armed with this information, I head to my desk to go online and figure out where on earth our missing posing table could be.

I can hear my cell phone ringing before I get to my office. I rush into the room and snatch the phone off my desk. "Hello."

"Hi, sweetie. Can you meet me for lunch?"

"Oh, Deb. Sure. Where?" Maybe she can give me advice on the Ross-Doris affair or lack thereof.

After we make our plans, I drop the phone into a drawer. On my keyboard there's a pink message slip folded in half.

Linda,
  I need to speak with you about an issue.
          Traci

What could this be about? I walk to the reception desk and check the sales schedule to see when we'll both be available. "Barb, when you see Traci, will you ask her to meet with me around one thirty?"

She glances at me like she's got a secret she doesn't want to share. She won't maintain eye contact, and her neck is colored with a blush that nearly looks painful. "Uh, sure." She immediately gets busy filing some information in a drawer.

How weird is that? "Is something wrong?"

Barb stares at me and then turns back to her work. "No. Why do you ask? I'm just very busy. The files got disorganized somehow over the weekend, and I'm trying to fix them before I get busier."

Barb only rambles like that when she's nervous. I'm sure I'll find out what's happening before long.

I return to my office to prepare for my first sale of the day. It's with Sherri Dunn, one of our clients notorious for viewing her images at least three times before placing an order. She was a big topic of conversation at our last staff meeting. Luke's adamant that clients need to place their order the first time they have an image presentation.

"Linda?"

I look up to see Katrina coming at me. She leans down and gives me a hug. "Did you know my mother came to town this weekend?"

It does my heart good to see this girl so thrilled. "Yes, Carol told me she was coming."

Katrina beams. "I can't thank you enough."

"I'm happy you had a nice birthday."

She gives me a wink and goes on her way.

I walk to the salesroom and load Sherri's file. Gorgeous images of a family of five burst onto my screen. And the additional portraits of the children together and separately and of Sherri and her husband simply must be matted into a collage frame. *Who wouldn't want that?* Those images will add at least four hundred dollars to the sale.

"Hey, there." Pam sticks her head in the door. "Your clients are here." She nods in such an exaggerated way that even her shoulders move. "Good luck getting them to place their order. The girls in the workroom are betting a box of Whole Foods chocolate truffles that you won't get them to make a decision."

I perk up at the thought of those creamy chocolate confections. "They're placing bets? What's in it for me?"

Pam twirls the long beaded necklaces she's sporting today. "Tell you what: if you close the deal, I'll buy you a box."

"You're on, sister. And I'll split it with you."

I follow Pam toward the lobby. As I pass a group of employees gathered outside one of the studios, their conversation ceases. *What's going on here today?*

The Dunns are without their children. *Great.* Maybe this will be the day their procrastination streak ends. They're wandering throughout the lobby scrutinizing all our samples. Sherri recognizes me and pokes her husband.

"Hi, folks. Are you ready to buy some portraits?" I smile and lead them back to the image presentation room. Let's hope this is an easy and profitable hour.

I march from the salesroom triumphant and with a credit card receipt for nearly five thousand dollars. Once the Dunns exit the building, I dance into the office to file the invoice. Wait until Luke hears about the Dunns' timely sale. I should get an award for this accomplishment.

I've got about fifteen minutes before I need to leave to meet Deb, so I stroll to the workroom to gloat about my victory.

When I enter, all conversation turns to whispers. Traci looks like she's swallowed a pickle. This sneaky behavior really makes my nerves tingle.

"Well, who wins the chocolate truffles?" Pam asks. "And do I owe you a box?"

The dear thing, I think she's trying to be so enthusiastic to make up for the cloddish behavior of my other coworkers. I can't help but smile at her. "I win. And they spent nearly $5K."

Pam raises her hand for a high five. I give her a limp slap and turn to Traci. "I've got a few minutes. Shall we chat?"

We walk back to my vacant image presentation room, and Traci closes the door. That doesn't bode well.

She slumps on the love seat and crosses her arms.

I sit on my office chair and wheel closer to her. "Well?"

"I wish you didn't make it so obvious that we needed to talk."

"You didn't mention in your note that this was to be a secret."

"Listen, Linda, there's some gossip going around about your son's girlfriend, and I think you should hear about it."

39

Traci is staring at me as though she expects I'll explode. Unfortunately she's going to be disappointed.

I hold my hand up. "Don't say a word."

She gapes at me. "But don't you—?"

I feel like sticking my fingers in my ears and singing *la, la, la, la.* "No. I don't want to know. If it's gossip, I don't need to hear it."

"Really?" Traci acts like I'm the most naive woman on the planet.

"Amber may one day be a part of my family. I know she's no saint, but I won't buy into the tea-table gossip running rampant in this building." I begin to pace. "If you're my friend, you'll put the kibosh on these rumors ASAP."

We look at each other, trying to ignore the shimmering tension in the room. Honestly, I'd like nothing more than to hear those juicy tidbits about Amber, but I know I shouldn't take any stock in gossip, and if she does become a permanent fixture in our lives, that gossip will forever simmer in my mind, waiting to boil over if I should let my temper overheat.

I thank the Lord that I've been paying attention when He whispers into my heart because listening to this gossip would definitely not be a loving thing to do.

"Okay." Traci chews on her lower lip as if she's mulling over what to say next. "I can see your point, and I respect your position."

Tension rolls off my shoulders, and I no longer feel like I'm carrying around a backpack full of rocks. "Thank you. And will you—?"

"I'll squash those rumors." She stands, walks over, and gives me a hug. "Don't worry about anyone breathing another word."

"Thank you."

"Listen, honey, you go have lunch, and I'll put an end to that little game of whisper down the lane that's been going on around here."

A thought makes my heart pound. "Does Luke know?"

Traci shakes her head. "He's been holed up in his studio all morning. And I doubt he'll hear of it. Especially after I'm finished."

We leave the salesroom, and I can feel the eyes of my coworkers rake my back as I exit the building. I wonder if they're curious about my reaction to whatever dirt someone may think they have on Amber.

On the way to the restaurant to meet Deb, I wonder if I should even mention the drama in the studio this morning. A catch in my spirit tells me that I know I'll never speak of that gossip to anyone. Not even Jer.

It's been nearly a week since I spoke with Deb. I wonder if she's sold her house. Or maybe they've reconsidered this cross-country move. *I wish.*

Her car is parked right in front of the restaurant. I find a spot for my Taurus and hurry inside.

The hostess snaps to life when I enter. "Are you Linda?"

"Yes, I'm meeting—"

She walks out from behind her podium. "Your friends are right this way."

Friends? Who else could be here? I follow her into the dim interior. She leads me to a booth by a window. The bright Colorado sun obscures the features of the two women sitting across from one another. From my perspective, all I see are silhouettes. Who could that be with Deb?

Deb pauses in her conversation. "Hi, Lin. I hope you don't mind, but I'm finishing a little business with Pauline. She said she knows you from Dream Photography."

Really? I turn to this mystery client, and my smile freezes on my face.

"You know Pauline Lincoln, don't you? She said you helped her with an order."

Oh yeah, I remember this haughty, demanding cheapskate who absolutely hated our huge logo on her son's portraits. "Hello, Pauline." *And if you'd like to, why don't you grind your stiletto into my foot? That will make lunch even more enjoyable.* I smile brightly as I turn to my so-called friend. "I didn't know you were acquainted with Pauline."

Deb scoots over so I can sit next to her. "Yes, she's our new Realtor. The best in the city, so I've heard. Amazing."

"Oh, good for you." I slide into the booth, and a pang of regret at my harsh thoughts toward Pauline pierces my conscience. Suddenly my appetite's gone. I wish I could make a graceful exit.

Pauline grins. "It's delightful to see you again. You were so very helpful to me."

I grin back and nod. "I'm glad I could assist you."

Pauline picks up a huge brown Louis Vuitton messenger bag from the seat next to her. I recognize the brand from the gold monogram. I bet that bag's worth a thousand dollars if it's worth a dime. That is, if it's real. If it's a knockoff, it's fabulous. I observe Pauline while she shuffles papers around, concern etching her forehead. "This is it." She pulls out a handful of papers and pushes them across the table to Debbie. "Let me know what you think after you've had a chance to speak with that handsome husband of yours."

The way she refers to Keith makes my stomach clench. *Just who picked out this amazing Realtor?*

Pauline bounces to the edge of the seat. "Well, girls, it's been wonderful. But I have to go." She stands next to the booth looking like a million dollars.

Oh, now I know who she is! The Million-Dollar Realtor. The one who only brokers the best homes in the metro area. And I hate to say it, but she smells as good as she looks.

Pauline struts away from the table, and I slide into her vacated seat. Maybe this lunch can be redeemed. "So, what's new?"

The natural light illuminates the worry lines along the edges of Debbie's eyes. *Were they as pronounced before as they are now?* Despite the strain this move is having on her, she's still my beautiful best friend. Her makeup has been applied with an expert hand, and her pressed jeans and soft blue sweater look like something out of a J. Jill catalog.

"I miss you already." She leans across the table and pats my hand.

A lump forms in my throat. "Oh, Deb." I pause before I embarrass us both with tears.

She snaps her fingers. "Enough of that stuff."

Okay, I can play this game. I take a sip of water. "So, I need a little advice to stir up some romance."

She gives me the look that says she's up to the challenge. "You've come to the right place, honey. What's going on?"

40

The Ross-Doris problem is on my mind all stinking afternoon. Every bit of advice I'm getting feels too clunky to execute. Ross is no dope, and within about three seconds, he'd see right through all the contrived plans everyone's dreaming up. And then he'd be even angrier.

Since I spent Saturday working, I'm doomed to an after-work expedition grocery shopping at Wal-Mart. My nerves are on edge. Not only did I have to drive through the parking lot for nearly five minutes to find a parking space, but the store is way too crowded. Is everyone doing their Thanksgiving shopping tonight? *Oh, joy.*

I race up and down the aisles, crossing items off my list and tossing food in my cart as quickly as I can. *Supermarket Sweep* contestants have nothing on me. After about ten minutes, I'm really in the groove.

I turn the corner and stop short. *Was that Doris who just walked past the end of the aisle?* I switch gears and neglect my list to chase after that sweet lady. I'm like a downhill racer swerving around poles to get to her destination as I veer left and then right to go around the other shoppers in my path. I take a left toward the front of the store. *Where could Doris have gone?* I stride with purpose, gazing down the aisles as I pass them.

Doris is nowhere to be found. I spin around and trudge back into the torture that is holiday grocery shopping.

When I get home, I toot the horn for some assistance bringing in my grocery haul. Jerry comes shuffling out in his slippers.

I pop the trunk. "Where's Emma?"

He loads up on plastic bags. "She's studying for a test, but I yelled to Nick."

I squeeze between the two cars in the garage and go inside the house, holding my bags as a barrier to Belle, who wants to run out the door. She catches a whiff of the cold cuts and trots into the kitchen with me. I drop the bags on the table and head back out for more.

Just as I'm about to call for Nick, he comes down the stairs wearing a big grin. "I've got good news for you."

"What?" I follow him out to the garage.

He pulls the remaining bags from the trunk. "I just got off the phone with Amber, and her roommate's decided to spend Thanksgiving with her family. So we'll be eating with you."

"Great." I close the trunk and trail him into the house, feeling better than I have all day. Maybe we'll finally get to know Amber better.

Nick returns to his room, whistling as he runs up the stairs, and Jerry and I put away the groceries.

Jerry has his head in the refrigerator, putting the veggies into the bin, when he says something about Ross.

"What? I didn't hear you."

He closes the fridge and turns to me. "I talked to Pop tonight. He's not as angry as he was yesterday, but he's really hurting."

He doesn't need to press the issue. "I feel terrible. We've got to get them back together. Maybe when Doris comes over for dinner on Thursday they'll smooth things over."

"Are you crazy? Doris isn't coming for dinner."

"No?" I was holding out hope that she'd come. "Are you sure?"

"There's no way. Pop told me he tried to convince her to come as a friend. But she was adamant that she would make other plans."

I stack junk food on the pantry shelves. "There's got to be a way to make her reconsider."

Jerry gives me the look.

I shrug and finish clearing the kitchen. He should know by now that I'm not the kind of girl who gives up easily.

"Mom?"

I lay my book on my lap and turn toward my bedroom door. "Hi."

Emma strolls in and sits on the edge of my bed. "Cole and I have another plan."

I almost laugh. "This isn't like a high school crush gone wrong that can be glossed over with friends running interference. Grandpa and Doris are mature adults. They can't be tricked into resuming their relationship."

"Well, I don't care what you say. I'm not the kind of girl to give up so easily."

Now she does make me laugh. She certainly is my daughter. "Don't worry. If it's meant to be, it will work out."

Her expression clouds. "Does Grandpa still hate me?"

"Oh, Emma, Grandpa never hated you. He was hurt, and unfortunately he spoke out of turn."

"I just wish it was like last year and Grandma was still with us."

I lean forward and draw her into a hug. When we lost Theresa, I lost a close friend, a second mother. "Me too. But that's not the way things are. We've got wonderful memories of Grandma. And you know what?"

Emma pulls back and waits for the answer.

"The best way to honor Grandma's memory is to take good care of Grandpa. Don't you think?"

"Yeah." She runs her hand through her hair. "Do you think Grandpa will find another girlfriend?"

"I don't know. If he's lonely, he probably will."

"Hmm." Emma looks like she's organizing her thoughts. "I think I could really like Doris. I hope they get back together."

41

The mattress gently rocks when Jerry gets up. Belle's whining from her crate by the stairs. No doubt she's Jer's reason for leaving our warm bed.

I stay snuggled under my blankets until the coffee's brewing, then get up.

Jerry is looking out the back door when I walk into the kitchen. He's holding a steaming mug and watching the dog dance on her hind legs under the aspen trees, barking at a squirrel.

I wrap my arms around his waist and rest my cheek on his shoulder. "Are you trying to annoy all the neighbors?"

He places the mug on the counter and pats my hand. Fresh, cool air washes over me when he opens the door and calls our little dog inside.

"Do you want me to do anything before I go into the office?"

I scowl. "You're working today? Isn't school closed? I thought you'd help me prepare for tomorrow."

"There are some things I need to get to. I won't be there all day."

I pour a cup of coffee and pop a frozen bagel into the toaster. I know it's juvenile to pout, but I'm disappointed.

Jerry leans against the counter. "I spoke with Emma, and she said she'll give you a hand."

"I never made a Thanksgiving dinner all by myself."

"I just told you Em will help, and I won't be gone all day."

That's not entirely the point. "Theresa—" The lump in my throat prevents me from finishing my sentence.

A sad look settles on his handsome features. I walk to him, and he welcomes me into his arms. I allow him to hold me tightly. Neither of us speaks. *What's to say?*

Emma's got Christmas music blaring from the CD player. I can barely think over the noise. Our trusted family recipes sit on my counter, and I gather my thoughts on what I should do first.

My daughter comes dancing into the kitchen. For a moment I'm transported to previous years, recalling Theresa singing and dancing as she wielded a wooden spoon or carried eggs from the refrigerator to the counter. My vision blurs. I swipe at my eyes before Emma sees my tears.

What a bittersweet day. Memories are both a blessing and a heartache. In the past, Theresa would come over with her apron, recipes, favorite potato peeler, and her delightful sense of humor and would keep us all amused through peeling pounds of potatoes, squash, and turnips and throughout the baking of pies. How empty the house feels without her.

A key turns in the front door. *Is Jerry home?* I start to walk toward the foyer as Nick announces, "I've got pizza!" He strolls down the hall. With Amber.

I smile. "Hi, kids."

Nick shrugs out of his jacket, takes Amber's hoodie from her, and drapes them over a chair in the living room.

We all sit at the table and share the cheese pizza. Emma sprinkles her slice with crushed red peppers. "What are you guys doing this afternoon?"

"I told Amber that my family makes a traditional Thanksgiving feast from scratch. She's pretty impressed." Nick looks at his girlfriend, who gives him a coy smile. "Anyway, I told her she could get the total experience by coming over today to help out."

"Oh, thanks." It's not that the help isn't appreciated, but this is one more reminder that life changes too quickly, and I don't always have a say in the matter.

We finish our lunch, and Nick and Amber tear bread for the stuffing. The recipe is on an old index card in Theresa's handwriting. *What a treasure.* Emma mans the food processor and starts to cut up onions and celery while I brown a pound of sausage.

When it's time to throw the ingredients together, Amber takes the big wooden spoon out of the crock that sits on the counter and picks up my large bowl. That was always Theresa's job. She would mix ingredients, adding liquid as she saw fit. And now Amber's decided to do that? I know she's only trying to pitch in, but I can't help but feel overly emotional today.

I swallow the words that threaten to emerge. I don't want to sound like I'm taking out my sorrow on this unsuspecting girl.

Amber really knows her way around the kitchen. Her forehead furrows in concentration as she reads the recipe and measures the right amounts of herbs.

The three young people banter as they make quick work of preparing our meal. I let them sit together to peel the vegetables while I stand at the sink to clean up our messes.

A chair scrapes across the floor. I look to see Nick get another glass of cola. He glances at the girls' near-empty glasses and gives them a refill too.

I turn back to the sink to scrub my frying pan.

"Look out!"

I jerk toward the table in time to see Amber's elbow connect with the bottle of soda Nick just put down.

The kids are all on their feet, and Nick reaches for napkins to wipe up the sticky brown soda that rolls across the table.

I grab the roll of paper towels and mop up the mess. "Oh no." I snatch the index cards that were stacked on the edge of the table. Cola discolors the yellowed cards. They're completely soaked.

"Look at these! These were Nick's grandma's recipes." I rush to the counter and blot the old recipes with a damp sponge.

Amber's at my side in a moment. "I'm sorry. I'll rewrite them all for you."

I shake my head, not trusting myself to speak kindly. It's painful to see the words written in that lovely, familiar handwriting fade and blur.

"Mom, it's okay." Emma's face is red. She's probably embarrassed by my outburst.

"I didn't get enough sleep last night. It's a poor excuse, I know. I'm sorry, Amber."

The poor girl is on the verge of tears, and Nick looks like he wants to strangle me.

I'm such a clod. "I'm just being sentimental. Please forgive me."

We finish cleaning up the table, and Emma takes the towel from my hand. "Why don't you take a nap? We'll finish here."

"Really?" *Nothing sounds better.* "Thanks." I give Amber a hug on my way out of the room. "Thanks again. Don't feel like you need to do any more work."

It's surprising what an hour of rest can do for your disposition. I come downstairs to find Nick, Amber, and Emma watching a reality TV show. The fragrance of fresh pumpkin pie hangs in the air.

"Feeling better?" Nick gives me a smile.

"Yes, by about 100 percent. Who baked?"

Nick puts his arm around Amber. "She did." He sounds as proud as if he baked the pie himself.

Well, bless her heart. Her pie doesn't smell quite like Theresa's. But I'll never say that.

42

The alarm goes off, and I bolt from bed as usual. It takes about five minutes before I realize it's Thursday and that I had only set the alarm to remind myself to put our bird in the oven. I exit my closet wearing my favorite velour pants and comfy T-shirt, thrilled that I don't have to pick out something professional and trek into the studio.

Belle scratches to go outside, so I turn the oven on and let her out the back door. I glance toward the dining room. The table is set for six, but it doesn't feel right.

I take a tube of cinnamon rolls out of the fridge, pop them in the oven while it heats for the turkey, and brew a pot of coffee. I toss food in Belle's bowl and call her inside, then move to the living room to sit in my prayer chair.

The house is blessedly still, and I search my heart to come clean before the Lord. I'm guilty of not appreciating what I have. A warm house in the winter and a cool one in the summer. A cozy bed, electricity, clean water. These details constitute the basis for my comfort. I have a frustrating job at times, but it pays the bills and gives me joy at other times. My family enjoys good health, and I enjoy the love of a wonderful man. My children are good people who love the Lord. *Oh, why do I dwell on my needs? my wants? my desires? Why do I too often forget the hurting world outside my doorstep?*

By the time Jerry joins me downstairs, the coffee's brewed and the rolls are sitting on the table, taunting me with their sweet aroma. I'm reading the holiday edition of the *Rocky Mountain News*, and my sweetheart walks by on his way to the coffeepot and tugs at a piece of my hair. I smile at him.

He sits across from me. "What's the plan?"

"Breakfast, then cooking. I plan on eating around one, so we'll probably start munching on appetizers around noonish."

Jerry nods and reaches for a section of the paper.

I slide open the back door a bit. Why do I always forget to turn down the heat when I'm cooking all day and we have a full house?

I survey the scene in the family room. Nick is sticking to Amber like glue, same as yesterday. Ross and Jerry are parked on the couch watching football. Ross has a distant look in his eyes. *Is he thinking of Theresa or Doris?* Emma is chatting with Amber and Nick. Of course Amber is wearing that sweater she bought a week ago. *Has Nick already seen it on her bedroom floor?* Thankfully my mind blanks before those images can rise up.

"Em? Want to help me get dinner on the table?"

She gets up, and out of the corner of my eye, I see Nick nudge Amber.

I organize my helpers and we mash, slice, plate, and carry the meal to the dining room. I light the candles in my mother's crystal candelabra, put a CD with Christmas music on the player, and call the guys to the table.

The cheerful music does little to enhance the ambience of the day. Jerry and Ross stepped outside about an hour ago to have a private chat and have barely spoken. Nick's falling all over himself to make Amber comfortable, and Emma is chattering like a monkey, no doubt with the same goal in mind. I just want to get through the day without tears. Holidays will never be the same.

We take our seats, Jerry and Ross at the ends of the table, Nick and Amber on one side and Emma and I on the other. Jerry asks a blessing on the family, the food, and prays for those less fortunate. I'm glad I don't have to say anything right now because my tears are just under the surface. Theresa always sat next to me for Thanksgiving dinner.

Ross holds up a glass. "I would like to make a toast."

We raise our glasses and look at him.

He clears his throat. "To love. The love of family and—" he glances at Nick and Amber—"to new love."

I must look like an idiot, batting my eyes the way I am. Nick and Amber lock eyes. Everyone is smiling. I glance at Ross and know he's thinking of Theresa as well. He nods ever so slightly and winks at me. I sigh to stifle a sob.

We all busy ourselves piling turkey, potatoes, cranberries, dressing, and green beans on our plates. The conversation turns to food. Bland, safe conversation. I'm good with that. Everyone has too much to say about the turkey. It's the kind of conversation strangers have in line at the grocery store. For the first time, we've cooked a natural turkey, in deference to Amber.

"Thank you, Linda." Amber sounds open and sincere.

Did she just read my mind? "You're welcome. I'm glad you could join us this year."

Jerry kicks my foot. His sideways glance tells me he didn't care for my response.

"And I hope you'll be with us for many years to come." I smile at her as she leans closer to Nick, who beams at me.

Ross puts his hand on Emma's arm. "Are you finished with all your college applications, sweetheart?"

She engages him in conversation about the pros and cons of the schools she's interested in.

Jerry nudges my foot again, then reaches over and catches my hand. I feel the sting of tears again. *Oh my. I've got to get ahold of myself.*

"You know, I invited Cole over for dessert." Emma pauses in that infuriating way of hers to make sure she's got our attention.

"And . . . ?"

"Well, I was wondering what time I should tell him to come."

I don't know what the big deal is. "You know Cole's welcome anytime."

She rolls her eyes. "Since he knows where Doris lives, perhaps he could—"

"No," Ross says. "Thanks for thinking of me, but I don't think we need to pester Doris."

My daughter's face colors. "Oh, Grandpa, your breakup was all my fault. Can't I try to make it better?"

Ross stands. I fear he'll run out like he did at Sunday's dinner, but instead he leans over and kisses the top of Emma's head. "Excuse me." He walks to the powder room.

Jerry turns to Emma. "I know you mean well, but you've got to stay out of it."

"But, Dad . . ."

I put my arm around her shoulders. "You've got a good heart." She crumples against me when I give her a hug.

When Ross returns, we resume our conversation as if we don't know he's got a doubly broken heart.

After a moment, Jer lays aside his flatware. "Every year during our Thanksgiving dinner we go around the table to express what we're thankful for this year. Shall I start?"

I wish he didn't bring that up. It's been a hard year. A familiar tug at my heart lets me know he's right, though. I sigh and try to get on top of the emotion that's been roiling inside me for the past few days.

He smiles at me. "I'm thankful that we're all healthy. And that in May, Emma and Nick will be graduates."

My turn. "I'm thankful for my loving home. As usual."

"I'm thankful that the college application process is over." Emma makes us all laugh with her funny expression.

"I'm thankful that God brought Amber into my life."

Amber dips her head. "Ditto."

Sheesh. Was that really an act of God or a hormonal reaction?

We all look to Ross. He lays his hands on his lap. "I'm thankful that God gave me an incredible woman to love for more than half a century. And . . ." His voice trails off in sorrow.

There's not a dry eye in the room.

43

Just when we fall into a somber mood, Belle comes along, sits next to Ross, rears up her front paws, and begs with her big, beautiful brown eyes.

Of course Jerry is horrified that she's misbehaving in front of company. "Belle! No!" He jumps up and rushes toward the dog.

She's getting old, but she's pretty spry. She tears off in the opposite direction, and for a moment it looks as if Jerry will be playing a game of duck, duck, goose, chasing her around the table. Silly girl that she is, Belle dives under the table, only to come out barking behind him. Jerry halts and she runs right into his legs. Before he can grab her, she dives under my chair.

Belle couldn't have choreographed this scene any better if she tried. Everyone breaks into laughter.

Ross rips off a piece of his dinner roll and holds it down by the side of his chair. "Here, Belle."

She pops out from under the table, chomps down on the roll, and scoots back out of reach.

We all laugh again at her antics. Even Jerry. Under normal circumstances he'd make sure he was the alpha dog, but I think he's glad for the comic relief too.

Before he can take his seat, the doorbell rings. He turns toward the foyer but is nearly knocked over by Emma, racing him to the door. "It's probably Cole."

The young man comes in carrying a bouquet of flowers. *How sweet.* His mother raised him right. He nods hello to everyone and thrusts out his right hand to Jerry; then he strides across the room to me. To my surprise, he presents me with the flowers. "Happy Thanksgiving, Mrs. Revere."

"Thank you very much." I stand and give the dear boy a hug. "Emma, why don't you run down to the basement for a vase?"

She's all perky and smiley. "Sure. Come on, Cole."

It appears as though everyone is finished with dinner. "I'll start the coffee and bring out dessert."

Again Nick nudges Amber. They both stand and start to bus the table. This, I like.

I plug in my coffeepot, pour half-and-half into the creamer, and carry it with the sugar bowl into the dining room. When I get back to the kitchen, Nick and Amber are hugging. I manage to keep any comments to myself. Amber seems startled while she wiggles out of Nick's arms.

"Should I cut the pies?" She gazes at me with anxiety in her eyes. *Is it because she's embarrassed by her lack of etiquette? Or is it because she's afraid I'll fly off the handle, shouting that pie cutting was Theresa's job? Who can blame her for being cautious after my insane outburst yesterday?*

"Yes. Thanks." I open the drawer and give her the pie server and a knife.

Amber turns away from me and gets on with her task.

I grab a pair of scissors and trim the ends off the flower stems over the sink. *Where is Emma?* I don't even hear any conversation coming from downstairs. I walk to the basement door and swing it open.

The sight that greets me gives me a jolt. "Excuse me?"

The two lovebirds spring out of their passionate embrace and stare at me with expressions of shock and guilt. Cole wipes Emma's lip gloss from his mouth.

I shake my head and return to the kitchen.

"Mom?" Nick smirks knowingly.

As if I need a lesson from him. I pick up the stack of dessert plates and take them to the dining room.

"Everything all right?" Jerry asks.

I smile at him and hope he can read my don't-ask look. "Fine." I raise an eyebrow for emphasis.

His lips twitch with a hint of a smile. Perhaps he's figured out what's going on.

Emma comes into the room, looking somewhat flustered and dragging a kitchen chair. I move my chair closer to Jerry so Cole can join us.

The poor boy, his face is as red as can be. He makes sure Emma takes the seat in the middle, next to me.

Amber comes in with a pie in each hand. "Pumpkin or chocolate?"

Everyone gets busy claiming a slice of pie, and I slip into the kitchen for the coffee. When I come back, Jerry's taking his first bite of pumpkin pie. Ross is having my chocolate pie.

"This is delicious, hon." Nick winks at Amber while he shovels pumpkin pie into his mouth.

I take a small slice of the pumpkin pie, but I'm not optimistic that it will be better than Theresa's. Even I don't know the special combination of spices she used to make her pie so wonderful. And a part of me hopes to never eat a pie that's better than hers. Some memories are best left intact.

Cole has a slice of each pie on his plate. I don't doubt that he can polish them both off. He lays down his fork and looks toward Ross. "Mr. Revere, will you be going to the winter concert?" Both Cole and Emma are in the advanced choir at the high school.

My father-in-law breaks into a big smile. "Wouldn't miss hearing my baby girl." He turns to Em, and she basks in his love.

Cole continues, "Did you know that this year we're doing several community concerts?"

Where is he going with this?

Ross shakes his head. "Didn't know that, but let me know the dates, and I'll be there."

"One of the concerts is tomorrow at town hall." Cole looks hopeful.

I lean in. "Ross, don't feel obligated to go to all of Emma's concerts. You'll be run ragged."

"Nonsense. It's my pleasure. Besides, what else does an old man like me have to do with his time anyway?"

"Grandpa, you're not old," Emma says. I think she fears losing him as well.

Ross winks at her. "Hanging out with you keeps me young."

Amber says something that makes everyone laugh.

I pull myself back from my musings and look at her. She seems to be trying to find a way into our hearts. An echo of the mandate the Lord gave me at church on Sunday resounds in my brain, *"Love her, Linda. Like I love you."*

I'm not even sure how to do that. I resolve to pray for her when she comes to mind and also to pray for her when we touch. We're a physically affectionate family, and I think Nick's been advising Amber to get in on the hug action. She's been forward about giving me and Jerry hugs when she comes over, despite the fact that you can tell she's moving out of her comfort zone. Each time I embrace her, I'll say a short prayer.

We drain the last of the coffee, and I rise to clear the table.

"No, Mom. Sit down. We'll take care of this." Nick's on his feet, and he motions to Emma and Cole to join in.

The four young people clear off the table and go into the kitchen talking and laughing. I twitch at the sound of dishes clattering on the counter. Someone turns on the faucet.

I hope my good china survives their help.

44

I walk Ross to the foyer, and Jerry hands him his jacket.

"Thank you." Ross gives me one of his extra-tight hugs and kisses my cheek. "Grandpa!" Emma sidles up to him. "Don't forget we're singing at the town hall tree lighting tomorrow at one. Will you be there?"

"Sure thing. Bye, Cole. Jerry." He shakes his son's hand and yells toward the family room, "Bye, Nick. See you around, Amber."

They're both on the couch playing a video game. The game pauses, and they walk over to say their good-byes. Ross opens his arms, and Amber rushes past me into his hug.

The door shuts and everyone scatters—Nick and Amber return to the family room, and Emma and Cole slip on their jackets to go out for a walk.

Jerry takes my hand and leads me into his study. I wonder what's up. He sits on the old love seat, and I flop down on his upholstered chair. He leans over and pushes the door closed.

I get comfortable. "What's on your mind, big boy?"

His mouth twitches. I can only guess at the thought that runs through his head. His gaze becomes intense for a fun moment, but then he seems to switch gears as he returns to his agenda. "Get your mind out of the gutter, girl. We've got some things to discuss."

I hate these discussions. They usually involve the *B* word— *budget*. I cross my arms.

"Pop and I have been talking about his final wishes."

"Is there something I should know? Is he sick?" I don't know if I could bear losing him right now.

Jer shakes his head. "Sorry. I didn't mean to upset you. He wants us to know how to plan his funeral should he become disabled."

"Jerry! Do we need to have this discussion today?"

"They're his wishes. Pop and I talked about it a few weeks ago, and today he asked if I spoke with you about it."

Oh. Why do I feel so emotional lately? My eyes sting with tears, and I pluck a tissue from the box on his desk. *And I thought this day was improving.*

Heaven help me, I appear to be listening, but in reality I'm nodding and watching Jerry go on and on about power of attorney, do-not-resuscitate orders, and funeral decisions. I hope these instructions are written somewhere, so when the time comes I can find them. I gaze out the window. The day is closing in on us. Dusk is settling, and the lights on our street are winking on. The sound of laughter comes from the family room.

"Lin?"

I jerk toward Jerry. "What?"

"Do you understand Pop's instructions?"

"Uh, yeah. Where did you say you were putting the documents?"

He grabs a magazine, rolls it up, and gives me a playful swat. "You don't want to think about this, do you?"

"You know this is a difficult holiday for me this year. I can only imagine how hard it's been for you."

Jerry grabs my hand and pulls me next to him on the love seat. He puts his arm around my shoulders. "I know, dear. It's hard for me too. But I want to honor Pop's wishes."

Darkness falls fast, and we remain where we are. Neither of us moves to turn on a light, and the gray evening sifts down upon us. I lean my head back on his arm and place my hand on his leg. We're breathing in unison. Peace comes back to my world.

The front door slams, and I hear Emma and Cole being invited
to play along with Nick and Amber. I think that Guitar Hero
is one of the most annoying games ever—discordant music and
shouts of frustration from the players. Why they are so crazy about
it is beyond me.

Jerry looks at me and grins. "I'm getting hungry."

I shake my head. Theresa used to tell me it was nearly impossible
to satisfy Jerry's appetite. And his son is just like him. "Let's go. I'll
set out a sandwich buffet. Besides, if you're ready to eat again, I'm
sure Nick is too."

The kids did a great job cleaning up the kitchen. Plastic tubs
filled with leftovers are stacked in the fridge. I take out the dressing
and cranberry sauce and slice turkey for sandwiches.

While I'm bringing the sandwich fixings to the table, I look into
the family room. Emma's standing by the couch with the plastic
guitar-game controller strapped around her shoulders. She's deep
in concentration as she tries to strike the right chords to the notes
playing across the television screen. Cole is sitting on the edge of
his seat, shouting encouragement. Nick and Amber snuggle in a
way that suggests a little too much familiarity. It makes me uncomfortable.

"Anyone ready for a sandwich?"

Emma groans and untangles herself from the guitar strap. "And
not a minute too soon. I was going to lose that round."

Cole follows her to the table.

I pass around napkins while my family joins me at what's left of
our Thanksgiving meal.

I don't even want to consider the amount of fat and calories I
ingested today. I wish I could crawl up the stairs and sleep it off.
I wipe off the table and put away the leftovers.

"Thanks again, Mrs. Re—I mean, Linda." Amber stands in the
hallway.

I dry my hands and go over to her. "I'm really glad you joined us today."

We walk to the foyer. She grabs her jacket out of the closet, turns, and smiles at me. We stand waiting for Nick to escort her out the door. *How awkward.* It sounds like he and Jerry are wrapping up their conversation in the study.

Amber steps toward me. *Is she going to give me a hug?*

The minute she's in my arms, I know what to do. I silently begin to pray. *Lord, I trust You've allowed this girl to come into our lives. Bless her. . . .*

"Mom?"

Huh? Oh, for goodness' sake! I let go of Amber and take a step back. "Yes?"

Nick looks at me as if I'm suffering a turkey hangover of ginormous proportions and I've totally lost contact with appropriate behavior. "We've got to go."

I slink farther away from Amber. "Well, good night, Amber. See you soon."

Note to self: stop praying when the girl tries to escape the hug. How embarrassing.

"Mom? Dad?"

Jerry jerks awake and takes me along for the adrenaline ride.

I sit straight up. "What? What's wrong?"

The dim light from the hallway casts frightening shadows in my room. Nick's sitting on the edge of the bed.

My hand flies to my heart. "Where's Em? Is she all right?"

Nick chuckles. "I'm sorry. I didn't mean to frighten you."

Jerry pushes his pillow against the headboard and leans against it. "What's going on?"

I reach out and brush the back of my hand on Nick's cheek. His skin is cool, as if he just came home. I glance at the clock. It's 3:40 a.m.

He catches my hand and holds it in his. "I wanted to talk to you both before I go to bed."

Well, he's certainly got our attention. "Yes?"

He shakes his head as if he can't believe what he's going to say. "I'm in love. I know in my bones and deep in my heart that I love Amber."

I'm speechless.

Jerry is not. "Wow."

I clear my throat. "Are you sure?"

He laughs again. "How does someone make sure of love?"

Does he have to keep using that word?

"And I'm going to ask Amber to marry me."

45

The alarm jars me awake. It's the day after Thanksgiving, when most of the population is sleeping in, eating leftovers, starting their holiday shopping, and decorating their homes for Christmas. But I work in the portrait photography industry, and this is one of those days when families are together. And what better time to have a family portrait taken or to purchase a portrait package than a holiday when everyone (else) is off work for the day? *Humbug.*

It could be worse, though. Luke has finally found a heart, and we are able to use flextime and share our jobs with one another for the day. I'm working a half day, and Traci is sleeping in and taking the afternoon shift. This way I can leave in time to watch Emma's concert at town hall.

Belle and I are the only ones up. I brew a small pot of tea, enjoy my quiet time, and eat a bowl of oatmeal.

I'm out on the road a few minutes early. Good thing, because all those crazy Black Friday shoppers are tearing down the highway in search of a great deal.

I wish Jerry had gotten up to have breakfast with me. That way he could assure me that our nocturnal visit really did occur, and it wasn't a nightmare caused by eating too much carbohydrates and sugar.

My son's in love. I wish my heart were soaring with the news. But it's not. It's every parent's dream that their children find good spouses who will love and cherish them. But Jerry and I also dream that whomever they choose will also love our Lord and that their marriages will be based on eternal truth. Amber doesn't fit that description. Did Nick even pray about this decision?

To retain my sanity, I can't think about that right now. I walk through the studio doors, where I'm greeted with the fragrance of a pumpkin spice candle. I clock in and check the schedule. I should have an easy morning. I'm working the reception desk, and fortunately most people assume all businesses are closed today, so I expect the phone will be silent.

The morning progresses peacefully. Except for the few clients coming in for portraits or groups stopping by to view their images, the lobby is quiet.

I'm organizing files for next week when the strap of jingle bells hanging off the door announces more clients. I watch a familiar-looking, attractive woman in her late thirties come in. She's all alone, a strange sight today when every other client is traveling en masse with their families.

"Good morning. May I help you?"

She sits down. Her huge diamond wedding set sparkles in the light when she zips up her gray velour jacket as if she's chilled. She's wearing matching velour sweatpants and carrying an Asian-looking backpack. Despite the casual attire, you can tell that her clothes are costly and she can easily afford our products. "I'm picking up a portrait. The name's Winston. Cara Winston."

"Sure, Mrs. Winston." I recall her. She and her family came into my salesroom about two months ago. I remember that her young children were very well behaved, and she and her husband were so kind toward one another.

She passes me her invoice, and I glance at it to see the sizes of portraits in her order. *Wow.* She's picking up a forty-by-sixty-inch portrait. I move to the left side of the storeroom, where we keep the large portraits, and have no trouble locating it. I maneuver it out of the vertical file and give it a brief inspection to make sure it's up to our standards. For the price our clients pay, we like to provide them with perfection.

The portrait is stunning. A lovely family of five is sitting on a gigantic rock outcropping in the mountains. Behind them is a vista that takes your breath away—pine trees, mountaintops, bright blue skies, and puffy, white clouds. Cara did a wonderful job selecting their wardrobe. They are all wearing a combination of green and navy blue. The artwork, as usual, is exquisite.

In addition to the large wall portrait, they've ordered a smaller wall portrait of the children and one of Cara and her husband looking into each other's eyes. They all look so happy.

I hoist the large portrait and walk out to the lobby, where I present it to our client. "Here you go. Your family is gorgeous. And you picked out the perfect frame. Your portrait is stunning." I smile and wait for the usual agreement that our clients give us. Everyone loves to have someone gush over their beautiful portraits and lovely family.

Apparently everyone except Mrs. Winston. She silently contemplates the family portrait and looks downright grim.

Oh no. What could be wrong with the order? I examine the portrait again. Nothing seems to be amiss—no upturned collars, wandering eyes, awkward positions.

Cara continues to stare at the portrait as if it's the last thing in the world that she wants to bring into her home.

"It's a magnificent portrait—don't you think?"

She studies the image a few seconds longer before turning her gaze on me. "I'll pay for it and probably keep the frame, but could you please dispose of this portrait for me?"

My eyes must pop out of my head. This is an absolute work of art. "Why don't you want to take it home?"

Cara drops into a chair, reaches into her backpack, and pulls out a tissue. She frowns and then her face crumples in tears.

Thank goodness there's no one else in the lobby. "What's wrong?" I pull the extra reception chair close to her and put my hand on her back. Cara covers her face with her hands, and her body shakes with silent sobs. I move my arms to her shoulders.

After a moment, she mops her face and takes a deep breath. "Please forgive me. I can't believe I just lost it here in your lobby."

"You don't need to apologize. Can I get you something to drink?" She swallows a sob and nods.

The lobby door opens, and a happy family enjoying the holiday weekend comes in.

Cara appears stricken. I'm sure she's mortified that she's in such disarray in public. I stand, pull Cara to her feet, and position her in front of me, facing away from the other clients.

I turn and smile at the group getting settled on our couch and upholstered chairs. "I'll be right back to help you folks."

I drape my arm around Cara's shoulders and guide her down the hallway. "There's an empty image presentation room. You take a seat and I'll be back in a moment with some water for you. Okay?"

She looks at me with gratitude in her blue eyes.

I hustle to the workroom and ask Jill to take over for me while I sort things out with Cara.

When I come into the room, Cara's emotions are under control again. I give her a bottle of water and take a seat. "Is there anything I can do for you?" I'm dying to know what the issue is. Could her husband have passed away? It won't be the first time someone's died before their order is delivered. But why wouldn't she want that beautiful portrait to keep as a family heirloom?

Cara leans back into the couch. "My husband and I are divorcing."

"I'm sorry."

"Not as sorry as I am. Nor as sorry as he and his pregnant little girlfriend will be after my lawyers are finished." She laughs bitterly. "I just can't bear to take that portrait home."

"That's okay. I understand. I'm sure Luke will discount your bill."

"Oh no. I'm happy to pay for it—with my husband's credit card."

Ah, vengeance.

Cara stuffs her tissue in her pocket. "I want the portrait of my children, though."

"Yes, it's lovely." I fall silent for a moment and then come up with an idea. "Other than having your soon-to-be ex in that portrait, do you like it?"

She looks at me as if I'm daft. "I love that picture. It's perfect."

I stand. "I'll be right back."

I go to our workroom and consult with one of our imaging artists, retrieve the family portrait, and hurry back to Cara. "Great news! See the way you're sitting on this rock? You're facing left and he's facing right. The children are sitting in front of you."

Her expression displays confusion.

I gesture toward the portrait. "There were enough images captured that we can remove Mr. Winston from the image, reconstruct the background, and create a portrait of you and your children. Alone. Without him."

Cara's face lights up. "You're a genius! Do it. And I don't even care what the artwork fee is."

46

It's a pleasure to walk out of work with daylight still illuminating the sky. I have just enough time to drive home, change my clothes, and head off to the community concert with Jerry.

Jerry's sitting in the living room reading a magazine when I arrive. Nick's gone out. My husband folds the periodical and lays it on the side table. He glances at our grandfather clock. "Hurry up."

I shake my head. "I'll be four minutes. I want to change into my jeans."

He rolls his eyes and picks up his magazine.

I'm almost as good as my word, and we're on the road in about six minutes. "So, where's our son? With Amber?"

He frowns. "You better tread lightly. If she says yes to his proposal, she'll be our daughter-in-law."

"But did you speak with him today? Did you talk about their future, especially since she doesn't share his faith?"

His expression fades. "He thinks everything will turn out well for them."

How naive can he be?

We ride in silence the rest of the way, find a place to park, and walk toward town hall. The weather has cooled enough to put a nip in the air but not enough to chill our toes. The kids who are singing have gathered together. I spot Emma talking with a group of girls. Funny thing, I don't see Cole, although his parents waved to us when we were joining the crowd.

"Do you see Pop?"

I raise my hand to screen my eyes from the sun and scan the gathering crowd. "I don't see him. Why don't you call his cell?"

Jerry pulls his phone from his pocket just as it begins to ring. He glances at the caller ID. "It's Pop." He pushes the button to accept the call. "Where are you? . . . We're to the south of the building. . . . Uh-huh." He raises his hand and turns to the side. "See ya!" He hangs up, and we watch Ross pick his way through the crowd to join us.

Emma's suddenly by our side. "Hi!" Her cheeks are colored with a blush of the season, and her eyes are shining. "If you stand over there, you might be able to get a better view." She begins to herd us over to a small rise in the landscaping.

"Where's Cole? Isn't he singing too?"

She flashes me a look that tells me something's going on.

I pull my gloves out of my pocket and slide them on my hands. "Did you and Cole have a fight or something?"

She nudges me. "Shh."

I glance behind us to make sure Jerry and Ross are coming. They're chatting as they follow us. "What's going on?"

Emma points across the street. "There he is." Cole's easy to spot, being as tall as he is. He seems to be shepherding an older woman with him.

"Is that a relative with him?"

She gives me a coy smile. "No."

I turn to regard the couple coming toward us. The older woman seems familiar. *Oh no.* I lower my voice. "It's Doris."

Emma nods, looking pleased.

I pull her close to me. "What are you up to? Weren't you told to leave this situation alone?"

She smiles. "Love will find a way."

Dare I hope this could turn out well? I look at Jerry and Ross, still in conversation. Jerry winks at me. He's going to be steamed when he figures out what his daughter's been up to.

My heart flutters like a bird flying away from a pouncing cat as I watch Cole and Doris come closer to us. I can tell that she has no idea she's walking directly toward Ross. I steal a glance at Ross. He's oblivious as well.

Jerry spots Cole, and his smile freezes when he sees that Cole's bringing a guest. This could be awkward.

I step forward to greet Doris.

She sees me and smiles warmly, then looks behind me right where Ross is standing. Her hand flies to her heart as her gaze darts around our little group.

Ross's expression holds a mixture of hope and disbelief. He approaches Doris with a tentative smile and clears his throat. "This is a pleasant surprise."

Doris smiles for a moment, and then as quickly as it appeared, it is gone. She begins to back away and bumps into Cole. "You should be ashamed of yourself, young man. You have no right to play with other people's lives." She turns and walks toward the sidewalk.

"Doris?" Ross follows her. "Doris, wait. Please."

Emma and Cole rush off to join the choir. Jerry's face is red, and I don't think it's from the cold. As much as I didn't want another woman to take Theresa's place in our lives, it breaks my heart to see Ross chasing after someone who seems to have no interest in a relationship with him.

Despite his years, Ross manages to catch up with Doris, and he grabs her arm. When she turns to face him, you can see that she's begun to weep. *Oh, maybe . . .*

The a cappella choir begins to sing "Jingle Bells." Jerry and I are the only ones in the crowd who are not watching the kids perform.

Ross reaches into his pocket and produces a handkerchief. He holds it out to Doris. She hesitates and then accepts the offering. When she dries her tears, Ross moves a bit closer to her. His hand rises as if he's going to touch her, and she takes a step back.

I'm glad I can't see his face. I can only imagine the hurt reflected in his expression. Can't that woman see how he's reaching out to her?

Ross thrusts his hands in his pockets. He bows his head, but I can tell he's still speaking. Doris hikes her purse on her shoulder and wraps her arms around herself. I don't know if I've ever seen two more miserable-looking people.

Doris starts to talk and her head bobs in an exaggerated fashion. She points toward the choir and then back to Ross.

Jerry nudges me. "Let's watch the concert. They need their privacy."

He puts his arm around my shoulders, and we focus on the choir. A moment later, I sense movement beside me and look to see Ross standing there. He appears somber as he stares at the kids singing.

I gaze off to the distance and see Doris walking down the sidewalk, a cell phone at her ear.

The next song begins. It's "Have Yourself a Merry Little Christmas." I feel anything but merry, and this song has never sounded so much like a dirge.

I snake my arm through Ross's. With his other hand, he pats my arm. I give him a sideways glance, but he's avoiding eye contact.

A spotlight illuminates the choir standing beside the lit Christmas tree. Emma's expression looks pained, and tears slide down her cheek.

This is hardly a good way to welcome the season.

47

We tried to convince Ross to come home with us and have turkey sandwiches, but he was adamant that he needed to get home. I could barely get two words out of him about his conversation with Doris.

"You're a sweetheart," he said, "but Doris is convinced that I need more time to get over Theresa."

The whole situation is just so sad.

After the concert, Jerry had a brief talk with Emma and Cole. They seemed contrite. A lesson learned, I guess.

When we get home, both Nick's and Amber's cars are parked outside. Emma and Cole follow us into the house. Before we can take our coats off, Nick and Amber come out to the foyer, their faces shining with joy.

I try to mimic their good mood. "Yes?"

Nick reaches for Amber's left hand and holds it up. A tiny chip of a diamond sparkles from a ring on her third finger.

"Congratulations, Nick. And best wishes, Amber." I open my arms and capture them both in a hug.

"What's going on?" Emma crowds us. When she spots the engagement ring on Amber's hand, she squeals in delight. She hugs Amber and gives her brother a kiss on the cheek. "I'll call Grandpa and tell him to come over right now."

Oh, I wish I'd thought of that.

We're all sitting together in the living room, Christmas songs softly playing as background music to this happy event. I would never behave in a way to cause lifelong regrets, but my heart really isn't in this celebration.

Ross has joined us, and he seems genuinely glad. "So, have you selected a date?"

Nick's expression alters to reflect an important announcement. "Actually, Grandpa, we decided on June 9."

Ross looks as if he's going to tear up. "Thank you. That's sweet."

I glance at Jerry to see his reaction. He looks very pleased. June 9 was Ross and Theresa's anniversary.

The couple tells us their plans. They want to give themselves a month after graduation before getting married. That way Amber will be out of her lease with her roommates, and hopefully she and Nick might have found some job leads.

"Where will the ceremony take place?" I always dreamed that my children would be married in a church.

Nick turns to me. "We're not sure yet. We'll see what's available."

I sit in the midst of my family, listening to news I never wanted to hear, trying to put up a happy front for the sake of my relationship with my son. And with my husband.

Everyone's staring at me. *Oh, I got lost in my own thoughts again.* "I'm sorry. What?"

Nick laughs. "Amber was asking you a question."

I focus back on the moment. "Yes?"

She dips her head a bit in a nervous motion. "I was wondering . . . I mean, Nick said I should ask you . . ."

Is it possible she wants to borrow my wedding gown?

Finally she spits it out. "I was hoping I could borrow the, um, pretty Christmas sweater you wore last Saturday when Nick and I had our Christmas pictures taken."

"My sweater?" That beautiful cashmere sweater I bought at Macy's? I've only worn it a few times myself.

"Mom." Nick's expression is a censure.

Jerry is scrutinizing me too.

As if I really have a choice. "I'm sorry, Amber. Of course you can borrow that sweater. I know it will look lovely on you."

She appears relieved and smiles. "Thanks."

If she gets a snag or a stain on it, I'll be heartbroken. It's a classically dressy holiday sweater that I plan on wearing for years to come.

"Mom?" Nick's staring at me as if I need to do something. "Tonight?"

"Tonight what?"

He sighs. "May Amber borrow the sweater tonight? We're going to a holiday party."

I stand. "Oh. Let me run up to my room and get it."

I go upstairs, pluck the sweater from my closet, and give it a good perusal to make sure it's in pristine condition. If it's altered in any way when she returns it, I'll know.

Nick and Amber are on their way. Our little party moves to the kitchen, and I brew a pot of coffee. I was afraid things might be awkward between Ross, Emma, and Cole, but they've seemed to smooth over any problems.

Jerry leans back in the kitchen chair and crosses his arms. "Do you have any plans for the weekend, Pop?"

Ross takes a sip of his black coffee. "Might do a little shopping, the sales are too good to pass up."

Jerry winces. There's nothing he hates more than shopping. Especially on one of the busiest shopping weekends of the season.

I love to hear my guys talk to one another. How dear their conversations are to me. They make me feel like a child, eavesdropping on my parents' exchanges. The comfortable give-and-take about everyday things inspires a feeling of security.

Emma and Cole move to the family room, where they can play that annoying video game again.

"Uh-oh. What's this?" Cole springs from the couch and holds up the piece of paper he sat on.

Emma takes it from him. "This is an invitation to the party and driving directions. I hope Nick didn't need them."

I shrug. "He'll call if he needs us to give him directions."

Emma stands in the middle of the room, still reading the sheet of paper. Her eyes meet mine, and then she looks back down at the paper and folds it up. She tosses her game controller on the couch and throws the paper in the garbage.

"Don't do that." I walk over to the trash to retrieve the invitation. "What if Nick calls and needs directions? I'm about to empty the coffee grounds, and then we won't be able to read the directions to him."

She seems nervous. "Don't worry about it. They probably know where they're going."

Better safe than sorry. I fish the small, folded paper out of the trash and open it. I'm about to lay it on the counter when I notice the words:

Come one, come all to Toby's annual ugly Christmas sweater party!

48

"Are you kidding?" I look from the invitation to Emma. "You weren't going to tell me about this?"

"Mom . . ."

"So it's okay to let me look like the fool?"

Jerry and Ross suspend their conversation and both jerk toward me as if I had shouted "Fire!" in a movie theater.

"What's wrong?"

I turn on Jerry, barely able to speak, so angry I could spit. "That little . . ."

He rises and I hand him the paper. He scans the sheet, chuckles, and passes it to Ross.

I can't believe what I'm seeing. I stand with my hands on my hips and get even more annoyed when he laughs so hard that he plucks a tissue from the box on the counter and wipes his eyes. I face Ross. *Great, now they're both laughing. At me.*

"This really isn't funny." The sting of my blush further wounds me.

Apparently I'm the only one who doesn't think it's hilarious. Emma is doing that silent laugh thing, her shoulders are shaking, her face screwed up in laughter, but no noise is coming from her. Cole looks as if he may burst from holding in his mirth.

I bolt into the living room to nurse my wounded feelings. Sure, it's easy for them to laugh. They're not the butt of the joke. And to think that I thought Amber and I had turned a corner on our relationship. *I don't lend out my clothes to just anyone, you know. Humph.*

Jerry takes my hand and pulls me up from the couch. "Don't be angry. It's—"

"Don't be angry? My, it's awfully easy for you to say. I thought—"

He puts a finger to my lips and walks me into his study and closes the door. "It's okay. I'm sure she's not trying to make you look like a fool."

Knowing Jer, he led me out of earshot before I could spout off something I'd regret. Dear man, he lets me vent. And, boy, do I vent.

When my anger has cooled, I lean against his chest. "What really bothers me is that Nick put her up to it."

"You're reading way too much into this. Amber just needed a sweater to wear to this party and didn't want to buy one."

I stare at him, unable to know what to believe. I've got laundry to do, and anything would be better than being the object of pity from my family. I exit the room.

Emma comes into the foyer just as I step from Jer's study. She walks over to me and gives me a hug. "Honestly, that sweater is pretty ugly."

The air sucks out of my lungs.

Before I can let her have it, she shakes her head and says, "How many college students do you see wearing Christmas sweaters?"

"What?"

"Think about it. The only people who wear Christmas sweaters are kids up to about middle school and older women."

"Older women?"

"You know what I mean: grown-up women."

"Whatever." Attending to my mountain of dirty clothes is looking mighty appealing right now. I need some alone time to digest the thoughts and emotions churning through my brain. I feel as though my children are marginalizing me. Like I'm no longer important to them.

I stew about that for a few minutes and realize that this is the way it should be. My birds are getting ready to fly the nest. There are new worlds for them to explore and new people to fill their lives with. But despite it being normal, that doesn't make it any easier for me. Especially when they're making choices I can't agree with.

I sort, wash, dry, and fold a load of laundry while simultaneously cleaning my room. I hear Emma and Cole go out for coffee, and I run down to the foyer to give Ross a hug before he goes home.

Back in my bedroom, I hear Jerry's laughter as he watches television in the family room. I start down to join him but stop halfway and take a seat on the landing. Belle strolls by the front door, looks up, and sees me. Her collar tags jingle as she climbs the stairs.

We sit side by side on the landing while my mind swirls. I stroke Belle's soft ears and pet her head that rests on my lap. Pretty soon it will be just me, Jerry, and Belle rattling around the family home. My kids will go off on their own. Who knows what direction Emma's life will take? And Nick—what kind of a life will he and Amber have? Amber. How will I ever have a healthy relationship with her? She obviously doesn't respect me.

I stand and walk down to spend some time with Jerry. What a perfect way to redeem this pitiful day.

• • •

I lie in bed, occasionally glancing at the clock, wondering what happened at the party Nick and Amber attended last night. Did they have a contest for the ugliest sweater? Did mine win? For most of the night, sleep eluded me. I'm still weary, but I promised Emma we'd get a jump on our Christmas shopping. I hear her footsteps as she walks down the stairs. *Good.* If I stay in bed another five minutes, the coffee will be brewed when I get up.

Snow is falling when we pull out of the driveway. We didn't get quite the early start I expected. By the time I stripped our beds and started laundry and answered a long call from work, it was nearly ten thirty. It's a good thing we're staying in Pine Grove to do our shopping. We won't have to slide up the highway to the mall.

Our first stop is Mountain Man to purchase baskets of candy and snacks to send to out-of-town friends. Then we rush to the Christian bookstore on Main and Pine Grove Road. As usual, that stop takes longer than planned. But what can you do when there are so many books to look over? When we finish, it's lunchtime. Even though it's not far, neither of us wants to go home. We duck into the Gray Pony and warm up eating soup and Mexican food.

We head to our last stop of the day, Target, with our lists in hand. I can't believe how crowded the parking lot is. I thought all the shoppers were out yesterday. When we get inside, we go to the toy department to buy a present for the angel tree at church. I leave the job of picking out something suitable for a nine-year-old girl to Emma and go on my way to find Christmas cards. Three beautiful boxes of cards later, I'm ready to resume shopping. I can't believe Em hasn't joined me. I pull out my cell phone and dial her. The phone rings three times and then goes to voice mail. *Oh, well.* She'll call me back.

I sail down the big aisle and see my daughter halfway to the other side of the store. She's talking to someone and holding on to the woman's cart.

I'm about thirty feet away from Emma when I realize she's talking with Doris. I hope Emma's not up to her matchmaking again. If she doesn't knock it off, Ross really will get angry.

When I pull up alongside them, Doris gives me a sweet smile. "Hi, dear. I heard you had exciting news in your family."

"Yes. We can't say we were too caught off guard." *And I'm not so sure it's exciting in a good way.*

We chat for a few minutes longer and go our separate ways. Emma and I toss items into our cart and cross them off our lists. We wait in a long line to check out and venture back to the parking lot. The sky has grown darker, snow continues to fall, and the temperature has dropped considerably while we were shopping.

I open the trunk and unload our bags from the cart. The car across the lane from us makes a repeated clicking noise. I glance up and see a woman's silhouette as she continues to try starting the engine. It sounds like a dead battery.

"Mom, it's Doris."

We cross over to her and I tap on the driver's window. "We have jumper cables, Doris. Can we help?"

Relief washes over her face. She unlocks the door and steps out.

I toss the keys to Emma and instruct her to drive around the lot and into the newly vacated spot adjacent to Doris's.

"Jerry insists I carry cables in case of an emergency, but I'm not sure how to use them."

She makes a face. "I don't know either. Perhaps we should ask someone in the store."

The thought of finding assistance in a crowded, understaffed store isn't all that attractive. When Emma returns, I give her that job.

"No need to do that." She exits the car and explains to Doris. "I've already called the cavalry. Help is on the way."

I invite Doris to sit in our warm car while we await help. Thank goodness Jerry is only five minutes away.

Doris and I talk about inconsequential things. She's really a lovely lady. I glance into the rearview mirror. Emma is looking out the window, smiling.

49

Like the strangers we are, Doris and I make bland conversation. But I feel compelled to take our relationship further. "I hope I won't offend you, but . . ." I look into her eyes to gauge her reaction.

She draws in her breath ever so slightly. "Go ahead. What would you like to know?"

As if he were Jiminy Cricket whispering in my ear, I can hear Jerry telling me to mind my own business. But I can't help myself. "Do you think there's ever a possibility that you will consider dating Ross again?"

It seems as if she smiles in spite of herself. "Ross is a wonderful man. I have immense respect for him. And I'm not getting any younger." Doris stares at her hands, clasped around her purse. "I had a wonderful marriage. Very happy. Blessed. I miss being a part of a couple."

I plunge in. "Ross is lonely too."

She studies me. "I know that. But is he ready to move on?"

I start to explain, but she cuts me off. "You can't imagine what it's like to lose your spouse. It takes time before you can even think straight."

"I think Ross is ready to find love again."

Doris pats my arm. "I know you do. And maybe you're right. But you could just as well be wrong."

"Will you consider seeing him?"

She laughs. "It sounds like you're asking me on a date for Ross."

Perhaps I am, but before I can say anything, her smile dims. "Like I said, I'm not getting any younger, and actually I'm running late to get ready for a date I have later."

"Oh no!"

I'm shocked by Emma's response and try to cover up her gaffe. "Sorry, Doris. She's a young romantic." I glance at Emma in the rearview mirror. She looks genuinely concerned.

We're all silent for a moment, watching the ebb and flow of traffic in and out of the lot.

"Here he is!" Emma hops out to flag Jerry down.

Doris and I climb out of my Taurus. I scan the lot but don't see Jerry's SUV. *I can't believe it.*

Emma steps into the lane and waves her arms.

Ross's car slows and then pulls into a spot a few cars down from us. He salutes me, and I'm certain that he doesn't see Doris standing alongside her car.

I turn to my devious daughter and in a hush say, "Emma."

She shrugs and smiles at Ross and me.

Ross puts his keys in his pocket. "At your assistance, ma'am." His smile remains constant when he sees Doris, and his eyebrows rise. "What a pleasant surprise."

Doris smiles and nods. "Hello."

"What about Dad?" I ask Emma.

She tries to affect a casual pose, but I know she realizes I've got her number. "Oh, didn't he say he had his own errands to run today? I didn't think he was available, so I called Grandpa instead."

As if anyone would believe that story.

Ross and Doris are standing about two feet apart, looking into each other's eyes. Maybe there is something here.

"Ross?"

He doesn't acknowledge my presence.

"Ross?" I try again.

He faces me. "Yes?"

The cold is beginning to frost my toes. "How about getting this car started?"

"Oh." He rubs his hands together. "Sure. Where are the cables?"

I toss Emma the keys. "Would you get them out of the trunk?"

The snow crunches beneath her boots as she walks to the back of the car. The trunk creaks open. "Uh-oh."

Ross and Doris are still gawking at each other, but I face Emma. "What's wrong?"

She holds up her arms. "They're not here."

"Did you look well enough? There's a coat back there. Are they under that?" I walk over to help her dig them out of my messy trunk.

"No, Mom. I let Cole borrow them about a week ago."

I give her a look that lets her know how aggravated I am. "I don't care that Cole borrowed them, but why didn't he return them?"

She cocks her head. "Sorry. Now what?"

We both turn to Ross for direction. He and Doris are talking quietly.

"Grandpa?"

He blinks and focuses on Em. "Yes, baby girl?"

Hmm. He's not in a bad mood if he's calling Emma by that term of endearment.

"I forgot that I let Cole borrow the cables. Do you have any?"

A smile splits his face. "No. I don't." He takes Doris's gloved hand. "How about I drive you home?"

Is she going to break his heart again? I think both Emma and I hold our breath waiting for her answer.

Doris hesitates, gazing into his eyes to seemingly investigate Ross's intentions. Then her eyes crinkle and she smiles. "Yes. Thank you, Ross. I would love a ride home."

Emma leans toward me and whispers, "Isn't this romantic?"

She's right. Standing beneath the parking lot light, the snow swirls and dances around them as if they're statues in a snow globe. If this were a movie, sweet, tinkling piano music would start the soundtrack that ends in swelling violins. They are in a world unto themselves.

What a scene Emma and I are witnessing. Neither of us speaks as Doris reaches into her car and takes out her shopping bag.

"Bye, girls." Ross winks at Emma and me.

We bid them good-bye and watch them drive off, the brake lights blinking through the snow. I wonder about the man who has a date with Doris tonight. But that's not my concern.

"Oh, Mom. Isn't this fantastic?"

I nod and put my arm around Emma's shoulders. "And quite a surprise. It could have ended up entirely different if you hadn't loaned out the jumper cables."

Her smile broadens.

"Em?"

"The jumper cables?" she practically sings. "They're under that old ratty coat in your trunk."

50

This seems to be the season for romance.

This week I've sold three wedding portrait packages at work. Nick and Amber are on cloud nine telling everyone about their engagement. I know they're excited, but they don't seem to understand that we can't all think and talk about their wedding 24-7. Emma and Amber have stacks of bridal magazines they've been poring over for a week straight. Each periodical is dog-eared to keep track of a wedding gown or bridesmaid's dress. And Amber's been talking about her girlfriends who will be in the bridal party.

I can tell you one thing—every time I hug Amber, my prayers get more and more urgent. If the Lord's going to move in her heart, He'd better get going on the project. In a little over seven months, she will be my son's wife. I've had a few more sticky situations that involve my prayer hugs. I'll be hanging on to her for dear life, imploring heaven to move, and she'll have thrust her arms by her side in an effort to escape my hug. Still awkward. But it's a vow I made to God, so she's going to have to endure it. One day I'll tell her what it's about.

The big news is that Ross and Doris are officially an item. Ross was like a teenager when he told us that he and Doris went back to her house last Saturday and had a long talk over coffee and cake. Then Doris took her phone into another room and broke her date with that mysterious stranger. Ross even asked her if she'd date him exclusively. *Wow. Going steady.*

It's Saturday night. Date night. As usual, Nick's out with Amber, and Emma and Cole are at a friend's house. Ross and Doris have gone to Denver to see a play at the Center for Performing Arts.

It's going to be a quiet night at the Revere homestead, and nothing could suit me better. The house is decorated for Christmas and feels all warm and cozy. Thick green garlands dotted with white lights and red and gold ribbon cascade down the upstairs railing. In the dining room my Dickens' Village sits on the side table, inviting you into a Lilliputian world of merry old England. The only thing missing is our Christmas tree, but we'll get to that soon. Tunes from a Christmas CD filter through the house. Even Hallmark couldn't create a more inviting scene.

Jerry and I shared a cheese pizza, and now we're wrapping the Christmas gifts I've already bought. We work well as a team. I size and cut the paper to fit the package, then pass it off to Jerry to seal it and put on a gift tag. This is a system we've perfected over the years.

"What about Amber?"

I look up at him. "What? What about Amber?"

Jerry shakes his head as if he expects me to understand his cryptic language. "Did you buy her a Christmas gift?"

"Not yet. Any ideas?"

"You'll think of something." He writes out a gift tag as though the task is off his plate.

I don't think so, buddy. "Excuse me. But I think *we'll* think of something."

Jerry laughs and then his smile tempers. His gaze holds mine, and he gives me a naughty look. "Actually I'm thinking of something right now."

Good gravy, this man still makes my stomach flip. "Stay on task. We've got a few more gifts to wrap."

"And then . . ."

Footsteps on the front porch command our attention. I scramble for a bag to throw over the unwrapped gifts when the dead bolt turns. Romance will have to wait until later.

Nick and Amber come into the house. Something's wrong. They appear agitated, and Amber's eyes are red. They both turn to us as if the weight of the world is crashing down upon them. Nick helps Amber out of her coat and tosses it, along with his, over the back of a chair. They stand looking at us, mute.

Now I'm getting concerned. "What?"

Nick cracks his knuckles. An annoying boyhood habit that signals trouble. "Can we talk?"

"Shall I make coffee?"

No one answers, so I take that for a yes. I get up from my place on the floor and go to the kitchen. I'm surprised when Amber doesn't follow me. She's been Little Miss Helpful ever since the day before Thanksgiving. I set the coffee to brew and place mugs, sugar, and half-and-half on the dining room table.

They're gathered at the table when I bring in the coffee.

Jerry and I sit across from the miserable couple. Nick takes Amber's hand in his. They're still silent. Amber sniffles and bats her eyes. "Excuse me." She pulls her hand from Nick's and goes to the kitchen. A moment later she returns with a box of tissues.

My blood runs cool in my veins. She's not just bringing these tissues for herself; she's placed them in the center of the table.

Nick grasps her hand again. "Mom, Dad, there's something we need to tell you."

Jerry fills a mug. "You both seem so serious. I want you to know that we'll support you and help you through whatever is upsetting you. Planning your future is a tricky task and—"

What's with his rambling on? "Jerry! Would you let them speak?"

He nods and gives them his attention.

"Our plans have changed a bit." Nick pauses to pour coffee.

His eyes are downcast. When he returns our gaze, there is emotion being held in check. He takes a sip of coffee and sets his mug down. He puts his arm around Amber as she plucks a tissue from the box.

"I don't know another way to tell you this." He looks at Jerry, then me. "Amber and I are going to have a baby."

51

"I beg your pardon?" *Could I really have heard that statement?*

Jerry, for once, is speechless. Amber looks as if she's going to cry.

"We're going to get married as soon as we can arrange it." Nick sounds resolute.

This was the last thing I expected to hear, although their lifestyle certainly wouldn't preclude such an outcome. "Oh." I close my mouth before the wrong thing comes out. All I've ever wanted for my children was for them to share their lives with a spouse who loves them and also loves the Lord. Amber doesn't seem to fit that bill. But I've always assumed Nick would be married to the mother of his child. My heart is at war with itself.

We sit quietly for a moment, letting this news seep into our consciousness. This is life-changing. How will they manage? Where do I fit into this situation? Could this be an opportunity for me to get closer to Amber, now that she's preparing to become a mother?

A disturbing thought occurs to me. "Nick, how will you handle a new baby and your last semester of college?"

His shoulders slump. "I'll have to finish college later. I'm going to have to get a full-time job to make this work."

"But you're so close to finishing."

Jerry leans in. "There may be another way."

Oh, good. I knew I could count on Jer to come up with a

solution. Maybe they can wait until May to get married. After all, Amber can't be more than a few weeks along.

"I have an idea." Jerry sounds optimistic. "How about if you get married and live here until you can get on your feet? That way Nick can finish college, and maybe Amber could too."

What! The thought of having them living with us as newlyweds just seems wrong. And awkward. "Do you really need to get married so quickly?"

Everyone looks at me as if I'm insane.

"Well, when's the baby due? Maybe you can finish school and still get married before the baby comes."

"Linda!" Jerry's expression is a cross between anger and disappointment.

I don't blame him. I know I'm grasping at straws. "I'm sorry. I'm still trying to sort this out."

Amber sighs. "In May."

"What?"

"The baby's due in May." Amber sounds weary.

It's difficult for me to concentrate. "That can't be right. That would make you almost four months along. And you're just now realizing it?"

"Mom!"

I'm not handling this well. *Help me, Lord.* "Sorry."

Amber's face colors. "I've always been irregular. It didn't faze me until last week."

The grandfather clock chimes, the CD changes, and John Denver sings a beautiful song about Aspenglow. If we hadn't just heard Nick and Amber's news, this would be a lovely, peaceful moment.

Jerry stands and walks over to Amber. She looks at him with big, scared eyes. He holds out his hand, and when she grasps it, he pulls her to her feet and embraces her. She melts into his arms.

Wow. Tears spring to my eyes, and even Nick appears affected. This poor girl has had no one to support her other than Nick. No mother, father, or any significant adult that we know of. *What kind of jerk am I?*

I leap up, and when Jerry releases her, I take her in my arms. *Heavenly Father, bless Amber. . . .*

A hand on my back brings me back to the moment. It's Jerry's. Amber is leaning away from me. *Yikes—I'm still caught up in my prayer. Oh, fudge. I did it again.*

I let go of her and return to my seat. It's bad enough that she's going through a trauma; now I've probably freaked her out with another one of my unending hugs.

We all sit again and nurse our coffees. Nothing could have prepared me for this moment. How embarrassing will this be? A rushed wedding, a new baby. We can't even pretend this child's coming early.

Jerry stirs his coffee. "Well, tomorrow we can call Pastor John and see what the availability is for a church wedding. Okay?"

Nick smiles. "Sure."

"I hope we can get a date soon. Christmas is such a busy season." Everyone stares at me while I ramble on. This isn't a happy group. I keep further thoughts to myself.

I glance at Amber and see her staring at one of the bridal magazines that Emma left in the living room. I guess she won't be wearing that beautiful wedding dress after all. And will she ever wear her graduation gown? Circumstances like this can change the direction of a life. Like a pebble tossed into a pond, I can see the ripples affect our lives for years and years. This is not what I dreamed of for my son.

I find my voice again. "I know this is a shock to us all, but remember—we're a family and we'll handle it together." I may stray off the mark occasionally, but I usually find my way back.

We talk for a while longer; then Nick takes Amber home. Jerry mumbles something about calling Ross and telling him the news. I wrap the remaining Christmas presents by myself.

By the time I'm cleaning up my wrapping supplies, Nick comes home. He stands in the foyer, jingling his keys, and nods toward the family room, where Jerry's watching television. "Can we talk for a moment?"

I join them at the kitchen table.

Nick crosses his arms. "I know you're probably disappointed with me."

I look to Jerry to respond. He'll probably be more diplomatic than I will.

"Well, yes."

I'm stunned by his terse answer.

"Amber and I love each other, and we're committed."

"That's not the issue." Jerry isn't giving an inch.

"Look, I know you're concerned because Amber isn't a believer, but she's more open than ever to investigating faith."

As I've done many times before, I get in the middle of their discussion. "You stepped outside your beliefs to have a good time."

"I guess that's true." Nick sighs. "So what do you want me to do? Desert her?"

"No." Jerry sounds as weary as I am heartsick over the situation. "I would never suggest that. I just want you to realize that you have a lot to deal with, and it won't be easy. Your mother and I love you and we'll help you as much as we can, but it's your responsibility." Jerry rises and claps Nick on the back.

Nick stands and walks to his room.

I remain at the table, listening to Nick's footsteps on the stairs and Jerry flipping through the television channels. I understand how our influence over our children is limited. They grow, fall in love, and make their own lives. I've lost control of Nick. I can't make his decisions for him, and I can't protect him from his own choices. With God's help I'll learn to live with this revelation.

I can only think of dragging myself upstairs to shower and relax in my bed with a good book. If there's one thing I do well, it's to allow myself the luxury of slipping away from reality and into the release of an intriguing story. Do I ever need that right now.

I jerk awake when Emma lifts my book out of my hands. Her brows are knit together, and her ready grin is absent. I wonder what's wrong. Remnants of a bad dream shimmer in my memory.

Oh no. It's no dream. Nick and Amber are going to have a baby.

Emma sits on the side of my bed. She looks so sad.

"Did Dad tell you?"

She sighs. "Yeah. It will be all right, though, won't it?"

It's my turn to sigh. "Yes. One way or another."

We sit together, lost in our own thoughts.

"Well, there're going to be a lot of changes around here," I say. "Another person in the family and—"

"No. Two."

I know I just awoke, but I'm having a hard time understanding her. "What?"

"Two new people in the family. The baby."

"Yes, the baby." A warm bundle of love to hold and to cherish. It seems unreal to me that in about five months Nick will be a father.

Goodness. That means Jerry will be a grandfather—and I'll be a grandma!

"Mom, what's with the funny look?"

52

I punch on the radio and turn up the Christmas music on my drive home from work. My spirits need lifting. I can't believe it's Wednesday and more than half the week is over. Since the bombshell Nick dropped on us last Saturday, time has been evaporating like the tiny snowman on my neighbor's south-facing front lawn.

Nick and Amber are cooking dinner tonight, and Ross and Doris will be joining us. I've spoken only briefly to Ross since he found out about the baby. As usual, he's a rock. Just like his son.

My street looks like a fairyland with all the Christmas lights on the houses winking in the cold, dark night. I pull into the driveway and see Ross's car parked on the street behind Nick's.

Laughter greets me when I enter the house. Nobody seems to notice I've come home, except for Belle. She urges me into the kitchen, where everyone is gathered. A delightful fragrance is coming from my oven. "That smells wonderful. What did you cook?"

Nick smiles at me. "Amber made ziti."

That's one of my special recipes. Nick's favorite. "Great. Excuse me while I run upstairs and change."

I think they barely notice I've left the room.

On my way upstairs, Jerry's happy whistle filters from our room. I walk in and close the door. When he sees me, his pucker turns to a grin. I start to walk past him toward the closet, but he grabs my arm. "Why the long face?"

Are you serious? "Stuff." I try to continue on my way, but my arm remains in his grasp.

"You're going to be the most beautiful grandma in Colorado."

In spite of my mood, I smile. This guy knows how to handle me.

Jerry pulls me close and gives me a kiss. "Hurry up and get changed. Dinner's ready. Oh, and leave your sourpuss up here."

I screw up my mouth and scowl at Mr. Cheerful. "Whatever."

When I come downstairs, Doris is sitting in the living room with Amber. They both startle as if I'm interrupting. *Did their voices lower in their conversation?*

I hesitate. *Shall I ignore them and seek out Ross?*

Before I can act, Doris comes toward me with her arms out. "Thank you for the invitation."

"Oh, you're welcome." We untangle from one another. "It's not as if I even made dinner. Nick and Amber took care of that."

Doris looks to Amber and smiles. "From what I've heard, the meal was all prepared by this young lady."

I wonder what recipe she used. *Did Nick give her mine?* "Well, I can't wait to sample it."

We head toward the kitchen.

Amber lingers on the couch. "Uh, Doris?"

The older woman returns to her, and I continue on. I know it's silly, but for a moment I feel excluded.

Emma's chattering as she helps Ross lay the silverware. The oven timer dings, and I'm surrounded by everyone grabbing for a seat. I step back and watch this new dance. We've never had both Doris and Amber join us for dinner. Will I even get my usual seat?

Jerry pulls out my chair and gestures. At least my guy's looking out for me.

We all settle in, Nick carries dinner to the table, and Jerry says a blessing.

The garlic bread Amber's prepared smells divine. I'm one of those girls who can never have too much garlic. Fragrant steam rises as I pull a piece off the loaf. I take a bite. "Mmm. This is wonderful."

Amber smiles as though she expected that response.

"We've got news."

Everyone focuses on Nick. *More news?* His last few announcements have been doozies. What more could he have to tell us?

"We're getting married in two weeks." He grins.

"How can that be possible?" *Heaven forbid—is he going to be married by a justice of the peace?* "Where? Who will perform the ceremony?"

Amber puts down her fork. "We're getting married at Doris's house."

"I have the room, and I would be honored to host the wedding." Doris couldn't look more pleased.

This is a surprise. "Who will officiate? Is Pastor John available?"

Nick shakes his head and speaks around a mouthful of ziti. "No, but we've got a great guy to perform the ceremony."

A great guy? What kind of great guy? "Who?"

He mentions a name I've never heard of. "But he comes on Pastor John's recommendation."

Whew. One less worry.

"Amber?" Emma sounds tentative. "What about a wedding gown? What will you wear?"

She reaches for the shaker of cheese. "Uh, I think I have a gown. A friend is getting it for me."

Something seems amiss, but I'm not going to get into the middle of that.

Emma's not finished with her questions. "Will you still have bridesmaids?"

Amber blushes. "Those plans have changed." She takes a bite of bread.

I know Emma had her heart set on being a bridesmaid. This could cause a problem.

Amber washes her food down with a drink of tea. "But I still want you in the party, Emma."

I'm beginning to feel more like an observer than a participant in this affair. "What can I do to help?"

Amber smiles at me. "Oh, I don't want to intrude on you. Letting us move in is more than we expected."

She doesn't want to intrude on my time or she doesn't want me involved in their plans?

"Won't this be a wonderful Christmas season?" Ross is ever the diplomat. "A family wedding. How exciting."

I'm feeling less than excited and more than excluded. "What about a shower? We could do one of those Jack and Jill showers, and you could both attend."

"I'm not sure about that," Amber says. "After all, isn't it considered bad form for a parent to host a shower?"

I quietly fume. I bet my face is as red as the ziti sauce.

The conversation falls silent for a moment until Jerry says, "What color paint do you like, Amber?"

Why would he ask a question like that?

Amber glances at him as if she's got the same question on her mind.

"Let me explain," Jerry continues. "If you're moving in, we should paint Nick's room and get it ready for you."

Amber beams. "I like blue."

"That's great," Jerry says. "We have some left over in the basement. Just a few weeks ago I bought—"

Is he crazy? "Please don't tell me you're considering that discounted paint you bought for our room."

"Dad!" Emma looks like she could shake him. "That color is hideous."

Nick gets a good laugh out of the situation. "I'll take Amber to the store to pick out paint. And I guess we better get some new furniture."

I must have a question in my glance because he continues. "Well, for one thing, we both won't fit in my single bed."

That's a conversation stopper if I ever heard one.

Jerry smiles one of his plastic grins. "Pop, would you please pass the garlic bread?"

53

I settle into my Victorian chair and listen to Debbie scold me for not calling her sooner with our big news.

"I'm telling you now." The tone of my voice conveys my emotion. "Sorry. I don't mean to sound so shrill."

"Do you really think I would judge or condemn Nick and Amber?"

"No, I just haven't been broadcasting the news."

"Telling your best friend isn't broadcasting."

"I know. Well, what are you doing the third Friday in December?"

"Of course I'll come."

My nerves are soothed just knowing Deb's coming to the wedding. "You'll get an invitation. I believe the RSVP will be my e-mail address." I guess that's what you have to do with a quickie wedding. "One more thing. I told Tammy and Steve from across the street, and Tammy's going to host a bridal shower."

"Let me know when, and I'll be there." I hear the sound of her chiming doorbell in the background. "Gotta go, hon. I'm showing the house."

I hang up the phone and look at the to-do list that taunts me from the refrigerator door. I usually go nuts cleaning when we're going to have houseguests. You won't believe how thoroughly I'll be cleaning before Amber moves in. I can't risk her scrutinizing my housekeeping abilities and thinking I'm not clean enough.

Today's a day off because I'm working Saturday. I'd like to clean my baseboards—no, wait, I don't *want* to clean my baseboards, but the dust buildup in the bathrooms is unbelievable. Anyway, instead of doing that, we're going to get a tree. We usually pick it out together, but Em has a cheerleading meeting this afternoon and Jerry's stuck at school, so the task will fall to Nick and me.

I'm loading my lunch dishes in the washer when I hear Nick come in the door. I dry my hands and meet him in the hall. Amber's with him. "Hi, kids."

They're both bright eyed and red cheeked. "Listen, Mom. I know you were expecting me to help you with the tree, but I was able to get an extra shift at work tonight."

I guess the holidays are busy times for baristas. But it's a job with flexible hours that accommodates a student. Still, I'm disappointed.

"I was really counting on you, Nick."

He smiles at me. "That's why Amber's here. She'll go with you to buy the tree."

I would much prefer to have Nick with us, but maybe it's a good thing that it will be just the two of us. We'll have time to bond. "Wonderful. Will you be ready in five minutes, Amber?"

"I'm ready now."

"All right, then. Let's go." I pull my coat out of the closet.

Amber's at my elbow. "Do you want to take my car?"

Hmm. Can I picture myself driving the streets in town with a Raft Naked decal on the rear window? I don't think so. "That's okay. I'll drive."

As we climb into my car, I wonder if I should put on the radio. *What will we talk about?* "Oh, my girlfriend from across the street would like to host a bridal shower for you. She's known Nick for years, and she's a dear friend. I know what you said, but I think her feelings will—"

"That's okay. That will be nice." Amber looks pleased.

I'm relieved. One less hurdle to handle. "Would you give me a list of friends you'd like to invite?"

She nods.

"Amber, may I ask you a question?"

She glances at me in a nervous sort of way. "Sure."

"What about your parents? Will they be coming to the wedding?"

Amber gazes out the window as if she never heard my question. After a moment, she sighs and says, "I had a falling-out with my mother about three years ago. We haven't spoken since."

"Where is she now?"

The look Amber gives me breaks my heart. "I don't know. I wrote to her about a year ago and sent the letter to our old address in Indiana, but my letter came back undeliverable."

"What about your dad?"

Amber shrugs. "My mom's the only family I've known."

"Oh." I don't often find myself speechless, but I don't know what to say.

Amber runs her hand over her seat belt. "My birth certificate says 'father unknown.'"

My nurturing instincts kick in, and a wave of pity washes over me for the poor girl. I recall my father, gone for years now, and the richness he brought to my life. I can't imagine what life would be like without the context of a person behind the title *father*. To have never known his love, his laugh, his hugs would have left me with an empty place in my heart.

I think back to the first time Amber and I met, when I thought she acted as though she was better than me. It looks like I've jumped to the wrong conclusion again. She doesn't have a superiority complex; she's a lonely and sad girl.

"What about grandparents, aunts, and uncles?"

She shakes her head. "My mother was estranged from her family before I was born. I've gotten the impression that they wanted her to have an abortion. So she left."

OUT OF HER HANDS

My hand flies to my heart. "That's terrible." What a burden for a child, to know you're unwanted by those who should love you. "I'm very sorry."

"I'm okay with it."

"That knowledge must be so difficult to bear." I wonder how someone, without the help of the Almighty, can withstand such sorrow. "I can't imagine being utterly alone at such a young age. You're a very strong woman."

A smile creeps back to Amber's face. "I'm not alone. I've got Nick."

I reach over and pat her knee. My eyes mist, and I talk around the lump forming in my throat. "That's true. And now you've got me and Jerry and Emma."

It looks like I'm not the only one with a tender heart. She bats her eyes. "Thanks, Linda."

Soon she'll be a Revere. She'll be Nick's wife, and they'll be their own family unit. That's the way it should be. I understand that it's God's plan that Nick leaves us and becomes one with Amber, but that old things change causes sadness to creep into my heart. I glance at Amber's profile and know that I have to let go of my son and establish a relationship with Amber. I need to be a mother to her.

"Amber?"

"Yes?"

"I'm glad we have this time together. I hope we can always make time for our relationship."

Amber seems touched by our conversation. "Me too."

We both try to control our emotions, and I pull into the lot of the home improvement store.

The fresh Christmas trees are displayed in the home and garden center at the right side of the giant building. It's an area that is attached to the main store and is enclosed with a front wall, plastic ceiling, and heavy-duty plastic sheeting on the back and side.

The sun breaks through some clouds just as we walk inside. It smells divine. The trees are stacked like toy soldiers up and down the aisles. The choices are overwhelming, the trees nearly blending together as they lean against one another, standing upright. We stroll through the store, inspecting the inventory, tugging on needles, pulling the occasional tree out from the others.

We turn a corner. *Oh, be still my heart.*

"Wow." Amber stops beside me.

So she notices too. About fifteen feet in front of us, a brilliant sunbeam falls onto the most exquisite tree I've ever seen.

We approach the tree at an almost reverent pace. One could imagine a choir of angels singing as we're drawn to the beauty in front of us. The noble fir beckons us forward by the sheer magnetism of its perfection. What a tree. I've never seen such a paragon of symmetry. If you saw it in a photograph you would assume it was artificial.

"What did Nick say about the size we were supposed to get?" Amber's voice pulls me from my trance.

"I think he said we usually get a six- to eight-footer."

She reaches for the plastic tag. "Oh no. This is an eight- to ten-foot tree."

A pang of disappointment passes through me. "Well, our living room has a volume ceiling. Height really shouldn't be a problem."

Amber's expression brightens. "Why don't you hold it up and I'll step back to see how big it really is."

"Good idea." I drop my purse and move the tree a few inches so it stands straight. I think it's calling out to me. *Take me home. Take me home.*

She walks about ten feet away and turns around. I feel the gentle light fall upon my head as I stand beside the fir.

Amber's face is a study in rapture. Her ethereal smile sets her face aglow, and she clasps her hands over her heart. "It's perfect, just perfect."

"I couldn't agree more."

"You hold on to the tree, and I'll get some help."

Amber returns with a young man who appears a little too eager to help her. He grasps the tree and, in a manly display, carries it to the front of the store, where he cuts a few inches off the bottom and runs it through a machine to encase it in plastic mesh.

I pay an attendant. The young man comes up to us and stands the tree on its end, holding it out to me. "Here ya go."

I have to tilt my head back to see the top of this large conifer. "Uh, could you please tie it to our car?"

He winces. "I'm not allowed."

"Sir, we couldn't possibly hoist this tree onto the roof of my car, and—"

Amber puts her hand on my arm and steps forward. "Oh, please? Please can't you help us?" She smiles and dips her chin.

Wow. This girl is good.

Before you can say *merry Christmas*, this young buck has the tree slung over his shoulder and is following Amber's attractive form outside.

Now, I know a 1999 Ford Taurus isn't a huge car, but this tree, when strapped to the top, dwarfs the vehicle.

Could it be possible that we've gotten a little carried away in choosing this beauty? Nah.

54

Well, surprise, surprise. Nick and Amber joined us at church this morning. It seemed awkward at first with her there, but by the end of the service, I was grooving on having a larger family surround me. I know the Lord's been moving in my heart, and combined with the bonding experience we had Friday buying our Christmas tree, I think Amber and I are truly making progress. After all, if you can agree on the perfect Christmas tree, that's got to say something.

By the time I got home from work yesterday, the tree was almost entirely decorated. Amber seemed so proud of herself for taking charge that I couldn't mention I would have strung the lights a little differently. And she didn't hang the doves at the top of the tree like I do each year, but whatever.

Emma and Cole are having dinner with his family, so it will be only the four of us for lunch. We meet in the kitchen, and I wash my hands to set up our sandwich buffet. Amber hangs her jacket over the back of a chair and opens the refrigerator. Isn't that a little presumptuous? I remember the progress our relationship has taken and try not to get ruffled. After all, in a few weeks this will be her house too.

"What shall I take out, Linda?"

"You can step aside. It'll be faster for me to grab our fixings."

She smiles and lets me get to work. Nick calls her into the living room, and I hear him giving her a history of our family's ornaments.

A thought occurs to me. I wonder if I should launder that little seersucker suit of Nick's that I've been holding on to? Maybe if their baby's a boy, he'll wear it just like his father did.

When the table's set, I call the kids to join Jerry and me for lunch. It almost feels normal to have Amber with us. When we're nearly finished with our sandwiches, Jerry retrieves a cheesecake from the fridge.

I'd be happy to just sit and savor the calories, but I've got something to discuss with my future daughter-in-law. "Don't forget. Your wedding shower's this Friday night."

Amber looks at Nick, and they grin at each other like a couple of lovesick puppies.

• • •

"Mom, are you ready?" Emma yells from the foyer.

Tonight my friend Tammy is hosting the wedding shower. After all was said and done, it was decided it would be a girls-only affair. I guess that's a good thing. Jerry looked at me as if I asked him to go bungee jumping when I suggested he would attend the shower. So Emma and I will join the women across the street while my manly men go to the Gray Pony for dinner.

"Give me a sec. I'm still wrapping." I step out to the top of the stairs. "I have another gift that I just thought of this afternoon."

Emma trots up to me. "What is it?"

I shake my head. "Just a little surprise. A sentiment, actually."

She knits her eyebrows. "What?"

"Never mind. You'll see." I'm so thrilled about this little idea that I practically float down the stairs.

We leave our jackets in the closet and dash across the street before the chill of the evening has the chance to sink into our bones. Tammy's house is dressed for Christmas, and the fragrances of cider and fresh pine drift throughout.

Tammy greets us at the door. "Emma, go see what's taking Lyndsay so long to get dressed."

My daughter runs upstairs to her friend's room.

Several young women have made themselves comfortable in the living room. I follow Tammy to the kitchen. There are platters of snacks on the island counter. Everything looks delicious.

"Thanks. This is wonderful of you." I catch Tammy in a hug.

She pats my back. "I'm glad to help. This wedding is making for an exciting holiday season, isn't it?"

"Yeah." *But excitement like this, I really don't need.*

As I carry a tray of cookies into the living room, headlights wink through the front windows. I walk to the door and see Deb park in front of my house and Amber pull into my driveway.

As they cross the street, it looks like Deb's introducing herself to Amber. They shake hands and enter the house together.

Amber's friends mob her when she comes in, and Deb gives me a hug.

I take her coat and put it in the closet. "Thanks for coming."

She adjusts her glasses. "Wouldn't miss this for anything."

The doorbell rings. Lyndsay and Emma skip down the stairs to answer the door. A lilting voice bids everyone good evening. Doris carries a large, professionally wrapped gift as she steps inside. One of Amber's friends takes it from her and places it with the other presents on the dining room table.

Amber rushes through the crowd to give Doris a hug. "I'm so glad you could come. I've saved you a seat by me." She leads her over to the couch.

Interesting. Why don't I have a special seat?

Music begins to play, and we all settle in for an evening of that ceremonial feminine rite of passage. Someone asks Lyndsay for a paper plate and scissors. Are they really going to make one of those goofy hats for Amber?

The same girl who sent Lyndsay off to find the plate and scissors continues to be bossy. "Talia, here's a notepad. Take notes on who gives what gift. Make sure you write down what Amber says when she opens it and the comments other people make."

I glance at Tammy. She smiles at me as if she's relieved to not have to play hostess.

The dictatorial girl commands someone to carry in the stack of gifts and place them by Amber's chair.

I grab a seat next to Deb. I can't wait to see what gifts Amber gets. And I can't wait to see what she thinks of my little present.

55

Amber's pushy friend is named Millie. She's got the gifts stacked and has appointed herself as the person who decides the order in which gifts get opened.

"Open this one. It's from me." Millie places a large gift bag on Amber's lap.

My future daughter-in-law eyes the gift suspiciously. I think that says something about Millie. Amber gingerly removes the tissue paper from the bag. She pulls out a canvas tote bag with bawdy images that says, "Stimulate your senses."

Some of the girls start to hoot. "Open it. What's inside?"

Amber's face colors, but she peeks inside and begins to assemble the products from within on the end table next to her.

Edible body paint. *Really?*

Herbal bath salts. Scented candle. *Now, those I can approve of.*

A Do Not Disturb sign. *No comment.*

The last item is a bottle of flavored body massage oil. I hope Talia's editing the comments that are being made about that gift.

The next package Amber opens contains a pair of tiny white thongs with the words *Blushing Bride* spelled out in rhinestones. *Blushing bride, my left foot.*

"Those are Swarovski crystals on that thong," one of the girls yells out.

Too much information. Okay, next.

Finally, a package large enough to contain something other than play toys for the happy couple. The beautifully wrapped package is carefully opened. From inside, Amber pulls another beautifully wrapped package and another. Finally inside the last package, which is the size of a box that would hold a pair of earrings, she withdraws a . . . I guess it's a negligee. It's about the size of a thimble.

I'm relieved to see Deb's gift presented to Amber. At least this one won't make me sweat. It's a KitchenAid mixer. Nice gift. And it's such a pretty shade of green.

The present from Emma and me comes next. Amber removes the paper. "What's inside the box?" She looks at me.

What does the box say? "It's packaged in the box it arrived in from the factory. That's the gift." I'm a little disappointed, and I'm sure Emma is too. She helped me pick out the nativity set.

Amber has the good sense to remove the lovely manger from the box. She appears puzzled.

I try to clear up the confusion. "You know, Nick loves Christmas. I thought it would be nice to start you on a collectible." *Has she never seen a nativity set?*

Amber nods as though she's beginning to understand. "Thanks."

Emma rises onto her knees. "It's called Fontanini. It's made in Italy. Hand-painted. It will be an heirloom."

I notice that Talia's not writing down much of our conversation.

Millie covers the awkward moment by passing more gifts to Amber. One girl gave her a cookbook. That's nice and safe. Then she opens a lovely silver photo frame. *Thank goodness, another normal present.* Next comes the gift from Doris. It's a large juicer.

Amber gives the older woman a hug. "Thank you. I've always wanted one but could never afford one as nice as this."

Tammy and Lyndsay give her a toaster oven. My relatives from back east sent mixing bowls, a coffeemaker, and kitchen goods.

"Is that it?" Millie looks disappointed that the opening of the gifts is over. She looks at one of the girls behind her. "Is that hat finished?"

Poor Amber. One of the girls has put all the ribbons and bows together on the paper plate. How ridiculous. It looks like something you'd see a horse wear trotting around Central Park in New York City.

"Wait. There's one more." I go to my big purse and take out the small box. It's wrapped in the same paper I used for the nativity set. I hand it to Amber. "This is from me."

I take my seat and wait to see her reaction to my gift. She gives the box a little shake. Somewhere along the line, the music ended. And now conversation is suspended. All eyes are on Amber as she opens my special surprise.

She runs her finger along the Scotch tape and releases one end of the packaging. The box slips out, and she lifts the top of it and folds back the tissue paper.

My pulse is skipping with anticipation. I hope she appreciates the sentiment this gift embodies. This could be a turning point. At least I hope it will cement our nascent relationship.

She peeks into the box and then tilts it toward Doris for her to see. Doris raises her eyebrows. *Why isn't Amber saying anything? Why isn't she taking it out of the box?*

Talia cranes her neck. "What is it?"

Amber picks up the cotton paisley material and holds it in front of her with the fabric hanging down. She glances at me. "I don't get it."

One of the girls speaks up. "Is it something torn? What's with the threads?"

Oh, honestly. "No, it's not torn. I took it apart."

They all stare at me as if I'm a kook.

I walk over and take it from Amber. "It's apron strings. And here's the apron." I grin at the gaggle of girls gawking at me. *Are they all really that dense?*

Doris puts her hand to her heart. "I understand. How nice."

Finally. "Thank you."

Most of the people in the room still appear clueless. Deb smiles as if she's embarrassed for me, and Emma truly looks embarrassed.

"It's a symbolic gesture."

They all continue to gape.

"I cut the apron strings and gave them to Amber. I'm saying that my son is hers now."

A voice from the back of the room pipes up. "I'd say he's been hers for months now."

Her nasty friends all titter. *Swell.*

From the corner of my eye, I see Doris poke Amber with her elbow. They exchange a private glance, and then Amber gives me a hug. "Thanks, Linda. That's sweet."

I accept her hug, but it seems too little, too late. Why is it that we take two steps forward and three steps backward in our relationship? And why am I left to feel like the awkward one most of the time?

56

Deb and I just finished a five-hour shopping marathon to find—
ugh—a mother-of-the-groom dress. After trudging from store to
store, we finally picked an appropriate one that didn't cost an arm
and a leg. I can't wait to wear it. It's an elegant and shimmering
dress and appears to be both sapphire and black at the same time.
This gem has a square neck, long sleeves, and a flared skirt that falls
below my knees. I think Jerry will like it.

Emma joined us just long enough to pick out a new dress for
herself and have me pay for it. She and Talia will be Amber's only
bridesmaids. Because of the time crunch, Amber's only instruction
to them was to wear a silver dress. Silver wouldn't have been a color
I would have thought of, but then it's not my wedding.

I think Emma's beauty will rival the bride's. She chose a gorgeous, full-length dress that makes her look stunning. The regal
satin gown has a demure scoop neck and an empire waist. When
she modeled it in the dressing room, she walked as though she
were floating on air.

In less than a week, my son will be married. If someone told me
a wedding could be planned in a few weeks, I'd have thought they
were nuts. But apparently it can be done, and Doris is the woman

to do it. She won't even hear of me helping her. I think it's an overwhelming task, but Ross said to let her be.

We didn't even stop for lunch during our shopping spree. Now my stomach is beginning to protest. "Let's find somewhere to get a bite to eat."

Deb smiles her approval. "I can't wait to sit down. My feet are screaming."

We settle on California Cafe. A young hostess leads us over to a cozy booth. Behind us, a circular fireplace infuses the atmosphere with warmth. Christmas music is a subtle background to the hushed conversations of other diners. A waiter greets us, and we order an appetizer to split and hot tea.

Debbie stares out the window, watching shoppers bustle through the mall.

"Deb?"

She looks at me with a hint of a smile playing at her lips. "You know what I was thinking about?"

"What?"

"Christmas trees in playpens."

We both laugh, and Deb continues, "Remember that year when we were afraid our toddlers would pull the trees down on top of them, and you read that a solution was to put the trees in our kids' playpens?"

What a year. "Wow, that was so long ago, but it really feels like just yesterday. What made you think of that?"

"You'll be blessed to spend next Christmas with your grandbaby."

I peer into the future with dreamy eyes. I can't wait to hold that warm bundle of love.

Before I can respond to Deb's amazing statement, the waiter stops by and delivers our tea. He places our teacups and pots just so and leaves.

I pour steaming orange and spice tea into my cup. "You know, a baby's first Christmas ornament caught my eye in one of the stores today."

Debbie reaches across the table and takes my hand. "There will be so many blessings to come from this marriage. You know that, don't you?"

I don't know if I'd go so far as to say that. I open my mouth to temper her enthusiasm.

But she continues, "I know how much you love your family and that you would do anything to protect them. But you've got to get on board with these changes. I've been listening to you and watching you, and I can see you're resisting. This is reality, and if you don't throw your heart into being the best mother-in-law and the most wonderful grandma, you'll be the one missing out."

Irritation creeps into this lovely moment. "I'm trying. You saw the shower gift I gave Amber and the lukewarm response she gave me. And—"

"Stop!"

Her passion stuns me into silence.

Deb lowers her voice a notch. "Stop saying you're trying, and just do it. Just act as if she's the girl you always dreamed Nick would find."

I scoop my jaw up from the floor and snap my mouth shut. Within moments, several replies form in my mind, but fortunately they never make it out of my mouth.

Deb's gaze holds mine. Her beautiful face is full of love as she scolds some sense into me.

Warmth from my pounding heart floods to my face, and a grin takes over my frozen features. I will be the loser if I can't change my attitude. *Oh, goodness, I'm going to weep.* "You're right."

She shakes her head like she's relieved I'm finally seeing the light.

The waiter delivers our order of chicken ginger spring rolls. Deb helps herself to one, and I search for a tissue in my purse to dry my tears.

• • •

When I get home, Jerry and Emma are eating Chinese food.

"Hey, we've got leftovers. Want some?"

"Nah. I'm more weary than hungry. Deb and I stopped for a bite." I kiss the top of Jerry's head and go upstairs to take a bubble bath. Nothing sounds better right now than soaking in warm, fragrant water.

When I finish bathing, I hear voices in the kitchen. I throw on my robe and go downstairs to investigate.

Ross and Doris are sitting at the table, watching Jerry make a pot of coffee.

Ross gives me a hug and pulls out a chair next to Doris.

Doris inclines her head toward me. "Hi. I heard you had a successful shopping trip today."

"Sure did." I think about my talk with Deb and my forced revelation. "It was a good day in more ways than one."

Doris has a kind smile. She absentmindedly fingers one of her small hoop earrings. She's wearing a pale green matching sweater set, and a shiny Christmas brooch on the lapel of the sweater glimmers in the light.

"What about you?" I ask her. "Do you have a dress for the wedding?"

"When you get to be my age, you've got stacks of clothes piled up in your closet. I'm sure there's something for me to wear and look halfway decent in."

I grin and agree. I hope her offer to host the wedding isn't putting a strain on the dear woman. Jerry brings the coffeepot to the table. After I heat my mug in the microwave, I turn to my husband. "Decaf?"

He nods.

Ross gazes at Jerry and me with concern in his eyes. "I'm still planning on going to California with Doris for Christmas."

I force a smile. "We'll be fine. You and Doris have a wonderful time."

He puts his hand on Doris's back. "She's going to need a getaway after this wedding's over."

I take a sip of coffee and hold the warm mug in both hands. "Are you sure I can't help you, Doris? Maybe help clean or decorate? Anything?"

"No, I think I've got it covered. I occasionally hosted parties for my late husband's company, and I'm sure I can handle this."

Ross beams at her. It looks like he has all the confidence in the world that she can do it.

I take another drink to keep from saying the wrong thing. I hope hosting the wedding won't be too overwhelming for Doris.

57

This day is passing much too quickly. I have more work to complete than time in which to do it. Especially since I'm leaving early for the rehearsal dinner and not working at all tomorrow on the big day. I'm still awestruck that Nick's getting married.

The door chime calls me to the lobby. This is one of our busiest weeks, and a steady stream of clients has been passing through, each eager to pick up their portraits in time to wrap and send off to friends and family out of town. I hustle out of the office to greet another client.

"Hello, Linda."

Oh, what's her name? That woman was so nice to me a while ago when I was having a bad moment. The Lord must be whispering in my ear because before the moment gets awkward, my overstuffed brain cycles through the data inside. I smile. "Hi, Joyce. It's nice to see you again."

She looks pleased I called her by name.

"Did you receive a call saying your order is ready?"

"You must have a crack staff because I got a call yesterday, and I didn't expect it to be ready until after the holidays."

Whew. I would hate to have to disappoint this woman. "What about your parents' order?"

"Yeah, that one too."

I leave her and go in search of the portraits. Our storage room is jam-packed with orders ready to be picked up. If everyone who has portraits due comes in, next week will be murder too. I don't have any trouble locating the Roarks' order and the one for Joyce's parents, the Sullivans.

I spread out the portraits on our delivery counter, and Joyce and I scrutinize them. I inspect each image with an eagle eye, wanting these clients to get error-free portraits. I'm relieved that the workers in the back room are doing their jobs well. "Everything looks perfect. Are you pleased?"

Joyce stands with her hands clasped. "They look beautiful. I'm thrilled to have them ahead of schedule. Mom is too."

I put them back into their boxes and bags. "May I help you to your car?"

"Thanks." Joyce scoops her keys out of her pocket and picks up the large wall portrait.

I grab the big bag full of smaller boxed prints and follow her out the door. She loads the large portrait into her trunk, and then I hand her the other bag. "Well, have a wonderful Christmas."

"You too." She looks at me as if she's going to say something more.

I start to walk away, then pause. "And please give your lovely parents my best regards and wish them a merry Christmas."

Joyce turns as she opens her car door, her expression filled with joy. "This may be the merriest Christmas in decades."

Her smile is so dazzling that I can't help myself. "May I ask why?"

"We're having a family reunion."

"How nice." I'm glad good things are happening to this sweet family.

Joyce drives off, and I hurry back into the warmth of the studio.

"Oh, there you are. Luke's been looking for you." Barb is manning the reception desk as I come inside.

"Thanks." I tear down the hall in search of my boss. Today of all days, he's got company at the studio. A photographer from Philadelphia is in the state for a ski vacation, and he's stopped by to see how Dream Photography runs. Why couldn't he have taken his vacation in January like other photographers?

I find them both in Luke's office, hunched over the computer. My boss looks up and leans back in his chair. "There she is."

"What can I do for you?" *As if I don't have enough work to finish so I can get out of here on time.*

"Linda, this is Adam Flint," Luke says. "He's got a studio in suburban Philadelphia. I would like you to give him the nickel tour, and then he's going to join me in the studio for a joint photo session."

"Sure, I'm happy to give a tour." *As long as it only takes a few minutes.* I guess he'll get the three-cent tour.

I lead Adam out of the office. We start in the workroom, and I give him an explanation of each workstation, barely taking a breath throughout my speech. "Any questions?"

Before he can formulate a response, I usher him out the door and into a vacant salesroom. I begin my brisk explanation. The poor man, his head is jerking this way and that as I gesture throughout the room and explain our process.

We leave the salesroom and work our way through the gallery hallways. I sneak a peek at my watch. I've got to wrap this up and get out of here in thirty minutes if I hope to shower before dinner.

"This is an interesting image. May I ask how this effect was accomplished?"

I force myself not to grind my teeth. "I think perhaps one of the imaging artists would be the best person to help you with that. Let's finish the tour. I know Luke wants me to explain our file protocol. Let's go to the lobby so I can show you some examples."

Adam follows me at a snail's pace, pausing to inspect the images displayed on the walls. "Now who did you say you purchase frames from?"

Fortunately my back is to him, so he doesn't see me roll my eyes. "I'll be happy to supply you with one of our vendor lists. All the information you'd want is there."

When we get to the lobby, it's filled with customers clamoring for their portraits. Barb looks overwhelmed as she sorts out who needs assistance.

Drawing in a deep breath, I turn to Adam. "Can you give me a minute? I really should help some of these clients."

He smiles broadly. "Actually, I'm happy to be a fly on the wall."

I greet the client who appears the most annoyed, assuming she's been waiting longest. She passes me her invoice, and I head to the storage room.

After locating the portrait I need, I return to the lobby and place it on the easel sitting on the display counter.

The client stares at the image with rapture. "Oh, it's perfect."

I conclude our business and retrieve another order from storage, then heft the large wall portrait onto the easel.

The client puts her purse down and cocks her head as she studies the portrait. "Um. What about this?"

I don't see anything. "Where?"

She points to the background. "Shouldn't that be a little lighter? You can barely make it out."

Of course like usual, whenever a client complains, you can hear a pin drop in the lobby. Everyone else wants to know what's going on.

"Well—" I move closer.

"Excuse me." Adam steps between us. "I'm a friend of Luke's, also a photographer. May I give you some advice?" He smiles an absolutely disarming grin and discusses a theory of making the subject of the image more prominent with lighting effects and placement in the studio.

Within two minutes the client is thrilled with Adam's explanation of the artistic rendering of her portrait. She thanks him profusely and exits the building.

I smile at Adam. "Bravo."

"Glad to help."

"Sir?" We both turn to another client who watched his previous interaction. "Can I get your opinion?"

I'm glad Adam's here to deflect some of the client attention. I watch him weave his magic for a moment, then turn my attention to another gentleman who's been waiting patiently. Between me, Barb, and Adam, we help all the clients who have descended on the studio.

What an afternoon. The door chimes again, and the client scheduled to have a photo session with Luke and Adam enters. Barb greets her, and I offer to run to the studio and retrieve Luke.

When we return to the lobby, Adam and Rachel are chuckling like old pals. Luke escorts them both back to the studio.

I can't believe it, but all seems quiet in the studio. I glance at my watch. *Goodness, where did the day go? I'm outta here.*

58

"Can I borrow your cubic zirconia earrings?" Emma's standing barefoot in the cutest black skirt that stops just short of her knees. Her ivory sweater has strands of sparkling gold shot through it. She looks gorgeous.

"Sure." I gesture to my jewelry box. "Top drawer."

She rummages around until she finds the jewelry. As she pokes her left earring in, she sits on my bed. "Make sure you watch for Cole. He said he'll be at the restaurant by seven thirty."

She's such a little mother hen. "Don't worry. We'll find him."

"Emma, let's go." Nick stomps down the stairs, jingling his car keys.

Em runs out and yells that she needs to put on her shoes. They're out the door in about ninety seconds.

Since it's such a small wedding and it's going to be a simple ceremony, only those in the wedding party are going to Doris's house for the rehearsal. Really, how long can it take? It's not as if it's a church wedding with ushers and pomp and ceremony. *Sigh.*

"What's wrong?" Jerry's hair is still wet from his shower. *Boy, he's cute.*

I remember my pledge to Deb and act as if this is what I've wanted all my life. I smile. "Just thinking. I always thought our kids would have a church wedding. But I'm getting on board with this one."

He nods his approval and I further explain. "Deb helped me understand that I'll be the loser if I don't extend myself more to Amber and fully accept Nick's choices."

"That's my girl." Jerry gives me a wink and walks into the closet to retrieve his clothes and finish dressing.

Bless me, Lord, with the right attitude.

I finish dressing, feed Belle, and meet Jerry in the living room. We drive the short distance to the restaurant and park on the other side of Main Street, behind the park.

I feel as if I've stepped into another world as we wind our way through the lit-up park to the street. Strands of illuminated white icicles dangle from the edge of the gazebo's roof, and clear lights strung on garland are draped around the charming pavilion. Gigantic white snowflake lights hang high above, suspended from the lofty cottonwoods, some blinking as if they're an illusion in the night sky. The trunks of the tall trees sparkle with a cloak of tightly wound white lights. The entire downtown twinkles in the December air, and even the Victorian streetlights dazzle passersby with necklaces of greenery accented with red velvet ribbons.

Jerry speaks over the passing traffic. "Did you tell Pop we'd be here by seven fifteen?"

"Yeah."

"At least it's not snowing."

"Yes, that's good."

Our breath hovers in puffs of vapor and dissipates as the words fall from our mouths. The conversation is awkward, an unusual circumstance for us, but then we're walking in new territory.

Jerry rests his hand on my back as we stroll through the double set of doors and into the Gray Pony Inn. The hostess greets us and leads us to a large table that runs down the center of the room. Santa's elves have visited. Each window is adorned with a swag of fir and an electric candle. A fire blazes in the fireplace. The mantel holds fresh greenery and glass bulbs; above it hangs a huge wreath.

Jerry sits at the head of the table, and I claim a chair next to him. We drape our coats over the chairs and pick up the menus. Conversation from nearby tables drifts by, and a log in the fire pops. I glance toward the door in time to see Ross walk in. He speaks to the hostess, then looks around. His expression lifts when he catches sight of us. He makes his way through the room with a young man at his elbow.

I stand and give him a hug.

He gestures to the good-looking fellow. "This is Kevin. He's the maid of honor's date this evening. We met up at the door." He takes the seat next to me.

Kevin sits next to Jerry. While we introduce ourselves, Cole joins us.

We order our beverages, and as they are being delivered, the wedding party comes in. We first notice Scott, the best man. He gives a small salute as he leads the group toward our table. Nick looks like he just found a million dollars, Amber glows with happiness, Emma smiles, Talia waves at Kevin, and Doris brings up the rear, looking like a fairy godmother who has just bestowed her best wish.

They join us chattering. If Nick or Amber are disappointed that their rehearsal dinner is less than anything they dreamed, they're not letting on. I can't help but compare it to Deb's son's rehearsal dinner last year. It was almost as extravagant as the reception the next day. They had at least fifty guests at that dinner, and it was held downtown at the Westin on the 16th Street Mall.

And here we sit with tables strung together in a casual atmosphere on rough plank wood floors. No glamour, no glitz, no waiters in pressed black trousers. I glance at the people who are so important to me, and heat floods to my face as tears form. Everyone here is healthy and content. They're all gathered for a joyous occasion. So what that we're not in an elegant, upscale dining room. The ambience of this cozy inn is perfect. It's warm and fragrant with the aromas of a burning fire and fresh Christmas greens.

The sound of footsteps on this wooden floor is a part of our family memories. We've spent so many happy moments at this restaurant. And here's another one unfolding before my eyes. *Thank You, Lord, for this blending of our lives with Amber's.* I determine to make more of an effort to grow close to Amber. After all, I'll be the only mother she's got.

Nick grins while Amber talks and gestures. I recognize the light of love in his eyes. Emma leans in, hanging on every word. Amber delivers her punch line, and everyone laughs. Doris claps and shakes her head. Ross adjusts the collar of his sweater and relaxes his arm across the back of Doris's chair.

Maybe this marriage won't be the worst thing to happen in our family. Maybe Deb was right. Maybe many blessings will result from this union. My heart's greatest desire is for Nick and Amber to have a marriage as rich and wonderful as mine.

Jerry's fingers brush my cheek, pulling me back from my reflections. I smile as I lean toward him. "Yes?"

"Are you okay?"

I put my hand on his and slowly nod. "Uh-huh. Finally."

"That's my girl."

When our waiter comes over to take our orders, conversation pauses. I'm not surprised when Jer asks for the naked burger. He's such a creature of habit. A cell phone chirps. Amber fishes around in her purse until she finds the phone. Her eyebrows rise, and she gives Nick what looks like a knowing glance. She answers the phone and walks to the end of the room, then puts a hand over her free ear and turns her back.

My heart thumps. *What's this about? Why would she leave her party? Is this something bad?* I study Nick. Concern clouds his features. The mood of the party shifts from celebration to one of guardedness. No one speaks.

Nick scrapes his chair back and crosses the room to his fiancée. He puts his arm around her shoulder. She's speaking and nodding.

Time stretches out like a rubber band as we watch the young couple. I hold my breath, fearing that either the rubber band will break and toss us into a world of anxiety or it will snap back with a disarming force. Either way, this can't be good.

Tears glisten on Amber's face when she ends the call and falls into Nick's embrace. He gives her a squeeze and leans down by her ear. *What could he be saying?* She nods and they walk back to the table. *Is she smiling through her tears?*

Amber picks up her napkin and blots her eyes. She drags in a deep breath. "Well, I've got unexpected news."

59

I look out the window for the tenth time this hour. Snow? This wasn't forecast. And the wedding starts in two hours. Most of Nick and Amber's friends are coming from Denver, and I worry about them sliding down I-25.

I'm wrapped in my fluffy robe, sitting in Grandma's Victorian chair, trying to focus on prayer. My house is buzzing with activity. Nick is like a little boy, all fired up and talkative. Earlier he and Jerry were sequestered in the study. I think I heard them praying as I walked by. Emma seems so excited as she primps and sings.

I try to clear my mind, but all I can think about is Amber's extraordinary news. It seems she does have family who want to include her in their lives, and believe it or not, they live in Denver. She'll be meeting them for the first time after their honeymoon. Extraordinary. There was some talk about them coming to the wedding, but Amber's family was concerned that it might make for too emotional a reunion. I know Amber's disappointed. She can't wait to meet them. Turns out Nick has been searching for her relatives for the past few months. Amber knew that her mother left Colorado as a pregnant and angry young woman. She had a huge falling-out with her family and never spoke to them again. She barely told Amber anything about her roots and even led her to believe her relatives were all dead. I wonder if curiosity about her family drove Amber to come back to Colorado for college?

Good news: they want a relationship with her. Bad news: we don't know what kind of people they are. They could be doing this out of idle curiosity. Or maybe they think they can get back at Amber's mother through her.

I'm afraid that this could be a big disappointment for my future daughter-in-law. She was absolutely glowing when she returned to the table last night and told us her news. It will be a crime if her dream turns into a nightmare.

Apparently her elderly grandparents have been hoping to meet her before they die. And that story about them wanting Amber's mother to have an abortion? It couldn't be further from the truth.

We all pile into Jerry's SUV. It's been a long time since the four of us have driven anywhere together. Nick's leaving his car home. Amber spent the night at Doris's, and she and Nick will take her car on their honeymoon weekend.

The windshield wipers squeak as they fight to banish the onslaught of snow. Nick says it's only six miles to Doris's house, but part of it is uphill, and this weather is not making the short drive easy. I hope the guests arrive in time.

We turn east off Pine Grove Road. This is a pricey part of town. I never imagined that Doris lived here. We slowly ascend the hill to her street, our headlights illuminating dancing snowflakes.

"There it is, Dad. On the right."

Oh, sweet Christmas pie! This house is gigantic. Jerry puts on his turn signal and pulls into the driveway next to Ross's car.

I see the curtain shift by the door, and out comes Ross, grinning and carrying a huge umbrella. We manage to make it inside without getting too wet. Doris greets us with a hug. She seems to be relishing the role of wedding hostess.

I'm sure my eyes are as big as snowballs, gawking at this beautiful home. The foyer has a curving staircase, and the railing is adorned with fresh garland, grapevines, twinkling lights, and silver ribbon.

Every tabletop I see is filled with Christmas bouquets. The colors of the holiday are repeated in elegant decorations everywhere my glance rests, and the fragrances are delightful—pine, orange, spice, and carnations.

Never in my wildest dreams did I think Doris was so wealthy. And that's got to be an understatement. This home is dripping with money. The art hanging on the walls look like original pieces. *And is that an O'Keeffe?* Before I can edit my actions, I cross the enormous foyer to look at the colorful painting. "Is this real?"

Doris laughs. "If by that you mean is it an original, the answer is yes. My late husband and I owned a home in Santa Fe for a while, and we picked it up there."

A small woman hovers nearby and takes my coat.

Doris hired in help for the wedding? This is overwhelming.

"Now, Linda, make yourself at home. If you need to touch up before the ceremony, go upstairs to the first room on the right." Doris smiles in dismissal and joins Jerry and Ross.

Emma grabs my arm. "Wait till you see the rest of this house. It's amazing!" She leads me into the living room.

Doris's Christmas tree is covered in crystal and silver ornaments and white lights. The massive fireplace holds a gas fire, and the mantel is decorated with fresh greens and Byers' Choice caroler figurines. Rented silver chairs are arranged in rows facing the fireplace. Tall vases with red and white flowers are accented with sprigs of greenery and sparkly silver twigs.

"Let's go upstairs to Amber," Emma says. "Kim said Talia hasn't arrived yet."

I follow her down a wide hall to the kitchen and another staircase. "Who's Kim?"

She glances over her shoulder. "That's Doris's live-in help. Isn't she nice?"

Live-in help? I climb the stairs behind my daughter, almost numb with disbelief.

The top floor of this mansion is as gracious as the first. Thick carpet muffles our footsteps. Elegant side tables hold delicate lamps and bouquets of flowers and greens. Emma knocks at a door at the end of the hall, and Amber invites us in. She's dressed in a floor-length white slip with a white terry cloth robe over her shoulders. Her hair and makeup are perfectly styled.

We stand about four feet away from each other, regarding one another. I don't know what she sees, but I see a motherless girl about to make the most important decision in her life. Her expression is one of hope. I remember my wedding day and waiting for that big moment to go to Jerry while sitting with my dear mother. And here's Amber all alone.

Or maybe not. I'm here. My heart warms within my breast, and I open my arms. As if she was holding her breath, waiting for my invitation, Amber flies into my embrace. It feels so right, so perfect, to hold this young woman.

When we pull away, I give her light kiss on the cheek. "Well, are you ready?"

She throws her arms up. "I've been ready for this day since I first met Nick!"

She looks so happy and so strong. Jerry volunteered to escort her to her groom, but she was adamant that she was leaving her old, lonely life and would walk toward a new beginning all by herself. It makes my heart squeeze just to think of it.

A knock at the door announces Talia, and we all help Amber into her dress. Wait until Nick sees his bride. She is stunning in her white, crushed velvet gown. The softly fitted empire dress has a scoop neckline and silver satin ribbons that cascade down her back from the bustline in varying lengths. The most amazing snowflake sparkles made of tiny Austrian crystal beads are randomly arranged on the skirt. Her veil is held on her head with a silver comb and is accented with more Austrian crystals. To top it off, her bouquet is a gorgeous combination of deep red roses, pure white calla lilies, and more silver ribbons. Her dress was a gift from Doris.

The doorbell continues to announce more and more guests. It's about time for me to leave to go downstairs. "Amber? May I pray with you?"

She looks at me in pleasant surprise, I think. Emma and I hold Amber's hands, and Talia stands by. My daughter and I take turns praying blessings on this young woman, and I know my eyes are not the only ones misting up.

". . . and, Lord, please bless Amber. Help her to always stand by Nick and walk with You. Amen."

Just as we finish praying, my friend Traci returns to take more photos.

I repair my makeup and hurry downstairs. Jerry is standing in the foyer. *Goodness, he's handsome tonight.* He captures me in his glance as I walk down the stairs, and the look in his eyes makes my tummy do flip-flops.

Most of the guests are seated. *Oh, sweet Chopin—that's not recorded tunes.* Doris hired a harpist and a violinist for the wedding music.

Kim rushes to answer the door. Cold air blasts my back, and I turn to see the new guests.

I feel disoriented to see those four familiar faces at the door. Their expressions seem to reflect my confusion.

60

What are they doing here?

Jerry steps closer to me, sensing something's happening. He takes control of the situation, gesturing for them to come out of the cold. "Welcome. Please come in."

The little old lady shuffles in, pushing her walker in front of her. Her husband follows, blinking his one good eye. A middle-aged lady holds the door for them to pass.

Behind them, a hand extends toward Jerry. "Nice to meet you. I'm Harry Roark. This is my wife, Joyce, and her parents, Slim and Bert."

Joyce steps forward. "Linda? From Dream Photography?"

I nod like a ninny. *Why are they here?*

Bert maneuvers her walker in front of me and smiles. "That's why you look familiar." There's a hint of a tear in her eye. "Do you know my granddaughter?"

"Yes, I do." I'm feeling emotional enough today without this sweet, shocking bit of news. My eyes sting with tears that cannot be contained. *Oh, what a blessing.* Amber's family is that loving Sullivan clan. I turn to Jerry. "They're clients. I met them at the studio."

Joyce wipes a tear from her cheek. "We decided at the last minute that we couldn't wait through the weekend to meet Amber. I hope it's okay that we've come unannounced."

"Of course. And I'm sure it will make the night that much more special for Amber and Nick."

Slim struggles to maintain his composure. We've got to move out of the foyer. Already guests are craning their necks to see what's happening.

"Is there somewhere we can go?" I ask Kim.

She nods. "The office. This way."

We follow her down the hallway and into a wood-paneled room. I glance over my shoulder and see Nick on our heels.

Nick closes the door. His expression is guarded. "You're Amber's family?"

Jerry goes out to tell Doris that the ceremony will be delayed a few minutes. We've installed Bert in a wing chair. She's trembling with excitement at the thought of meeting her long-lost granddaughter.

I take a tissue from a box on the desk. "I'll go upstairs and get Amber. Nick, you've got to leave."

He jerks my way. "What? Why?"

I shake my head. My statement didn't come out right. "Sorry. I meant that Amber may be sentimental and might not want you to see her before the ceremony."

He looks a bit relieved.

I put my hand on the doorknob. "If she wants you here, I'll get you right away."

A million thoughts race through my mind on my way upstairs. Amber was disappointed that she would have to wait until after she returned from her honeymoon to meet her family. Won't she be surprised?

She and the girls are laughing as I rap on the door and let myself in. They glance at me, and the mood in the room dims. It could be my teary eyes.

I think of the blessing this lost family will be to Amber, and my expression softens with a smile. "Amber? You have some surprise guests downstairs."

Her eyebrows rise, and she flings a hand to her heart.

I won't keep her in suspense. "It's your family. They're in the den. Do you want to meet them before the ceremony?"

She nods furiously as she walks toward the door. "Where's Nick?"

"Do you want him there?"

"No. I don't want him to see me until I walk down the aisle."

I hold the door for her. "Good. That's what I thought. He won't see you if you take the back stairs."

I wish I could press my ear to the door to hear what's going on in the office. Amber's decided to meet her relatives alone. She said the wedding will start in ten minutes. I hope she's right.

We've all taken our seats. This is one of the loveliest sites for a wedding I've ever seen. It feels like something from a movie—the snow, the magnificent home, the tasteful Christmas decorations, the fire in the fireplace, and the classy background music.

Jerry grabs my hand. I think the beauty of the evening is affecting him too.

The song being performed comes to an end, and after a pause, the harpist starts to strum "Christmas Canon." *Oh, blathers. I'm going to cry.* Jerry passes me a tissue.

Nick stands by the fireplace with Scott and the minister. My son appears eager. Everyone stands and turns to see the bridal procession. Talia and Emma walk down the hall and into the room.

After a few moments, Amber is in sight. She's on her grandfather's arm. How radiant she is, and Slim couldn't look prouder. She steals a glance at her grandmother and then focuses exclusively on Nick for the rest of the way.

The music ends, and you can hear a pin drop when the minister asks, "Who gives this woman?"

Slim clears his throat as though he's trying to control his

emotions. "Her grandmother and I." He bends down and kisses Amber and places her hand in Nick's.

The ceremony begins, and it's as though we're all caught up in the same glorious dream. It couldn't be a more touching moment.

When they exchange vows, Amber offers Nick a small, shy smile. She pauses to gaze into his eyes. "Nick, as we start our new life together, I could tell you I'll give you my heart, but it's been yours since we first met. I could tell you I'll give you my dreams, but they've been yours since we first dared to plan a future together. So all I can give you is my unending love one day at a time and the promise of discovering future memories as we journey together through life to a destiny known only to eternity. I will love you forevermore."

Jerry hands me another tissue as Nick declares his love for Amber.

Poor Emma—she's standing in front of everyone, sniffling away just like her mother.

The magical evening continues. After the ceremony, two young men remove most of the chairs, and guests drift to the dining room and family room for refreshments.

I make a point to search out Amber's relatives. They seem as happy as the bride and groom.

Bert pats the seat next to her on the couch. When I sit down, she takes my hand in hers. "I couldn't be happier to find out that Amber's married into your family."

Emotion makes my voice quiver. "I'm thrilled too."

Traci approaches us with two cameras strung around her neck. "Time for family photos."

We gather together in front of the fireplace and listen to Traci direct us where to stand, when to smile, and where to look.

Nick and Amber glow with joy. Especially Amber. She went from being alone to finding a loving extended family.

And I went from resisting this union to believing God wants me to welcome Amber with open arms instead of with a cold heart and a disapproving spirit.

61

I haul the last of the boxes of Christmas decorations down to the basement. It seems that each year the season passes more quickly than the last. As I walk back upstairs, my timer lets me know that my pot of tea is steeped to perfection. I pour a cup and take it to the living room.

I'm glad to be home alone this mid-January morning. I take a moment to think about all the changes we've endured the past few months. Between Nick's proposal, news of the baby, moving up the wedding date, and having Nick and Amber living under our roof, we've had to make quite a few adjustments to say the least.

I wrap my hands around the warm mug and savor the memory of their wedding. It was like a fairy tale. My mother's heart was blessed when Nick told me that a verse came to him as he was dressing for the wedding: "Though your sins are like scarlet, they shall be as white as snow; though they are red as crimson, they shall be like wool." I'm glad to hear he's consulting with the Almighty. I hope that Amber will want to know more about the God her husband serves.

I finish my tea and haul my dirty laundry to the washer. It's filled with Amber's wash. Again. I drop my basket and run for the ringing phone. It's Jerry.

"Hey. You're not going to believe what's happened. Amber left her laundry in the machine and went out. You know, she could have—"

"Hang on." His deep laugh filters through the line. "Be patient. It will take a while for us to work out the kinks."

I can't stuff down my irritation. "That's easy for you to say. You're not the one who has to deal with these kinks."

"Hon, we knew this wouldn't be without conflict. Try to remember that it's only for a few months."

He's right, but it still doesn't solve the current problem of transporting her laundry out of my washer. "I know. Why did you call?"

"Can't I call to check in on my wife?"

"Sure . . . " But I know him well. Something's up.

"Are you going out today?"

Bingo. "Yeah, I'm meeting Deb for lunch."

"Good. Would you take the gas cylinder and have it filled up? It's disconnected from the grill and is sitting by the side of the garage."

• • •

Deb's car is in the lot of TeaTime when I arrive. I push through the door and spot her right away. She's talking on her cell phone. Chamber music plays softly in the background. The restaurant is full of women enjoying a break in the day.

I wind through the tables, pull out a chair, and plop down.

Deb finishes her call, then winks at me. "Hi, hon. What's new? How's the happy couple?"

I try not to roll my eyes. "They're fine."

She laughs. "What's the rest of the story?"

Am I really that transparent? "We're still going through a period of adjustment. That's all."

Our conversation pauses while we place our order. When the waitress walks away, Deb leans in. "And . . . ?"

"I try to be patient, but it's hard to know how to act sometimes. For Christmas, Amber bought me a cookbook. Can you believe it? As if I don't know how to cook. Now I'm nervous when I prepare meals. She's always judging my culinary skills. Did you know she only eats organic produce and natural meats? Have you any idea how expensive that is?"

"Don't they contribute to the household?"

"Yeah, but not as much as they consume." My face prickles with a blush. "I don't mean to sound like such a shrew. To be honest, I think I'm having issues dealing with all the changes."

Deb pours her tea. "Don't stress. I'm sure you'll get over it. And before you realize it, they'll be gone."

"I know. I know. But in the meantime, it's awkward at times. The smallest issues seem to blow up out of proportion. Did you know that there's a wrong way to hang toilet paper? Apparently I've been doing it wrong forever."

"So tell me. What is the correct way to hang toilet paper?"

I can't believe I'm having this conversation. "It's with the square rolling over the top of the roll and not coming from under the roll."

Deb gestures, rotating her hands until her palms face up. "Of course. That's the way I've always done it."

We laugh, and then her expression changes. "Well, I have news for you." She leans back. "We've gotten a contract on our house."

"It's sold?" My heart pounds. I knew this day would come, but it hurts to think of losing my best friend.

"Yeah, it's a good offer. We're going to take it."

"So that means you'll move soon?" A lump forms in my throat.

"I'll move in two months, providing the house closes according to schedule. It will be nice for me to move to Keith. I've missed him so much."

I bite back any unkind words about her darling husband. "Oh."

We both fall silent. I gaze at the other women enjoying lunch with their friends.

"Lin?"

I look at Deb. She leans toward me and grins in encouragement.

I push my mouth into a smile. For her sake I hope I'm a good actress.

62

I drive down our street in the fading light of day. Both Nick's and Amber's cars are parked in front of the house. I pull into the garage and leave the door open so Nick can take the gas cylinder to the backyard.

The house is in darkness. "Nick? Amber?"

Maybe they've gone for a walk. Amber's always getting Nick to take her out for fresh air. I walk upstairs to the laundry room. I need to put my clothes in the dryer. If it's empty. I open the machine. It's full of laundry—no doubt by now all too wrinkled to simply hang in the closet. I may not be the sophisticated chef that my daughter-in-law is, but I know how to efficiently do laundry. I toss their clothes into the plastic basket and put my laundry in the dryer.

What was that noise? I step into the hallway. Belle lies at the top of the stairs. She sees me and wags her stumpy tail. There can't be an intruder in the house, or she would be on the job and protecting us with her nineteen-pound self. I shake off a feeling of unease and close the laundry room door.

There. I heard it again. I inch down the hall.

Oh, good gravy. It's Nick and Amber. Behind closed door.

I go downstairs to make dinner.

Emma comes home. "Why's the garage door open? Do you want me to close it?"

"Uh, yeah. Close it please."

She disappears for a moment and comes back into the kitchen. The sound of the garage door closing follows her. "Did you leave it open on purpose?"

I take a pan out of the cabinet. "Yes, I left it open for Nick to take the gas tank around back."

Just as I'm about to explain that the tank's still in the car, laughter drifts from the stairway. Nick and Amber walk into the kitchen.

Emma gets a glass of water. "Nice job, leaving the garage door open, Nick. Are you trying to freeze us out?"

"What?"

Emma gestures toward the door. "After you took the gas tank out of Mom's car, you didn't close the garage door."

His head swivels my way. "What's she talking about?"

"I need to have someone take the gas cylinder out of my trunk."

"Why didn't you ask?" Nick sounds irritated.

What shall I say? I tried, but you were, uh, busy.

Comprehension dawns in Amber's eyes. She puts a hand on Nick's arm and has the good grace to blush. She leans in to him. "She may have called, but we didn't hear her."

"Uh, sorry." Nick sounds rattled.

Emma looks between us all. Her expression moves from confusion to amusement. "Oh, you've got to be kidding."

• • •

Somehow we've all found a way to make this arrangement work. And fortunately, we haven't had any incidents like the one with the gas cylinder in the past three and a half months. I've also been given a reprieve on my farewell to Debbie. The family buying her house ran into trouble, and the deal fell through.

Spring is blooming in Colorado, and Amber's blooming as well. We've got only about three weeks to go before the baby arrives.

Amber's been madly reading parenting books and scouring Web sites for tips on being the perfect mother. Of course I want nothing less than for Amber to know the Lord. She remains skeptical. But still I pray.

This past Wednesday, Amber had the sweetest baby shower ever. All the decorations were pink, in honor of little Lily, my grand-daughter. I forgot the wonder of tiny booties and frilly dresses. Her corner in her parents' room is all ready for her arrival. The crib is outfitted with pink and green bedding, and a pretty mobile hangs from the rail, waiting to amuse Lily with a sweet song and floating dragonflies.

I had the brilliant idea of taking Jerry away for a weekend before the baby comes. We're headed to Beaver Creek in the Vail Valley. We've cashed in all our credit card points to be able to afford our little getaway. Deb highly recommended the area, and their slogan is to die for—"Not exactly roughing it." Surely that's my kind of resort. Of course Deb and Keith stay in the Bachelor Gulch side of the resort, but when I checked the prices online for that expensive real estate, I nearly choked.

Our drive through the mountains is beautiful. The day couldn't be more spectacular. The few puffy clouds sailing above look like orphans in the big blue sky. I'm content to simply watch the gorgeous scenery.

"Whatcha thinking, Grandma?" Jerry glances my way. He seems relaxed and happy.

"I'll grandma you." I give him a punch on the arm.

His right hand slides to my thigh. He gives me a little squeeze. "I tell you what—you're the sexiest grandma west of the Mississippi."

"Really? Only west of the Mississippi?"

"Later on I'll give you the opportunity to persuade me that you're the sexiest grandma in the entire USA if you'd like."

Oh, this man.

We turn off the highway onto a winding road that leads farther up the mountain. The lane is lined with colorful flags of the nations. It looks like we've arrived at our destination. We find The Pines Lodge without any trouble. *Wow.* Deb didn't mislead us on this pick.

We check in and take a walk through the village to get our bearings. I feel as if I've been transported to a European alpine wonderland. Beaver Creek is situated in a little valley surrounded by amazing mountains. The vista is shades of green with a backdrop of snowcapped peaks. *Awesome.* As we wander along the twisting roads, stunning brass sculptures placed between quaint shops wink in the sun.

I pull Jer close to me. "Did you see that?"

He glances around. "What?"

"I think we just walked by Newt Gingrich. I wonder where he's staying."

"Lin, hurry up. Our reservations are for six."

I finish primping and grab my purse. We don't have far to go. The Grouse Mountain Grill is right downstairs.

It's everything you'd hope for in an award-winning restaurant. We sip our drinks and wait for our appetizers to arrive. Jerry leans back and sighs. I put my hand on his and give him a wink. This day has been perfect. Our walk was exhilarating, and before dinner I was able to persuade him that I'm the sexiest grandma in the world. Or so he said.

I'm surprised when he leans toward me and gives me a tender kiss. He's not the kind of fellow to be affectionate in public.

If this is what it's like to be married to a grandpa, bring it on.

• • •

A delicious breeze dances through open windows, carrying the fragrance of springtime in the Rockies. The sounds of chattering squirrels and birdsong further drag me from slumber. I nudge Jerry. Before breakfast we want to take the chairlift up the mountain for a hike.

There are only a few early risers walking through the village, and there's no line to ride up the mountain. The morning sun warms our backs on our ascent.

"Over there!" Jerry points below us where a small red fox picks his way up the mountainside.

It's quiet up here. We choose a path among the spicy pines and scruffy spring grasses. Around a curve, the sight of a hillside covered in yellow balsam root flowers takes my breath away. An aspen grove borders the beautiful scene.

Jerry leads me over to a downed aspen tree, and we sit on its long, smooth trunk. The wind hums through the mountains while he reaches into his pocket for his small, worn devotional book. I'm not surprised.

I close my eyes and lean into him while he prays for our family and for our precious little Lily, whom we will soon hold in our arms.

63

"That was a fast weekend." I adjust the sun visor as we head east, out of the mountains.

Jerry smiles. "Back to our real life. No more Belgian waffles with applewood smoked bacon for breakfast. No more pretzel-coated pork chops for dinner."

"That's all this weekend was to you? A smorgasbord of delicious food?"

His glance warms the pit of my stomach. "And other pleasures as well."

I'm glad we took today off.

I must have dozed because the change in sound from driving through the mountains and into the Eisenhower Tunnel stirs me. I roll my shoulders to work out the kinks. *Good.* We'll be home in about ninety minutes.

• • •

I'm pleased to see that the garbage can and recycling bins are back in the garage. It really annoys me to come home on garbage day to find that stuff sitting at the curb. Amber's car is the only one at the house.

We find Amber sitting on the couch watching television. Her face lights up when she sees us. "Hi. Did you have fun?"

I bet my grin tells it all. "Yep. How are you?"

"I met Grandma for tea this morning." She pauses as if she's recalling time spent with Bert; then her expression dims. "But ever since I got home, I've had a backache that won't go away."

I sit next to her. "Did you call the doctor?"

Amber stares at me as if I'm an idiot. I know we've been watching her like she's a ticking time bomb, but this is something that should be checked out. She waves me off and struggles to rise from the couch. "Don't worry. My regular checkup is this afternoon."

Jerry and I watch her waddle from the room. I've grown to love her, but she's still the most stubborn girl I've ever met.

She hesitates in the foyer. "Linda, do you want to go to my appointment with me? You can hear Lily's heartbeat."

"I'd love that. Thanks."

Amber continues on her way, and a lump forms in my throat. I've asked her once before if she'd like me to take her to the doctor, but she said no. This could be another signal of a change in our relationship. *Thank You, Lord.*

Jerry looks pleased at our exchange. He gives me a sweet kiss and carries our luggage upstairs. I load the dishes left on the counter into the dishwasher and search the fridge for dinner ideas. I've got ground beef and chicken. Neither appeals to me.

Jerry comes downstairs and sorts our mail.

I talk over my shoulder to him. "Burgers?"

"Nah."

"Chicken?"

"I'm not in the mood for chicken."

I lean against the counter. "You know what? I just don't feel like cooking." I cross my arms and wait for his reply.

He shakes his head and laughs. "Okay. Let's get some pizza."

About ninety minutes later, my laundry is folded and put away. I follow Amber downstairs and pluck my purse from the table.

"Jerry! We're off to Amber's appointment. We're each taking a car. I'll pick up the pizza, and Amber is stopping at the grocery store. We'll be back in about an hour."

I hear his muffled response come from the basement, and we let ourselves out the door.

I follow Amber's car, and we wind our way north toward her doctor's office.

Traffic is beginning to pick up in town as rush hour approaches. A few cars squeeze between mine and Amber's on the crowded road. We get as far as the intersection at Hillside Avenue and sit at the red light, waiting to turn left.

The light turns green. I'm at the end of the line, so I'm not optimistic that I'll get through before the next red light. I watch the familiar Hyundai creeping forward, waiting for a break. This is the intersection that Jerry complained about to town hall. He says it will take a fatality before a turn arrow is put on the traffic light.

A car behind me honks. I hope Amber's not influenced by that impatient person. Sunlight glistens off the windows of her car as she moves forward.

Fear chills my heart. Cars in the two turning lanes on the other side of the intersection can block any view of oncoming traffic. I hope she waits until she can see the oncoming traffic.

More horns. A squeal of brakes and the screech of tires on asphalt fill the air. An awful shattering crunch resounds as an SUV plows into my daughter-in-law's little car.

I put my car in park and race across the intersection. The sound of car horns surrounds me, and oncoming traffic whizzes past. My legs feel numb like I'm running through an ice-cold riptide as I rush toward the crumpled vehicle.

Someone yells to call 911. A teenage boy stumbles from the SUV, obviously dazed.

I make it to the driver's side of the car. The door is locked. A deflated airbag lies across Amber's still form.

Cracks in the window make it look like a crystal web. It's rolled partway down, so I try to reach in to unlock the door. "Amber!"

Her eyes are closed. If her chest wasn't rising, I'd think she was dead.

"Lady, don't move her." A man dressed in a business suit is by my side.

"She's my daughter-in-law. She's pregnant." I continue to claw at the fragmented window. "Amber!"

A woman wearing a camouflage jacket grips my arm. "Calm down. I'm a nurse. Let me see her."

Strong arms drag me back, and I flail against their hold. A man says, "An ambulance is on the way. This lady's a nurse. She'll help."

I grow still. *Help. Someone is offering help.*

Nurse Camouflage turns to me. "What's her name?"

"Amber."

Somehow, someone gets the door open. Her car is turned off and the nurse is leaning over Amber.

Help our girl and Lily, Lord.

I feel like a rag doll, and if it wasn't for the businessman holding me up, I'd be crumpled on the asphalt.

"She's responding!"

Thank You, Lord. I step closer and see Amber's dazed eyes. "Honey? How do you feel?"

She glances at me and then winces and shuts her eyes.

I put my hand on her shoulder. "Don't move. An ambulance is coming."

The businessman on my right taps my arm.

I turn toward him to see him holding out a cell phone. *Right.* I have to call Jerry. And Nick. My hands tremble as I punch in Nick's number. Are the last two digits four-six or six-four? Without speed dial, I can't figure out his number. I call home.

The phone rings and rings. I'm sure Jerry's there, but he may not bother to pick up an unknown call. The answering machine kicks in, and my voice comes through the line. Finally the tone sounds. "Pick up, Jer. It's me. There's been an accident. Amber's—"

64

"What?" Alarm edges Jerry's voice.

I cup my hand over my ear to muffle the sound of sirens. "Amber's been in an accident. We're at that intersection at Hillside and—"

"I'll be right there."

"No, wait! Call Nick."

He promises he will, and we end the call.

I quickly step aside for the EMTs. They lift Amber from the car and gently place her on a gurney.

A police officer begins to direct traffic. "Whose vehicle is this?"

I reach into the car to grab Amber's purse.

"Ma'am? Excuse me?"

A hand on my arm gets my attention. The cop peers into my eyes. "That vehicle needs to be moved. Is it yours?"

"Uh, yes." I can't seem to think straight.

"If you give me your keys, I'll park it over there." The policeman points to the lot in front of an electronics store.

"The keys are still in the car."

He gives me a salute and runs over to my car.

I move closer to the ambulance and catch the eye of one of the technicians. "This is my daughter-in-law. May I ride in the ambulance with her?"

They heft Amber into the vehicle, and he turns to me. "You can ride up front."

I climb into the passenger seat and quickly realize that my purse and cell phone are still in my car. I scoot from the ambulance. *Where's my car?* Traffic is snarled up and down the road. A tow truck approaches on the shoulder of the road. Several men and women in uniform walk around, managing the scene.

"Ma'am, we're ready to go."

I scan the area. *Where did that cop say he was moving my car?* I hope he locks my keys inside with my purse.

A police officer gestures toward the ambulance as if he's clearing a path for us through the traffic.

I scramble back inside. As I'm putting on my seat belt, a knock at the window startles me. I look up to see the policeman holding my purse. "Oh, thank you," I say, rolling down the window.

He passes me my bag, and the ambulance creeps out of the intersection, siren blaring.

I pull out my cell and speed-dial Jerry. "Did you reach Nick?"

"He's on his way back to town. I assumed you're going to Pine Grove Hospital, right?"

"Yes, that's where we're going."

I pray all the way to the hospital. *Will Amber be all right? Will Lily survive?* My mind churns in all kinds of directions, and some of them are very frightening. I don't know what will become of my granddaughter, but I rest in the assurance that God does and that He holds her in the palm of His hand.

When we arrive, there are nurses standing by the door to receive Amber. I get pulled over to Admitting. I give them what little information I can.

I glance up and see Jerry come through the door.

He gives me a hug. "How is Amber? What happened?"

I take his hand. "She tried to turn left at Hillside. She must not have seen the SUV."

Jerry shakes his head. "Maybe now the town will fix that death trap." He looks over my shoulder and nods. "Nick."

I turn to see my son barreling through the door.

"Where's my wife?" His face is drained of its usual ruddy color, and worry lines frame his eyes.

Jerry claps him on the back, and we all hurry to the ER.

A nurse walks out the double doors and points to Nick. "Are you Amber Revere's husband?"

He nods and she ushers him inside. Before the doors close, she directs Jerry and me toward the waiting area.

Jerry takes out his cell. "Did you call Slim and Bert?"

"Oh no. I—"

He scrolls through his contacts and calls. He talks briefly and disconnects. "Did you call Emma?"

"I didn't. She'll be worried."

Jerry flips open his phone and calls her.

We sit and wait. *How long has it been? Why isn't Nick coming out to give us information?* My mind races ahead of my faith, and I imagine the worst. *What if Amber's seriously hurt? What if the baby doesn't survive?* I chase that sad premise and envision Lily dancing in Theresa's arms in a beautiful heavenly garden. The thought both comforts and sickens me at the same time.

Soon Slim, Bert, and Emma arrive. We huddle together in the beige, antiseptic island of anxiety that is the ER waiting room.

Every time the door opens, we suspend conversation and glance up.

This time it's Nick. He strides over to us. "She needs to have an emergency C-section, but the doctors think it will be okay. She wants to see Bert and Mom."

I help Bert with her walker. We follow Nick down the wide hallway into a small exam room. He shows us to Amber's room and heads back to update the rest of the family.

Amber's head is bandaged, and dried blood clings to a strand of her hair. She looks terrified. "Grandma! Linda!"

A nurse behind her interrupts. "I thought it might ease her mind to see you ladies before we take her up to Surgery. Your girl's been through a scare, but the doctor thinks mother and baby will be fine."

I scoot around to the far side of the bed and allow Bert to shuffle to Amber's bedside.

Bert kisses her forehead and grabs her hand. "It's wonderful news that you'll both be okay. Just think, in a few hours you'll be holding Lily in your arms."

Amber shakes her head. "This isn't right. I know Lily was going to be born on a Saturday."

She makes me chuckle. "Honey, these babies have a mind of their own. When they want to come, they come. And now's the time."

Bert takes charge of the room by bowing her head. We fall silent while the older woman prays for a safe delivery, a healthy baby, and a quick recovery for Amber. Just as she finishes, Nick reappears.

Amber turns to her grandmother. "I'm still scared. I've got . . ." She looks at Nick.

He steps forward. "The doctor says it's placenta abruptio."

"What's that?"

The nurse working on Amber's IV speaks up. "That means the placenta has separated from the uterus. Sometimes that happens when an expectant woman is in an automobile accident. But Amber's so close to her due date, we're not too concerned."

"It will be all right," Bert tells Amber. "We're all staying until Lily's safely in your arms. And we'll be praying."

The nurse takes the brakes off Amber's bed and pushes her from the room, Nick following closely behind.

Bert and I rejoin the family and take the elevator up to Labor and Delivery. *Good grief, another beige waiting area.* We settle in. Who knows how long this will take?

I've never seen a minute hand sweep around a clock more slowly. Every once in a while, someone goes in search of more coffee. The suspense is killing me. I concentrate on images of silken hair, skin as smooth as satin, and a tiny fist clasping my finger. I'm going to be a grandma.

65

As Jerry, Emma, and I walk through the hospital parking lot, Em holds tightly to the pacifier, lamb, and stork balloons we picked up at the grocery store. They bounce against one another in the spring breeze.

It was a long night. Lily Bertha Revere made her appearance at 4:08 a.m., all six pounds fifteen ounces of her. Nick sent us home around midnight, but now that we've all slept a few hours and had breakfast, we're ready to meet this new little lady.

When we make our way to Amber's room, Nick is sitting on the bed beside Amber, who is holding our Lily.

Emma ties the balloons onto Amber's bed railing. She bends over and gives her a hug. "I can't wait to hold Lily, play with her, build a snowman with her, and teach her how to wear makeup. . . ."

We all laugh. Hearing my daughter gush over Lily takes my breath away. I thought I would have all the time in the world with my children. *When did they grow up? Where did those years go?* I glance at Jerry, and he raises his eyebrows. Tears sting my eyes.

Emma notices. "Get a grip, Mom."

"You know me. I'm a weeper." I pluck a tissue from the side table. "And now I'm a grandma. Oh, she's beautiful."

Jerry shakes Nick's hand. "Congratulations, Son."

We stand in awe of this gorgeous baby. I look from Lily to Amber. She's glowing, casting her gaze from her daughter to her husband. I run my hand over Amber's head and give her shoulder a squeeze. "And how are you, honey? You gave us quite a scare yesterday."

Her joyful expression changes. "It wasn't my fault, Linda!"

I'm taken aback. "I didn't say it was."

We stare at one another. I feel my face color. *Why is she attacking me?* "Amber, I didn't mean to imply—"

"So is this where the party is?"

We turn to find Slim and Bert Sullivan standing in the doorway. What a welcome diversion. Bert pushes her walker forward with Slim following.

"Congratulations." Slim kisses the top of Amber's head and looks tenderly at his great-granddaughter. "She's a beaut. Just like her mother."

Bert clears her throat. "God is good to let me see this day."

I slip behind everyone.

Jerry comes to my side. He leans close to my ear and whispers, "Don't pay any attention to what Amber said. She's been through a lot in the past eighteen hours."

I nod. "It's probably the result of hormones."

We fuss over the baby for another half hour, then leave to let Amber and Lily rest. By the time we go, I've probably taken thirty photos.

Jerry and I go directly to work, Emma heads to school, and Nick says he's going home to shower and nap.

Tomorrow afternoon our little family comes home. I can't wait.

• • •

All day long I tell my coworkers and clients about my adorable granddaughter. I can't stop thinking about how she looks just like Nick when he was newborn. Her fuzzy light brown hair frames her sweet face. Her loud cries, I suspect, come from her mother's side of the family. *Oops.* As soon as that nasty thought flies into my mind, I repent. Amber's never known an unconditional mother's love, and I'm determined to love her like that. Even if it takes more energy than I ever had to put into a relationship.

After dinner, I tidy up Nick and Amber's room. I strip the bed, and while the sheets and the dirty clothes on their floor are in the laundry, I vacuum and dust. When I finish making the bed, I pause by Lily's crib. It will be wonderful to have a baby in the house.

I look forward to when we'll be awakened by the sound of Lily's cries in the wee hours. I always loved nursing my babies during the night. It was a private, peaceful time when I had them all to myself. I hope Amber treasures those moments with her daughter too.

It's around ten o'clock when Nick arrives home.

I go downstairs to the kitchen, where he's getting a glass of tea. "Did you have dinner? Can I make you a sandwich?"

He puts down his glass. "No thanks. I ate at the hospital. I'm only looking for a snack."

"Want some nachos? Or cheese and crackers?"

"On second thought, I'm beat. I'll just go to bed." Nick starts to walk out of the room and pauses before me. "I'm sorry Amber snapped at you. And so is she. I think she's feeling guilty for getting in the accident."

"I don't hold her responsible. I was sick with worry for both of them."

"That's okay. I know that."

Jerry snores peacefully. I would have liked to talk about Lily some more, but he's worn-out. I e-mailed photos to everyone we know. She's so beautiful. I already made an appointment for Nick, Amber, and Lily to have their first family portrait taken at Dream Photography. As a favor to me, Luke made sure to have them scheduled in his time slot. Maybe I should make a special dinner for Amber and Lily's homecoming tomorrow.

• • •

I could barely keep my head in the game at work today. It's a good thing I can practically do my job in my sleep. All I could think about was going home and knowing my granddaughter will be there. I couldn't wait to hold her again.

It looks like there's a party going on at my house. Cars are lined up along the sidewalk. I don't know if I have enough chicken to feed this many people. I slip into the house and head to the living room, where everyone is gathered. Bert and Slim and Joyce and Harry Roark are leaning over a bassinet that no doubt holds Lily. Jerry is standing off to the side, grinning.

I'm greeted by the masses.

"Look what Aunt Joyce and Uncle Harry gave us. Isn't it gorgeous?" Amber gestures to the lace-covered wicker basket that holds our little angel.

"It's lovely." I move closer and stroke Lily's cheek. "How long has she been sleeping? Do you think she'll wake soon?"

Amber shakes her head. "I kept her up long enough for Grandma and Grandpa to see her. She'll probably sleep for a couple of hours."

Oh, well. I'll have plenty of time to spend with her.

66

I didn't find out until last night that Nick had invited friends over to visit Saturday. Since he decided on a party, I invited a few of my own guests. After all, I want to show off Lily too. She's been with us for only three weeks, yet I can barely remember what life was like without her.

Our backyard is filled with family, friends, and neighbors. Many of Nick and Amber's friends laugh around the picnic table. Deb is in the kitchen, cleaning up from lunch. We had enough food to feed an army, which is a good thing considering the way Nick's friends eat.

Amber lies in the hammock in the corner of the yard. I think she's finding the demands of motherhood to be more than she expected. I'm a bit surprised at how short-tempered she is with the family at times.

I stroll across the grass to Amber. "Can I get you anything? a sandwich? a glass of tea?"

She glances at me as if she's in another world and isn't part of the gathering. For a moment, I wonder if she actually heard. She brushes a piece of hair off her face. "No. Thanks." She closes her eyes and turns her face to the sun. I guess she's giving herself a bit of a time-out.

I walk inside the house. Deb is standing at the sink, looking out the window at Amber and drying her hands on a towel. "I think that's about everything that needed to be washed. The rest of the stuff is disposable. I put leftover fruit salad in the fridge."

"Thanks, Deb." I pull out a chair and sit.

She joins me. "Well, Grandma, you've got a beautiful grand-daughter."

"I couldn't agree more."

Joyce comes in from outside. "Am I intruding?"

I shake my head and motion to the chair next to me.

She reaches over and pats my hand. "I haven't seen my mother this happy in years. She nearly shriveled up and died when my sister left pregnant and angry. For years we wondered what happened to her, what happened to the baby. But now we've found Amber. It's a dream come true."

A burst of laughter on the patio draws our attention. Amber's sitting on Nick's lap and telling a story to their friends. She must be refreshed from her nap.

The sound of Lily waking comes from the baby monitor on the counter. I hop up to get her.

Joyce stands. "May I?"

We go upstairs together. I'm a little embarrassed at the condition of Nick and Amber's room. I hope their mess doesn't reflect on me. Dirty laundry is tossed behind the door, tissues litter the night-stand, and the bed is unmade. I try to ignore the obvious disarray and raise the shade while Joyce picks up the baby.

When we walk downstairs to the kitchen, Emma's chatting with Deb. Our doorbell rings, and Emma kisses Lily on the head and rushes off.

Deb looks pensive for a moment. "If I had a grandchild in the area, I don't know if I'd be able to pick up and move."

"I hope your son and daughter-in-law have plenty of children to lure you back to Colorado."

Joyce passes Lily off to me when she gets up to answer her cell phone. I'm snuggling my little darling when the door opens and Amber comes inside.

"Why didn't you tell me she was awake?" Amber snatches Lily and goes back out to the patio.

Deb looks at me and shrugs. I'm a little embarrassed to have Amber treat me so rudely in front of my friend, but I bite my tongue to keep from saying something that would cause an argument.

• • •

May has drawn to a close. We've gotten into a routine around Lily's schedule, making sure everyone is quiet during nap time, and we've started to childproof the house for safety. I try hard to be loving toward Amber, but she's still the stubborn, independent girl she was the day she married Nick. As much as I've opened my heart to her, she seems to be holding me at arm's length. Jerry says to give her some time since she's been through so many changes so quickly. I strive to be patient.

Emma's graduation from high school was a week ago. We had a graduation dinner for her at the Gray Pony Inn. The party consisted of our new group, including Doris's and Amber's relatives.

Nick graduated from college but decided to skip the ceremony. I was disappointed that he didn't want to commemorate the event. He worked so hard to earn his degree. From the conversation I overheard coming from their room, I suspect that because Amber didn't get her diploma, she wasn't interested in seeing his accomplishment celebrated. He has a few good leads on a new job and hopes to hear about some interviews he's had. In the meantime he's moved on from his part-time job and is working as a temp.

Jerry wrapped up his semester and is teaching summer school. As usual, I stuck to my regular schedule at Dream Photography.

Deb closed on her house and moved away. She promises to keep in touch. I know we will, but still . . .

We push on, accepting each day as it comes. I pray we'll be a healthy, happy family living together in harmony under one roof. With God's help, I think that's happening.

• • •

My mind won't stop racing tonight. I can't stop thinking about Amber and Nick. They've had a few bumps in the road of their relationship. Having to move up their wedding to accommodate the coming baby, Amber taking an incomplete on her spring semester due to morning sickness, paying the hospital bills from the baby, and having to pay to repair Amber's car after the accident have taken their toll. They've had a few counseling sessions with Pastor John, and I see a renewed sense of purpose in my son. If only we could reach Amber. She and Nick have begun to argue about silly, inconsequential things.

It's nearly one o'clock. Jerry snores beside me. I give up. Maybe a cup of herbal tea will help me sleep.

The lights are on downstairs, and voices carry from the kitchen. It's Nick and Amber. A cabinet door slams. They must be having another argument.

"For goodness' sake!" Amber sounds angry. "Living in this house is like living in culinary Siberia. There's never anything good to eat."

The hairs on the back of my neck stand up. I quietly go back to bed.

• • •

When I arrive home from work, the table is set with only four place settings. I walk to Jerry's study and sit in his easy chair. "What's going on?"

He looks up from his computer and pinches the bridge of his nose. "Amber's taken Lily and has gone to stay with Bert and Slim for a while."

"How's that going to help? We've been walking on eggshells around that girl, and from what I've seen, Nick's been trying to be a good husband and father."

"Don't get all defensive. This isn't about us. It's about Amber."

I settle back. Jerry may be right, but this will crush Nick.

Children walk by outside wearing bathing suits and shooting one another with water pistols. The everydayness of life comforts me.

The doorbell rings. I push out of the chair to answer it.

Ross and Doris are standing on the porch. "Can we barge in?"

I swing the door wide. "Sure. We're having burgers tonight. Join us."

Jerry comes out of his study, gives Doris a hug, then shakes Ross's hand. We make our way to the back of the house. I set two more plates on the table. "The salad's already made, so we only have to grill the burgers. Let's get some iced tea and keep Jer company while he cooks."

We move out to the patio with Belle at our heels. She struts around, allowing each person the honor of stroking her head. Jerry explains the Amber situation as if it's no big deal. Ross shrugs at the news.

Emma arrives and bounces out of the house and straight for Ross. "I didn't know you were coming for dinner." She plants a kiss on the top of his head and smiles at Doris. "Hi."

Jerry puts the burgers on the grill, and Emma bends down for the Frisbee that lies by her feet. She tosses the disc out into the yard, and we all watch Belle tear out to catch it.

"Grandpa, are you staying for dinner?"

"Yes, we are."

Emma glances at the table. "Then why are there only six place settings?"

I look to Jerry. He picks up my hint and answers. "Amber and Lily have gone to stay with her grandparents for a while."

Her face contorts in confusion and sorrow. "Why?"

If only we knew. The sound of sizzling beef fills the empty space.

Ross leans over to Doris and takes her hand. "I think this family could use a little good news." The two of them smile like teenagers.

Emma's expression moves from disappointment to delight. "Grandpa, do you have a secret to share with us?"

67

In answer to Emma's question, Ross holds up Doris's left hand. "We're engaged."

We all rush to offer congratulations. Doris's ring is not a traditional diamond. It's a gorgeous oval ruby, surrounded by small diamonds.

"Oh, it's lovely." I grasp her hand and bring it closer.

She squeezes my fingers. When I look at her, she's wearing an expression that asks if I'm being serious or just polite.

A rush of emotion brings tears to my eyes. In the past few months we've grown more than comfortable with one another. "I'm so glad you're joining the family."

Her watery smile tells me she feels the same way.

I dash tears from my cheeks and gaze at Jerry. He's standing by the grill watching the scene. He gives an almost imperceptible nod. He's okay.

Emma's got her arm around Ross. She's the most transparent person I've ever known, and she seems thrilled at the prospect of her grandpa remarrying. *Boy, we've come a long way with this girl.*

"Grandpa, when's the wedding? Where are you getting married? Will the ceremony be in Colorado or in California? How will—?"

"Hold on. One question at a time." Ross puffs up with pride.

It's been such a long while since I've seen him this happy. As much as I resisted the idea of another woman taking Theresa's place, I'm thrilled that he's found someone to love and be loved by in return.

Ross glances at Doris, and—*oh my goodness*—the look he gives her leaves no doubt about his feelings. In return, she blushes. It's charming on her.

I completely understand her reaction. After all, I love a Revere man too. My thoughts turn to my absent daughter-in-law. I've seen Nick gaze at her in that same tummy-tumbling way. How could Amber walk away from that?

"No way!" Emma laughs and looks to me for agreement.

But I got lost in my thoughts. "No way what?"

"Grandpa says they're going to Vegas to have an Elvis-themed wedding at the DooWop Wedding Chapel."

"Grandpa's kidding." I give him a look that says he better be. I can't imagine him taking such an important step and not having his family surround him.

Doris laughs. "Don't worry, honey. If he's going to marry me, there had better be a familiar minister and lots of family and friends present."

Ross throws his hands up. "I'm busted."

We move the celebration into the kitchen. While I'm bringing the rest of dinner to the table, Nick comes home. The mood of our gathering becomes a little subdued.

Emma grins at him. "Grandpa and Doris are getting married."

It seems as if the news takes a moment to register, but then Nick smiles and gives them both a hug.

Emma continues her interrogation. "So, have you decided on a location for the wedding? Will it be at Doris's house?"

Her question is asked in innocence, but I can tell that everyone is thinking of the family wedding that took place there not too long ago.

If Doris senses the discomfort, she masks it well. "I always thought it would be special to be married outside in a beautiful garden. Ross and I thought—"

Emma clasps her hands. "Then you're getting married soon? When the weather's still nice?"

Jerry's glance scolds our daughter. "Don't interrupt."

Doris waves her hand. "That's okay. I'm excited too. I hope to find an available date to get married at the Denver Botanic Gardens."

Knowing Doris, she'll get her date and the wedding will be spectacular.

Nick sits in the midst of the happy chatter. *Is he thinking of his failing marriage?*

68

I daydream while I stuff deviled eggs. My grandfather clock intrudes on the silence of the house. It's three o'clock, and Doris's Fourth of July party starts in an hour. She told me I didn't have to bring anything, but to tell the truth, I simply cannot show up empty-handed at a barbecue.

Nick left the house early this morning. He's been so secretive lately, it makes me uncomfortable. Jerry thinks that's his way of dealing with the stress of his marriage. All I know is that we hardly see him. He's either working one of his temp jobs, out with friends, or in his room.

I wish Amber would join us at the picnic. I've called her a few times, offering to babysit and asking her out to tea. But each time she politely declines my offer.

Since I worked on Memorial Day, I have this holiday off. It's a welcome break in my week. Yesterday at work, Thomas was gossiping again. He scurried away when I came into the workroom, and everyone else's face got red. Traci spilled the beans. Apparently Thomas was hinting that he saw a certain young man having coffee with a beautiful blonde. I guess he was talking about my son. It hurt to hear that rumor, and I doubt Nick would cheat on Amber.

At 3:50, Jerry and I head to Doris's house. Emma and Cole will meet us there. They're at another barbecue now. I'm not sure if we'll see Nick, Amber, and Lily. My family feels splintered. I try not to think about next month, when Emma leaves for New York. I thought that by now Nick's family would be searching for an apartment nearby and Emma might change her mind and go to a local college, but life never goes according to the plans I dream up.

Doris's house could be a stop on a political tour for the next presidential candidate. Red, white, and blue bunting ripples in the breeze from the porch railing, and the front walk is lined with small flags stuck into the flower border. Beside the front stairs leading to the porch, Old Glory unfurls in the wind.

Doris comes to the door wearing that cute T-shirt I saw at Nordstrom. The one that was too rich for my budget. Her earrings are shiny red, white, and blue stones set in the shape of a flag. I'm not even going to ask if they're really tiny rubies, diamonds, and sapphires.

"Hello, darlings. Oh, Linda, you didn't need to bring anything."

Jerry raises his eyebrow at me. Not even ten minutes ago, he said the same thing.

We join the rest of the party in the backyard. Doris's deck is huge, and at one end is a screened gazebo with a table and plenty of chairs. I'm pleased to see Amber's family already here. I crane my neck to spot my son and daughter-in-law.

"They're not here." Joyce gives me a sad smile and a brief hug.

"Just hoping." I move around the deck to greet the folks I know and take the empty seat beside Bert.

She smiles and pats my knee. "How are you?"

"Fine." I'm not able to elaborate any further. My mood is too low, and I don't want to be the wet blanket of the gathering.

Bert inclines her good ear to me. "What?"

I smile and speak louder. "I'm fine. How are you?"

She takes a sip of lemonade. "As well as an old girl can be. Have you seen our Amber lately?"

I shake my head. "I know she and Nick have been seeing each other, but she doesn't come around."

Slim's out on the grass, tossing a ball with some of his younger grandchildren. It just doesn't seem right that his great-granddaughter isn't here too. I wish Nick and Amber could solve their problems. Then I might be sitting here, holding our precious Lily, perhaps dandling her on my knee while she marvels at the red, silver, and blue pinwheels stuck in the planters on the deck. But instead I'm pretending my heart isn't broken for that little family.

My cell phone chirps from my purse. I fish it out and walk to the side of the deck to answer. It's Nick.

"Mom?"

"What's wrong?"

He clears his throat. "Nothing. I just don't want you to expect me at Doris's house anytime soon."

"Why? Where are you?"

"I'm with my family."

"How are they?"

"They're fine. Lily's sleeping. Amber and I are talking."

"Oh, Nick. I want—"

"I'm calling to let you know we won't be at the barbecue for about an hour or more, okay?"

"Take all the time you need."

"Sure." He rings off.

Voices rise, and I see Emma and Cole have arrived. They're greeting other guests.

Doris and Ross come out of the house with Doris's daughter, Adrianne, in tow. They introduce everyone to her and her family. I pretend all's well with the world and smile like everyone else.

I can't believe we'll have another family wedding next Thursday. The ceremony will be at the Botanic Gardens just as Doris had hoped.

Dinner is served, and I nibble on a burger and potato salad. Jerry's deep in conversation with his future stepsister. Who would have thought he'd finally have a sibling at the age of fifty?

I keep watching for Nick and Amber to arrive. They must have changed their minds.

"Mom?" Emma startles me out of my ponderings.

I smile in response.

"Cole gave me a ring." She holds out her left hand and splays her fingers.

I grip her fingertips to take a closer look. "It's beautiful."

"Cole has one just like it. They're our friendship rings. They're titanium."

I inspect the silver ring. It has a polished finish, and in the center of the band is a circle of dark blue Maltese crosses.

Emma wiggles the ring off her finger. "Look."

I angle the ring and see an inscription inside. *Priceless memories.* I can live with that. It's not a promise ring or something that's meant to bind them together while they're at opposite sides of the country. Cole's going to Seattle Pacific University.

The party continues with good food and lawn games. Before you know it, the afternoon ends with a glorious sunset. Citronella candles that skirt the gardens surrounding the deck are lit. Doris's deck is perfectly positioned to see a nearby fireworks display.

Jerry gets a sweater out of the car for me. We sit on the deck and watch the beautiful show. Emma and Cole are lying on a blanket on the grass. Conversation ceases except for an occasional exclamation when a particularly stunning display lights the sky above.

I study Jerry's profile in the flickering lights.

He must sense my gaze because he faces me. "What?"

I smile, and he lays his arm across my shoulders. I stare at the pyrotechnic sparkles shimmering in the heavens. They remind me of my fractured family. *Are we all splitting apart and fading away too?*

69

The quiet morning makes me feel lonely. Emma is out getting a manicure, and Nick is at work. Jerry's taken my car and is having the oil changed. Later this afternoon, we'll go to Ross's wedding. Doris says it's going to be a small, low-key affair. I'll believe it when I see it.

Jerry and I talked about Theresa this morning, of all days. I think my husband's at peace with his dad's new marriage. And honestly, this is what Theresa would want—for Ross to be happy and loved.

I start to dust but get sidetracked by photos of Nick, Amber, and Lily. They went to Dream Photography for their first family portraits when Lily was just eight days old.

The little family looks so perfect. Amber's cradling Lily, and Nick has his arms around his wife. They're both gazing at their sleeping daughter. Oh, how I miss having them all under my roof. My heart breaks when I think of how much I miss Lily. The portrait mesmerizes me as I study the curve of Lily's cheek and her fluffy puffs of light brown hair. Her tiny fist. Her upturned nose.

As Bert says, *"God is good all the time. All the time God is good."* I truly believe that. But I want my family happy and loving one another. Bert reminded me at the picnic that God knows our pain for the young family, and He hears our prayers. I try to believe her, and I think her pep talk is working on me. I've begun to notice the

sun shining again in the blue Colorado sky. I think I've even seen
Nick's eyes lose that lingering sorrow he's had since Amber and Lily
left.

I finish putting on my makeup and give my hair a spritz of spray.
My new dress hangs on the back of the closet door. Jerry's already
dressed. He looks too handsome in the tuxedo he rented. He's
Ross's best man, and Doris's daughter, Adrianne, is the matron of
honor.

   I pick up my small satin purse and go downstairs to wait for
Emma. Jerry's in the living room, keeping Cole company.

• • •

The ceremony starts at six. When we park the car, the day's patrons
are streaming out of the gardens. We walk against the flow and
stroll through the grounds to the Woodland Mosaic garden. Jerry's
whisked away by the wedding planner, and Emma, Cole, and I take
our seats in the front row beneath the lattice gazebo.

   Candles flicker in staggering displays along the front of the pavilion and on a simple altar. Dear Doris, she hired the same musicians
who played at Nick's wedding. I could sit in this spot for hours
listening to the soft music, enjoying the gentle breeze, and breathing in the sweet, competing fragrance of hundreds of blooms.

   I wave at Doris's son-in-law and grandchildren, familiar faces
from church, and friends of Ross's.

   Jerry and Ross walk to the front of the gazebo. Ross looks like a
million bucks.

   Emma nudges me. "Where's Nick?"

   I wish I knew. "He wouldn't miss this. I'm sure he'll be here any
moment. Maybe he was delayed leaving work."

   The harpist's strum announces the beginning of the wedding
march. *Oh no. Where is my son?*

We stand and watch Doris and Adrianne come toward us. Doris is glowing. Her champagne-colored dress flows to just below her knees. The bodice has an eyelet satin overlay, and the skirt is gauzy silk. A small spray of flowers sits on the side of her silver hair. She carries long blooms of mixed flowers.

Where is Nick? He'll never forgive himself if he misses his grand-father's wedding.

Emma pokes me with her elbow. "Tissue."

I pass her a tissue and hold one in my palm.

Cole whispers to Emma, and she leans toward me. "There he is."

I follow her gaze and see Nick in the distance, rushing along the path to our pavilion. Relief floods my heart. It wouldn't be right without him here. He pauses, turns back, and gestures to someone behind him. A tall blonde girl hurries to catch up with him.

My heart turns to stone. *Was Thomas's gossip correct? Has Nick moved on to another woman?* I can't believe that he would choose to bring her here of all places. This is not the time to introduce Amber's replacement. And he's not even divorced.

I catch Jerry's eye and incline my head in the direction of Nick. Jerry's expression dims. I hope this doesn't ruin the day for the happy couple.

Emma elbows me. "Wow."

Yeah, she's got that right. I glance at her. *Why is she smiling?* I thought she loved Amber.

Our view of Nick and his friend is obscured by bushy landscape. *This is going to be so embarrassing. Is he going to sit with us in the front row?* There are four empty seats beside us. I hope he has the good sense to slide into a seat in the back.

The minister clears his throat, and we all focus on the event. Ross and Doris face one another and look as if they're in a world of their own. The phrase "they only have eyes for each other" could have been invented for this moment.

The sound of high heels clacking away on the cement breaks the spell. Nick and that girl sidle up the end of the aisle. I mask my emotions, not to take away from the solemnity of the event. Nick plops down beside me. I feel like kicking him but instead focus on the ceremony being performed.

Jerry's studying at his dad, love written in his expression. His gaze flickers to me, and he winks. *The flirt.* I smile back.

His head jerks to Nick. I suck in my breath. I hate that something unpleasant would intrude on this joyous time. But Jerry's face warms in a smile. *What's going on?* I crane my neck to the right.

The beautiful blonde nods at me and puts her hand in Nick's. *When did Amber dye her hair?* Nick switches her hand to his left one and puts his right arm over the back of her chair. More movement from the sidewalk behind us catches my eye. It's Bert and Slim approaching the ceremony, and Joyce and Harry are with them, pushing Lily's carriage.

Thank goodness I stuffed a whole package of tissues in my purse. The one in my hand is soaked already. My heart soars. My whole family is here to witness this late-in-life miracle of love.

When Ross and Doris are pronounced man and wife, they embrace and kiss. Instead of walking down the aisle together, they hold open their arms for family to join them. We all crowd around with hugs and kisses.

70

Peace. Finally.

As soon as I plopped down on the chaise to relax on my patio, all the surrounding neighbors decided to mow their grass. That's Saturday in Pine Grove for you. Fortunately, our yards are small, so the inconvenience lasts only a short while. The tinkling of my fountain and the music of birdsong lulls me to a state of calm.

Jerry's voice drifts out from the kitchen. He's asking Emma if I walked to the mailbox today. I close my eyes in case he pokes his head outside to ask me. I'm not in the mood to talk right now.

My thoughts turn to the wedding two nights ago. I was so happy to have Amber and Lily there. Things seemed good between her and Nick, and they even danced a few times at the reception. But at the end of the evening, Amber and Lily went home with Slim and Bert.

Still, Nick seems a lot happier. Today he even cleared the mountain of dirty clothes from his floor and did a few loads of laundry. My prayer is that his heart doesn't get broken again. He's such an optimist. Does he think one pleasant evening will restore his marriage?

A squirrel in one of the aspen trees must spot Belle sprawled in the shade. The stinking rodent lets loose with that annoying staccato barking. Belle's up for the challenge and barks right back. There's no way I can pretend to be napping any longer.

The screen door slides open, and Jerry steps out. "Hey, sleepy-head."

I smile at him. The I'm-okay charade is better than showing my true emotions and causing him worry. "Yes?"

"Let's go for a walk."

Sigh. "Oh, I just feel like vegging out."

Jerry grasps my hand and tugs. "Come on. It's a nice day. We haven't gone for a walk in a long time."

"Emma may need help sorting out the stuff she's shipping to New York. We've got to get to the UPS Store later and—"

He bats my protest away with a swipe of his hand. "She's a big girl; she can handle it."

"And I was going to marinate steaks for dinner—"

Jerry laughs. "I'm in the mood for pizza. Come on. You don't have any good excuses."

The breeze stirs his hair. Despite the worn T-shirt he's wearing and the hint of gray at his temples, he's still my handsome hunk of a man. He looks hopeful.

Who am I to disappoint him? I can't for the life of me think why he wants my company, but whatever. "Okay. Let me change into my tennis shoes."

When I come back downstairs, he's wearing his sunglasses and holding mine. We lock the door behind us and head toward the Cherry Creek Trail.

It's crowded today. Families on bicycles compete with parents pushing strollers, joggers huffing along, and walkers like Jer and me. Alongside the concrete path, horses and riders mosey along. The wildflowers scattered among the prairie grasses bow to the heat of the afternoon sun.

I try to match his stride, but my legs aren't as long. "Slow down, bub."

Jerry slows and we fall into a good rhythm.

"Jer? What are you thinking?"

"Thinking about the kids."

"Me too. I just want them all happy."

We walk for a few more yards, and Jerry steps behind me to allow a group on bicycles to pass us. "It's not our job to make our kids happy. They'll be fine."

"I know." My gaze follows a flock of barn swallows as they dip and weave among the swampy creek bed. "Emma's acting so brave about going off to college. I told her she'll be homesick. And that will be okay, but she will be homesick."

He seems to be inspecting me. "It sounds like you're worried about missing her. And that will be okay."

Humph. We tramp along in silence.

"Pop's wedding was nice."

Good tactic. Change the subject. "It was lovely. Doris is a sweet lady. A godsend, really. I think Ross looked younger at his wedding than he has for the past year."

Jerry gives me a playful shove. "That's what love will do for you. Look at me. People mistake me for a thirtysomething all the time."

As if. But he makes me laugh.

We continue our stroll, talking about Emma and the new life she'll have on Long Island. My heart bumps against my ribs when I think of my little girl wandering into New York City for an adventure. I breathe a silent prayer for her safety.

We reach the spot on the path where we usually turn around. The sun is warm on my back. "So, do you really want pizza for dinner?" I ask Jer.

He chuckles. "Not really. I wanted you to myself for a while." He locks his eyes on mine, and I'm lucky not to stumble as I'm held in his gaze. This man knows how to maneuver my emotions. My stomach does a swan dive.

When the path joins our neighborhood, we veer off onto our street. I see our house from a distance. "What's that in front of the house?"

Jerry squints. "It looks like boxes."

"Why would Emma put her boxes on the street?"

As we get closer, I can tell that they're used boxes, some from a liquor store and some with grocery logos.

"Why would someone put boxes there?" Jerry sounds offended, as if one of our neighbors is playing a trick on us.

The garage door is open. "Oh, look."

We both stand in the driveway like two idiots, staring at the white Hyundai Elantra with a scuffed back bumper parked in the garage. The one with the bright red Raft Naked decal on the back window. The open trunk has bags and boxes thrown inside, and more clothes are hanging inside the back of the car.

My hand flies to my heart. "Has Amber come home? Do you think she's really home?" *Could the Lord have brought her and Lily back to Nick? to us?*

Jerry gestures toward the door. "Only one way to find out."

We file through the garage. As I'm opening the door to the house, laughter greets me. More boxes are piled in the foyer by the stairs. We stand by the door absorbing the wonderful sounds coming from the next room. I grab Jerry's hand, and he squeezes mine.

Amber's voice carries from the kitchen. I had forgotten how lyrical it is. My heart soars at the sound of her loving banter with Nick.

"Oh, for goodness' sake," she says.

Lily's baby squeals sound like she's trying to get in on her parents' conversation.

I hear cabinet doors closing and Amber's laughter. "I'm starving. And living in this house is like living in culinary Siberia."

ABOUT THE AUTHOR

Megan DiMaria has fond memories of the days when her mother would pile the kids into the car to take their weekly trip to the Troy, New York, public library. There under the mural of *Gulliver's Travels* and amid the stacks of books began a lifelong love of the written word.

Megan is an active member of several writers' groups and enjoys encouraging other writers in their pursuits. She volunteers her talents to her church and local nonprofit organizations and speaks to writers' and women's groups. When she's not tapping out another story on her computer, she loves to hang out with her husband and three adult children.

Megan holds a BA in communications, with a specialization in mass media from the State University of New York at Plattsburgh. She has been a radio and television reporter, a Web content editor, a contributing writer for local newspapers, and has worked for a weekly newspaper. Megan has sold magazine articles locally and nationally. In her day job, she works in the marketing department of an upscale Denver portrait studio.

Out of Her Hands is the sequel to *Searching for Spice*.

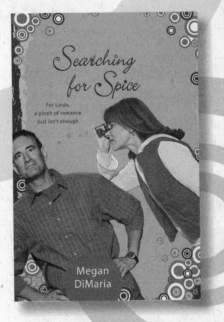